SEND THE WORD

A Novel by James Hockenberry

James Hockenberry

Published by HN Books, LLC, James Hockenberry and Colleen Nugent
HN Books, LLC, P.O. Box 4214, New Windsor, New York 12553, USA
Copyright © 2020 by James L. Hockenberry
Endpapers, interior and cover illustrations by HN Books, LLC
Hockenberry, James L.
Send the Word/James Hockenberry
384 p., | c22.86 cm.
ISBN: 978-0-9915612-4-7 (paperback)
ISBN: 978-0-9915612-5-4 (e-book)
Library of Congress Cataloging-in-Publication Data has been applied for.

1. Action & Adventure, 2. Suspense Thriller, 3. Thriller, 4. Fiction, 5. Literature &
Fiction, 6. Spy Stories & Tales of Intrigue, 7. Contemporary Literature & Fiction, 8.
Mystery, Thriller, Suspense, 9. Historical Thriller, 10. Teen & Young Adult, 11. World
War One, 12. War, 13. Military History
Printed in the United States of America
Book Design by HN Books, LLC

First Private Edition 2020

For

All the Doughboys

Who Died So Needlessly

Organization

- Epigraphs
- Historical Background
- Text
    - Section I: April 1918 – May 1918
        - MAP: Ground Gained by German Offensives of March and April 1918
    - Section II: May 1918 – June 1918
        - MAP: Ground Gained by German Offenses of May, June, and July, 1918
        - MAP: Belleau Wood, 2nd Division Operations, June 4 – July 10, 1918
    - Section III: June 1918 – July 1918
    - Section IV: July 1918 – August 1918
        - MAP: French-American Counter-offensive, July 18, 1918
    - Section V: August 1918 – September 1918
        - MAP: Saint Mihiel, Plan of Attack of First Army, September 12, 1918
    - Section VI: September 1918 – November 1918
        - MAP: Meuse-Argonne, Plan of Attack of First Army, September 26, 1918
        - MAP: German Defensive Organization in the Meuse-Argonne Region
        - MAP: Meuse-Argonne, Operations of First Army, November 1-11, 1918
- Appendices
    - I.   Cast of Characters
    - II. U.S. Military Organization
    - III. Key Terms and Abbreviations
    - IV. Acknowledgements
    - V.   Author's Note
- First chapter, *So Beware* (final book in the World War I Intrigue Series)

"I am inclined to think we are going to have a very hard day."

– U.S. General William Haan, Meuse-Argonne

~

"We can kill them, but we can't stop them."

– German officer facing onslaught of U.S. troops, Meuse-Argonne

Historical Background

<u>Spring 1918:</u> The Great War on the Western Front has been raging since the summer of 1914. Following their failed offensives in 1917, Britain and France are reeling. Their only hope to win the war is America. But America, which declared war in April 1917 with a standing army of only 200,000 soldiers, needs time and heavy equipment before it can have a military impact on the battlefield. It is building up fast.

In the east, Germany has knocked Russia out of the war with the signing of the Brest-Litovsk treaty, a virtual capitulation by Russia to German demands. Now free of a two-front war, Germany has sent more than 500,000 soldiers west. For the first time since 1914, Germany holds numerical superiority over the Allies of men on the battlefield.

The other Central Powers (Austria-Hungary, the Ottoman Empire, and Bulgaria) are on the verge of collapse or surrender. At home, the German people are starving. The government is in turmoil due to rising socialist sentiment and war-weariness. Germany knows it must win now before America can send enough troops to turn the tide in favor of the western democracies.

In America, support for the war grows, galvanized by an effective propaganda campaign led by George Creel's Committee on Public Information (CPI). President Woodrow Wilson dreams of American greatness and has idealistic plans to restructure the post-war world. But in order for America to have a major role in shaping these plans, he understands that the American Expeditionary Force (AEF) has to make a significant contribution on the battlefield.

In New York City, German agents have been chased out, but support for Germany and Irish independence remains in certain areas. In 1916, the Irish Republican Brotherhood launched a poorly led and under-resourced uprising against the British with its Eastern Rebellion. It failed. However, Ireland remains a weak point for Britain. A successful Irish revolt could cripple Britain and maybe force it out of the war.

America has formed a national Bureau of Investigation, based in

Washington, D.C., to coordinate efforts to stop spies, pro-Irish patriots, and Central Power sympathizers.

On March 21, 1918, German General Erich Ludendorff launches the first of his Spring Offensives ("Operation Michael") in an all-out gamble to strike the British and destroy them. If successful, France, alone, will have to capitulate.

This book opens as the German army sweeps across the British lines.

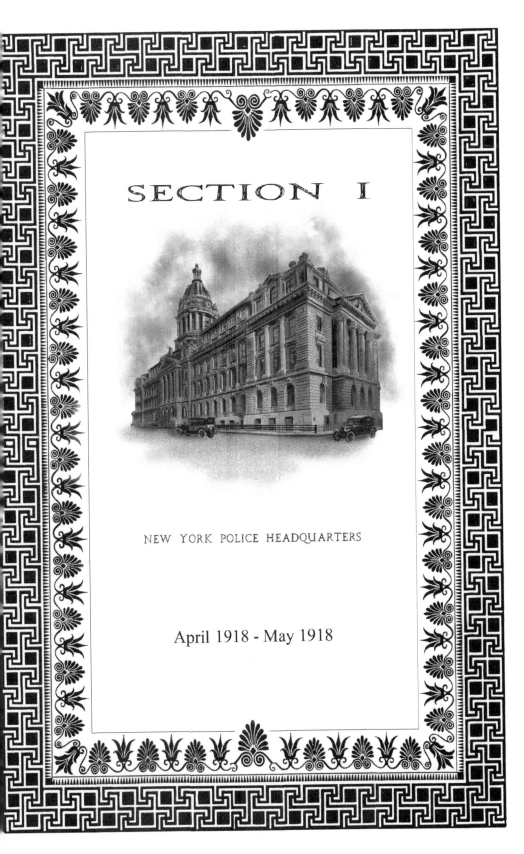

SECTION I

NEW YORK POLICE HEADQUARTERS

April 1918 - May 1918

Chapter 1

The Inconceivable

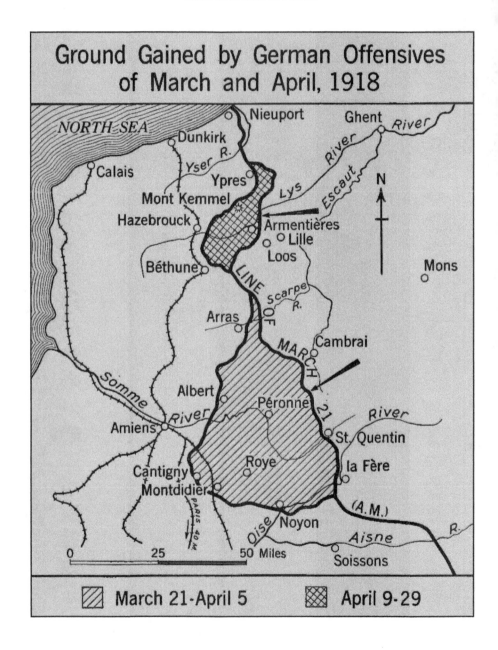

Ground Gained by German Offensives of March and April, 1918

March 21-April 5   April 9-29

The Western Front, Flanders, British Second Army HQ: April 10, 1918
U.S. Army Captain Gil Martin felt the cold ripples of panic shiver down his spine. A former detective on New York City's elite Bomb Squad, Martin had witnessed panic in other men. But panic in an army was altogether different. Like a flooding river, it was powerful, deadly, impossible to stop. The British officers thronging into the briefing room at General Herbert Plumer's Second Army headquarters were caught in its rush. Unsteady voices reinforced doubt; misdirected energies magnified errors; fear-induced body odor confirmed the impending crisis.

Martin peered out of the open second-floor window of the 18th-century château and sensed the gravity of the British Expeditionary Force's (BEF) drowning retreat. To his horror, weaponless soldiers were running past. "Stand firm, men!" he shouted, knowing his words meant nothing in the face of the German onslaught. An Allied victory meant more to him than his life, but all he could do at the moment was pray.

A sharp whistle quieted the room. A sergeant-major pushed through the ranks of officers, three deep, and pounded his rifle stock four times, jarring the length of the floorboards. The tremors vibrated up through Martin's boots. "Listen up," the sergeant-major barked. Martin felt the air turn heavy.

Dusk was turning the room the color of a dead man's skin exposed too long to the elements. Chief of Staff General Gerald Cobb stepped forward, the only sound the rasp of his boots against the naked oak planks. Martin's heart pounded with anticipation and dread as Cobb moved to the center of the dimly lit room. "Gentlemen, let me detail our predicament."

The gravity of the understatement was clear. Martin had faced desperate situations before but nothing compared to this. He turned to the American officer as his side, Lieutenant Paul Keller, his best friend, army intelligence assistant, and long-term partner on the Bomb Squad.

No words were necessary between these men. He trusted Keller with his life. They agreed: *disaster*.

"We're in a bit of a scrape," General Cobb said, trying to sound confident. "The Huns have bashed us hard."

Martin reached into his uniform blouse for his Camel cigarettes, his one pleasure. Life was short on the Western Front. Exposed to poison gas in New York two years before, he didn't care what effect smoking had on his weakened lungs. What if cigarettes made him cough? Whether he died by a bullet or lung failure, he would be just one of the millions who had perished in the Great War. Who would care? He had no one left back in The States.

General Cobb cleared his throat. "I won't mince words. The Germans have caught us unaware and crushed our front-line defenses. They struck first toward Amiens and are now attacking north in Flanders across the Lys River Valley. The enemy is more than 200,000 strong. In one day, he has established a bulge in our lines ten miles wide and five-and-a-half miles deep. We are evacuating Armentières."

"That's the fastest breakout on the Western Front since the trench lines were established," Martin whispered to Keller.

Thunder rumbled in from the east, jolting Martin's attention. Undoubtedly an artillery duel. Cobb stopped, turned his ear to the sound. "Formidable," was his only comment. He turned back to his men. "The enemy has captured thousands of men and hundreds of cannons. Our Second Corps is down to half strength. The Germans have formed a bridgehead across the Lys, and threaten to push to the junction at Hazebrouck."

Hazebrouck? The extent of the debacle exceeded Martin's worst estimates. The Boches were approximately twenty miles from the vital railway connection that supplied the BEF from the Channel ports of Calais and Dunkirk. Understanding the daily need for vast amounts of materiel, Martin realized that if the British lost Hazebrouck, their army would be starved of the ammunition and supplies needed to prosecute the war. The entire Flanders defenses would be compromised. If those defenses collapsed, the Germans could push to the Channel and destroy the entire British army.

"All is not lost," Cobb said. "The Germans are running ahead of the supplies. They have taken losses and have expended huge quantities of munitions they cannot quickly replace. Their men are tired; their reserves are depleted. We have taken their best punch and are still standing. Our secondary defenses are stiffening. The French will send help, but we do not know when they will arrive. The next two days will be decisive."

The artillery battle intensified. Outside the window, explosive flashes lit up the horizon like so many city lights. Ear-splitting booms followed. Martin's entire being was vested in winning this war, regardless of the cost. He'd tally that in the end if he survived.

Cobb's eyes turned fierce. "We control our fate. Get to your posts. Rally your men. Do not yield. Make the Huns pay for every foot of ground they have taken. We must save Hazebrouck!"

The men cheered in unison. They stood taller and moved with renewed resolve. They scrambled out of the room and returned to their desks. Telephone lines heated up. Questions became answers. Answers became orders. Orders renewed confidence. The British army was fighting back.

The sole American officers in attendance, Martin and Keller stood isolated in the empty room. Martin finished another cigarette and reviewed his options with his usual calm and methodical approach. He noticed Keller repeatedly pounded his right fist into his left hand, a baseball gesture he habitually used. The familiar tic suggested his impetuous old friend was anxious to get going.

"Forget staying here, Gil. We need to join this fight. Our headquarters don't need us."

Major Simon Dillard, their BEF liaison officer, approached. They exchanged salutes. Dillard had the look of a beaten man.

"How can Lieutenant Keller and I help, Major?" Martin asked.

"You Yanks might be too late. The war may end before you have a chance to reach the battlefield."

Keller spoke first. "Surely you don't mean —"

Martin shot Keller a disapproving look that stopped him in mid-sentence. Keller was fast into a fight, fast with a knife, and fast with his opinions. He was usually correct, but why challenge Dillard in the crisis?

"We're calling up our last reserves. Luckily, it's the 1st Australian Division. They are the best we have, but our defenses are thin. A breakthrough is probable. We may have to retreat further. Shorten the lines. Keep them intact."

"But the French," Martin said with unjustified hope. "Surely they will arrive in time."

"The Huns threaten the entire front. The French will defend Paris before they help us. We must stop them ourselves."

"I'm sure you will," Martin said, mustering the remnants of his confidence.

The growl of artillery shells grew louder in the distance. Martin took two deep breaths and straightened his equipment belt. "What are our orders, Major?"

"I have no authority over you. You are American liaison officers with no direct responsibilities in the British Second Army. We have enough staff here. Infantrymen, no. You may stay and answer telephones, or, if I were you, I would grab a rifle and head to the front. The Aussies need men. God be with us all."

As he left the building with Keller, Martin had but one thought, inconceivable a week ago: The Allies might lose the war.

Chapter 2
Backs Against the Wall

1st Australian Division Front Line: April 1918
Martin and Keller's staff car sputtered along a narrow dirt road two miles behind what Dillard's maps indicated was the Australian position. The night was clear, a becalming prelude to the battle to come. The Ford's engine backfired, spit oily exhaust, and rolled to a halt. Martin hopped out, threw his campaign hat on the ground, and kicked the tires, a rare display of emotion. A light breeze cooled his brow but failed to lessen the hissing steam pouring from the engine. Another casualty of war, but one Martin had sacrificed willingly, having pushed the Ford beyond its limits to get to the front lines. *How long before the Germans attack?* "We'll have to walk the rest of the way, Paul." Martin reached for a cigarette. "No turning back."

"Way I want it." Keller appeared resolute. "We'll fight it out here, or —"

"We need to hurry."

Assigned to General John Pershing's American Expeditionary Force (AEF) intelligence staff, Martin and Keller had been in Europe three months. In March, they were transferred to General Plumer's Second Army to learn tactics and foster relationships with the British. As cops, their combat experience was limited to small engagements, except for one pitched battle between their Bomb Squad and German agents in New York.

Keller, one of the best marksmen in the AEF, picked up his 1903 Springfield, fitted with an A5 sniper scope, and Martin grabbed his Winchester pump action shotgun. For close combat, nothing matched it. They donned their "battle bowler" steel helmets and secured their .45 semi-automatic Colts in their side holsters. Their cartridge boxes bulged with ammunition. Keller strapped a knife scabbard to his calf, and Martin slung a haversack of grenades over his shoulder.

From a distance, they heard shovels hacking into dirt and the orderly bustle of men preparing for battle. Australian accents confirmed their destination. Sandbags filled and positioned. Logs cut and shaped into defensive barriers. Mortar and machine-gun crews readying their weapons. A large ruddy-cheeked man with a captain's authority and an infantryman's informal gait approached, but he lowered his rifle when he noticed their uniforms. "You Yanks lost?"

"No," Martin said, a bit surprised by the Aussie's relaxed demeanor. He acted as if he were on a stroll with friends on a pleasant evening. In the moonlight, the stripe of a bullet scar, deep and long across his cheek, became apparent, testament to the difference a couple of inches make between disfigurement and death. Stress lines along his brow made him look older than his athletic body would suggest. Martin saluted and introduced Keller and himself.

"Captain Maddison. You joining our party?"

"Yes," Martin said, adding his military credentials.

"Intelligence officers? Hah. We don't much like staff officers in my outfit. Don't matter whose army. They got the brains of a wombat and the common sense of a roo."

"Former cops," Keller said.

"Cops? Me too. Funny war. My best soldiers are stockmen, plumbers, teachers. Social ranking don't mean shit on a battlefield. What's important is what's here." Maddison touched his heart. "And here." His head. "Rich man's war. Poor man's fight."

"It's America's fight, too," Martin said. "War to end all wars."

"An idealist? Here it's man against man. No honor. No mercy. No glory. The better killer wins. I just want to get home to my family. You married, Captain?"

"Widowed. She died in childbirth. Worst day of my life."

"Sorry." Maddison ran his hand over his short brown hair. His ring finger and half his pinky were missing. Noticing Keller's look, he said, "Gallipoli. Grenade. Not many of us left. Caught shrapnel in my chest at Passchendaele. Luckier than most. Tomorrow?" He shrugged his shoulders. "Who knows but *Him*?" He lifted his head to the sky.

Tough man, Martin thought. The reputation of the ANZACs as the shock troops of the British army was well represented in this man. If the rest of his unit were like him, maybe they had a chance tomorrow. "We're here to fight," Martin said.

"More than I can say for those Pommy bastards. They get into a fix, and we got to save their English backsides."

"I hate the Huns," Martin said.

"For me, the war is about my mates." Maddison's focus shifted to Keller's rifle. "You good with that, Lieutenant?"

"Won some marksman awards in the police force."

"You won't be shooting targets."

"I've killed men before, Captain."

"Good. Call me Vic. First names around here. None of that King George formality. Welcome. Need every bloke we can get. Fritz will be here by mid-morning. At least that's what Intelligence tells me. For once, they might be right. My scouts tell me the same thing. I trust them. I'll have my sergeant sort you out. Start with some food."

"Food we'll take, but let us help. Tough day tomorrow," Martin said.

"If the hardtack and plonk don't kill you first … . Bill," he called to his head sergeant. He opened a pack of cigarettes. "Want a fag?"

After Martin enjoyed the cigarette, he and Keller followed Bill and set to work.

~

At daybreak, Martin saw the Aussies had situated their position well, along the natural curvature of a small hill that surveyed an open pasture. The grazing animals were either hiding or dead. Shell craters dotted the ground, remnants of prior battles. The tree line concealed and protected the unit; the hill's elevation gave them a tactical advantage and the contours of the ground, a bowl-shaped depression in front of them, provided an excellent killing field. If the Germans came straight at them, they would have to pinch their lines tighter to cross the funnel-shaped valley eight hundred yards deep that narrowed into their position. A shallow lake protected the right flank, and a soggy onion field provided a small obstacle on the left, the most vulnerable part of their line.

The Aussies had improved their defenses overnight, building rifle pits, erecting log barricades, and camouflaging their position. No time to construct deep trenches or reinforced bunkers. The battle would come down to numbers and each side's willingness to die. Would their sacrifice buy the Allies the time they needed for the French to arrive and save Hazebrouck? Martin had no doubt about the Aussies' courage but was sure the Germans were equally determined.

The sun was coming up; the Diggers had done what they could. Maddison told his men to drink water and eat — no hot food, fires could give away their location — and rest. Twenty minutes later, he ordered his company of two hundred or so men into position in a curved line along the contours of the hill, anchored on both ends with portable Lewis machine-gun teams. His men were spread thin. The two mortar teams, deployed one hundred yards behind the main line, had spent the night studying their field of fire. Behind them, no one. If the single line were pierced, all would die.

Martin and Keller joined Maddison in the "glory hole," sandbags and a clump of rocks that served as the company command post thirty-five yards behind the front line. Maddison seemed relaxed and confident, surprising Martin, whose pulse was quickening.

Maddison rolled his neck, producing a cracking sound that seemed to satisfy him. "I've done this dozens of times," he said in his broad accent. "Accept what you can't control, do what you can, and don't sweat the rest. My men are bloody good and fight like a mad croc after a fat pig. We've been in harder scraps. My only worry is artillery. But I think the Germans are advancing too fast for their heavy guns to catch up. This will be an infantryman's fight."

Martin confessed that he had learned more about advanced infantry tactics in the last five hours than he had in five months in the U.S. Army.

"Put it to use," Maddison said. "Survive and pass it on."

Keller admitted that he had formed a bond with the Aussie men.

"They like you too," Maddison said. "You're more like us than the Pommies. Whatever you Yanks do, fight under your own generals. British high command sacrificed us. Stupidly. Wastefully. Constantly. *Bastards*. They asked us to do things they knew their men couldn't. Or wouldn't. If you get slaughtered, at least let it happen under your own officers." Someone called from the rear and Maddison jumped up to answer. He returned clutching a piece of paper and chuckling. "A note from General Douglas Haig," he said, referring to the commander-in-chief of the BEF. "Special order of the day, April 11." He read:

There is no course but for us to fight it out.
Every position must be held to the last man:
There must be no retirement. With our backs
to the wall and believing in the justice of our
cause, each one of us must fight on to the end.
The safety of our homes and the Freedom of
mankind alike depend upon the conduct of
each of us at this critical moment.

"I guess Haig doesn't want us to lose, the butcher. He claims the glory; our remains get a hole in the ground and a nameless grave." Maddison's expression turned somber. "Do you know what the top brass call our attrition rate? *Wastage.* Five thousand men a week across the British army, like scrap from a meat packing plant, discarded and replaced with fresh grindings." He called for Bill. "Pass this along to the men. For what it's worth. Tell them they can use it for ass-wipe."

Bill read the order. "Fancy words don't matter. I'm worried about ammunition. It won't last long."

"Depends on how many men attack. How's the minefield coming along on our left flank?"

"Need more time."

"We can help you," Martin said. "We're explosives experts."

"Take him, Bill. When you're done, Captain, I want you by my side during the battle. I'm down to two other officers. I might need you. "But get rid of those officers' bars. You too, Lieutenant. They attract unwanted attention."

Into the valley of death, Martin thought.

"Stay here, Lieutenant." Maddison's eyes narrowed. "I need a sniper. My best one is in the hospital. A good one is worth ten privates. You that man?"

"Yes." Keller tried to sound confident despite his cotton mouth.

"Good. I want you on our left flank. There's a clump of poplar trees thirty yards behind our front. Some rocks will provide cover. It's the highest point on our line and should give you a good line of fire. Find a few places to dig in. Keep moving. Camouflage yourself. It's dangerous. You could make the difference today."

Keller had already scouted the defenses. "Exact spot I was thinking of."

Chapter 3
This War Will Change You

1st Australian Division Front Line: April 1918
Maddison studied the ground in front of him like a riverboat gambler assessing his cards. He shook his head and lowered his field glasses, but Martin noticed his concern. "What do you think?" he said, as much to himself as to Martin.

"Three men. Advance party," Martin said. The lead man pointed to the tree line that anchored their position. "Wait, they're stopping."

"They sense something." Maddison called Sergeant Bill. "Get Malcolm over here. Now." He turned to Martin. "That Abo can track anything. Forty years old, and he volunteered. Other blokes didn't want him, the bigoted fools. He's saved us more times than I can count."

Three minutes later, Malcolm arrived. Martin had never seen an Aborigine before, but the toughness and inner calm that came from living in the outback was immediately recognizable. Maddison gestured as he gave Malcolm his orders. "Circle around to our right — find out what you can. Count how many men. When will they get here? What weapons? No risks, we need you back, mate." Maddison patted him on his back. "I'll give you ten minutes." He looked up and down his line, assessing weaknesses.

The German scouts peeled back out of sight.

"Shit. They're reporting back to their commander," Maddison said. "They sense we're here; just don't know exactly where."

With each passing minute, the tension mounted. Martin flexed his hand around the trigger guard of a borrowed rifle, the smooth metal cool against his finger. His shotgun rested nearby.

Malcolm returned as catlike as he had left. The lines around his leathery face seemed deeper. "Bad news, Captain Vic. Battalion strength heading straight at us. Didn't see mortars, but they have a 37mm field gun and several machine guns."

"Good job, Malcolm. Stay three hundred yards behind us with the motorcycle. If they break through, go to HQ and tell them we did our best."

"No, Captain Vic. I'm staying here with me mates. You been good to me. Another rifle on the line could make a difference." Malcolm headed toward their weak left flank.

Maddison gestured for Bill. "Sergeant, go tell Lieutenant Keller he is authorized to shoot anything he can hit. Our friends will be here in a few minutes." He looked at Martin. "They outnumber us more than three to one, but our defenses even the odds a bit. Now it's a fight. Man for man, my men are as good as they are. Better. But if they get close enough to throw grenades, ..."

"How will they come at us?"

"First they'll probe. Then hard."

"From what direction?"

"All of them."

~

Hidden in his rock-protected sniper's nest, Keller leaned against a tree and wondered whether he was about to act as an executioner or a vengeful protector of freedom. He'd been in a number of shootouts, but this time the other side was equally armed, equally trained, and equally German. A multiple generation German-American, Keller had already reconciled himself to killing fellow Germans. This was war, and these men were his enemies. America was his country, not Germany. Keller had personal reasons for fighting: competition, the thrill of adventure, and the life-on-the brink challenges of the Western Front. But he strongly felt compelled to right wrongs, as well. Germany had acted horribly in this war. Justice must prevail, and he was its protector.

He took his knife from its ankle holster and ran the blade against a stick. It helped him concentrate. A good marksman had patience. Whittling was an old trick to pass time he had learned from his grandfather during summer hunts in Pennsylvania. "You and that rifle are one," his grandfather had preached, a lesson never far from Keller's thoughts.

The rising sun pierced the shade of the trees. Sensing the impending fight, Keller secured his knife, sipped from his canteen, and poured cool water on his face. Maddison's instructions were clear: "Shoot the leader first. The Germans are taught independence of command, but your kill will disrupt them. Get the man who takes his place next. After that, aim for their heavy weapons people." Keller looked across the field and understood he had graduated from hunting game to hunting men. He readied his Springfield.

~

Behind his cover, Martin prayed, asking forgiveness. A devout Catholic who had struggled in the past with his faith, he followed the Ten Commandments and expected others to do so. Murder was one thing, he reasoned, but killing Germans did not qualify. This was war. Just in case he was wrong, he wanted permission from a higher authority for the sins he was about to commit.

Maddison spoke, bringing Martin back to the present. "This war will change you. See how you are after you've been shelled for twelve hours straight. The air vibrates so hard you think you're in an earthquake. The gas. Choking, blinding, smelly gas. Every second could be your last. Minute by minute. Hour by hour." The Aussie took a deep breath, then added, "You'll be a different man when this war is over." His comments were wise beyond his years and seasoned with experience.

"I just want to beat the Huns. After that … ." Martin shrugged.

"Look at me," Maddison said. "I've seen my share of death. My mates maimed, blinded, killed in places no one ever heard of. Hell, I can't even pronounce most of them. Some men turn to quivering wrecks; some harden; some die on the inside. Me? I just want to forget this war ever happened. Go home to my wife and daughter. Raise her generation better."

Martin had no one to go back to.

He fell silent and wondered. *What will I be like at the end of the war?*

Chapter 4

Live Today, Die Tomorrow

Flanders, Front Line: April 1918

Three squads of German soldiers moved into the clearing facing the Australian lines seven hundred yards away. Crouching low, armed with carbines and hand grenades, they moved at an even pace five yards apart across the two-hundred-yard, wide-open field. Their eyes moved constantly, their senses sharp, their weapons ready. Step by careful step, a sergeant led the way. A flock of birds escaped the woods behind them, squawking high-pitched warnings.

The Australians, equally vigilant, remained hidden. Martin calculated the Germans could cover the distance to the dugout post in ten minutes, less if they charged. Grenade throwing distance in maybe seven. Did the Diggers have enough firepower to hold them back? Martin could only guess and knew enough not to try.

"Patience," Maddison said. "I'm doing the same math as you. These bastards are methodical. They're probing us. Small force. See what they're up against. They'll hit us good soon enough." Maddison spoke with the conviction of a newly ordained priest and the confidence of a veteran soldier. He had ordered his men to use just enough force to keep the Germans at bay. Conserve ammo. Open up with the machine guns when absolutely necessary, then mow them down. The longer the fight, the worse the odds.

Martin scanned the Aussie line in front of him. Maddison's men seemed to share his strength. No hesitant looks. No jittery movements. No sounds. A tense quiet settled over the area. He could hear his timepiece: tic, tic, tic. The heavy machine gunner at the center of the line shot a thumbs-up. The mortar men behind them signaled *ready*. A light breeze danced through the tall grass and caressed Martin's face. His confidence grew.

The German sergeant gave a hand signal: *down*. His men

dropped as one. He studied the terrain.

"What's wrong?" Martin asked.

"He senses something, trying to see what's what," Maddison said. The Aussies remained still.

Twenty-five seconds later, the German sergeant signaled again, and his men stood and continued forward. This time moving slower, crouching lower, expecting danger. They'd advanced another sixty yards when the crack of a rifle echoed on Martin's left. The German sergeant fell.

"Good shot," Maddison said.

Yeah, Martin thought. *Keller always did have perfect timing.*

~

The recoil of the Springfield slammed into Keller's shoulder. *Target down. Work bolt. Aim. Relax. Caress trigger. Man and rifle one. Fire.* The soldier attending to the fallen sergeant grabbed his chest through a spray of red mist. Keller blinked three times to refocus. The hair on his arms stood up. The German infantrymen returned fire, forcing him to duck. He poked his head up and saw the Germans pull their two comrades away. No time for another shot. Move to another position.

~

Martin saw the Germans retreat in orderly fashion with their wounded comrades.

"They know we're here, somewhere," Maddison said. "We're an unknown force. They're trying to figure out if they're up against a regiment or just a single sniper."

"What's next?"

"Depends. How much pressure are they under to attack? How confident is their commander? How reckless? How much firepower does he have? The German infantry has been moving fast. Let's hope he won't have time to bring up heavy guns." Maddison took a deep breath. "They'll regroup and attack with more force. Measure their success and react accordingly."

Martin began to understand this was a contest of wits as well as weapons. Who is the better predator: the Aussie crocodile hiding in waiting, or the aggressive German bear? Martin flexed his fingers to relieve the tension. He craved a cigarette.

Two German crews rolled forward a heavy Maxim machine gun with a front metal plate. Maddison lowered his binoculars. "Shit. I hate those things. Can't stop them with bullets."

A moment later, more than three hundred stormtroopers specialized in attack and infiltration emerged into the clearing. Potato masher grenades weighed down their equipment belts, and each fifty-man platoon carried a portable machine gun. Behind them, the Germans set up their 37mm field gun.

Maddison wiped his brow. "Nothing subtle about their commander." His voice was dry. The stormtroopers maneuvered forward in a scattered pattern. "He means to take this hill, and *fast*. We'll open up when they reach three hundred yards." His men remained silent.

Crouched low in their glory hole, Maddison opened a pack of gum and offered Martin a piece. "Have a cigarette if you prefer."

Martin lit a Camel.

"Any second now."

~

Watching the advance from his sniper's nest, Keller saw he did not have a clean shot at the 37mm crew. But he had to try, even if it meant exposing his location. He fed another clip into his Springfield. Squeeze trigger. Miss. Squeeze trigger. Miss. *God damn it.*

The Germans retaliated with machine-gun and rifle fire. Their volleys were as intense as a summer deluge and just as loud. Bullets careened into the stones in front of him, spraying chips of rock in all directions and stripping the overhead branches clean. Bullets flew over his head so thick they seemed to block the sky. He curled into a fetal position and waited. *Let them think they've got me.* He peeked through a narrow crevice between two rocks and saw the Germans approach the Aussie line while the 37mm gun pounded them from afar.

~

At three hundred yards, the Aussie riflemen opened fire as their machine gunners remained silent at the ready. Twenty Germans fell, but rifle fire alone could not hold back the attack. The Hun machine guns hosed the Aussie line. Their casualties mounted.

Maddison ordered all his men to fire, reluctantly committing his strongest weapons so early in the fight. The mortar lobbed a shell, killing six Germans. The Lewis and Vickers machine guns sprayed death. The Germans accepted the casualties and kept coming: 250 yards, 200, 125.

A 37mm high-explosive shell silenced the Vickers machine gun. The next shell blasted a five-yard gap in the center of the Aussie position. As the Germans dashed toward it, Martin grabbed his shotgun and ran to stop them, alone. He threw a hand grenade and dived to the ground. Three Germans fell as they stepped through the Aussie defenses. Martin rose up and pumped four rounds in quick succession, stopping two more. He reached his front line, reloaded, and kept firing, cursing and shouting like a man possessed.

The Hun infiltrators scattered.

Along the rest of the line, sustained bursts from the Lewis guns and determined rifle fire halted the German advance as well-placed mortar fire prevented reinforcements from crossing the field. Keller continued to pick off individual soldiers. A whistle signaled *retreat*. Thirty minutes into the battle, the Aussie line had held — barely.

~

Surprised to be alive, Martin fell to his knees in grateful relief and emptied half his canteen in three gulps. After sustaining more than a hundred casualties, the Aussies were in desperate shape. Martin figured that one-third of their men were gone. The mortar team was running out of shells; their Lewis gunners had few drums of ammo left;

and the center of their line was exposed. The heavy German machine guns continued to rake their position, making any movement risky. The 37mm gun remained a threat. Impossible to survive another sustained blow.

Undeterred, the Diggers continued to fire back, momentarily forestalling another attack. Martin knew something had to change. *Retreat?* No defensible position to fall back to. *Surrender?* Worse than running. He'd rather commit suicide. *Fight it out and die?* If it came to that, hoping they would inflict enough German casualties to slow them down. *Yet —*

Martin headed back to the command post. Maddison was conferring with a corporal when a 37mm round shrieked past him. Instinct or a voice from above — Martin would debate which for the rest of his life — caused him to dive against the outer sandbag and earthworks barrier of the glory hole.

The shell landed inside the dugout, detonating a haversack full of grenades. The explosion shook the area. Shrapnel and gore collided in midair. A thigh landed on Martin's back with surprising impact. Maddison's headless torso somersaulted and landed on top of the sandbags. The smell of cordite was overpowering. Dust and debris filled the air, making it hard to breathe.

Martin forced himself out of his daze and rose to his hands and knees on the hard ground. His ears rang and his head throbbed, but he was still in one piece. He tried to focus and assess the situation. Our line is still holding. In God's name, how?

The gunfire stopped. German bodies littered the open field; some moved. The rest had retreated. An eerie quiet enveloped the area.

Sergeant Bill dodged his way back to the glory hole. His face contorted at the sight of Maddison's severed corpse. "One of the originals," he muttered, referring to the men who had fought at Gallipoli. A wet streak rolled from his eyes, clearing a narrow strip of battle filth from his cheek. "You hurt, Yank? You're covered in blood."

"Not mine. I'm okay. What's our situation?"

"Our mortars just got that damn 37mm gun a few minutes ago. We've got no more rounds. The Vickers is gone, and we got maybe eighty men standing. You're the last officer left."

"The Germans?"

"We pushed them back to their jump-off point. We got maybe a third. If I know them, they ain't giv'n up. Any ideas?"

Martin tried to collect his wits. "How's my man? The sniper."

"He took out his share. Can't say if he's alive or not. Haven't heard that Springfield of his in a while." Bill hesitated. "That don't mean shit."

Martin recalled a tactical lesson from the War College. "How are the Lewis gunners? They got enough ammo?"

"Not for long."

"Your men willing to risk everything?"

"Better than dying in a hole."

"Attack. Surprise them." It was a desperate tactic. "Half our men will sneak around that lake to our right and hit their flank. Push them into that minefield we set up."

"Sir?" Bill gulped hard. "You crazy? We're outnumbered four to one or more."

"It's our only chance. Put every wounded man who can fire a rifle in the center line. Take every available man from our left and the two Lewis gunners and bring them here. That gives us what, forty men?"

"Maybe. But our left —"

"They'll think we've weakened it to fortify the rest. They'll push right toward it, and we'll help them."

Bill scrunched his face in apparent doubt.

"Wait 'til they've committed the bulk of their troops. When they do, our attack force will charge. Hit them with all the firepower we can muster. Like reinforcements just appeared. Drive them forward into our trap. Blow them to pieces."

A wry smile crept across Bill's face. "You got bigger balls than any man outside of Melbourne. We'll lose a lot of men — but, yeah, it might work."

"Make those men sound like hundreds. Be ready in five minutes. Get me Malcolm. I got a special request for that Abo — and my lieutenant, if he's still alive."

~

Keller watched the Germans shifting in the line below him, regrouping for an attack as Malcolm cruised through the bush, headed for the sniper's nest. "You're alive. Good." He breathed easily despite his demanding run. His face, determined yet placid, betrayed no fear. "Follow me, Lieutenant. We're going to infiltrate Fritz's line and kill us some officers. Your Captain Martin called us a two-man surprise party."

~

Four minutes later, they were ready. "The men and I are all behind you, Captain." Bill added that every man begged to join the attack party. They drew lots; the losers and wounded did what they could to fortify their positions. One collected ammo from the dead. Another risked a dash into the field to snatch whatever German rifles and grenades he could.

Martin loaded his shotgun and checked his .45. "Let's go."

Bill held him back. "That's my job, Yank. We need you here. You're in command. The men agree. Things will get tight. We need your cool head. There'll be plenty of killing to do here."

Taken aback, all Martin could say was, "Go."

"It'll take a few minutes to get in position while you hold the line. See you in Hell." Bill ran off with his troops.

~

A whistle sounded from the enemy and gunfire erupted on the front. Creeping behind the German lines, Malcolm saw them first, Keller, a second later. Five men moving fast, carrying a light machine gun. Malcolm pulled out a grenade, winked at Keller, and tossed it cricket-style. The carnage stunned Keller.

Malcolm grinned. "So much for surprise." He grabbed the machine gun and charged toward the German command post. Gray-clad men ran to the explosion amidst gunfire, screams, and dying gasps. Then there was silence. Still concealed, Keller crawled closer to the action. Malcolm had taken out a good fifteen Germans, but the rest had scattered and fired back. A volley knocked Malcolm to the ground. As he struggled to recover, an advancing private reached his twitching body and fired two bullets into his head. Keller shook with fury but forced himself to be still.

Keller disappeared back into the woods as thirty more Germans ran past. *Move on. Find their commander. That's my job.* A few tense minutes later, he had a major in his sights one hundred yards away, surrounded by five other officers. *Shoot now and I won't last thirty seconds.*

A minute later, a sergeant ran to the officers and an argument ensued, giving Keller his chance. Two shots in quick succession felled the major and a lieutenant. Keller crawled back thirty-five feet into thicker cover. Seeing indecision among the Germans, he squeezed the trigger. A German captain grabbed at his heart. Confused, the Germans fired wildly. A bullet nicked Keller's arm; another grazed his helmet; more hit the ground in front of him, spraying dirt in his face. Escaping became a 50-50 proposition, and Keller was not a betting man.

~

Newly positioned on the line, Martin sucked in a lungful of smoke as two hundred Huns or more moved confidently toward him. Aussie fire reduced their numbers as they advanced to one hundred yards. Just then, the Germans accelerated their pace, pounding the Diggers with concentrated fire. Every fourth Aussie rifle fell silent. At forty yards, the Huns reached for grenades. Martin would pay for his failed gamble with his life, but until then ... . He pumped off shotgun round after round, the hot barrel scorching his hand. Out of bullets, he reached for his .45.

Like a call from the heavens — maybe *He* existed after all — Martin heard gunfire and yelling to his right. Loud. Men seeking revenge for Maddison. Bill's attack sounded as if they were a whole company. Smoke grenades veiled their advance. The two Lewis gunners carpeted the field with bloody accuracy. The Boche heavy machine gun began to fire into its own men. Bill.

Confused, the Germans looked this way and that. A lieutenant ordered them to charge at the Aussie left, where resistance was weakest, just as Martin had planned. Bill's men pressed their attack. Grenades and reckless bravado forced the Huns further into the trap. Buoyed by their success, Martin's weak front line yielded no ground.

Given the light defense in front of him, a German lieutenant looked around and ordered one-third of his men to turn about to counter the Aussie charge. They died quickly. As the lieutenant waved the rest forward toward the weakened line, an Aussie engineer detonated the trap of explosives. Shrapnel scattered across a five-yard radius. More followed. The Germans were caught.

"Fix bayonets!" Martin cried, and the fifteen Aussies who could, charged and tossed grenades. Martin shot two men with his .45. What was left of the German force retreated to their original positions. Returning from the battlefield, Martin met Bill.

"Well done, Captain." Bill extended his hand. "They won't be back soon."

"We lost a lot of good men, Bill."

"What about your lieutenant? We sent him and Malcolm on a suicide mission."

"I need to find his body."

~

Martin patched up his wound and surveyed the carnage. A bright orange sun in a clear blue sky contrasted vividly with the green battlefield stained with red. Cries from the wounded knotted his stomach. He fingered the two aluminum identity tags hanging from his neck. A couple of inches either way and some staff officer would be looking at one to record his death. The other would be buried with his corpse.

Two Aussie medics scrambled around the dead and dying. "This man needs an amputation," one said.

"Put a tourniquet on it and hope," the second medic replied, turning away from a disemboweled man. His somber look betrayed his feeling of impotence.

Keller hadn't returned.

~

Forty minutes later, a British staff car appeared on the horizon. A major stepped out and approached Martin and Bill. His boots were clean, his buckle shined, his uniform neatly pressed. "Jolly good show, men. Who's in charge here?"

Bill pointed to Martin.

"A Yank?"

"We've taken 75% casualties, Major," Bill said.

"A relief column will be here in an hour. Can you hold?"

Bill laughed. "Does it look like it, sir? How about more ammo and some ambulances, *tout de suite*?"

"Humph." The major walked off.

Martin turned to Bill. "I like your candor, Sergeant. Couldn't get away with that in our army."

"Only way to deal with stuck-up arses like that. Don't take any shit. Remember that. You might ruffle some high-ranking feathers, but you and your men will live longer."

"Thank you, Bill."

"We held them back. For now. You made a difference today, Captain. I'd fight with you anytime."

"Today, for now is good enough. Victory is still a way off."

"You're learning, Captain. Live today, die tomorrow. Can't think about the future. Luck and the man upstairs decide. Accept it or go crazy."

"I need to find my man."

"You might not have to." Bill pointed.

Keller approached carrying Malcolm's body over his shoulder.

Chapter 5
Threatened

Manhattan, New York City: April 1918
Shannon Keller walked onto Park Avenue and headed to nearby Grand Central Station with the hope that a brisk stride and some fresh air would revive her flagging energy. She was tired after her talk at the Women's City Club luncheon, where, as a guiding light in the women's voting rights movement, she had addressed a room of three hundred suffragettes. No matter how often she had given her talks, the attentive faces and eager questions, especially among the youngest in her audience, never failed to inspire her. The women were stirred by her rise from humble roots to her work with the New York City Police Department's elite Bomb Squad unit and detective bureau.

Running late, she picked up her pace, anxious to get home. She was glad she had dressed practically and could move freely. Police work and the latest war-related fashions had dictated her choice of attire. Her low-heeled everyday Oxfords were sensibly laced and the hemline of her dress swished above her ankle. *Thank God*, she thought, as she boarded the train, *I've banished those cumbersome underskirts.*

Shannon barely made the 4:48 p.m. Harlem commuter train to the northern suburb of Bronxville. Face flushed, she sat down on a wicker train bench next to a partially open window, grateful that the recently installed electric service would get her home in just twenty-five minutes. A sweaty man sat down next to her and gave her a look, evidently admiring her fine features and beautiful, dark red hair. When Shannon ignored him, he pulled out a flask and opened the day's *New York Herald* with an ostentatious rustle. He took a swig and relaxed as the train started up, spreading his legs and crowding Shannon against the window. She nudged him away with a sharp elbow to the ribs. He pulled back with a startled grunt and proceeded to empty his flask.

The bumpy ride, the noise from the locomotive, and the

impudent man set Shannon's nerves on edge. She smoothed the long sleeves of her dress, as she often did when irritated, an unconscious habit that dated back to her time with the Bomb Squad when a German agent had kidnapped, tortured, and nearly killed her. Now, two years later, the cigarette burns on her arms were barely visible, but the mental scars remained a legacy of her ordeal. Shannon had looked her trauma square in the face and became an expert marksman as part of her recovery. Overcoming that ordeal had helped to make her the woman she was today. She was confident in a man's world. In any world.

As the landscape fled by her window, Shannon's thoughts shifted to the complexities of the Tammany Hall case she was currently investigating. The flow of money into and out of the bank account revealed unexplained discrepancies. The treasurer, Murdock Kittridge, was certainly corrupt and guilty of something — but what?

Interference from well-placed Tammany officials who had tried to block her work made Shannon suspect she was getting close — a suspicion that the unsigned note she had found on her desk this morning confirmed: *Cease or else.*

She had to admit that the threat had her worried. She was returning to an empty apartment near the Bronxville station. She and her new husband, Detective Paul Keller, had moved to Bronxville shortly following their marriage after working together on the Bomb Squad together for two years. Deeply patriotic, her impulsive husband was transferred to Army Intelligence at the start of the war and was now an untested lieutenant on the Western Front. The single letter she had received from him so far said he was excited to get into the fight.

The conductor passed through the carriage, startling Shannon from her worries. "Next stop, Bronxville."

She stepped off the northbound train and walked along the tracks toward the newly built pedestrian and vehicle underpass that crossed beneath the railroad line that divided Bronxville in two. Shannon approached the tunnel alone, walking against the traffic, as the other passengers headed east into the main part of town.

An acne-faced man she had never seen before stood by the entrance to the tunnel. He wore a worker's cap pulled low over his eyes — unusual attire for upscale and sleepy Bronxville. His behavior, too, was odd. Smoking a cigarette without inhaling, he turned his head from side to side as she neared, as if he were waiting or looking for someone.

Avoiding Shannon's attempt to make eye contact, he pretended to check his timepiece — far from the usual male reaction to her well-filled dress and stylishly bobbed hair. She continued straight ahead and passed him by, but he turned to follow as she entered the tunnel. Alert to his steps, she immediately turned back and lightly brushed by him to assess the threat. He jumped away with reptilian quickness, but not before she felt the weight in his pocket. Not a gun, but something sinister — a knife perhaps. A street tough or worse, with malicious intent. She was his mark, no question.

She mumbled a terse apology, turned, and followed the other passengers east. Except for a thick-necked gray-haired man farther down the quay, they had all moved on. Gray Hair scratched his nose and looked past her at Acne Face. A team. Shannon turned to head off the quay, keeping Gray Hair in her peripheral vision. He moved fast to block her path, as the sound of someone in heavy boots echoed closer behind her. Trapped between the two men, Shannon reached into her purse for her Webley Bull Dog revolver, then hesitated.

Looking up at Gray Hair, she said in an alluring voice, "Please, sir. Kindly move out of my way."

He put his hands on his hips and stood firm. "I'm lost. Can you help me?" he growled in an Irish-Brooklyn accent.

"Where do you want to go?" Shannon backed away, trying to maneuver, but the men matched her step for step. "Maybe the police can help you. The station's right around the corner," she bluffed.

Gray Hair stepped close. "We have a message for you, Mrs. Keller."

"What do you want?" She turned sideways to keep them both in view.

Acne Face sneered. "We could —"

"Shut up, stupid," Gray Hair snapped. He thrust his finger inches from Shannon's face. "You get one warning. This is it."

Shannon recoiled but kept her composure. "From whom?" she demanded.

Gray Hair looked her up and down. A jackal's smile filled his face. He reached into his coat and flashed his fist, twisted around brass knuckles. He drew his arm back as a whistle from a northbound train sounded in the distance. "Worse things are coming if you don't comply."

Shannon dodged his wild swing, pushed Acne Face hard, and ran. The train whistle grew louder as she dashed along the quay, the men right behind her, catching up. She had one chance, a calculated risk. Rapidly cutting sideways, she leapt over the tracks, only yards in front of the approaching train. The locomotive missed her heel by inches. She felt its power as it thundered by.

She left the two thugs cursing on the opposite side of the tracks, impotent to follow as she ran across the street to the safety of Lawrence Hospital. She arrived at the front desk out of breath and stood there gasping, her eyes on the tracks, as the last of the cars rolled by. No sign of the two men.

"Are you all right?" asked the receptionist in alarm.

Shannon straightened her clothes. "Yes, thank you, but could I use your telephone?"

A local policeman arrived in twelve minutes. Shannon described the two men in detail and reported they had attempted to rob her as she left the train. The officer checked the area and returned, assuring her the thugs had left. He escorted her home to nearby Alger Court.

Shannon collapsed into her favorite armchair and poured herself a proper Irish whiskey to calm down. "Takes more than two low-life fools to stop me," she muttered between sips.

One thought replayed through her mind: *Tammany Hall knows where I live.*

Chapter 6

The Shadower

Police Headquarters, New York City: April 1918
The next morning, Shannon sat at a tightly packed desk in the open squad room talking to Sergeant Joe Fernandez, her direct superior. "It's too dangerous, Shannon." Noise from the street outside and the clatter inside made the area sound like Times Square.

Fernandez was the lone detective of Spanish descent in a department full of Irishmen, Italians, and old-time Americans. He was the lead detective on Shannon's banking investigation of Tammany Hall. Wiry with black hair and a rigorous accountant's mind, he had become a shining star in the detective bureau. "Tammany Hall doesn't threaten unless they mean it."

"That proves we're getting close," Shannon said, ignoring her three-inch height advantage over Joe. "Kittridge is diverting large sums of money, that's for sure. Where's he going? Who is he talking to? I can learn a lot if I shadow him."

"You can also be killed if they catch you."

"If I do nothing, I could be killed anyway." Shannon trusted Joe but guessed he would reject her plan. Too fatherly. Her instinct told her shadowing Kittridge was the right thing to do. "Listen, Joe. I've shadowed Eugene Traub, and he was the best there was. He ran the dockyards for Germany before you arrived here."

"I'm familiar with that case, but you're fighting Tammany Hall."

"Back then I was fighting German spies. They were far more dangerous."

"You were kidnapped and almost died."

"We were betrayed. Those men last night were dumb brutes, not the subtle types Tammany likes to use. They are not going to stop unless they silence us. We need to take the fight to them." When it came to police work, Shannon was as naturally aggressive as her army lieutenant husband. "I'll be careful."

"Let me go with you."

"No thanks, Joe. You're better working on ledgers, not skulking around the streets. Let me start the field operation. Kittridge won't know I'm there. I'll keep my distance and learn his favorite haunts." Shannon paused and took a deep breath. "I'll back off at the first sign of trouble."

"I wish I could believe you. Don't go home to Bronxville tonight. It's too dangerous. Stay in the city. We'll put you up in a hotel. Deal?"

Shannon twisted her wedding ring as she weighed her options. "On one condition."

Joe groaned. "You're impossible. What?"

"I need some things at home, and I need to get my mail regularly."

"Your husband?"

Shannon nodded. "He doesn't write much, but his best friend does. And I have a few meetings to go to in town."

"Your suffragette work?"

"Not those. Talks at the church and library. The wives are scared for their husbands in the army. I want to encourage them and give them the same support I got growing up. Still do."

"Okay, shadow Kittridge, but take Sean Clancy with you. I'll get him transferred to us. He'll watch over you."

"I'll like that. Sean's an old friend."

~

When Officer Clancy walked into the detective room that afternoon, Shannon ran and hugged him. She had not talked with Sean since her wedding. A beat cop who had helped Gil Martin early in his police career, Sean was transferred to the Bomb Squad and had worked undercover closely with Shannon and her husband to snare a German agent. The old Irishman's hair was now white, and he walked with a stiff back, but he maintained his Leprechaun's charm and a longshoreman's quiet strength.

Everyone liked Clancy. His savvy and experience guided the younger officers, and his connections across the city were legendary. Scuttlebutt suggested he knew the comings and goings in the mayor's office better than His Honor's secretary. Sean did nothing to dispel the claim. He kept the detectives lingering for hours at The Headquarters, the popular restaurant and bar across from Police Headquarters on Centre Street, with his gritty tales and wit.

~

The next morning, when Murdock Kittridge left his office at 50 Broadway in lower Manhattan at 11 a.m., a paperboy packed up his unsold papers and followed him through the crowd. Shannon had used the paperboy disguise often. She was a superb shadower, not because she was a woman, though it helped — no one expected to be shadowed by a woman — but because she was a natural actress who could hide in any role, was expert with disguise, and a marvel at anticipating the behavior of her marks.

As she followed Kittridge across Broadway, Shannon adjusted her oversized cap, a signal to Clancy, sitting nearby in a dilapidated Ford. Kittridge strolled north among the crowds on Broadway at a leisurely pace, as if he hadn't a care in the world. He was easy to follow and showed no signs of concern about being shadowed. He was either untrained at the shadowing game or confident he was safe. Shannon rejected the third option — that he didn't care. Anyone working in the murky area of banking irregularities as he was would be naturally suspicious.

Had she lost some of her tracking skills? Was Kittridge setting a trap for her? Was he coaxing her into laziness, only to strike later, or enticing her into a mistake with his obtuseness? She flashed a look at Clancy, who signaled that no one was following. Her pulse returned to normal.

Kittridge raised his arm and hailed a yellow Electric Vehicle Company taxi. Shannon was close enough to see the white numbers on its maroon plates, then jumped into Clancy's Ford, undetected. "Gee, lass, it's good to be working with you again. I was getting lonely after all my Bomb Squad friends left for the army. Excitement follows you around."

She wished she had a change of clothes in the Ford, but she hadn't expected Kittridge to go uptown. To her knowledge, he rarely left the downtown area during the day.

Clancy stayed a half a block behind the taxi through midtown and up Madison Avenue on the east side. At Yorkville, a well-known German section, the yellow Cadillac stopped at Second Avenue and 87th Street in front of the Hanover Restaurant.

"I know this place, Sean. Park on the street and wait. I'll go out back to make sure he doesn't leave from there. If he doesn't come out in a few minutes, go into the restaurant and see who he's with. He doesn't know you; keep it that way. Let's meet back at the squad room at six."

Shannon hid in the alleyway behind the Hanover for two hours, but saw only a kitchen worker dumping garbage and a barman carrying out crates of empty bottles. A feral cat chased an oversized rat. She jumped. *Just rusty.* A light flicked on from a second-story window and she ducked behind a pile of trash. The curtains opened a crack. She did not believe in coincidences when police matters were involved. It was time to leave.

~

Back at the squad room, Clancy reported he had not seen Kittridge in the restaurant. He'd had a meal, then waited in the Ford until 5 p.m., but Kittridge never appeared. Shannon confirmed he had not left out the back.

"Is it possible he got by us somehow?" Clancy asked.

"No." Shannon said. "He had no reason to suspect we were following him. He must have gone into a back room for a meeting. A long meeting." She mentioned the incident at the window and her suspicion that Kittridge might have been the one peering out. "He couldn't have seen me, I'm sure."

"What's he up to, staying in there all day?"

"A secret meeting? In Yorkville? In a known location for German agents? Something strange is going on."

Chapter 7

The Health Inspectors

Police Headquarters: April 1918

Shannon confronted Fernandez the next morning. "Now do you accept that Kittridge is up to something?" She had slept poorly trying to figure out the ploy, but nothing made sense. Was he a Tammany stooge or something more sinister? Disappearing for hours in a German restaurant violated Tammany behavior — unless there was a political angle she had not considered. Tammany was always hungry to expand its political reach, and Yorkville offered juicy opportunities. With the war on and the ebbing influence of German-Americans, Kittridge could be expanding Tammany's tentacles uptown on the cheap. Influential Germans were too occupied cultivating their patriotic American image to contest Tammany's spreading web.

Clancy disagreed. His connections all confirmed that Tammany and the mayor had a solid understanding, and they would do nothing to jeopardize that relationship. Make money, win the war, expand later.

Yet Shannon insisted Kittridge was moving cash, large sums of it. But whose? And why?

"You are not listening," Fernandez said. "I agree Kittridge is a rotten apple, but I need more evidence before I can act."

"We know he's guilty. Let me loose. I'll get you the evidence you need." When Shannon sensed trouble, she turned aggressive and sought to obtain results any way she could. That's what they did in the Bomb Squad. She realized she was proposing to dance around the law but did not care, certain Kittridge's actions involved something big. She also resented the threat to her person and wanted to retaliate.

"I don't break the law. Neither should you. Everyone in this building knows I'm as tough on criminals as anyone else. I get my convictions with thorough police work. If you disagree, go to another department."

"Calm down, Joe." Shannon had never seen him so angry. "I didn't mean to imply that I would —"

"I have a suggestion," Clancy said, breaking the tension. "It's maybe not borax clean, but it might work."

"I'm listening." Fernandez visibly relaxed.

"Shannon, can you pass yourself off as a man?" Clancy asked.

"I'm tall enough."

"Joe, that restaurant is a health issue if ever I saw one. Cockroaches all over the place. Garbage in the back that smells like a sewer. Rats bigger than my shoe. What would happen if some health inspectors dropped by to look around?" Clancy flashed his wide-eyed smile. "Shannon and I could pretend to be answering complaints from the locals. Not sure who performs these inspections, but someone must."

"I'd have to check."

"We'll see what's in those back rooms. Talk to the staff, friendly-like. Don't think we'd break any laws. Maybe bend them a bit, but we just want to look inside. No arrests. Just in and out."

"Yeah, maybe I could arrange that."

~

Two days later, Sean Clancy drove a 1916 Model T Ford ambulance north from Police Headquarters. He was dressed as a doctor from Columbia Presbyterian Hospital. Next to him, Shannon adjusted the wig covering her pulled-back hair. "You sure this is the best Joe could do — pretending we work for the hospital?" she asked as the ambulance bumped up and down on the cobblestone road before turning onto Third Avenue. The Ford needed a new suspension. Shannon's stomach felt like churning butter.

"Said he didn't want to go through legal channels, nothing official from the department. So he called in a favor to get us identification. Unofficial visits from hospitals concerning local health issues do take place. We have no authority, but it should get us in the door. *Damn.*" He slammed on his brakes to avoid a kid running across the street.

"That was close." Shannon scratched her mustache. The rubber-based glue made her itchy. Makeup rounded out her high cheek bones and clever padding turned her feminine curves into rolls of manly fat. She wore common overalls and a white jacket.

Clancy looked over at her and chuckled. "If I didn't know any better, I'd say you were an overweight orderly. Where did you get that outfit?"

"I have an old college friend at the Met. She's a seamstress. She helps with my costumes." Shannon pulled up the collar on her jacket. "Can't disguise my lack of an Adam's apple, but you do the talking while I inspect the facilities. Keep them occupied while I snoop around."

The ambulance hit a rut in the road with a loud bang, and they both hit their heads on the roof. Clancy plowed forward as if nothing had happened.

Shannon rubbed her head. "You sure you're my bodyguard, Sean?" She put her hand gently on his arm. "Please drive more carefully. Otherwise, there's a good chance that neither this ambulance nor I will be in one piece by tonight."

"Sure thing." Clancy swerved to miss a mule-drawn wagon. "Watch out!"

"Sean!"

"Sorry. If anything happens to you, lass, I sure don't want to be around if your husband learns I was at fault. That man loves you something big." Sean took his hands off the wheel to make a gesture.

Shannon closed her eyes. Better not to look. Her mind drifted to Paul. She folded her hands on her lap and prayed. *Please be safe, my love.*

~

"Almost there. You ready?" Clancy asked as they passed the sign for 86th Street.

"Yes. My revolver's in the medical bag."

"No trouble, right? Back off at the first sign of danger." Clancy slowed down and parked by the curb on 87th, across from the Hanover.

He left the ambulance and checked his timepiece. 10:23. "Good. Shouldn't be too many people in there. Just staff."

~

It felt like walking into Little Bavaria. The walls were covered with pictures of the Alps, the Rhine River, and Munich. The restaurant smelled of sauerkraut, sausage, and beer. Small, maybe thirty tables were neatly arranged and nicely set. A large part of the wall showed less discoloration, where presumably a German flag had been removed, a sign of the current anti-German sentiment. The steins hanging on hooks featured men in lederhosen and rustic village scenes. A well-stocked bar covered one-quarter of the room.

Clancy reached into his hospital coat and withdrew the papers Fernandez had concocted with a friend in the district attorney's office. Legal nonsense. In the same voice he had used during countless raids, he pushed open the door to the restaurant, waved the papers in the air, and shouted, "Health inspectors. Where is the manager?" Authority backed with the proper amount of bluff and conviction always brought compliance.

Looking bored, Shannon followed him in, her hands in her pockets.

A tall thin man with a bowl-style haircut confronted them. "What's the meaning of this, sir?" he said in a heavy German accent.

"I'm from Columbia Presbyterian. This restaurant is a health hazard," Clancy said. He was performing his role perfectly. "The neighbors are complaining. Hell, I can smell your back alley two blocks away. The police want me to investigate. Here." Clancy aggressively thrust the papers into his hands. The proprietor took the papers but didn't inspect them. Shannon had bet Joe $5 that the manager would not even open the papers. Her winnings would go to the Red Cross.

"What's your name?" Clancy demanded.

"Mueller." He seemed uncertain. "Vass you intend to do?" he asked.

"My colleague and I have to inspect every room in this

establishment. We will report our findings. After that, it depends on what we see." Seeing himself unobstructed, Clancy shined, enjoying his role. Shannon stayed in the background.

Mueller stepped aside.

Clancy walked behind the bar, pulled out a notebook, and started scribbling. "Get moving, Louis," he said to Shannon. "Check out the back rooms, you lazy sod. I'll get the kitchen and outside."

"Mind if I follow you?" Mueller asked.

Clancy shrugged.

Shannon opened a door behind the bar that led to a dark narrow corridor. Three mice squeaked by. The walls smelled of grease. A few steps into the corridor, she reached a closed door marked "office." She knocked.

A gruff "What?" followed. Shannon opened the door. "Health inspector," she announced in the deepest voice she could manage. She coughed to mask any false inflections. The room was a twelve-foot square. Stout bookcases filled with ledgers, boxes, and papers circled the windowless room that reeked of stale beer. A man she did not recognize stood up at a desk in the middle of the room. An older man with his back to her sat in a chair facing the desk. Behind the desk she noticed a large safe at least four feet tall.

"Nothing to see here," the man at the desk said. "Get *out*."

A target for another day. She returned to the corridor and found steps leading to the second floor. Now to find the room overlooking the back alley where the man had peered out of the window the other day.

Halfway up the stairs, she heard footsteps. "You. Where are you going?" A voice she recognized, but not the man at the desk. "Upstairs is private. You have no permission to go there," he said.

Shannon looked down and saw the gray-haired man who had threatened her in Bronxville. "Sorry," she mumbled and walked away. It was not the time or place for a gunfight, but she was now certain something sinister was happening inside the Hanover.

Chapter 8
Return to HQ

Somewhere in France: April 1918

Martin and Keller headed back to AEF General Headquarters (GHQ), with Keller at the wheel. Martin sensed trouble. In his pocket were orders from his commander, Colonel Ewell "Nosehair" Grimes: "Report immediately." Grimes liked to keep things orderly and disapproved of junior officers gallivanting off without orders. Though a decent intelligence officer, he was a poor commander. A southerner, he also detested Yankees, especially former New York City cops, whose exploits far surpassed his own.

"Don't worry about Nosehair," Keller said. He winked and slowed the Renault, delaying the trip to aggravate the colonel. "Everyone knows what we did."

Martin chuckled. He liked Keller's cavalier approach to authority. They were a good combination: Martin's steady reserve and Keller's bravado. "Indeed, they do," Martin said. He felt proud. In their first combat on the Western Front, they had earned the respect of some of the finest soldiers in the British army. Martin had led the much-depleted Aussie company for three days after the battle, when their unit was finally pulled out of the line. The Germans had not returned to their sector and had failed to break the thin British front. French reinforcements had arrived; the German onslaught had been temporarily stymied. Hazebrouck had been saved.

Martin had brushed away a tear when the bodies of Maddison and Malcolm were carried out. Keller noticed and, with a sad smile, whispered he felt the same way. The rest of the Aussies watched stoically as the other rotting corpses were stacked three-high in an ambulance. Someone played "Waltzing Matilda" on a harmonica.

The country roads back to AEF headquarters were in poor condition and the bumpy ride jarred Martin from his rest. The arbitrariness of life and death on the battlefield had unsettled him. If that shell had landed one meter closer, he, not Maddison, would be dead. "I hope we never get as hardened as those Aussies."

"We can't judge them," Keller said, showing no signs of fatigue. "They've been at it for three years. Who knows what we will be like after that? We still have a lot more fighting to do and a lot to learn. More will die."

"I'm afraid you're right, Paul. The worst is yet to come." The Renault hit a bump that almost knocked them out of their seats. Only Keller's skill kept the car on the road.

Soon the roads improved. Martin steered the topic away from death to lessons they had learned — the use of firepower, the positioning of guns, German strengths and weaknesses — everything to make the AEF a better fighting unit. Keller, who had a natural awareness for the battlefield and an uncanny ability to anticipate the flow of the fight, spoke about the ferocity of the struggle, his heightened senses during the worst of it, and the thrill when the Germans retreated.

"You were born to be an infantry commander," Martin said. But he understood: *such men do not survive this war*. He wondered how he could uphold his promise to Shannon to keep her reckless husband alive. Martin needed him, too; Keller was his only friend.

"Same rules for a soldier as for a cop," Keller said. "Learn fast or die."

"And we have much to learn." Martin turned somber, remembering his first police raid as a rookie. It had ended badly. A pimp shot the first cop to rush in the door and then killed his whore. Martin, the second man in, shot him and took a bullet in the fleshy part of his thigh. He earned his first police commendation for bravery and recorded his first kill. Righteous killings did not bother him. From that day on, luck seemed to follow him on the job. His personal life was different.

~

Outside Grimes' office, Keller fidgeted. Those baseball gestures again. Martin checked his Waltham Officer's Trench Watch that he had bought in London. They'd already been waiting for thirty-five minutes. When they entered his office an hour later, Grimes did not look up. Shuffling and signing papers, he continued to ignore them for another forty seconds. Annoyed, he threw his pen down with a thwack and then looked with disgust at the ink bleeding across his desk. He gradually raised his head.

Martin could sense a growl building up in the colonel's throat. In a deep, steady voice and punctuated by a deliberately slow cadence, Grimes said, "You men should be court-martialed for that stunt." His gray eyes met theirs. "Who gave you permission to run off and fight the whole German army with a bunch of Australians?"

Keller jumped in. "But, Colonel, we —"

Martin cut him off with a wave of his arm. *Let him vent his anger. We can manage him when he calms down.*

Fired up by Keller's outburst, Grimes continued his reprimand: "You are liaison officers. You don't call me. You don't ask for permission to join the Australians. You just get in your car and drive to the front." Grimes paused. "By the way. Where *is* the car? My sergeant says you arrived in a Renault."

"Destroyed in the fight," Martin said.

Grimes jotted something down. "I'll add that to my list. So, on your own you decide to play General Custer and stage a two-man cavalry charge?"

"With all due respect, there was no time to contact you, Colonel," Martin said. "The situation was desperate."

"Did the British order you to go, Captain?"

"We made the decision. No one forced us. They needed every man who could fight."

"What if you'd been captured? American intelligence officers. You think of that? Your actions were madness."

"We made a difference. Without us, the Germans could have broken through," Keller said.

"That's a bold statement, Lieutenant. Didn't the Aussies have something to do with the outcome? Are you sure you weren't trying to be heroes again?"

Martin was incensed. "Do you mean ... ?"

"I know your record. 'Bomb Squad detectives save Wall Street.' I've seen your personnel file, and I'm not impressed. Could be propaganda to hide police incompetence."

"Our actions in New York are well documented, Colonel. As for last week, we did what we thought best. You were not at British HQ when a breakthrough seemed imminent. Lieutenant Keller and I have nothing to apologize for. We would do the same thing again in a heartbeat."

"You wanted to die that badly?'

"No. We wanted to fight Germans," Keller said. "That's why we came here, isn't it?"

The three men faced each other like marble statues placed too close together.

"What now, Colonel?" Martin broke the stalemate.

Martin waited quietly, suspecting vindication for Keller and himself and embarrassment for the colonel, who scratched his head and peered out the window. He mumbled something Martin did not hear, cleared his throat, and said, "It seems your exploits have reached high command. Complete with high praise from General Plumer. We've received several messages from the Australians thanking you, saying if all of us Yanks are like you two yahoos — my word, not theirs — the war is as good as won. Overstated, in my opinion, but I'm outranked." Grimes removed a note from his uniform pocket and handed it to Martin. "Here are your orders."

Martin stepped forward and took the paper.

"General Pershing needs interpreters and specifically asked for you. Lieutenant Keller is to interrogate captured Germans and relay the information back to me. You, Captain Martin, are also to work with the French as our liaison officer. I order you to keep your opinions to yourself. If asked a question, you will keep your answers short and to the point. Can I trust you to do that, Captain?"

"Of course, Colonel."

"Somehow I think this will not be the last time we will have this chat. Just remember, you're still *my* intelligence officers. You still report directly to *me*. Dismissed."

~

As Martin and Keller were leaving the building, a staff car pulled up bearing a flag with a single star perched on the hood. A brigadier general emerged. "Which way to General Pershing?" he asked the sergeant who opened the door.

"Shit," Martin said under his breath. "More trouble."

"Why?" Keller asked.

"That's General Donald Prescott, one of my instructors at the War College. He's got some fancy pedigree and more ambition than brains. We called him *Iron Head*. Arrogant and egotistical. Looks down on anyone who is socially below him. Old school West Point. By-the-book all the way. I'm in trouble if that barrel-chested fool is joining GHQ."

"Why's that?"

"I had a run-in with him at Leavenworth. I disagreed with his assessment of General McClellan at Antietam. 'A great victory,' he insisted. 'How dare you challenge me, Captain? I can have you court-martialed,' he said. I held my ground and provided facts to support my conclusion that a better Union general could have ended the war there. He walked off in a huff. His last words were, 'I won't forget this insult, Captain.'"

~

After dinner, Martin sat at the small desk in his room writing a letter to Shannon, knowing her husband would not. That was Paul's nature, though he would walk through the gates of Hell for her.

> *Dear Shannon,*
>
> *Paul and I are fine. He talks of you every day and keeps the locket you gave him close to his heart. I know you read the papers and understand things have been tense. We were assigned to a British unit, learning modern tactics, when the Boches hit us hard. With the will of God, the British held and French reinforcements have arrived to stabilize the line.*
>
> *As for us, we staff officers do not have front-line duty, so don't worry. We have returned to AEF headquarters. Our commander doesn't measure up to your Uncle Thomas.*

Martin stopped. He hated to lie to Shannon but did not want to worry her. Yet, he had to write what he felt.

> *War is truly Hell. In the last few weeks, we have seen the effects of the savagery and the human cost of the war. What we saw as cops is nothing compared to this.*
>
> *I wonder what kind of man I will be when this war ends. I see men who say God is dead; others who are so hardened they seem dead; a few so wounded they'd be better off dead. If you see the hollow, panicked look in the face of a man who has endured a nighttime bombardment, you will know what I mean. Our cause is just, and we will persevere.*

God be with you. With all of us.
– Yours, Gil

~

Shannon put down the letter and wanted to cry. Gil was rarely so honest. The newspapers had avoided such stinging details.

She was proud that Paul was fulfilling his patriotic duty. Some in the U.S. questioned the loyalty of German-Americans and had persecuted them, but Paul was anxious to serve. He and Shannon agreed. This was a righteous war; Germany had to be stopped.

What would happen if the Central Powers won? Shannon refused to contemplate the possibility despite the alarming German successes. Would she sacrifice Paul to defeat the Central Powers? She was not sure.

Chapter 9
The License Plate

Bronxville, New York: April 1918

Shannon looked across the main room of the Bronxville Village Hall and wondered how she had become a source of hope and a symbol of modernity. As a compelling speaker and a woman who worked in the New York City Police Department, she was respected and well liked. Having an army lieutenant husband in France helped her talk to women about their main concerns. She had just come from Lawrence Hospital, where she had visited patients and talked with nurses. One nurse had told her that she was the best therapy they'd had.

Cool spring air filtered in from the large open windows. Fifty wooden folding chairs filled the room. About thirty-five women, ranging from age eight to over sixty, looked up from their seats as if she had been Queen Victoria. A newspaper reporter stood along the side wall taking notes. Shannon didn't feel she deserved the attention. She considered herself normal, but lucky. Barriers had never deterred her. Her family had modest means, but her life seemed to be paved with success from her high school chess-playing days, to Vassar where she had graduated with honors, to working in the New York City Police Department, to a happy marriage with a handsome and good man.

To the audience, she was "a new woman": liberated, bright, and accepted in a man's world, a role model to emulate and admire. If she could succeed, so could they — if she told them how. She emphasized how women had answered America's wartime call in the fields, in industry, in hospitals, and in offices. And they had performed admirably. Now they demanded recognition, respect, and the vote. When the war was over, they expected to get it with women like Shannon Keller leading the way.

Sean Clancy stood in the back of the room in an ill-fitting brown suit. "Only one I got, lass," he had grumbled, when she'd chided him on the train ride from New York. "Put on some pounds since I last weared it."

"It's fine, Sean. It conceals your revolver well, but next time get it pressed, will you?"

"I guess an old widower like me needs some female guidance."

"Yes, you do, old friend." She smiled, and they continued the rest of the trip in peaceful silence.

Shannon concluded her talk to sustained applause, then asked if there were any questions. Excited hands shot up, and she picked the youngest.

"Can you shoot a gun, Mrs. Keller?"

A few muffled "Oh, my's" followed.

Clancy muffled a laugh; Shannon was as good a shot as anyone in the detective bureau.

Shannon ignored the audience's reaction. "That's a great question," she said. "Women in rural America have been using guns since the pioneer days. We should learn how to handle them. Practice. I have been taught by the best. I can handle a rifle and a pistol, but their power to kill scares me."

As Shannon was speaking, a young man wearing gray working clothes walked in, startling Shannon with a vengeful look. Acne Face. She shivered, but fought off her nerves and continued, her reaction seemingly unnoticed by the crowd.

~

Except for Sean Clancy, who recognized the slight change in Shannon's tone and demeanor. He followed her eyes toward the intruder and moved closer to him, his service revolver hidden behind his back.

~

Shannon relaxed, knowing Clancy had the drop on Acne Face.

Have you ever arrested someone? "I am not a police officer. I have no legal right to arrest anyone. I help with cases. Some people call me an analyst."

But you've been involved in some big cases. "Yes, but not in a big role," she said with her usual modesty.

Have you ever been scared? Shannon paused to think. "What a question. Yes, like all of you, I get scared. Courage is something you do in the face of fear. You really don't think about it when you act. How you react defines your measure as a person."

What's your most interesting case? "New York is full of bad people. I've seen my share. To me, all my work in the department is interesting." Hoping to dodge specific questions about her previous involvement in tracking down German spies, Shannon thanked her listeners and bid them goodbye.

On her way out, she noticed a small girl with wide, brown eyes clutching a Raggedy Ann doll. Shannon leaned down and asked the girl her name. "Grace."

"That's a lovely name," Shannon said. "I've got a wonderful aunt with that name. I had a doll just like that. She was my best friend for years. I'm sure you take good care of her."

Grace's mouth opened wide but no words came out. "Come on, Grace," her mother said. "We need to go. I'm sure Mrs. Keller is busy. Thank her."

"Just a second, Grace." Shannon dug into her purse and gave the girl a green satin ribbon. "I use this when it's windy, but you can have it. Here. The color suits you."

Grace whispered a timid thank you and continued to look back at Shannon as her mother pulled her away.

When Shannon reached the columns outside Village Hall, the weather had turned unseasonably humid. Clancy was nowhere in sight.

~

Bold, alert, and ready for anything, Clancy followed Acne Face along Pondfield Road, Bronxville's main street, moving cautiously like a good beat cop. His target gave no indication he knew he was being followed. Clancy wanted to wait for a secluded spot to confront him. When the man sped up and headed to an idling black Hudson Super-Six, Clancy moved in.

"You in the gray clothes, stop. Police." The man hesitated long enough for Clancy to catch up and kick his legs out from under him. He fell on his face, knocking the breath out of him. Clancy got on top of him, jammed his knee into the man's back, and reached for the handcuffs hooked to his belt. His captive fought like a roped alligator. Starting to weaken, Clancy grabbed the barrel of his revolver and knocked the handle against the man's head, silencing him.

He looked up just in time to see a stout man step out of the Hudson with a drawn .45. A shot from behind Clancy knocked the gun from his assailant's hand.

~

Shannon aimed her Webley again and shouted, "Freeze!" The stout man retreated into the Hudson and sped away. Clancy clamped the handcuffs on his adversary.

Shannon touched Clancy's shoulder. "You okay, Sean?" By now, a crowd had begun to mill around the scene. She turned and asked, "Anyone see the plates on that Hudson?"

Little Grace was the only one to move forward. "They began with a 3, a 1, and maybe a 5 and a 9."

"Good girl, Grace. You'll be a great cop someday, if you want to be."

Grace beamed.

Clancy roughed his prisoner to his feet. "We got some questions for you back in the city."

Chapter 10

Fishbait

In transit to Police Headquarters: April 1918

When a paddy wagon from New York Police Headquarters arrived in Bronxville, Clancy pushed his handcuffed prisoner into the back and bound him to a splintery bench. Shannon followed Clancy into the vehicle and was hit with the smell of stale air, urine, and sawdust. The floor was spotted with crusty, brown stains of dried blood and littered with jagged white fragments that Shannon discovered were broken teeth. Clancy ordered the driver to make it a long, uncomfortable ride — he wanted to sweat the kid. The driver complied almost too well. By the time they crossed into Manhattan, Shannon's bladder was bursting, but she refused to admit it to the men. Her stomach growled hungrily, but if they weren't complaining, neither would she.

Their prisoner said little and trembled during most of the ride. The only coherent words he spoke were his name, Fishbait Jackson. Shannon guessed he was no more than twenty. With acne scars on a baby face and what might pass for a two-day beard, he looked far less threatening as he cowered in the paddy wagon. His wrists were so skinny the handcuffs looked like they were about to slip right off him. How did a boy like this get mixed up in a Tammany Hall conspiracy with Germans?

Although he acted dim, Shannon guessed he was calculating what to do after they stopped. Tammany Hall did not employ idiots. Shannon leaned over to Clancy on the bench opposite Fishbait, and whispered, "Don't underestimate this one, Sean. He acts slow, but he's smarter than he looks."

"Don't worry, lass. We'll get what we need out of him. Best stay away when we interrogate him."

Shannon kept her anger to herself. "I've got more questions for him than you. I was the one he tried to assault, remember?"

"We got to get him talking. How we do that might be, uh, ... distasteful. If this gets to court, it would be better for you not to be aware of what happened."

The paddy wagon drove down Manhattan's west side, turned east toward Chinatown, and drove onto Centre Street. They pulled into the basement of Police Headquarters and stopped near the door to the cellblock. Two uniformed cops unlocked the paddy wagon and dragged a stumbling Fishbait out by his arms.

"What do you want us to do with this piece of shite?" one of the cops asked Clancy.

"Take him to the small room next to the shooting range. You know the one."

"Sure do." The cop smiled.

Fishbait's eyes widened. "Am I under arrest?" he asked. A good question. They had no grounds to hold him, but Shannon hoped he wouldn't know that.

Clancy moved so close his nose almost touched Fishbait's. "Nothing to be scared of, son," he said in a quiet but menacing tone.

"What you goin' to do to me?"

"Officer, tell Red to come down here as soon as he's free," Clancy said.

The cop whistled as he walked away. "Glad I'm not going off duty. Things get fun when he goes to work."

"Who's Red?" Shannon had never heard the name before.

Clancy pulled her to a quiet corner and said, "He provides special skills we sometimes need."

Red was full of mysteries, Clancy further explained. He was a former Texas Ranger whom the Comanches respectfully called "Chief with Missing Ear," after Red had a tussle with a tomahawk that ended with a bloody stump on the right side of his head and the scalp of an Indian in his left hand. Rumors said he once tied a Comanche naked to a cactus and tossed a handful of fire ants onto the man's groin. He laughed for a minute, then finished his cigar before he asked the Indian his questions. The answers came fast. Some said he left the Indian to die on the cactus. Others said he shot him in the head. One speculated he cut the Indian free out of respect for his courage. The version depended on the audience. Red never disclosed the truth.

He carried the biggest Bowie knife anyone in the department had ever seen. He talked little, always with a strong Texas twang. No one knew why he had shown up in New York, but a few of the more astute cops believed he was not wanted back in Texas. Red never mentioned his old home. Over fifty years old and with an ornery disposition, he claimed to hate three things: criminals, Indians, and his mother.

"Do what you need to, Sean," Shannon said. "This is a big case, and this Fishbait fellow is our first good lead. Excuse me." And she hurried to the toilet as ladylike as she possibly could.

~

The basement interrogation room was so small it could have been a closet. Sounds of pistol shots from the adjacent gun range reverberated through the walls like steady hammer blows. They seemed to make the room vibrate. Water dripped from the ceiling, feeding the pungent mold spreading on the floor. The overhead light provided enough brightness to see, just. The cops secured Fishbait to a rickety wooden chair with uneven legs and a cracked seat, one of only two in the room.

Fishbait raised his handcuffed arms and looked at Clancy. "What did I do? Why am I here?" He shut up when Red walked in.

Red was as short as Clancy, but projected the stature of a much taller man. His one-inch haircut did not hide the stub of his right ear, and his once-broken nose made him sound nasal. He gestured to Clancy, who stepped aside, allowing Red to approach Fishbait. "We got some questions for you, son, and you're goin' to answer 'em true. Ain't you?"

"I ain't committed no crime."

Red's hand swept around faster than a Christy Mathewson

fastball and passed over Fishbait's head, causing the breeze to ruffle his wavy hair. Red's hand landed on the handle of his Bowie knife. "No laws in here, son. Just us." He paused and partially withdrew his knife. "Understand?"

Fishbait sat up, seemingly ready to talk.

"Officer Clancy, I think we have his attention. What do you want to ask this nice young man?" Red stepped away but stayed close enough to strike.

"Mr. Jackson, you are not under arrest — yet. But we know you are involved in some bad business. First, tell me your full name and where you live."

Clancy quickly obtained Fishbait's information and moved straight to the heart of the matter. "Why were you in the Bronxville Village Hall today?"

"I wanted to hear the talk."

Red thwacked him hard. In a soft but threatening voice, he said, "We're here as long as you want. Me? I'm not tired."

"Who sent you there?" Clancy asked.

"Don't know him. I get messages to tell me what to do. I jus' does it."

"Who was in the Hudson?"

"Never seen him." Fishbait cringed, anticipating Red's next hit. "I'm telling you the truth. I know crap."

Clancy had been interrogating suspects for more than thirty-five years, and detected some honesty in Fishbait's words. He gestured Red to back off. "You ever been to the Hanover Restaurant uptown?"

"87th and Second? Yeah. Stood outside a few times. Some men having a meeting."

"Who?"

"Don't know no names. Big Negra fellow, lots of muscles. Another man dresses fancy. Last guy sounded Irish."

"Who is the older man, gray suit? The one you were with when you assaulted Mrs. Keller?"

"Never met him before. I were told to do what he says. Scare the red-haired lady."

A timely gunshot from the firing range made Fishbait hop an inch out of his chair.

Clancy stayed silent for a moment, then rested his hand on Fishbait's shoulder. "I can arrest you right now for the assault on Mrs. Keller in Bronxville. I know some friendly judges who will agree. Her word against yours. You lose. Then, I'm going to go to your house and look at every paper, every corner, and every hiding place. Believe me, I will not be neat. After that, I'm going to tell every one of your friends that you are a lying cheat. Make it up. Who cares? They'll believe me. I'm going to find out what you're up to. Finally, I'm going to leave you alone with Red and that knife of his. Understand?"

Fishbait nodded.

"But you got an option," Clancy said. "I can let you go, and you can work for me now. We'll make it look like you escaped on your way here, so your friends don't get suspicious. Get me names: the men at the Hanover, especially that fancy dresser and the Negra. The Irishman too. Also, the driver of that Hudson, your accomplice in the attack on Mrs. Keller, and everyone else you think might interest me. We'll meet every few days — I'll tell you where. Do that and I promise you won't see Red again. Deal?"

"What if'n I can't get what you want?"

"You will. You're clever. Be smart and help us."

"If I do, I'll be dead."

"Maybe," Clancy said, "but if you don't, I guarantee you will be."

Chapter 11
Abbeville

Abbeville, France: May 1, 1918

Two weeks after he returned to Pershing's headquarters, Martin stood in the back of the hallway as the heads of the Allied forces, the Supreme Council, filed into the grand dining room. It was the first day of discussions concerning how to incorporate the growing U.S. Army into the combined Allied war effort. Martin was restless. He understood the gravity of the meeting and recognized that, however unlikely, a direct hit on the building by a German zeppelin or airplane bombing attack could kill the heads of the Allied powers: Prime Ministers Lloyd George of the United Kingdom, Georges Clemenceau of France, and Vittorio Orlando of Italy, followed by General Pershing and Generalissimo Ferdinand Foch, the newly appointed overall commander of the Allied armies whose command of English was as basic as Pershing's French.

Two squadrons of British Sopwith Camel pursuit fighters circled Abbeville on the channel coast. Martin could not stop worrying until the meeting ended. Anticipating problems was his nature. He did not like leaving things to chance but had learned that in war, chance was a principal variable. To counter its capriciousness, he worked as hard as he could to anticipate and minimize risks, lower unfavorable odds, and trust the Lord above.

Faith in the Lord was proving harder and harder. Already his time at the front line had begun to change his thinking about the war. The Allied cause remained just, of that he had no doubt, but at what cost? To the army? To himself?

Martin did not have answers and wished that Keller was with him. Since their transfer, he had not seen much of Keller, who was busy training American soldiers. Martin missed his old friend's common sense and granite nerves.

The doors to the meeting room closed in front of him, leaving

Martin to guard the entrance with a squadron of Marines, elite French alpine troops, and Royal British Fusiliers. Sergeant Andy Cooper led the Marine Guard. Martin liked him. The mood was tense, their interactions limited to military concerns.

General Ferdinand Foch strutted in last, always the peacock. He looked at his watch, and his gray-blue eyes stormed. "We are two minutes late. This is unacceptable. We must start immediately."

~

That day, Keller was playing shortstop in a game against a pick-up team. After days of inspecting defenses on quiet fronts, listening to senior officers spout made-up crap to newsmen, and hearing instructors who had never been in a fight lecture about tactics, Keller was frustrated by the lack of action. He suggested to Nosehair Grimes that a baseball game would help morale. Surprisingly, he agreed, saying it would be good to showcase the skills of his staff. Their opponents were soldiers from a Negro regiment out of Harlem, and they came to win. They were scoring so many runs, the team captain called on Keller to pitch.

When the captain handed him the ball, Keller said, "I've stuck out a good number of people in my time, but I never pitched to a black man before."

"Throw one at his head, just don't give up a homer," the captain said. "We were expected to win this easy."

Keller shut them out the rest of the game, but his team lost 7 to 5, despite Keller's two-run double in the seventh. The captain of the Negro team called him over and congratulated him on a great game. Nobody had ever shut them out over six innings before.

As Keller left the field, Grimes, looking disgusted, walked over to one of the Negro coaches and reached into his wallet.

Despite the loss, Keller enjoyed the game, a welcome break. Tomorrow he had to return to normal duties: checking on newly arrived troops, many of whom did not know how to fire a rifle. He knew many of these men would die. The thought made him angry.

~

At dinner that night with his general staff, General Pershing confessed that the day had been contentious. Martin felt privileged to be invited. Luckily, Prescott was elsewhere. A captain, Martin was the lowest ranking officer there, but Pershing made him feel welcome by mentioning Martin's latest adventures with the Australians. Half-jokingly, he said so all could hear, "Now you've learned a few lessons on the front, Captain Martin, and managed to keep your head on your neck, I trust you can help us do the same."

Martin felt trivialized by the comment. "Of course, General, but this will be harder for some than others." A few chuckles eased the tension. As the only officer at the table with actual combat experience on the Western Front, Martin fielded numerous questions, answering with insight and candor. The senior officers complimented him for his modesty and intellect.

Cognac was served, and Pershing stood up to toast his fine soldiers. He cleared his throat and said, "The French and British were difficult today. I understand their position, but do they understand mine? The president has instructed me that the forces of the United States be a separate and distinct component of the combined Allied armies. American identity *must* be preserved. Where and how to utilize our boys is my decision." With that, his face turned red, and he pounded so hard on the table that the champagne glasses jumped. He sat back down with a distinct thump.

Martin agreed. The Australians had advised the same thing: The British will use you like cannon fodder and not think twice about deploying you where they would never position their own troops. The practical considerations of war had interfered with American political needs, but a solution had to be found.

Martin understood the need for adequate training down to the platoon and squad levels, experience the AEF did not have. The AEF needed the British and French as much as they needed the Americans if they were to win the war. Pershing's contention that he could train the AEF in *his* way of fighting was arrogant and short-sighted. It could lead to disaster. The war would not wait until Pershing considered his army fully trained to fight a major engagement on its own.

~

When the council convened the next day after breakfast, the doors were closed, but Pershing's voice vibrated through the walls. Martin, on guard, moved closer to hear. "I will not have my men be filler replacements in your armies," Pershing vowed.

Generalissimo Foch countered in French. "There is no choice, *mon général*. Time is short. We need troops at the front now. The Hun is hungry and still has teeth. You *Amis* don't have the personnel or equipment to make your army a fighting force that can survive a modern battlefield. The only solution is *amalgamation*."

Martin cringed. Amalgamation meant disaster: The French and British armies would bring in American soldiers as replacements who would report to French and British officers. Six British privates are wasted, six American soldiers would replace them. All sense of an American army with an American identity would be eliminated. American boys would become forgotten in the ranks of the other Allied armies. Invisible cogs to be used up and discarded. This was everything Maddison had warned against. *Don't give in, General Pershing, please.*

Pershing displayed his annoyance. "No. My president demands an American army with an American presence. Do you continue to believe you know how best to fight this war?"

"*Oui!*"

"I disagree. Maneuver out of the trenches. Open warfare is required."

"Do you not think we have tried that?"

"What I know is that you've been fighting for four years with few results. We need a new approach."

"And you Americans, who are new to this war, know better?"

"Yes. We will fight this war our own way. The rifle and bayonet forcefully applied. Maybe you can learn from us."

No, they can't, Martin thought. Pershing's approach called for 1914 tactics in a 1918 world. They hadn't worked then; they wouldn't now. Guaranteed slaughter. The Aussies had taught him how to fight: heavy equipment, grenades, coordination between infantry and artillery — not suicidal frontal attacks against formidable defensive positions packed with machine guns.

"You are a fool," Foch replied. "We return to the same problem. Our troops are exhausted. Our supply of replacements is dwindling. There is no question we need your men. When will they be ready?"

The critical question, Martin thought, knowing the limits of the AEF. He looked around and saw the other guards were listening too.

"The AEF will not be ready to fight as a unified army for several more months."

"Too late. The war will be decided before that. Are you willing to sit back and let Germany win?"

Tense silence.

Pershing spoke again. "We must reach some compromise."

"A suggestion? I understand the political considerations you face." Foch's tone had become conciliatory.

"My troops must be unified at the division level under an American Major General," Pershing insisted. "These divisions can join your armies under that basis. With existing French and British Corps, they can contribute immediately. That is the best I can offer."

"So be it. Every effort must be made to bring your soldiers to France with the utmost haste. Men we need. We can supply the artillery, planes, and tanks."

"With additional British transport, I believe we can land more than 200,000 men a month by July."

"*Bon.* The inexperienced units can take over quiet sectors. That will free up our men. Your combat-ready divisions will go into action immediately under our existing Corps."

Low-level chatter that Martin could not hear was interrupted by a final burst from Foch. "One last thing, General Pershing. *I* am the Supreme Allied Commander. On this, there is no compromise."

As Martin backed away from the door, a French major approached and saluted. Martin did not recognize him and feared he would chastise him for eavesdropping. Speaking French, the major said, "You are Captain Martin, *n'est-ce pas*? It is a privilege to meet you. I am Major Victor Fauchaux, General Jean-Marie Degoutte's aide." He paused and smiled. "I understand that your 2nd Division will likely be assigned to the general's XXI Corps. You will be our American liaison officer. We will work to integrate your division into our command. You will be most welcome. General Degoutte is skeptical of your ability, but I am not. I am a great admirer of your General Grant and have every confidence your line will not break."

"I vouch for the ability and fighting spirit of American soldiers," Martin said, surprised that Fauchaux was better informed than he.

"Excellent. The XXI Corps is moving into a sector we believe the Germans will soon attack in force. Paris could fall if we retreat."

"We will not let that happen."

SECTION II

HELLO GIRL WORKING THE
PHONE LINES IN FRANCE

May 1918 - June 1918

Chapter 12
The Hello Girl

Tours, France: May 1918

Twenty-two-year-old Emily Lange plugged into her switchboard and answered the call. "*J'écoute.* Number please." She made the connection and immediately moved to the next caller. Emily worked for the U.S. Army Women's Signal Corps at the Services of Supply Headquarters in Tours. She sat in a row of other women facing switchboards that ceaselessly growled for attention. Emily had been in France for two months. She was one of their bilingual telephone operators, known as "Hello Girls." They were expected to handle three hundred calls an hour during an eight-hour day; men managed half that.

Her work demanded long hours, patience, and concentration, but she was thrilled to be part of the war effort. Near the end of her afternoon shift, she looked forward to a weekend of much-needed rest. Tomorrow, her Uncle André would visit, bringing fresh eggs, apples, and vegetables from his farm. In exchange, she gave him a sack of American goods not available elsewhere in France. Everyone liked the kind, old, one-armed gent who moved slowly and often needed help, requiring Emily to ask for personal time away. She made up for her absences by working hard, taking extra shifts when the other girls were sick, and never causing trouble. Because she was well-liked and excelled at her job, her supervisors gave her liberty once a month, unless a big push was on.

A deep baritone voice distracted her. Emily turned and saw an attractive, dark-haired U.S. Army major speaking to her supervisor. She guessed he was in his early thirties. A captain stood next to him.

She made a new telephone connection but leaned back, adjusted the receiver over her ear, and managed to hear the major say, "Excellent work your group is doing here, Matron. Before the war, I would not have believed it possible, but your girls are doing a superb job. Your translations are vital to our efforts. General Pershing told me himself the communications network you've established has helped the AEF immensely."

General Pershing? He must work on the commanding general's staff. I want to meet him, Emily thought. His connection to the general was more important to her than his handsome appearance. She wanted to transfer from Services of Supply to the AEF's high-command General Headquarters (GHQ). She craved adventure and responsibility, and she suspected this man could help.

~

An only child, Emily grew up in a townhouse on the upper east side of Manhattan. Her wealthy father also owned an estate farther north in the Hudson valley, which she visited often. Raised to be a genteel, well-mannered lady, she nonetheless loved all things boyish: She could shoot a duck in midflight and butcher a newly killed deer; loved to scale cliffs and hike the Appalachian Trail; and could breast-stroke one hundred meters faster than most boys her age.

At the same time, she sewed, danced, and painted well. Her performance in high-school theater was so good, her drama teacher encouraged her to think of making a career of it. Emily had no time for trivialities.

As a young teen, Emily was tall and gangly, but her high cheekbones and aristocratic features hinted at the beauty she would soon grow into. By sixteen, her brown eyes radiated a mischievous sparkle, and her long, lanky legs had turned shapely. Recent curves provided an envious figure.

At her father's insistence, Emily learned French and German as a child and spent several summers with Uncle André in the Jura region of Switzerland. She visited Paris often with her equally independent cousin, now dead from influenza. She continued her language studies in college at Barnard, also studying math at neighboring Columbia University. Being the only woman in her class bothered her not at all.

She enjoyed outscoring the boys on tests.

Rebellious by nature, Emily was fiercely independent, but she shared her father's patriotism and wanted to serve the war effort. Nursing, the only certain opportunity for women in the U.S. military, did not suit her — cleaning up excrement, bloodied stumps, or shattered minds was other women's work. She had seen enough of that during her mother's struggle with cancer before her untimely death two years ago.

When she saw an advertisement asking for women volunteers to join the Signal Corps, her father encouraged her to apply. As a banker, he understood how a rapid and efficient telephone system could help a modern army. He also appreciated his daughter's intelligence, determination, and deft social skills. "This is your chance," he told her.

Emily agreed. Bored at college and anxious to fulfill the dreams her father instilled in her, she interviewed with the Signal Corps the following week. She used her mother's full maiden name and false documents her powerful father had procured. He was worried that people would perceive her differently if they knew she was the daughter of a powerful banker. She just wanted to be Emily and rise on her own merits. No one questioned her carefully crafted background or the forged papers, and she breezed through the French language oral exam.

Next, the interview. Emily impressed the Signal Corps recruiter. *Smart, good family, excellent education, pleasing voice, and socially skilled*, the recruiter noted. Her only concerns were Emily's strong personality and good looks. Emily had anticipated the questions and had practiced her response with her father. "I know what you expect of me, and I will do it to the best of my ability. I learn quickly and work hard. I will make you glad you hired me. I was raised to be a gentlewoman and to adapt to any situation. My looks are irrelevant to the job — switchboards don't have eyes. I can think of no better way to serve my country than to work in this job, and I am ready to give up a lot for the opportunity — the closer to the front lines the better. Bombs do not scare me." She wiped the wetness from her lower eyelid. "Please, I will not disappoint you."

The recruiter looked at Emily for several seconds as if she was trying to read her mind, then said, "You're hired."

~

Two weeks after her interview, Emily was fitted for her Women's Signal Corps uniform and reported to the American Telephone and Telegraph Company's offices in New York City for a short, intensive course in telephone operations. Her instructor recommended her for immediate assignment in France.

She boarded an old White Star liner that had been converted to a troop ship in New York. Having crossed the Atlantic frequently, she easily adjusted to life at sea, despite the crowded conditions and bad food. She had more important priorities in mind.

~

Emily had been in Tours for several weeks when she saw the attractive major. She finished her shift, put on her calf-length military-issue coat, and went outside hoping to find him. Disappointed not to see him, she needed a cigarette but only smoked in private. She walked around the back of the building near the woods, where, to her surprise, she discovered the attractive major talking to the captain. The conversation seemed heated, but the major stopped talking as she neared and approached to meet her halfway. He gave her a sort of salute, although she was not army. *Friendly or trying to impress*? She'd play along.

The major mumbled a few words Emily did not hear, but she smiled anyway. The captain dipped his head slightly and said, "Hello, *mademoiselle*. I'm Captain Gil Martin. This is Major Andrew Jameson. We are impressed with your work and want to thank you. We have the best communications network among the Allied units." He flipped his cigarette butt to the ground, took another, and offered her one.

Emily reached for it and thanked him, as the major rushed to light it. Captain Martin excused himself and walked a distance away, leaving Jameson and her to converse. He could not help overhearing Jameson say, "I'd like to see you again."

Chapter 13
Rendezvous in Paris

French Countryside, France: May 1918

The train carrying Emily Lange to Paris traveled through a countryside unmarked by war. Unbeknownst to her friends and superiors, she had arranged an illicit rendezvous with Major Jameson. If the army learned of her actual intentions, she could lose her job and be sent back to America. Personal relationships were off limits, as if the army's regulations could trump desire.

She had told them she would use her weekend pass to visit Uncle André, who had moved to the capital to avoid the fighting near his home. Paris was safe from conquest since the Allies had stopped the main thrust of the German advance. No one minded; they knew kind and feeble André needed help.

Jameson had started calling Emily the day after their first meeting. The calls sometimes lasted seconds, but that was apparently enough for Jameson. He was persistent and soon made excuses to inspect the Signal Corps Station. People noticed, but he did not seem to care, such was his attraction. Emily remained coy; she rejected his offers to meet outside of Tours, claiming that fatigue, rules, and time prevented anything but casual encounters at the station. Meanwhile, she learned as much as she could about him. Good family pedigree. Well connected. Had been engaged, never married. Rising fast.

When she was satisfied he could influence her transfer to GHQ, she mentioned she would be interested in meeting him in private. At his next visit, she suggested they have coffee in the canteen at the end of her shift. Shyly, she hinted they could have more time together if she worked closer to him. Could he arrange it?

He smiled broadly at the suggestion.

At their next meeting, he invited her for a weekend in Paris. She pretended to be shocked, but he persevered. When his offers melted into pleas, she knew she had control and accepted, making him think his manly charms and persistence had convinced her. Her "yes" so excited him that he readily agreed to arrange her transfer.

Knowing Paris from her teenage visits with her cousin, Emily arranged to stay in an obscure hotel in Montmartre where the owners were discreet, the beds were comfortable, and other guests had their own reasons for privacy. The hotel catered to unwed couples and unescorted women, whose room requirements were hourly, not daily. For love or profit, the proprietors did not care.

Emily entertained no qualms about the scandalous nature of the weekend. She had befriended the other Hello Girls by acting like an older sister, giving lessons in French and offering a sympathetic shoulder. But she neither cared what they thought nor was constrained by accepted morality. The war had dramatically changed conventions. The major would not be her first lover. She had lost her virginity at sixteen to Max, the son of her father's best friend. She and Max became close, as far as their own separate aspirations allowed, a relationship her father encouraged.

Max was an exquisite lover. He knew the right places to touch, when to be forceful, and when to be gentle. None since had surpassed him. She was sad when he left the country to fight in the war.

Max had taught her well, and Emily learned to love sex. On a physical level, she craved the tactile sensations that tingled across her skin as her body intertwined with her mate: the jolt of electricity that flowed through her body when her most intimate areas were caressed or licked, the pressure that led to climax, the waves of pleasure that flowed just after. If her passion was lacking, her raw animal lust provided gratification aplenty.

Emily knew full well she was beautiful. Clothed, men admired her. Among other women, there was envy. Naked, she became an object of unrestrained desire. She loved the power her raw sexuality gave her. Sex was a game. She understood it was a formidable weapon if applied correctly by a skilled practitioner, as she had become. Sexual conquest provided a means to advance, whether to help her father with an important client, to secure something she craved — be it money or information — or to obtain chits that she could claim later.

Her new prey was Jameson. When she arrived in Paris at the Gare Montparnasse, Emily went to the water closet, changed out of her Signal Corps uniform, and transformed herself into an aristocratic French widow about to have a weekend tryst. Makeup and expensive perfume completed the conversion.

As planned, Emily got to the hotel first and registered as Madame Jameson — not that anyone cared. She paid in the dollars Jameson had slipped her at their last visit. She worried that Jameson would not make it. Telephone activity had spiked in the last week, a sure sign of an impending offensive; railroad breakdowns were common enough; or she had scared him off, although this was unlikely, given the obvious desire of his last kiss. Maybe he was dead.

The room was small. The large double bed squeezed into the corner took up nearly half the space. A desk, two sitting chairs, a night table, and a mahogany chest of drawers took up the rest. An armoire served as a closet. Situated on the top floor of the hotel, the room's ceiling was low, slightly higher than that of a tall man, and angled down to the one window. Emily shut it immediately; the room was chilly. The room contained a private bathroom, an unusual amenity Emily had insisted upon. The room smelled of lilac, clean sheets, lingering odors of lovemaking, and Parisian air. The walls were thick enough to stifle any noises coming from the next room. Jameson's money was well spent.

When he failed to arrive by eight, Emily became restless and ate some bread and cheese, which she washed down with wine she had bought at the station. When nine o'clock passed, she put on her nightgown and robe, leaving her upper body largely uncovered. No undergarments. She'd be ready for him in case he arrived. Another forty-five minutes ticked away. She began to worry.

When the knock finally came, Emily was greatly relieved. She opened the door to Jameson, who was wearing his U.S. Army uniform and a nervous look on his face. She had advised him on the uniform — Parisians liked *Amis* and never questioned their actions. She reached up and kissed him on each cheek, French-style. "Come in, Andrew. You look tired."

"I'm sorry I'm late. Work. I —" He stopped in mid-sentence, excited by the sight of her welcoming cleavage.

She grabbed him by the lapels, pulled him into the cramped room, closed the door and locked it. He dropped his trench coat to the floor and reached for her breasts. She offered them up to him and threw her arms around his neck. She kissed him passionately. His nerves seemed to melt, and he responded. She pushed her tongue into his mouth and held him close. She felt his reaction move against her belly and led him to the bed.

She removed his uniform blouse and pushed him down. She straddled him, massaged his chest, and allowed him to untie her robe. She removed her nightgown and relished his hungry gaze at her nakedness. She leaned forward and kissed him as she unbuckled his belt. She reached inside his trousers, which he quickly slipped off and tossed away.

Her mouth was everywhere: his ear, his neck, his spine. Her hands rubbed his back using slow, delicate movements and a light touch. She blew warm breaths over his body. She intrigued him when she looked into his face and suggested *soixante-neuf* with a devilish look. He was not sure what she proposed until she moved into position, her mouth near his groin, her sex pointed at his face. He gasped and did not realize, or if he did, he didn't care, when she placed a French letter on his member with her mouth, a trick she learned from a Parisian courtesan. He finished quickly, spilling his wetness into the sheath. Unsatisfied herself, she used her own touch to reach the satisfaction she craved, first arousing her nipples with exquisite pinches and then with her saliva. She reached down between her thighs and stroked the button in a rhythm that aroused her to glorious delight. Her moans were quiet but intense.

Afterward, deep breathing, whispers, and pillow talk. Him: coos, sighs, and romantic nonsense. Her: practiced purrs, expressions of contentment, and boring nonsense. When their talking faded, Emily pulled the bedding up to her neck and fell asleep. Jameson woke up two hours later wanting more, saying he'd have more stamina. She complied. Afterward, he snored the rest of the night.

The next day they visited Paris, but the war had stolen its romantic allure if not its physical beauty. It was gray, quiet, and shaken by war. The dirty streets contained scores of Allied soldiers from all over the British Empire and French colonial world, grieving widows, and maimed veterans. Classic hotels had become hospitals or military headquarters. Church stained-glass windows had been removed or covered. Lights were blacked out. The restaurants lacked delectable fare. Talk was of fighting, not love. People were tired and feared what was to come.

Emily hid her sadness and steered Jameson toward talking about his work to find out all she could about AEF headquarters. "What is General Pershing like?" "What is your typical day?"

"Why do you want to know those things?" he asked.

"So I can do my job better once I'm assigned." She put her arm around his waist and pulled herself closer to him.

Contented, he shrugged his shoulders and answered her questions.

Chapter 14
A New Threat

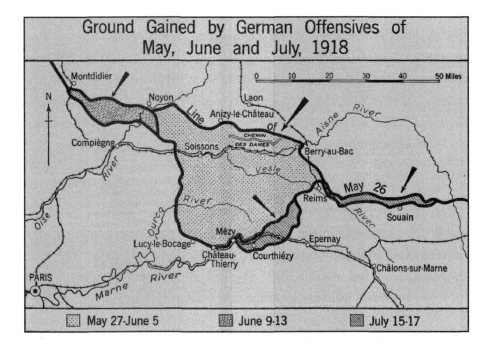

Ground Gained by German Offensives of May, June and July, 1918

May 27-June 5   June 9-13   July 15-17

Chaumont, Haute Marne, France: June 1, 1918

Waiting to hear the bad news, Martin sat outside the office of General James McAndrew, General Pershing's newly appointed chief of staff. McAndrew had been speaking with General Pershing, who was in Paris with the Supreme War Council, for more than forty-five minutes. A conversation that long indicated the situation on the front had worsened during the day.

Martin had grown accustomed to crises in France, and a new one was unfolding. Turning from the British position in the north, the Germans had launched a new phase of General Ludendorff's offensive against the French along the Chemin des Dames. Weakened by the transfer of units to support the British and the grinding war, the French lines were giving way.

The grandfather clock next to Martin chimed midnight. The twelve echoing chimes interrupted the stony silence in the hallway and startled the sergeant guarding the closed door. He looked at Martin with a face full of questions for which Martin had no answers.

Martin had already seen dispatches that reported the German onslaught had pushed the French lines back more than thirty miles in three days. He had discussed the situation with contacts in Paris and twice with Major Fauchaux, who expressed reservations about France's ability to stop the Huns. Later, at the Signal Corps telephone exchange, he learned that every Hello Girl had been called in to handle the high volume of calls.

General McAndrew opened the door and invited Martin to enter. "Sit, Captain," he said. "I have asked you here because you have established contacts in the French army, and experience tells me line officers often understand the real situation better than generals. What do you know? Tell me straight." The choppiness of McAndrew's tone and his taut facial muscles signaled the gravity of the situation.

"From the reports —"

"Screw the reports. I've read them. What have you heard, unofficially? What is *your* assessment of the situation?"

Martin cleared his throat. Giving bad news to higher-ups, even if that is what they needed to hear, was never easy. "Things are not good, General. Parisians are panicked. People are fleeing the city by the thousands. Major Fauchaux has told me General Degoutte is pessimistic. The XXI Corps may not rally. Many French soldiers have left their units without uniforms or rifles. A rout is possible."

Lines of despair etched into McAndrew's brow. "It is true then. Your information is consistent with mine. I had hoped you had better news."

Martin hesitated. Somehow there had to be an answer. "What is General Pershing saying? Surely he has not given up?"

McAndrew rubbed the bridge of his nose with his thumb

and index finger and closed his eyes. "I can only disclose this to the immediate staff. You're new but qualify, Captain Martin. You are under orders not to mention this to anyone."

"Of course."

"The general has cabled the President that we might lose Paris. The French government is preparing to evacuate to Bordeaux."

Martin was sickened. The situation was worse than he had imagined. *Could the Allies lose the war before America had a chance to participate?* "But certainly, General Pétain can order additional French units into the fight."

"I'm afraid the commander of the French army may have fought one too many battles. He claims that seventeen of his thirty-seven divisions are, in his words, 'completely used up.' Far too pessimistic. In his mind, France is already defeated."

"But we are not. Our troops may be green, General, but they are full of fight."

"Yes, Captain. This will be America's chance to show what we can do. The 2nd Division is moving forward as we speak. The 3rd Division is already engaged at Château-Thierry. If I'm not mistaken, your assistant, Lieutenant Keller, has been training men in the 2nd Division. I hope he has done a good job."

"No finer man in the AEF. The 2nd Division will do well," Martin said. *But would Paul survive?*

~

Being a soldier is like being a cop, Keller thought to himself during the all-night march: hours of exhausting drudgery culminating in minutes of life-or-death excitement. Even though he was army, Keller had been assigned to the 4th Marine Brigade of Major General Omar Bundy's 2nd Division. Jealousy between the Army and Marines was rampant, and their trust of staff officers thin. Keller initially resisted the assignment, but Martin convinced him to take it.

The Marines had reservations, too, but accepted him into their ranks. They needed him. He had proven his fighting ability with the Aussies, and he communicated his knowledge with confidence and clarity. More crucially, he was the only officer who had actually faced the Germans. He had much to teach, and the Marines had much to learn — and fast.

The march was strenuous. The roads were in poor condition and clogged with fleeing refugees and French army stragglers hurrying west. More than one said, *"La guerre est finie."* Keller refused to believe the war was lost, but the defeatist comments and mocking gestures from soldiers leaving the fight sowed doubt and apprehension among the Yanks. When the French told the Marines they were headed into Hell, Keller led the men in singing the Battle Hymn of the Republic, drowning them out. A few minutes later, one *poilu* stood on the road as the Americans walked by and ran his index finger across his neck again and again. Keller went up to him and punched him unconscious. The Marines gave a hearty cheer, stood straighter, and marched livelier.

As dawn approached, the sound of distant cannon fire greeted the Marines, making them uneasy. "You'll get used to it," Keller yelled, feigning false confidence. He had seen what artillery could do to men unprotected in dugouts. The image of Maddison's mangled body flashed through his mind.

Just before they stopped to eat cold rations, Keller's leg began to throb, the result of an old bullet wound from a German agent in New York. The doctor had proclaimed he was fully healed, but Keller knew better. He lost a step but refused to acknowledge the lingering pain. His leg sometimes cramped after exertion, but today he forced himself to walk without a limp. He could not afford to lose the confidence he had just won. He was grateful when the battalion commander ordered a rest.

Two hours later, the Marines reached their objective, the Metz-to-Paris road, and began to dig in. Even though this was a critical position, one the Germans would attack in force, Keller took care to remain nonchalant. He supervised the placement of forward barbed wire and made sure the machine guns supported each other with interlocking fire.

The company commander approached Keller and asked, "What do you think you are doing, Lieutenant?"

"Setting up our defenses."

"We are an offensive unit. We attack."

"Do you want to live?"

The captain crossed his arms.

"Captain, I was assigned to this unit to help prepare it for battle. The Germans are going to stampede in here like a herd of mustangs if we don't dig in. I know; I've fought them. Bravado does not stop bullets. Now, let me help save your men."

The master sergeant had been listening in. "You heard the lieutenant," he ordered the troops. "Dig in."

Keller saluted the captain and turned away to issue further instructions. As he removed his gloves and began to sight his rifle, one of the Marines noticed the ring on his hand. "You're married, sir? You sure don't act like it."

"Why do you say that?" Keller joked, but inside he was furious with himself. His pre-battle excitement, concern for the Marines, and the importance of the coming engagement had deflected his thoughts from Shannon, the one person who mattered the most.

He dug into his uniform blouse and lifted the locket that hung around his neck next to his aluminum identification tags. He flipped it open and lifted up the picture of Shannon, her red hair full, her high cheekbones prominent, her smile dazzling. A few men whistled; one man declared she belonged in the moving pictures; another said a dog-faced lieutenant like him must have kidnapped her.

Keller smiled. "She kidnapped *me*." He closed the locket and kissed it before returning it to its place next to his heart.

The whirl of airplane engines followed by machine-gun fire sent them all diving for cover. Fokker D-VIIs. The Germans controlled the air. As the stream of lead passed around Keller, a bullet skimmed off his helmet with a ting and a force that he felt down to his jaw. The Marine next to him took one in the shoulder. The company commander stood defiantly against a sustained burst. He fell to his knees, clutched his face, and screamed in agony, hands syrupy red. Eyeball missing, he was out of the fight.

The airplanes circled away. A corpsman bandaged the captain and sent him to the rear, escorted by a buck private, who couldn't believe his luck. The captain screamed protests as he was led away, leaving Keller the highest-ranking officer in the unit.

"Dig deep, men. Those planes were spotting our position. A barrage is coming. Be prepared." Drill instructors stressed that the machine gun was the queen of the battlefield, but Keller knew better. He had seen the statistics at the Army War College. By far the greatest numbers of field casualties were due to artillery and mortars.

The bombardment that came forty-five minutes later was just a softening-up to greet the Yanks. It lasted fifteen minutes. Due to Keller's foresight, the men suffered no casualties, although one became so terrified, he had to be sent back. The others handled the stress well. Keller praised them for their courage but did not tell them the attack was just a bee sting, with far worse to come.

Keller defied his standing orders to return to brigade headquarters once his company had established a defensive position. Staff officers belonged behind the front lines, but he was now the accepted company commander. He would not leave them to get slaughtered, nor would he forfeit the thrill to come.

God help me in this fight and return me to Shannon.

~

Six hours behind in New York, Shannon woke up in a sweat. Paul was in danger.

Chapter 15
Where Do We Stand?

Police Headquarters: June 1918
Clancy, Fernandez, and Shannon sat in a poorly lit interview room on the second floor of Police Headquarters and discussed the case. Fernandez had wanted someplace private to talk. The confined room was designed to minimize noise from the outside corridor and hardened the voices of the two men. To Shannon, the lack of elbow room made it feel like a tightly packed train carriage. The cold metal chair seat added to her discomfort. She hoped never to face an interrogation in such a place.

"Where do we stand?" Fernandez asked.

"Progress?" Clancy shrugged. "Slow. It's been two weeks since Fishbait's been with us, but he can't get close to learn more. All we have is the description of Kittridge's accomplices. Not much good without names."

"Kittridge is involved with the Germans," Shannon said. "That's clear. But to what end?"

"We broke up the German spy ring two years ago. Is Kittridge forming a new one?" Fernandez hesitated, then asked, "Could he be operating outside of Tammany Hall?"

"If Fishbait's description is right, he's also up to something with the Irish," Shannon said. "A German-Irish connection worries me."

"What about the listening device we planted in the Hanover?" Fernandez's tone conveyed his frustration.

"Hasn't helped." Clancy rubbed his tired eyes with his hand. "We were lucky to get it placed, but we can't use the health inspection disguise again."

"If they were using that restaurant to make their plans, they aren't now." Shannon tried to read Fernandez's expression. The investigation was not going well. Was he thinking about shutting it down?

"They on to us?" Fernandez asked.

"Maybe they suspect something, but I'm sure we haven't given ourselves away," Shannon said with as much conviction as she could muster.

"Last night, Red pushed Fishbait hard. Maybe too hard." Clancy said. "Risky, but necessary. We got to get something useful out of him. I hope the kid holds up."

"You think he's backstabbing us?" Fernandez asked.

"No. Too scared. Red says Fishbait's doing what he can."

"Kittridge has another meeting today. Fishbait will be there," Shannon said.

Fernandez stood up. With a reputation for excellence, he had overcome prejudice over his Hispanic background and suspicion concerning his five-foot-five stature with an engaging smile, hard work, and incorruptible morals. He attended Mass every day and handled the toughest cases with consistent success. His arrests brought convictions; convictions supported by irrefutable evidence and ego-breaking interviews brought promotions; and promotions gave him respect. "Keep me informed. The lieutenant wants results. Promotion time is near. He's counting on us."

~

Fishbait Jackson looked nervously over at the four men milling around the park bench behind Columbus circle in Central Park. He wanted to run, take a train to Chicago, start a new life, but he was trapped. "Get names," that one-eared cop had said in the stall of a public toilet at Grand Army Plaza. Fishbait could still feel the cold steel of the knife as it rested on his nose half an inch from his eye. Weeks had gone by since he'd encountered the man they called "Red" at Police Headquarters. Everyone had a last name but him. That knife of his gleamed sharper every time they met.

Fishbait's other worry was Silas Wood, "Mr. Wood" to Fishbait. Did his gray-haired partner really believe his fabricated story about how he'd escaped after he was arrested in Bronxville — that the old

Irish cop had failed to lock the paddy wagon, and Fishbait had tumbled out the back as they crossed into the city? Had the cut on his head, requiring three stitches, and the handcuffs on his wrists convinced Mr. Wood? Fishbait prayed that his wanted poster plastered on the wall of every local police station strengthened his story. To further suggest he was on the run, he began to grow a scraggly beard and pulled a cap low on his brow over his freshly dyed hair.

Over the last week, Mr. Wood had been watching Fishbait more closely every day. His frown had turned to a scowl, and he never left him alone during the day, even to urinate. Luckily, Mr. Wood liked women and lived with a whore in northern Manhattan near the Polo Grounds, where the Giants were midway into the baseball season. He permitted Fishbait to go home alone to Brooklyn, which gave him the chance to meet Red at night.

With Mr. Wood's scrutiny ever more intense, Fishbait realized he would not have many more chances to come up with the information Red demanded. He eyed the four men by the bench, evaluating them. Aside from Kittridge, there was an Irish fella they called Michael, a Nigra with sleeves rolled high over his biceps, and someone Fishbait had seen once before, a dandy-type in a bow tie, bowler hat, and expensive black leather shoes, spit shined. The black man, who looked like he could beat Jack Johnson in the ring, appeared bored as the others talked. Fishbait edged closer, trying to pick something up, anything at all, so Red would leave him alone. *Shit*, he thought. *Why did I ever get mixed up in this mess? The cops have nothin' on me but petty larceny. Life ain't never been fair.*

Mr. Wood turned to leer at a woman walking by, and Fishbait circled around the bench hoping to overhear their conversation. The Irishman handed Kittridge some papers. A passport? Fishbait bent low, pretending to tie his shoe.

"Everything you specified," the Irishman said. "From our best man in Boston. The diplomatic documents took a while. It'll cost you."

"They better be as good as the last ones, or you'll never get your money."

Fishbait waited, guessing Mr. Wood would soon go chasing after the dame. When Wood crept away, Fishbait approached the bench, remaining behind his targets' backs. Hot in debate, they failed to notice him.

"The deal's in the works; the down payment is made," the dandy said. "The German offensive has stalled. Should we continue?"

A cop sauntered by, tipped his hat, and wished them a good day. Kittridge waited until he was out of earshot before speaking. "Nonsense. The Germans have already knocked the British back. They're shelling Paris with that Big Bertha gun. Can you imagine? The French are reeling; the Americans aren't yet ready. Foch, the overall Allied commander? Ha! The Allies are in a panic — it's the perfect time to strike at Britain."

"What do you know about fightin'?" the black man asked. "Any of you ever kills a man? I have, and it ain't no game. I'm risking everything. How do I know I can trust you?"

"You'll be well compensated," Kittridge said.

"I agree with Gibson," the dandy nodded. "Can we trust you?"

The vein in the Irishman's head looked like it was about to burst. "This is not about money or trust. It's about freedom." He looked at the black man. "You should know this better than me."

"That's one reason I'se here."

"Maybe we should wait," the dandy suggested. "It's risky."

Gibson moved away and sat on the park bench. He glanced at the sky and the sun reflected off a gold front tooth. Fishbait eyed the three glittering gold rings that adorned both of the man's hands, wondering if they were diamonds. This man had money despite his working clothes and low-born ways. *Must have gotten it illegal.* A wave of self-pity and jealousy washed over him. Why should a Nigra have such success when he didn't?

The black man took out a razor-sharp dagger from some mysterious pocket, picked up a thick stick, and began to whittle. Each of his long, powerful strokes shaved off thin, precise slices from the wood. The man's actions were quick and deliberate, no wasted motion. He looked like a grizzly: powerful, agile, and dangerous when provoked. Without looking up, he said, "Decide soon or find someone else. I want half my money now."

"You'll get it." Kittridge glimpsed Fishbait from the corner of his eye and looked surprised. He switched to German, and the dandy and Irishman responded in kind. Fishbait walked off a bit, pretending to ignore them.

Mr. Wood returned, rubbing a red mark on his cheek. "That bitch," he muttered. "I should have slapped her back."

Kittridge stared at Wood's cheek. "Where've you been? It's always women with you. Good for you I like your work. Now do your job." He gestured toward Fishbait.

Fishbait understood the threat. Mr. Wood carried a gun and would not hesitate to use it. He could try to sprint away, but he couldn't outrun a bullet. *Best to play dumb.* He had to get away — he had important information for Red.

Mr. Wood understood too. "You been a bad boy?" he asked Fishbait.

"He's been listening to us," Kittridge said.

Fishbait gulped. "No! I haven't. With Mr. Wood gone, I came over 'cause I thought you needed protection. That's all. I didn't hear nothin'."

The dandy said something to Kittridge that Fishbait couldn't hear. They both nodded, and Kittridge called Mr. Wood over and whispered something.

The edges of Wood's mouth curled up in agreement.

Chapter 16
The Baron

Upper West Side, New York City: June 1918
Kittridge sat smoking his pipe in his plush West Side apartment overlooking Central Park. The neatly arranged furniture was mahogany, the China from Delft, the tapestry from Bruges, and the tobacco from Cuba. Though well organized, his apartment was a bit dusty. Not that he cared about cobwebs. No one was allowed to enter without his supervision, let alone a lowly cleaning lady. He gazed at the three pictures on top of his piano: his brother in the Alps, his beautiful daughter, and his wife in her wedding dress. Sad she had died so young.

The weather was unseasonably chilly, and the glowing logs in his fire place spit dying embers onto the hearth in front of him. The fire soothed his troubled mind. For the first time all day, he relaxed and enjoyed the solitude that surrounds midnight and the emptiness of the street five stories below. He looked at the moon and wondered where he would be in six months — here, in Europe, or in an unmarked, worm-eaten box six feet under?

After a few moments of calm, he reflected on the events that led him to his meeting today in Central Park with an Irish patriot, a *Schwarze* laborer, and an American gun merchant. He examined the papers Michael Donnelly had given him. They were perfect. His new identity as a Dutch diplomat, Harry Vandoven, was ready to use whenever he chose to do so. That would be soon, he guessed.

He had used his current identity, Murdock Kittridge, for so long that his real name seemed foreign to him: Baron Klaus von Stolberg. His great-uncle once removed, German Chancellor Otto von Bismarck, had sent him to America in 1888 at age twenty with orders to "become American — learn their ways, their weaknesses. Succeed and prosper. We will give you money. Build yourself a good life. Raise a family, but never forget who you are. Make sure your children know it too."

Though Kittridge was young, his many talents had not escaped the Iron Chancellor. Klaus's early genius at numbers, precocious business skill undoubtedly garnered from his steel-making grandfather, natural political gifts, and accent-perfect language ability made him the ideal candidate for an undefined, never-before-tried experiment. Von Bismarck planned for the long term, but he could not have predicted how von Stolberg's assignment, predicated on a forged American identity, would evolve. Or when Germany would need him.

Kittridge studied mathematics and law at the College of the City of New York. He started his career in accounting, then moved on to banking at the urging of an old family friend and Germany's future ambassador to the United States, Johann-Heinrich von Bernstorff, who predicted that money would be the lifeblood of the 20th century. At least twice a month, Kittridge corresponded with Uncle Johann, who encouraged him to advance and always be ready to serve the Fatherland.

Seeing the growing power of Tammany Hall, von Bernstorff advised Kittridge to apply for a position in their treasury group. A sizable donation to a few favored politicians secured the job. Kittridge's brains, savvy political skills, and ingenious ability to shuffle money around invisibly propelled him to the highest ranks in Tammany Hall. He actively became a corrupt city official, a thief, and a con man, but remained a German agent-in-waiting.

With the outbreak of the Great War, Germany activated its long-silent asset. Kittridge shifted his alliances away from Tammany Hall back to the Fatherland. For the last thirteen months, he had been skimming money out of their coffers to a secret account known only to him and von Bernstorff, now ambassador. When the U.S. cut off diplomatic relations with Germany, von Bernstorff's forced departure left Kittridge alone with mounds of cash to plot how best to serve Germany.

The seeds of the plot came to him as much by happenstance as by calculation. Before she died, Kittridge's wife, an American of German extraction, had been good friends with an Irish Catholic woman born in County Cork. Fiercely anti-British, Maggie Tullamore spoke angrily and often of England's subjugation of Ireland. Through her, the Kittridges feigned sympathy for the Irish cause. Kittridge pretended to be devastated when the 1916 Easter Rebellion in Dublin was crushed and the leaders were hanged.

Kittridge later met the Irish patriot Michael Donnelly at a Boston fundraiser that Maggie had urged him to attend, and he and Donnelly became fast friends. Donnelly had fought in the Easter Rebellion but, now wanted, escaped to America before Britain rounded up the rest of the revolutionaries. Fury erupted in the Irish-American community, and Donnelly did everything possible to promote the Irish cause here. His growing friendship with Kittridge offered possibilities, and he vowed to return to Ireland to fight for independence.

Kittridge's plan traced back to a late night in Flanagan's Bar after too many beers. He had the financial means; Donnelly had the contacts and soldiers in the old country. Procuring the weapons proved difficult until Ronny Ellison magically appeared, saying he had worked with Karl Bier, who ran the New Haven Projectile Company, a known German-run rogue operation. Ellison was one of their customers from Los Angeles, and Kittridge thought he needed to know more about him. Finding someone to ship the goods was easy: von Bernstorff recommended a black man called Gibson who had worked with German agents two years ago, as reliable, smart, and trustworthy.

The scheme matured into a viable plan just as the war had reached its climax. General Ludendorff's Spring Offensive had gained nothing strategic, but Kittridge's plan, if successful, would bring victory to the Fatherland off the battlefield, if not on it. Inquiries, legal and not, into Ellison confirmed his gun-running credentials.

Kittridge stood up, stretched his back, and added two logs to the fire. It crackled back to life and exhaled earthy warmth back into the apartment. He poured himself another glass of twenty-year-old single malt Irish whiskey, a gift from Donnelly, and savored its subtle blend. The second drink steadied him. He was living on the edge of an icy precipice, the waters below cold and angry. He was guilty of two capital crimes: robbing Tammany Hall to fund his enterprise, and violating the 1917 Espionage Act, written to deal with traitors plotting against the United States. His likely fate was a bullet to the head by some Tammany Hall assassin — Silas Wood? — or a hangman's noose by a servant of a U.S. court.

Kittridge finished his whiskey and tried to assess his chances. Donnelly confirmed that Ellison had procured seven thousand rifles, ninety machine guns, twenty mortars, hundreds of boxes of grenades and explosives, and a million rounds of ammunition. Enough to support a proper uprising. Michael swore the Irish revolutionaries were ready once the weapons reached Derry. Ellison had received 25% of his fee, the rest would be on delivery. Gibson assured him he could ship the goods without problems. He had arrived in New York a year ago with a recently purchased merchant ship and swore the Germans would never bother him. People laughed, but he never lost a cargo. And he never explained why.

A similar venture had failed two years ago, when the German cargo vessel *Libau* secretly sailed into Ireland carrying a huge cache of weapons. The *Libau* failed to deliver them due to poor communication between the German crew and the Irish insurgents concerning the exact delivery date. When British ships intercepted the ship, the crew scuttled it rather than surrender the cargo. Donnelly swore no such catastrophe would occur on this mission.

Kittridge was fatigued beyond sleep, but he still had one more thing to finish. He took out his fountain pen and began to write. Dissatisfied, he crumpled the first draft and let it fall unnoticed. His careless heel pushed it under the chair's fringe. He began again.

Dear Andy,

I am sorry I have not written sooner, but, as you can imagine, I am busy. The plans we discussed before you left are coming together. It is to be greatly hoped that the deal will merit the risks and bring great rewards.

If everything succeeds on my end, we may not need your help with the estate. Do your job and learn what you can. I am sure you are the best shot in your outfit; your skills will help our noble cause.

I trust your final days at Camp Merrick were not too stressful and your journey across the ocean was uneventful. These U-boat attacks are immoral.

By now, I assume you are settled in your post. A friend you know will contact you. He is a resourceful fellow.

Your Aunt Ruth is fine and asks how you are. I'm sorry to say that your dog McKinley is sick. He's old, and his kidneys are failing. He needs to be put down.

This should all be over by the year-end, and God willing we will see a righteous end to all this slaughter.

Everything is fine on my end. Proceed as we have discussed. All my plans are in the works and I see nothing that would forestall them.

Stay safe. I can't tell you how. Trust your training and listen to your superiors. Do your duty. Good luck, not that you need it. I pray this reaches you.

– Your loving Father

Kittridge sealed and stamped the letter. *The army censors will read this, but so what?* he thought. *To them it's just family news. But even if I fail, you, Andy, you remain — our one last chance to strike a blow against Germany's enemies.*

I have trained you well.

Chapter 17
Jelly

The Plaza Hotel, New York City: June 1918

Shannon pondered Fishbait's description of the conspirators. Gibson provoked the most curiosity. "I jus' can't figure out what he's doing," Fishbait had said. "He's more like a worker than a boss, and black to boot. Mystery to me why he mixed up with a rich man like Kittridge."

Maybe, thought Shannon, but this was a conspiracy, and Gibson was not there by accident. She had spent many sleepless hours trying to figure out his role, but for once she agreed with Fishbait: Nothing about him made sense. Kittridge could have obtained the services of any number of more suitable Irishmen, but he had chosen this man. Why? How did Kittridge find him?

Shannon had not yet questioned Clancy, who was busy chasing informants and monitoring the Hanover restaurant. The next morning, she enticed him into a conversation, bribing him with his favorite scones in exchange for his thoughts.

"I agree, Shannon," Clancy said between appreciative mouthfuls. "Something's not right. Tell me what you know so far."

"Fishbait didn't know if Gibson's name was real. Kittridge, who looked down at everyone but his betters, called him "you," if he called him anything at all. The black man was no business partner; he was still a slave — he just didn't act like one. Fishbait guessed Kittridge would rather do business with a white man, but someone big had selected Gibson, and Kittridge had no say about it."

Shannon related Fishbait's report that he would never forget three things about Gibson. First, he was a big man — 6'2" and over 200 pounds — who wore shirts too tight for his colossal chest and a scowl that seemed to separate the violent man inside from the outward appearance he presented to the world.

Gibson's deep baritone overpowered other men's voices when

he spoke, which was not often. He kept his distance during talks, but sometimes added a comment. He often seemed bored, and ignored the others while he whittled. He would slash anything that provoked his fury. When he did speak, though, everyone, Kittridge included, listened. Even Mr. Wood admitted that he was smart, and the dandy respected him too. Or maybe feared him. Gibson was a scary guy.

Finally, Gibson had a gold front tooth. He had a big face and a bigger smile, and that shiny tooth was the center of it. He wore a gold cross on a chain around his neck but didn't seem religious. Profanities made up half his vocabulary, and he'd sent any number of men to the hospital without a thought. Maybe he had his own code for living, but Fishbait never seen him near a Bible or any other book either.

Clancy rubbed his chin. "For the love of Saint Patrick, Shannon — that sounds just like Jelly Brown. But that's impossible. He disappeared."

"Jelly Brown? Who's that?"

"Some Negro who ran a dock gang and a lighter crew in Brooklyn two years ago. I worked that beat before I joined the Bomb Squad. That was about the same time as you, Shannon, if I recall. Brown had muscles and a gold tooth just like your Mr. Gibson. As I remember, he was a decent man. Honest, as far as dockworkers go."

"Doesn't sound like our Mr. Gibson."

"Maybe. Jelly Brown was fierce, just like this guy, stronger than a P.T. Barnum weightlifter. No one crossed him without paying a price. But like I said, he ain't been seen in a long time. Dead, most think."

"What do *you* think happened to him, Sean?"

"Not rightly sure. Won big on the numbers and just skedaddled is my guess. The story goes that one day Brown and his crew are buzzing around like flies over horse flop, all excited. Getting ready for something big. Two days later, him and his men go missing, his warehouse burned to the ground, his lighter empty. Nobody ever saw them again."

"When was that?"

"Hard to say. Everything got crazy after that bomb attack on Black Tom Island. Longshoremen were not a concern."

Shannon's analytical mind leaped to the central question. "Was it around the time of that poison gas attack on Wall Street? Some Negroes were in on that, you know."

Clancy's head snapped back as if someone had slapped him. "Whoa. Now that you mention it, could have been."

"Anything else you remember? Something that didn't seem right?"

"Yeah. Heard he had this fancy motorboat docked by his warehouse. Disappeared about the same time he did. He told people it belonged to some friend of his, a white fellow."

Shannon was as focused as a sniffer dog on a scent. "What white man? Forties maybe, soldier type? A loner — someone you'd never expect to be with Brown?"

"Maybe. What are you thinking, Shannon?"

"Can you take me to Brown's old warehouse?"

~

Shannon never liked the dockyards. They smelled of refuse, dirty men, and low tide. Men labored like ants at a picnic. Women did not belong, and no one hesitated to say so, either with cat calls, lewd remarks, or whistles. But today, no one bothered her out of respect for Clancy, who was remembered by all for running the best beat on the Brooklyn dockyards. A few called out to him and said they missed him, and Clancy waved back, addressing each man by name.

They walked for about ten minutes through manure, muddy debris, and river waste. Shannon felt grateful for Clancy's protection and her boots, gloves, and old clothes.

"That's it." Clancy pointed to Brown's old dock, a burned-out area thirty yards ahead that had remained empty since the fire — or was it arson, as some had thought? The lighter, too, was long gone, no doubt stolen. In the dockyards, where misfortune and superstition were common, people simply avoided the place.

Shannon determined the placement of the warehouse from the outline of the few remaining timbers and started poking around with a stick. Weather and time had turned the debris into unrecognizable muck. "Keep looking, Sean," she encouraged, feeling that a find was near.

An hour later, Shannon was still exploring. Clancy paused and looked around. The place was desolate. Coming darkness had begun to hinder the efforts of the lighter crews returning to dock. "Honestly, Shannon, for the last time — we've got to go," he urged.

"A few minutes more," she replied, moving to a new area and stubbornly plunging her stick into the ground for the hundredth time. *Ting.* Something metal.

"Sean, come help me. There's something down here." Clancy drove his shovel into the muck and the hard ground beneath it with a forceful push of the leg. Pushing again, and a third time, he unearthed a rusty tin container slightly larger than a cigar box.

Shannon gently pried open the flaking lid, hoping the contents were still intact. Maps and hand-made diagrams spilled out of a waterproof leather pouch. Shannon almost fell over when she realized the gravity of the discovery. "My God in Heaven," she said. "This is where they planned the attack on Wall Street two years ago."

"Impossible. We checked this area."

"Well, you missed something. Here's the evidence." She held up a map highlighting underground gas lines and key locations on Wall Street.

"Sean, it seems your Jelly Brown and maybe his white friend were ringleaders in the attack. Brown is our Mr. Gibson."

"We do know one man escaped the Wall Street shootout wearing a gas mask. No one could identify him. His crew neither. They were all shot up."

"What has Mr. Brown been up to for the last two years? And what is he doing with Mr. Kittridge?"

~

While Shannon was digging around his old warehouse, Jelly Brown sat in the office of the Hanover waiting for Kittridge to bring him his down payment and further orders. Kittridge was late, and Jelly had a bad feeling about him. He knew how to size up other men, a skill that had kept him alive longer than expected. Kittridge was holding something back, something important, and Jelly did not trust him.

While he waited, Jelly thought back to the attack on Wall Street in September 1916 — the event that had led him to this meeting — and how it had transformed his life. It had started out well, but ended in disaster. All his men were dead, his German agent friend likely dead along with them.

Jelly knew that the plan was risky: launch a poison gas attack, intercept an armored Sanford truck on its way to the Treasury on Wall Street, and steal its gold. The police reacted quickly and foiled the plan. The lone survivor, Jelly had escaped with his life and several gold bars. He rushed back to his dockyard, doused it with gas, and was digging for the metal box that stored his accomplice's valuables, when approaching voices caused him to flee. He tossed a match behind him, and, hidden at a distance, watched his old life go up in flames and float away with the ashes.

Knowing he was a hunted man, Jelly grabbed the first train out of New York and fenced the gold to a friend in New Jersey. The $20,000 was a tidy sum, but not the riches he had hoped for. He made his way to Cuba, arriving in October 1916, and began to live a gentleman's life in Havana.

Jelly quickly became bored lounging on the beach by day and chasing whores and drinking rum by night. He thrived on action but had to lie low and shut up about his past. A social man, he did not like hiding, but he knew all about prison life and swore he would rather die than rot in a U.S. penitentiary.

By June 1917, Jelly's money was running out and he became

restless and careless. One night, he met a man in a bar who claimed to be a former German agent who had escaped a New York Police round-up of German spies after the United States had entered the war. They became drinking buddies, and after another long night of debauchery, Jelly confessed that he'd been a longshoreman and had worked for a German agent in New York. He never saw his companion again.

Jelly did not think much of the encounter — such men came and went frequently — until a few weeks later, when the German ambassador to Cuba approached him on his veranda. The ambassador carried a letter of introduction from Johann-Heinrich von Bernstorff, thanking Jelly for his past service to Germany. His German accomplice must have mentioned him to his supervisors. The ambassador made a proposition that Jelly promptly accepted, favoring adventure to monotony.

The ambassador returned the next week with false papers, a wad of dollars, and instructions. Jelly was to pick up a cargo ship that had just been purchased in his name, return to Baltimore, and set up a shipping operation under his new identity to smuggle critical materiel into Germany. What he did outside of the smuggling was his business, but he was assured that German U-boats would never attack him. They set up a communications link, and Jelly's ship soon garnered a reputation for never losing cargo in dangerous waters.

Working under the name of Jerome Gibson, Jelly was doing fine: profits were excellent, the operation was running smoothly, and life was good. Then in early March, Murdock Kittridge had marched into his office with a special request from Germany, one that Jelly was compelled to accept or risk police inquiries into his past. Kittridge would be the one to pay him, but Jelly's real superior would be von Bernstorff.

~

The sound of footsteps alerted Jelly that someone was coming up the stairs. He pulled out his gun, but put it down when Kittridge appeared at the door of the restaurant office and handed over a heavy leather pouch.

Jelly did not bother to count the money. Not now. "When do I pick up the goods for Ireland?" Jelly asked.

"In a few weeks. Ronny Ellison is bringing them to Jersey in batches."

"After that, we done. That's right, isn't it, Mr. Kittridge? No more smuggling."

"Yes, as we agreed."

"If you or the others cross me, I'll kill you slow. Understand?"

Chapter 18
Belleau Wood

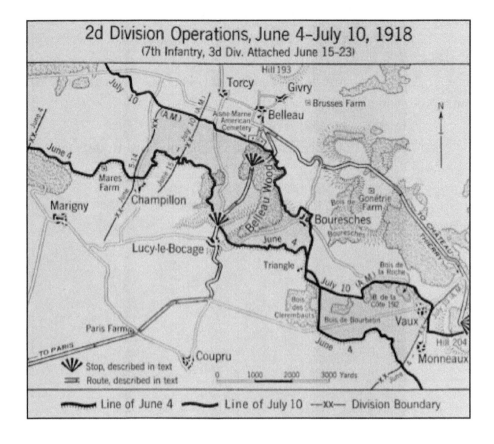

2d Division Operations, June 4–July 10, 1918
(7th Infantry, 3d Div. Attached June 15-23)

Allied Front Line above the Metz-Paris Road, France: June 4, 1918

08:00: Keller watched nervously as the last withdrawing French battalion filtered through his line. Now the de-facto company commander, he worried about his men. His Marines had been dug in for the last two days north of the village of Lucy-le-Bocage, on orders to relieve the outnumbered French, exhausted after a week of continuous fighting, and establish a line of defense at the Allied front. As his men prepared to face the advancing Germans, fighting had erupted to the northwest at Champillon: Keller knew their turn would come soon.

The French battalion commander approached in a torn, sweat-stained uniform. "Thank God, you are here," he said to Keller in good English. "The Boches are 1,200 meters behind and will advance through the woods. I officially hand command of this sector over to you. Paris is fifty-nine miles behind us. The war may be decided here if they break through. Do not fail."

"You can count on us, Major. The Germans will not get by even if it costs every man in this company."

"I pray that will not be the case. *Au revoir.*"

A mechanical noise overhead caught Keller's attention. A flock of high-pitched birds scattered. Flying toward the German advance were two French SPAD XIII reconnaissance planes with red-blue-white American rondel markings. One of the pilots tipped his wing to his comrades below. "Good to see you," Keller muttered. "At last."

He turned to study the position in front of him: a wheat field about one-quarter mile deep, with a woodland behind it standing on higher ground. The woods, about one square mile of rough, rocky terrain, were shaped like a wobbly rectangle. A retreating *poilu* had called it *le Bois de Belleau*. The trees were tall and tightly spaced. In the field, waist-high shafts of wheat swayed in the gentle breeze like ripples of water across a wind-swept lake. The land was flat; no ditches, no rock outcroppings, no cover.

There was nothing to stop bullets but human flesh. It was a perfect killing ground, and Keller had positioned his machine-gun teams for maximum effect. Let them come.

He did not have long to wait. Two German scouts at the edge of the woods appeared in Keller's sniper scope. Keller saw the flash of deliberate hand signals to an unknown number of men behind them, and ordered his men to hold fire until he signaled — two shots in quick succession. Attack-and-defense was as much a game of nerves as it was of weapons. A more resolute unit could prevail against a superior force if it could endure the pain inflicted on it and administer more punishment than its adversary could accept. In such a contest, Keller was confident his Marines would win.

Before the Germans could attack through the field, thunderous cannon booms erupted from the American rear. The Americans had brought up their artillery in time, sending streams of shells over the field into the woods and beyond. Keller heard the unholy screams of wounded men as the shells exploded amid the German ranks.

Predictably, a German counter-barrage commenced. The duel lasted for ... Keller had no idea how long. Who could think with such a deafening clamor? He soon realized that the Americans had sustained their bombardment longer and more powerfully than the Germans. Were the Krauts running out of shells? Had the SPADs' observation mission successfully targeted the enemy gun positions? Did the Americans have more field pieces in this sector than the Germans? Most important to Keller, no poison-gas or high-explosive shells had landed on his position. The Americans had won the first stage of the fight.

As the artillery duel tapered down, two under-strength German infantry companies emerged from the woods. It was far from the powerful force Keller had feared. He nestled his rifle into the crook of his arm and waited until they were halfway across the wheat field, then fired off two shots, killing the lead German sergeant.

The Marine machine guns opened up and cut down the advancing enemy as easily as a straight razor against three-day stubble. The riflemen finished the job. The remaining Germans retreated back into the woods, dragging their wounded and leaving dozens of dead on the field.

The Marines cheered. Keller warned them to prepare for a more powerful attack, but the situation was calm for the rest of the day all across their sector. The 2nd Division had stopped the German advance. Temporarily.

"You survive a day, good on you, mate, but if you want to keep your sanity, you got to take it day-by-day, hour-by-hour, minute-by-minute," one of the Aussies had told him. "Take in some air and enjoy it. Your next breath may be your last."

Thoughts of death and the battle sure to come led Keller's mind back along the path that had ended him up at Belleau Wood. His moral code had been set at an early age, when he witnessed his Uncle Ulrich beat his aunt bloody. Just thirteen, Keller had been staying with his relatives in Pennsylvania, working at the local mill during the summer. He tried to intervene in the fight, but his uncle threatened him with a knife, and later stole the money he had earned at the mill hauling scrap and debris. Paul came back to New York that summer determined to never again back away. He taught himself to fight and shoot, and got the local beat cop to teach him all the techniques: police methods, the dirty tricks of criminals, and everything in between.

Keller learned fast. He returned to Pennsylvania a year later an expert knife fighter and marksman. His hopes to even the score with his uncle were dashed when he learned that Ulrich was in prison for killing Pete Riley, his old summer league baseball coach. The motivation for the murder was unclear, but Keller's aunt was never the same.

Keller liked Pete; he was the first adult to tell him he had the talent to play big league ball, and Keller always felt he could have saved him had he been able to fight his uncle the year before. From that day on, Keller swore he would not allow bullies to win. That pledge made him want to be a cop. Never again would he hesitate to fight if necessary. Attack, not retreat, became his personal motto. As an adult, people would describe him as impulsive, belligerent, and hot-headed. He was none of those.

The one person who truly understood this was his wife. Keller thought of her, and breathed more easily.

~

All through the night and into the next day, Keller waited for a renewed German attack or orders from headquarters. Neither came. With each passing hour, the men became increasingly agitated. They had seen what American machine guns could do and suspected they would face the same from the Huns when the inevitable order to attack arrived. Keller spent the day on edge, breaking up petty fights and calming shaky nerves.

The situation worsened when the men received no hot meals for the third day in a row. The field kitchens had been slow to keep up with the 2nd Division advance. The men ate stale biscuits and something called dried meat that cracked their teeth and settled in their stomach like cement. Water was scarce; the mood of the Marines worsened. "Let's just attack," a private said. "I'd rather die from a belly full of lead than from this crap." Keller calmed him with some chocolate he had been saving for an emergency.

The shouts of German officers and the sound of men chopping trees across no-man's-land reached Keller's ears. The clamor of axes hitting wood told Keller the Huns were fortifying their position. They would not surrender Belleau Wood without a fight.

Keller had spent hours with the platoon leaders describing fighting tactics he had learned from the British. A few resisted, complaining that his approach contradicted everything they had been taught, but Keller's explanation and experience convinced most of them of his wisdom: no massed formation; move fast, zig zag, keep low. "Get rid of all non-essentials," he ordered. "Carry only what you need: rifle, ammo, gas mask, and plenty of grenades. Grenades, not bayonets and bravado, will prevail."

The moon was full in the sky when the runner from battalion headquarters brought Keller his orders: Advance on Belleau Wood and take it. Pre-attack bombardment begins at 03:45 tomorrow, June 6. Phase I attack on Hill 142 to your northwest begins at 05:00. You are to advance your company at 17:00. The entire 2nd Division would participate, and its brigade commander, General James Guthrie Harbord, had guaranteed success.

His success, our blood, thought Keller. Intelligence had reported that boulders and gullies provided excellent defensive positions in Belleau Wood. Visibility through the trees was poor and the pathways irregular and hard to follow. Fighting in there would be vicious. Of that and that alone, Keller was certain.

Keller ordered his men to rest before the attack, but few did. Tension built with each passing hour as the excitement and anticipation of naïve but zealous boys pulsed through the company. Some wrote letters; one studied his Bible. Others, more composed, played cards. Waiting created its own stomach-churning stress.

With nothing more he could do, Keller leaned back in his ditch and instructed his master sergeant to notify him at 03:00. Thoughts of Shannon kept him awake. He composed a letter, sealed it, and scratched "In the event of my death" on the front. He left the letter in his knapsack with instructions to give it to Captain Martin at GHQ. Feeling calmer, he fell into an exhausted sleep, his hand wrapped around the locket containing the portrait of his beautiful wife. He woke up sometime later, clutching his locket so tightly his hand had begun to cramp. He welcomed the pain. It meant he was still alive.

He was alert and rested when his sergeant appeared. "03:00, Lieutenant."

"I'm awake, thank you." Keller crept to the forward attack position. The moon's light reflected off the sea of wheat in front of him. The area had a disturbing calm about it — the same feeling one has looking at a tide rolling onto a sandy beach even though a storm out to sea is closing in.

He squinted through the moonlit sky and across the wheat field to the woods, a quarter mile away. The day was certain to bring carnage. He checked his watch: 03:40. Five minutes to go. The opening salvos appeared on schedule. Flashes arced across the horizon like deadly shooting stars as explosions rattled his teeth and shook the earth beneath him. The men hunkered down and covered their ears to little effect, their nerves taut.

Keller and his Marines suffered through the barrage, hoping the bombardment would soften up the German defenses. Master engineers, the Huns were ingenious with machine-gun emplacement. He expected the worst.

Keller waited all day to attack hoping Phase I would be successful and his company would move forward in unison with adjacent units. In actuality, it didn't matter: Orders were orders.

~

16:58: He signaled his men to prepare. Keller loaded full clips into his rifle and .45, tightened his chin strap, placed his whistle into his dry mouth and blew. The shrill sound pierced his line. "Come on, boys!" he hollered, and jumped over his earthworks. The rest of the company followed, with adjacent units entering the field simultaneously. Keller crouched low and moved forward at a steady clip, each stride bringing him closer to his maker. They'd advanced one-third of the way across when the Germans opened fire. Platoons that bunched together, ignoring Keller's warning, were ripped to pieces. Their screams seemed to reach into Hell.

The stream of German bullets forced Keller to turn his head and lean sideways. Soldiers on either side of him fell. A bullet clipped his leg, several zipped by his ears, shafts of wheat sheared free by waves of lead floated everywhere, but Keller kept running. First this way, then that, in unpredictable patterns, ignoring the searing crimson patch on his thigh.

A hundred yards from the edge of the woods, Keller dived onto his belly just as the machine-gun team facing him rotated the barrel of their Maxim and unleashed a sustained burst right at him. A flurry of bullets passed inches from his prostrate head. They would have cut him in two had he been standing.

Breathing hard, he pushed his face into the dirt and looked side-to-side across the attack zone. He and two Marines had reached the farthest, but elsewhere the attack was stalling.

"We're right behind you, Lieutenant," a familiar voice called. "We're pinned down. What do we do?"

"Stay down." Keller ordered." Put down your rifles and grab grenades." He signaled the men behind him to pour everything they had at the Germans. The Browning Automatic Rifles (BARs) spat out bursts of lead, and the riflemen worked their bolts feverishly, as Keller and the two Marines crawled forward under suppressing American fire.

Inch by agonizing inch, minute by torturous minute, Keller advanced using his legs and elbows. The man to his left stopped dead, a bullet hole drilled through his helmet, but miraculously, Keller kept crawling. He got within twenty-five yards of the woods and signaled the platoon behind him to stop firing.

One chance. He breathed hard, pulled the pin, popped up and tossed. He dived down and counted the seconds: three, two, one. The grenade exploded, lifting the machine gun and body parts into the air.

Keller reached for his .45 and charged. He spotted movement in the woods and reached for another grenade. Toss, duck, wait, charge. He repeated the drill two more times and reached the woods. His Marines were right behind him. He jumped over the sandbags into the machine-gun nest, firing wildly at anything that moved.

"Lieutenant, watch out!"

Keller turned to his right as a wounded German rose up and pulled back his arm. A studded trench club tomahawked toward Keller's head. He ducked and turned his head to the side, his helmet absorbing the blow. It felt like a sledgehammer. The attacker reeled back, arms flailing, as bullets slammed into his belly.

Dizzy, bleeding from the ear, Keller collapsed. Marines stormed into the woods to meet the German counter-attack. The last things Keller heard were shouts, gunfire, and the desperate wrestle of hand-to-hand combat. Blackness overtook him.

Chapter 19
The Mystery Man

Police Headquarters: June 1918
Shannon sat at her desk flooded with dread after reading the latest news about the bloody fighting in Belleau Wood. She took a deep breath, tried to suppress her fears about her husband, and returned to the case. Several days had passed since Kittridge's meeting in Central Park, and Fishbait's rendezvous with Red was coming up. Her task today was to garner insight into what he had revealed about Kittridge's associates. The lack of details frustrated her, and she vowed to secretly take pictures at their next meeting. Someone in the police force must recognize them.

The Irishman, the dandy, and Mr. Wood seemed to have no distinguishing features, but the most curious conspirator, however, had now been identified as Jelly Brown. The involvement of the man who had almost blown up Wall Street made Kittridge's plot even more treacherous. Shannon meticulously combed through the files piled on her desk hoping to find more about him, but police records provided little help. There was no information whatsoever on Jelly Brown after the New York attack.

Fernandez sat at the next desk, busily scrutinizing Kittridge's banking ledgers — those he had extracted from the bank despite their protests, and the more valuable ones he had obtained through Clancy's less legal means. To Shannon's amazement, he had determined that more than $50,000 had recently disappeared from Kittridge's Tammany accounts. It was a true testimony to his skills as a financial detective. His long hours had paid off.

An expensively dressed young man walked into the squad room with the authority of a major general. His face was narrow, his forehead high, his cheekbones well-chiseled. Sporting a carefully trimmed mustache with well-barbered hair parted in the middle, he looked boyish despite his commanding presence. Almost lost in his shadow was an older man carrying a thick briefcase.

Shannon gave the younger man a sustained look, then turned to Clancy at the adjacent desk. "Who's that?"

Clancy scratched his head, leaned over, and whispered, "Can't rightly say, but I'll be damned if that ain't the mayor's top aide behind him. Whatever it is, it's important."

The man spoke with a loud, confident voice. "Which one of you is Sergeant Fernandez?"

Fernandez stood up, his arms on his hips. "I am, sir," he fired back. "This is my unit, and I don't take kindly to the disruption. What is your business here?"

Good for you, Joe, Shannon thought.

The young man took a commanding tone. "Come with me. We have a meeting with the police commissioner. Now."

"I'm at work on a vital case."

"That's what we need to talk about."

Shannon's jaw dropped as they walked out the door. The squad room fell silent. She exchanged "what-the-hell-just-happened" looks with Clancy. It was no way to treat a detective sergeant, particularly a well-liked one with Fernandez's stellar record.

Clancy broke the silence. "I ain't seen nothin' like that in my thirty-plus years on the force, but nothin' around here surprises me no more. Let's get back to work. We'll find out what's happenin' soon enough."

~

An hour later, Fernandez returned and asked Shannon and Clancy to join him in private. His face was pale, and the furrows between his eyebrows had deepened. His voice trembled just enough for Shannon to detect his concern. They walked to the nearest interview room in silence. He slumped into a chair and paused a moment before speaking. "I don't know how else to say this, but we have just been ordered to halt our investigation of Kittridge."

Shannon tensed, wanting to explode, but managed to hold back her Irish temper.

"Under whose orders?" Clancy asked.

"Officially, the mayor. Kittridge, Fishbait, and the Hanover are off limits. The police commissioner was adamant. Our 'visitor' was not introduced, but the mayor's aide kept glancing at him."

"What went on, Joe?" Shannon asked. "You were in there a long time."

"Not really. We waited a while for the commissioner. He was not in a good mood, and seemed annoyed. The meeting was merely a formality. The commissioner had no say in the decision. The verdict was in; this was just his official declaration. The mayor's aide did most of the talking."

"That arrogant young whipper-snapper had something to do with this," Clancy declared.

"He kept a poker face. At the end, he looked at me and said, 'So, it is agreed, Sergeant Fernandez. You will cease your investigation and hand over all your files to the mayor's office.' Then he adjourned the meeting."

"The hell we'll give them up." Clancy began to turn red.

"So the young man was the real power," Shannon concluded.

"That was clear from the start," said Fernandez.

"Who is he?"

"Someone connected to the top people in Tammany Hall. All I can think of," Clancy said. "They bought off the mayor and twisted the commissioner's arm. Good day's work, I'd say."

"You're all dismissed for the day," Fernandez stood up. "I'll see what I can find out. I'll talk to the boss. Come back tomorrow, and we'll regroup."

~

Freed from duty, Shannon went uptown to Times Square to see the latest Chaplin movie, *Chase Me Charlie*, accompanied by Clancy as her bodyguard. The movie strung together several shorter Chaplin films, including Shannon's favorites, *The Tramp* and *The Bank*. Both she and Clancy felt they could use a laugh.

As they were leaving headquarters, the desk sergeant asked if they had seen Red. Shannon smiled blankly. "No, Sergeant," she said, masking her concern. "You know he keeps his own hours."

That was a half-truth. Red worked for the New York Police as a civilian, and pretty much made his own schedule. He was known to like his liquor and go on a bender now and then, but he was never drunk when there was work to do, and their case was at a vital point. *Hadn't he arranged a meeting with Fishbait?* She had not thought about it during the excitement with the commissioner. Was it only a coincidence that Red was absent when that young man marched into their office? She suppressed the thought. *Surely, Red could not have had anything to do with the case being dropped. But where was he?*

"You know Red has a weakness for the ladies," Clancy reminded her.

Maybe. Shannon managed to push Red out of her mind on the subway ride to Times Square. She surrendered two dimes for two tickets at the box office and scooped up four pennies change. Prices had risen everywhere since the war, and in New York City more than anywhere else. She and Clancy settled in the half-filled theater, their minds still troubled by the day's events. Unlike the audience around them, neither of them laughed.

The house lights went up at the end of a reel, and a middle-aged man walked to the front of the theater. A volunteer from the Committee on Public Information (CPI) led by George Creel, he was there to stir up support for the war as part of President Wilson's propaganda effort. Shannon, who went to the moving pictures often, could predict what he would say, so often had she heard "Four-Minute Men," as they were called, deliver their patriotic message during the minutes it took to change reels.

This man, like the others, was an accomplished public speaker, and better than most. No worn-out phrases like "doing your bit" marred his perfect delivery as he extolled United States fighting men and their cause. He went on to explain rationing in simple, but convincing terms that an average, poorly educated audience could understand, and wound up with an appeal to buy bonds: "Earn the right to say *I helped win the war.*"

Shannon had come to the movies to escape and did not want to be reminded of the war. She sat through his appeal with her hands over her ears, looking down at the floor. She knew the stakes and horrors of the war better than any Four-Minute Man.

She left the theater still trying to understand the day's events. *Suspend the case? Impossible. Ordered by the mayor's office? Makes no sense unless Tammany Hall did indeed buy him off. Still, given what we know, it's a big risk for the mayor, and he is not one to take risks. Fernandez said the mayor's aide knew details that no one outside of the team could have known. Curious and more curious. And who is that brash young man? Whoever he is, he's the one with the answers.*

Chapter 20
A Long Night

Along the Subway Line to Brooklyn: June 1918
Midnight: Fishbait rode the subway back to Brooklyn preoccupied with thoughts of Red's knife and Mr. Wood's .45. He was running on time for his meeting with Red, but something wasn't right. Not nerves, but something more. He needed a drink but had to keep his wits together. Fishbait's senses and well-honed survival instinct told him that something was about to happen. What, he didn't know, but something. Armed with the information he had gathered, he hoped to keep his eye and maybe escape to Chicago. He'd done all he could for the police. He still had dreams.

He was surprised he still drew breath. Although Mr. Wood continued to cast threatening looks his way, the days had passed uneventfully since the meeting in Central Park. No meetings today — Kittridge had mostly stayed in his office, as Fishbait and Mr. Wood sat parked on Broadway, consuming coffee and stale cheese sandwiches in the Hudson. Twice, a local beat cop ordered them to move on. Fishbait was tempted to yell for help, but remained silent, remembering the .45 inside Wood's coat. The cop must have sensed danger. He gave Wood a warning and left.

Wood flashed Fishbait an "I know what you're up to" look. Fishbait expected Wood to shoot him at any moment. Was he waiting to administer a worse fate?

Alone on the subway, Fishbait could not stop his knees from shaking. As the old car shook and shuddered, clanging its way through lower Manhattan, each screech of the wheels reached deep into his ears, every bounce jolted his spine. His clammy hands grabbed the grimy strap hanging overhead. As the car rounded a bend, the sway nearly toppled him over. He sat down and eyed the few people still on the train, wondering which one, if any, was there to throw him onto the tracks or drive a knife into his liver.

The people around him were a tired, faceless lot, just the usual midnight riders. The stable hand with horse dung on his boots was half asleep; the doorman with the fancy red coat from a hotel Fishbait had never heard of was reading the paper; a musician hugged his violin case; the kitchen worker gazed out the window. The few others were not worth a look.

Fishbait left the subway two stops early to avoid being followed as Red had told him to do. The stable hand got off at the same stop, but walked in a different direction and was joined by a hunched older man in a black coat. Fishbait saw only his back, but did not think he had been on the subway. He watched the two turn the corner, then walked three more blocks and waited for a tram to take him the rest of the way to Flatbush Avenue to meet Red at Kevin's all-night diner.

He jumped off the tram and looked in all directions. No one following.

When Fishbait walked into Kevin's, Red was at the counter eating pancakes. Fishbait removed his cap and stuffed it into his left back pocket, the signal to Red that it was safe to meet. He headed to the men's room; Red followed.

Before Fishbait had a chance to speak, the door to the toilet slammed open. Shotgun in hand, the stable hand with the dung on his boots appeared with Mr. Wood in a black coat right behind him. Fishbait froze; Red reached for his revolver. A flash. A loud noise. Volleys of lead. Silence.

~

At the end of their shift the following day, Shannon and Casey arrived at a vacant lot on 45th Street between 8th and 9th Avenues as twilight began to shroud Brooklyn. "Why is this *our* case, Sean? Shouldn't homicide be called in?"

Clancy merely grunted; he was in a bad mood. "A Brooklyn cop called it in. The captain wanted *us* to investigate. Didn't say why."

Shannon suspected the worst — Red had failed to report since his meeting with Fishbait. She and Clancy identified themselves to the roundsman at the scene, who was unsuccessfully attempting to console two sobbing girls who'd been playing in the lot. The younger girl, shivering, pointed to the old wine barrel. "*I'm scared,*" she wailed. "It's ..., it's ..., *horrible.*"

Shannon hugged her, told her she was safe, and asked the roundsman to escort the girls from the scene. She stiffened herself for the sure-to-be disturbing sight, but the reality was worse than she expected. A cowboy boot stuck out of the barrel. "Jesus Christ, *no!*" she cried, one of the rare times she had ever used His name in vain.

"*Damn it*! Just what I feared," Clancy said. "It's them or us. This is personal."

"Who's *them?*"

As they approached the barrel, the unholy stench of stale wine, human remains, and carrion seekers grew overpowering. "Here," said Clancy, handing Shannon a can of tooth power. "Rub it over your upper lip. Reduces the smell." He lit his torch and pulled away the burlap that covered most of the body. A large rat scurried out with a gob of flesh in its mouth.

Shannon jumped back. "I *hate* those things."

Clancy gazed inside, then paused to collect himself. "That's Red all right. He was a tough one. Shotgun blasts to the midsection. Close up. I'm amazed his body is still in one piece. "*My God!*" Clancy jerked back and crossed himself. "They cut off his head."

"I need to look," Shannon said. Clancy cast her a sorry glance, but stepped aside. Holding her breath, she peered in. Her stomach immediately revolted, sending up a burning gush of bile into her throat. She swallowed it back down and quickly backed away. "We need a photographer. I want as much evidence as we can get."

"We know who did this," Clancy said, "but we'll never prove it. These people wanted us to find him."

"Do you see his knife?"

Clancy checked the barrel again. "No. But if we do find it, we can nail the bastards." He narrowed his eyes and looked hard at Shannon. "Some big shot might have ordered us off Kittridge, but nobody said nothin' about no murder. Red's one of *us*. I don't care what the commissioner, the mayor, or anyone else says. I'm goin' to kill the people who did this."

~

A few hours after Red's death, Mr. Wood and the man called Dusty escorted Fishbait to a point north of the Brooklyn Bridge overlooking the East River. His clothes were soaked with blood, the front of his pants wet with urine. The sun was just coming up.

Fishbait relived the last six hours. It had been a long and grisly night. The assassins had forced him to drag Red's body from the toilet to the alley behind the diner. It made a stinking mess of blood, gore, spilt liquor, and grease. They heaved the body in the trunk of the car and sped off before the police arrived and stopped at a warehouse on 45th and 9th Avenue overlooking a vacant lot. Fishbait was ordered to carry Red's body around to the back. The 180-pound corpse was too heavy for him, but Dusty's taunts and Wood's threats gave him the extra dose of adrenaline he needed. He dragged the corpse to a dingy room filled with spider webs and mildew, let go of the feet, then half-stood, his hands on his knees, totally exhausted.

Mr. Wood handed him Red's knife. "One more thing — the head."

Cutting off a head, even with Red's big knife, wasn't easy. The two assassins laughed at Fishbait, ridiculing his failure to cut through the neck. Wielding the knife like an ax, he delivered four hard chops with all the force of his fury and frustration. Red's head broke free and rolled over with a sickening thud.

"Put it in here." Mr. Wood tossed Fishbait a burlap sack.

He grabbed a handful of hair and pitched the head into the sack as if it were a hot iron. It weighed more than he had expected.

Mr. Wood seemed pleased. "We'll dump the body nearby where the cops can find it."

~

Sunup: When they reached the Manhattan side of the river, Mr. Wood told Dusty to stop the car. The sun shone bright on Fishbait's face as he tossed the sack with Red's head into the river. He was greatly relieved to be rid of the ghastly thing. They watched it sink into the dank water, then drove to the Bridge Café on Water Street near the Brooklyn Bridge. "I like this place," Dusty announced as he unlocked the door. "Full of ghosts. The owner owes me, so he looks the other way during unannounced visits."

After an hour of joking and several rounds of beers, Mr. Wood turned serious. "We got some questions for you, Fishbait."

Fishbait jumped up to run but slipped on spilt day-old beer. Dusty was on top of him before he could cry out. They stripped him naked and took him to the basement. They tied him to a straight-backed chair. The coarse, thick ropes dug into his skin and burned his wrists and ankles as he struggled. When Fishbait finally gave up, Dusty pulled out Red's knife and began to flay razor-thin strips of Fishbait's pale skin from his legs and arms as Fishbait screamed in excruciating pain.

Mr. Wood held up his hand. "Thank you, Dusty. I think our friend gets the idea." He raised his arm and punched Fishbait in the face, knocking out three teeth. Dusty followed with a blow to his gut. Four rounds of beer spilled out.

Mr. Wood's questions followed fast. "What did you tell the cops? How long you been talking to them? What do they know?"

Fishbait poured out everything. How he was arrested in Bronxville, the faked escape, the meetings with Red. Everything. Truth was his only hope. A faint one.

~

Twelve Minutes Later: Fishbait gagged on the metal barrel as Mr. Wood jammed the .45 into his mouth. He pulled the trigger, splattering

Fishbait's brains on the wall. "They'll collect the garbage around here pretty soon, Dusty. Wrap him up and toss him in with last night's waste. He'll rot in the dump 'til the worms shit him out. No one will ever find him."

"What about the cops?" Dusty asked.

"I expect we are at war."

Chapter 21
A Lead

Police Headquarters: June 1918
A week had passed since Red's murder. Despite the warnings to stay away from Kittridge, Shannon and Clancy continued their search, certain his murder was connected to Kittridge's plot. To his credit, Sergeant Fernandez looked the other way — he, too, took Red's murder personally — and assigned them a light case load. Everyone helped when they could; no one kills a cop without retribution. When the crime scene yielded nothing, Clancy quizzed every informant and called in old favors, but no leads developed. Shannon stayed in the city and worked late into the evening. She napped on whatever couch she could find.

The investigation sputtered. Fishbait had disappeared and was presumed dead. Kittridge's office claimed he was out of town. The Irishman and dandy remained unidentified. Nothing further on Brown. Efforts to find Mr. Wood through contacts familiar with Tammany Hall's New York political machine had failed. No one in the mayor's office would acknowledge the existence of the narrow-faced man who had managed to stop their investigation of Kittridge.

Shannon was further distressed by the course of the war. The U.S. 2nd Division continued its assault on Belleau Wood and casualties mounted. *Was Paul involved? Could he be maimed? Had he even survived?* The papers claimed the Doughboys were winning. Not in terms of casualties, but after three-and-a-half years of stalemate, what constituted a victory? Gaining ground previously lost was a tangible measure regardless of the cost. The Allies had managed to halt the German advance, and tens of thousands of American soldiers were flooding into France every week. Shannon prayed that the papers were right, that the end seemed to be a question of time. But it was also a matter of how many lives it would cost.

She sat down at her desk, plagued by the feeling that something bad had happened to Paul. She pushed aside her thoughts of the war and picked up her old notes, hoping she might see something fresh. She combed through the files for half an hour or so, then stopped short and cursed her folly. With all the drama surrounding the case, she'd neglected a simple piece of evidence: little Grace's memory of the first four numbers on the license plate of the getaway car: 3 1 5 9. It was not much, but it was all she had.

A series of questions quickly flipped through Shannon's mind. *How many black Hudson Super-Six autos were registered in New York State? How many of their license plates bore the four numbers? Was New York's record keeping up-to-date and accurate? Had the little girl remembered the numbers correctly? Had the assailants changed or altered the Hudson's plates since?* Who could say how helpful the answers would be, but Shannon prayed they'd provide a lead.

~

The New York Police wanted Red's killer too. By the next day, the whole department was aware of Shannon's lead and eager to help. The plan was to start at the nearest motor vehicle departments. That morning, as Shannon opened the door to the one in Manhattan, Clancy entered Brooklyn's, and two other members walked into those in the Bronx and Westchester. Each team had two volunteers from the secretarial staff to help. Fernandez had approved the assignments and overtime, with ready authorization from the captain.

Shannon introduced herself to the manager in charge and explained what she was after. He chuckled. "That there's a first. Always wondered why we issued them plates. Thought it was to charge them owners." He yawned. "You're welcome to search, but our files ain't all that neat or up to date. Kinda like finding a sober Irishman in a bar."

The manager showed her the boxes and loose paper registries and described how they were supposedly organized. At least the date of issuance was part of the filing system. He implied there might be some connection between the plate numbers and the date the plates were issued, and added, "I never seen no pattern or clear correspondence. No state-wide coordination of plate numbers as far as I can tell. Reckon the plates are reused. Different locations issue different plates." He wiped his brow and sighed. "We just process 'em and box 'em."

Shannon was left to contemplate his words as she stared at the overwhelming stacks of paper. *Surely, there must be some connection between the plate numbers and the dates*, she thought, as she tried to figure out her approach. First, she decided, was to assign a volunteer the task of searching the files for plates starting with numbers 3 and 1.

Next, she tried to guess when the plates would have been issued. Shannon closed her eyes and struggled to visualize the Hudson. She'd never had much interest in autos, and a lot had been going on that day. *Was the Hudson new?* The paint looked shiny, the tires unworn. She compared her observations with Clancy, who knew more about autos, and particularly liked the powerful Super-Six. Guessing that the Hudson was less than a year old, they started in on the records for the last half of 1917.

Finding the boxes for the period was an effort in itself. At the end of the day, her team had found nothing. The next day, and the next, they combed through different periods. Three days of work, three strike-outs.

~

She sent her team home and returned to the squad room to see how Clancy and the others were faring. The Bronx group filtered in fifteen minutes later wearing the same long faces. "We're not giving up," Shannon declared, despite her private concerns.

Clancy appeared, having found a potential lead. A Hudson bearing plates with two of the numbers was registered in Brooklyn Heights but belonged to a retired banker who rarely drove it and never lent it out. Clancy admitted that the chance of finding the right Hudson was slim.

Shannon held out hope that the Westchester team would return with more encouraging news. There were fewer registered autos in Westchester, and their department's records might be in better order. The area was wealthy, so their chances of finding an expensive Super-Six in Westchester might also be better than in the city.

A few minutes later, Fernandez entered the squad room. Sensing the feeling of defeat, he dismissed everyone but Clancy and Shannon. Given the pressure he was under from his superiors, Shannon expected a reprimand or at least a demand for faster results. Instead, he said, "You'll get them. Let me know how I can help," and returned to his office. She wondered how long his patience would last.

Shannon and Clancy waited for the Westchester team. Shannon fretted. Clancy paced. Across the room one way, and back again the other. The heel of his shoe loosened and began to squeak. At the next pass around the room, he cursed the offending shoe, pulled it off, then chucked off the other one. He continued to pace in his stocking feet, mumbling. Shannon put down her pen and told him to sit down. They needed a new approach for tomorrow.

At 6:30, the leader of the Westchester team, the young detective Gordon Abbott, bound into the room with electric energy. "I think I've got something."

~

The next day Abbott drove Shannon and Clancy north in an unmarked Ford to New Rochelle in southern Westchester County, eighteen miles from the city, where a Hudson Super-Six was registered to one Edgar Willis residing at 7 Oak Drive. They arrived on Main Street at 10 a.m. and turned east toward Long Island Sound. Willis's house overlooked Little Pea Island on a lovely tree-lined street whose houses ranged from grand to grander.

"We're just looking. Correct, gentlemen?" Shannon reminded them. "We'll confirm it's the auto we're after and leave."

Clancy fumed and tightened his face muscles. "If the killer is there —"

"Sean."

"Just a thought, Mrs. Keller." He only called her that when he was angry.

Abbott nodded and kept to the speed limit. There was no need to arouse suspicion. He parked two blocks from Oak Drive and adjusted his derby as Shannon donned a wide-brimmed sunhat. Clancy remained in the Ford while Shannon and Abbott set out on foot. All senses alert, the two strolled arm-in-arm down the street, looking like a married couple out to enjoy the view.

Willis's house was at the end of the street. Shannon spotted the black Hudson in the driveway as they approached, and Abbott reached for his service revolver. "Easy, Gordon. No need. They can't identify us under these hats. Just keep walking." She confirmed the license number out of the corner of her eye, and silently nodded.

As she and Abbott turned away, the front door to the house suddenly opened. Shannon glanced back and saw the man who had tried to assault her in Bronxville squinting at them, but she was too far away to be identified. Fishbait had told her his name: Mr. Wood.

Shannon had her man.

SECTION III

PERSHING'S HEADQUARTERS IN CHAUMONT

June 1918 - July 1918

Chapter 22
Missing

AEF Headquarters, Chaumont, France: June 1918

Martin was assessing the progress of the Belleau Wood offensive when the latest casualty lists arrived. He turned from his situation maps to look for information about Keller. He was still praying that Paul was alive, although he was listed as "missing, presumed dead." Initial battlefield reports indicated that the Marine company Keller had led, one of the first American outfits to reach Belleau Wood, had been driven back by a fierce counter-attack and "virtually wiped out." The few witnesses from his company still alive reported that Keller had single-handedly destroyed an enemy machine-gun position but was wounded in the head and fell, unconscious or dead.

When the Marines regained possession of that part of the wood days later, Keller's body was not found. The Germans could have removed him during their withdrawal or his body could have been obliterated by an artillery shell. Martin requested permission to search the area to look for Keller's identity tags or locket but was denied. Recovery teams had looked. What was one more dead Doughboy when so many others had perished?

Martin promised himself that he would interview every remaining soldier in Keller's company and any German prisoners who had defended that sector. He owed it to his best friend and Shannon to learn every detail of Paul's last minutes, and he regretted that he had not fulfilled his impossible promise to protect him. He would not contact Shannon until he had definitive word of Paul's fate.

The generals may have thought in terms of tens of thousands of men, but to Martin the war was about the buddy next to you. Despite the mass slaughter, individual life still mattered. Part of his humanity remained intact.

~

By the end of June, the fight for Belleau Wood was nearly won, and Martin was hoping the latest information would contain some conclusive news. Unfortunately, the report contained no word about Keller. Resisting the temptation to rip it up, Martin silently handed it back to the sergeant and returned to work. Martin felt numb, as if he had been injected with a powerful dose of morphine. He reached for a Camel and tried to concentrate on the maps.

Aside from Martin's gloom, the mood at headquarters was jubilant. In their second major engagement of the war, the U.S. Army and Marines had taken their Belleau Wood objective and stopped the German advance. That's what Pershing's propagandists were telling the thirsty American press. Yes, it took longer than expected, about three weeks, with more casualties than anticipated, but the Germans had fought hard. The Yanks had stood toe-to-toe with them and prevailed, surprising the French and Germans alike. It was a major psychological victory if only a marginal military one.

Major Fauchaux mentioned that the French would rename the wood *le Bois de la Brigade de Marine*. A publicity gold mine. Headquarters was quick to reveal that captured German prisoners commented on the guts and dogged determination of the Marines. Another morsel for the press to feast upon.

A voice caught Martin's attention. "What does Intelligence think, Captain Martin?" Full-of-himself General Prescott, the last person Martin wanted to deal with.

Martin replied with as much respect as he could muster. "Belleau Wood is in our hands, General. I believe the German advance has been halted. A victory for sure, but a costly one."

"Ha. A victory is a victory. The French and British have had precious few in four years, and we've bagged one in our first big try. I'd say we've done splendidly." Prescott puffed out his big chest.

How little Prescott understands. How did he ever become a general? Strong political connections to Midwest meat packers, Martin had heard. Prescott would of course interpret this battle to reflect his propaganda narrative. Leavenworth all over again, but Martin refused to back down. "But General, we have suffered more than 5,000 casualties. That's a high price for a bunch of trees without much strategic value."

"Nonsense. You sound more like the defeatist French every day. You spend too much time with that Frog major, Forshoot."

"*Fauchaux* has helped us tremendously. The French were part of this fight too."

"But not in Belleau Wood. That was all *us*. We protected the road to Paris. The French would have retreated to Africa without us."

Martin knew this was false. The German offensive was beginning to stall by the time the Americans arrived. They had made an impact, but the Americans had not won the battle alone. "I agree; we made a difference."

"Damn right, Captain. We engaged four separate German divisions and took 1,700 prisoners. One hundred years from now, Americans will remember the name Belleau Wood with pride."

"Yes, General." Martin would not have admitted it to a self-promoting braggart like Prescott, but it was clear the tide of battle was changing. The Boches knew they couldn't win with American soldiers pouring into France. Captured Germans seemed demoralized. They were short of food, equipment, and munitions. The offensive was supposed to bring final victory; instead, it brought a new stalemate. "I believe the Allies have fended off the best Germany can throw at us. They will not win."

"That's the most positive thing I've heard you say since I joined headquarters, Captain." Prescott checked his watch. "I need to see a newspaper man from Chicago." He straightened his uniform, lifted his chin high, and strutted out. Martin shook his head. With generals like that, the U.S. Army would suffer far worse than Belleau Wood.

~

Martin slumped onto his cot at 01:45, his tired mind giving way to drifting thoughts. He had seen men become blood-lusting savages, crossing the boundary between humanity and beast. The senseless slaughter on the Western Front would have been unimaginable years ago.

Raised to hate Germans, even he was bending to the animalistic barbarity he had recently witnessed. The enemy was not human but a dark form of ogre to be starved, beaten, and strangled. Never before had he felt such loathing, not even for the most despicable rapists and murderers he had arrested. His growing insensitivity shocked him.

His parents had immigrated to America after the Franco-Prussian war when Prussia stole Alsace-Lorraine from France. Two of his uncles had died in that war. The first words Gil learned were "cursed Boches." He grew up poor in the slums of Brooklyn. Milk was scarce and meat a luxury, but unlike many of the neighborhood kids, he never stole. An only child, he was often alone at home. His sickly mother preferred the church to family responsibilities, and his father favored liquor to work and spent more time at bars than with his son. A scrawny French-speaking child, Gil had few friends.

Young Gilbert sought refuge with the priest of his local church, Father Joseph, whom he helped to clean the building. Since he was excellent at mathematics, young Gil also helped the good father to manage his budget. In turn, Father Joseph taught Gil to box.

When he was thirteen, two neighborhood teenagers tied a bell to a stray cat's tail and laughed as it tried to free itself. Martin ran over to stop the abuse only to be pushed away by the older one. Martin stunned him with his first punch and knocked him to the ground with his second. The other boy threw a rock that grazed his cheek. Martin blackened the second boy's eyes with two quick blows. No one taunted him after that.

Gil spent his most pleasant hours in Father Joseph's library. The books shaped his quick intellect: James Fenimore Cooper's stories of the American West and Conan Doyle's mysteries fascinated him; Dickens, Hugo, and Upton Sinclair taught him the ways of the world. Through his reading, he became a keen observer of people; through the church, an excellent judge of character; through his talks with Father Joseph, an empathetic and thoughtful man.

He broke free from the slums when he was accepted into the police academy for reasons he never learned. Gil suspected Father Joseph, whose brother was a lieutenant in the New York Police, had helped.

He drifted to sleep thinking war was considerably harder than police work.

~

By July 2, the AEF brigade and division commanders had straightened out their lines, rushed supplies to the front, and repositioned their artillery. The famished soldiers received their first hot meal in days. GHQ had a brief respite during the lull, giving Martin a chance to visit the 2nd Division's main field hospital.

As his staff car neared the hospital, Martin was met with the smells of rotting flesh, overflowing latrines, and newly washed sheets and bandages hanging out to dry. He had visited numerous hospitals in his days as a cop, but had never seen anything this appalling. The intensity of activity around the facility resembled a New York dockyard. Coffins waiting for burial stacked up like so many cords of wood. Amputated limbs were piled outside the surgical area. Flies and rats circulated through the compound enjoying the feast despite the best efforts of the exhausted staff.

Inside, Martin explained to the harried head nurse his desire to find a missing friend, an army lieutenant with a Marine unit who had suffered a head injury on the first day of the battle. She laughed at the sheer folly of his mission. "My goodness, Captain. We have lots of men who fit your description. More likely, you'll find his name over there on the burial lists," she said, directing him to the desk that received and released patients. "That is, *if* his body came through here."

Martin checked the names on every list going back to June 4, but did not find Keller's name. At least that was consistent with the casualty reports. He asked permission to walk through the recovery rooms. There was no indication that Keller had ever been there.

He visited two more hospitals that day and experienced the same frustration. Refusing to accept the likely chance that Keller was gone, he held onto the outside possibility that somehow the casualty reports had gotten his name wrong. The New York Police routinely confused or misspelled names, and the AEF was many magnitudes larger and notoriously less efficient.

Hoping against hope, Martin reviewed the Belleau Wood casualty reports yet again, this time with a different eye. The new Hello Girl transfer, Emily Lange, whom he'd told about Keller's plight, volunteered to help. Politely refusing her offer at first, he finally accepted when he realized how much work was involved.

One night after her shift, Miss Lange was working in the records department with Martin when she spotted a notation: Lt. P. Keltner, U.S. Marine Corps, poison gas. Hospitalized June 16.

"It can't be him," Martin said. "He suffered a head wound on June 6. Besides, he's Army."

"He was fighting with the Marines. I'll investigate anyway to make sure. Strange things happen in war." She moved to the death records file. After a few minutes she looked up, horrified. "So many are listed *unable to identify.*"

"Yes, Miss Lange. The injuries are unimaginable."

"They die for their country and not enough of them is left for a proper burial. Only God knows who they are. What has this world come to?"

At midnight, Martin suggested they stop for the night. He thanked her for her efforts and continued searching alone for another hour. He despaired that he would ever find his friend, but vowed he would never stop until he had answers.

Chapter 23
Three Concerns

Chaumont, France: July 1918
Emily was pleased how events had progressed since her weekend with
Major Jameson. True to his word, he had helped secure her promotion
to the Woman's Signal Corps Unit at AEF's GHQ in Chaumont. Although
she was as busy as she had been in Tours, she felt new excitement to be at
the center of America's effort to win the war. The calls she handled were
more urgent, made by higher-ranking officers, with higher stakes. She
detected the importance of a call by the tone of a voice, the abruptness
of the demand, and the impatience with delays.

The life-and-death nature of her work drove her to become even
more efficient. The few seconds it took to connect each call allowed her
to eavesdrop, but she had to suppress her curiosity and concentrate on
the next call. In addition to the confidential documents she translated,
she had a veritable wiretap on all American operations, an intelligence
treasure trove. *If this intelligence should fall into the wrong hands ... .*

Emily had three immediate concerns. The first was Major
Andrew Jameson. After their weekend in Paris, she knew "Andy" would
insist on further liaisons. Now that she worked within walking distance
of him, she would have a harder time rejecting his advances, but she
still wanted his help.

She remained silent about his interest — no sense sparking
jealousy among the other Hello Girls — but she could not hide his
frequent visits and puppy dog looks, so uncharacteristic for an otherwise
decent officer. He was smitten; she had that effect. It was only a matter
of time before he would become a burden.

She continued to see him after shifts, but rejected further
weekend meetings as too dangerous. If caught, she'd be sent back home.
Luckily, the war provided credible excuses. The AEF was preparing its
first major offensive as a completely independent army, from General

Pershing down to the lowest private. It would be a test to prove American capability, and the Allies and the public were watching.

Emily satisfied him temporarily by confessing that she cared for him. She got a reprieve when Jameson was promoted to Lieutenant Colonel and transferred to the U.S. 1st Division in the Marne, a sector where fighting was intense.

Her second concern was Captain Martin, who had accompanied Jameson when they first met. He visited her Signal Corps Unit often, such was its importance to the AEF, and remained a curiosity to the Hello Girls. She tried to be friendly, but he remained distant and focused on his work, probing with questions and observing every detail. He once asked Emily's matron to explain how the equipment worked, sought her advice, then followed up to make sure her recommendations were completed. *Imagine that. An officer asking a woman for her opinion.*

The other Hello Girls whispered he was a widower and found him attractive in his quiet, confident way. Not for any distinguishing features, which were rather plain, but for the mystery surrounding him. His competence was obvious, and he projected more authority than his rank conveyed. He never failed to spot something amiss and was always polite and respectful. *Intense and taciturn*, Emily privately thought, but she admitted to her mirror that he intrigued her in a way that Jameson did not.

"He looks sad," one of the girls commented at dinner.

"No, troubled," corrected another.

"He's been on the front lines. Seen a lot. That changes a man," a third said.

"Everyone says he's a brave soldier and an excellent officer," Emily said, trying to gauge reactions. She would listen and say no more.

"He must have a vice."

"Work. He's married to it."

"I'd love to meet him. He's a man I could marry."

"Enough of this nonsense," their matron scolded. "Are you all lovesick teenagers? You know army officers are off-limits. We are not here to gossip. We are at war, not some cotillion. The captain is a fine soldier. He's here to insure we do our jobs well, and we won't if we have silly thoughts about men."

Emily winced. During the conversation, she had learned the captain was supposedly a hero in New York City before America entered the war. She did not recall seeing his name in the papers, but she was busy in college at the time. Well respected, he was rumored to be a trouble shooter for General Pershing. Jameson had described him as a pain in the neck to him and his patron, General Prescott. To ingratiate herself to Martin, she had volunteered to help him find his missing friend, but he remained distant.

Emily's third concern was her father, from whom she had not heard in weeks. His last letter hinted he was working on a big project for the war. His was a small part, but time-consuming. *Just like him — modest and patriotic.* He was always interested in her achievements, but his letters did not ask about her. *Men, always staying away from their emotions.* She wished her mother were still alive. At least she had Uncle André.

~

After her shift ended late that afternoon, Emily sat on a bench tucked in the nearby woods overlooking some train tracks and the grassy area in front of the château and the compound around it that served as Pershing's headquarters. She pulled her coat tight against the unseasonable wind and smiled blankly at the few passersby, but she discouraged approach by folding her hands on her lap and avoiding eye contact. Her coworkers understood that the normally social Emily wanted to be alone.

Uncle André rode up on a rickety bicycle. She marveled at how he managed to ride with one hand, using a bicycle with brakes on the pedals, not the handlebars. She stood to meet him and kissed him on both cheeks. André was breathing hard, his face an unhealthy red, his now-gray hair looking thinner than ever. "Here," he said, handing her a big basket of fruit, vegetables, and eggs he had strapped to his bicycle.

"Uncle André, you don't look well. You should see a doctor."

"These are harder to get each time. I'm not much of a farmer with this wooden hand, but it's important your friends think I appreciate their concern."

Walking a few minutes, they moved deeper into the woods where no one could hear them. "Seriously, how are you doing?" she asked.

"I've settled in close by. We do what we have to do. Everything you gave me last time was useful."

"Yes, we do what we have to do. I'm still waiting to hear what to do next."

"Communications are slow. Things on our side are becoming more difficult." André tapped the side of his coat as if he had forgotten something. "Oh, here. Something special for you." He reached into his pocket and handed her a glass bottle of clear liquid. "Your favorite. Uncle André's special schnapps."

"Oh, thank you! You don't know how much I need this." Emily opened the bottle and lifted it in a toast. "*Santé!*" she exclaimed. "To our success." She took a long drink and passed the bottle to André, her throat burning delightfully.

André took a big gulp. "To business. How are you holding up?"

"I'm happy here. I like the job — right in the thick of AEF activity."

"That's good."

Emily hesitated a moment, unsure whether she should mention a subject she felt she needed to bring up. "What do I do, now that Jameson has transferred?"

"We'll have to find someone new," André said. "I'll investigate."

Emily took a swig from the bottle. "Do you have word about Max?"

"Your old lover? I thought that was over."

"I still care."

André looked away.

"André, what do you know?"

"The truth?"

"Of course."

"He was reported missing in action around Amiens this spring. His company was wiped out, his body never recovered. Presumed dead. I'm sorry."

Emily collected her thoughts, remembering her lover's delicious body and hairy chest. Fighting back her emotions, she said, "He thought we'd win."

"We still can. Our plan will succeed. We'll *make* it succeed."

"Time's short. I sense it."

"Don't take unnecessary risks," André said. "This is not a suicide mission, *Fraulein* Andrea Kittridge von Stolberg."

Chapter 24
The Annihilator

Police Headquarters: July 1918

Once they had located Mr. Wood, Shannon, Clancy, Abbott, and Fernandez disagreed on the next step. Clancy wanted to kill him and worry about the rest later; Abbott suggested they investigate the ownership of 7 Oak Drive; Sergeant Fernandez preached caution, reminding them they had been ordered to stay away; Shannon wanted to tail the auto and the two men they had spotted. Bigger fish than these two thugs were lurking in a Tammany Hall plot.

Fernandez asserted his authority. Clancy and Abbott would shadow Wood. Shannon would investigate 7 Oak Drive — the bankers, real estate people, and lawyers. He would press the mayor's office and his stool pigeons inside Tammany Hall for more information.

The New York Police had withheld details about Red from the public, taking special care to hide his association with the force. All the newspapers knew about his killing was that a vagrant had been brutally killed in a vacant lot in Brooklyn. Shannon could not figure out how all the pieces fit together: Kittridge and Tammany Hall; Kittridge and the Irishman; the mayor's office and the mysterious young man with powerful connections; Jelly Brown and the dandy; and Red's killer with the others. Yet, she was sure they did. As much as she wanted justice for Red, Shannon needed to decipher the puzzle, but all she had were disconnected pieces.

~

Over the next week, Shannon learned that 7 Oak Drive had been bought for cash two years ago and owned by a fictitious company. Dead end. Fernandez was summoned to the commissioner's office and forced to stop the investigation into Kittridge once again. All of their contacts remained mum.

Only Clancy and Abbott reported progress. Except for Wood, no one had visited Oak Drive. Most nights, Wood frequented the Bridge

Café, a bar near the Brooklyn Bridge, where he seemed to have many friends and admirers. Some good detective work identified one of his associates as Edgar "Dusty" Muldoon, a notorious ruffian who hired himself out for a hefty fee. Abbott, sitting at the bar in disguise, had observed Wood and Muldoon hold court, and had overheard Muldoon brag with drunken bravado that he had the largest knife in New York. He flashed it from his scabbard, slicing the cheek of the man next to him through to the teeth. Ignoring the man's howls of pain, he admired the cut and licked the blood off the blade. Abbott immediately recognized the knife as Red's, and had all he could do to prevent himself from shooting Muldoon on the spot.

~

The next morning when Fernandez heard the story, he told Clancy and Abbott to arrest Muldoon and his likely accomplice, Wood. They were to use force if necessary, but not get into trouble. "Get what you can out of them, but I didn't tell you that. Got it?"

"Understood." Clancy stood to leave. "Got to do something first. Be back later today."

Shannon caught up with him on the stairs to the main entrance. "Where are you going, Sean?"

"Some friends at the armory goin' lend me some artillery."

~

That afternoon, Clancy returned carrying a rifle the likes of which Shannon had never seen. At about 32 inches, it was shorter than the standard American Springfield rifle, with a wooden stock and a pistol-like grip instead of a trigger guard. A round drum magazine fed ammunition into the gun, unlike the box magazine of a Lee-Enfield rifle.

"What the hell is that?" Shannon asked.

Clancy's smile was so big it looked like he'd found a pot of Leprechaun gold. "A Thompson sub-machine gun, but my friends who are testing it call it the *Annihilator*. The gunnery sergeant let me have it for a couple of days. Cost me a bottle of good whiskey." Shannon walked around from behind her desk to get a better look.

"It's a prototype of a weapon for our Doughboys," Clancy explained, holding out the rifle for Shannon to admire. "I can change this here fifty-round magazine in seconds. Allows me to spray hundreds of bullets a minute. Designed to sweep out trenches. Imagine the firepower this gives an infantryman. Portable. Here." He handed the tommy gun over to Shannon.

"About eleven pounds." Shannon cradled it in her shoulder as if to shoot and looked down the sight. "What's the range?"

"Maybe 150 yards. Not a long-distance weapon, but up close — *wow*. Devastating .45 caliber slug. Gives one Doughboy the stopping power of twenty riflemen. Takes some practice to handle her right, but I've been shootin' her all morning."

"Dare I ask what you're going to do with it?" Fernandez inquired, walking into the conversation.

Clancy jumped in front of Shannon, attempting to block his boss's view of the gun. "Uh, what are you talkin' about, Sarge?"

Fernandez apparently understood Clancy's intentions. "I was talking about that report you promised me later today." He disappeared back into his office.

Clancy took the tommy gun from Shannon and pulled her aside. "I aim to go huntin' tonight," he whispered. "Kill those bastards who got Red. I know where they'll be. I might be outnumbered, but with the help of the divine Virgin and this here weapon from Hell, I sure won't be out-gunned."

"You're not going after them alone, Sean."

"Sure am."

"I'll go with you."

"No, lass. I ain't goin' to arrest them. I know what the sarge said, but this ain't a police matter. It's jus' me and them. Red was a friend. If I get tossed off the force or thrown in jail, don't matter shit so long as I get revenge."

"We need to talk to them, Sean."

"Time for talking is over, Shannon. You got a great future ahead of you. Don't mess it up with this business. I want to finish my days drinking at a bar with my cop friends knowing I did the right thing and sent Red's killer to his maker. He'll get justice there."

"I can go as a sniper, keep a distance. I'm in this too."

"No, lass. You're a great target shooter, but you never kilt a man. It's more dangerous if you go. You might miss and ..., well ..., you could regret the consequences for the rest of your life. This is goin' to be a close-up fight. That's why I got this." He raised the tommy gun. "If you insist, I'll bring Abbott. Me and him'll be fine."

~

The streets were quiet that night, but the Bridge Café was crowded as Abbott parked the Ford across the street. Clancy sat next to him dressed in dark clothes to blend into the night. He hid his badge, fed the cartridge drum into the tommy gun. "Closing time in forty-five minutes," was all he said.

Abbott looked directly into Clancy's eyes. "You sure about this, old-timer?"

"This is personal. If these bastards don't want to go quietly, and I hope they don't, me and this here trench sweeper goin' cut them in two. And anyone else fool enough to interfere."

Wood and Muldoon came out of the bar laughing. They walked unsteadily, in an alcoholic stupor, followed by several other men. Clancy approached them, the tommy gun hidden at his side. Abbott took cover behind the auto, a Springfield rifle at the ready.

This was Clancy's play, reckless as it was. He was once again a roundsman facing up to bullies, prepared to back his authority with whatever means necessary. Back then, it was a night-stick; tonight, it was the *Annihilator*. At twenty-five yards, he raised the tommy gun. "You — Wood and Muldoon. Come with me."

They laughed.

"Now! You're under arrest."

Wood reached for his .45, Muldoon for Red's knife.

Clancy squeezed the trigger, full automatic, releasing a fusillade of bullets.

~

The next day's papers had the story faster than Shannon had expected, but she already knew the grim truth. The reports were accurate in one respect: They called it "street-side carnage." Some sort of gangland vendetta that turned murderous. Four men presumed dead and many more wounded, though both sides removed their own before police arrived. Investigators found a surprising number of spent .45 caliber shell casings scattered around a pool of blood, far too many for a semi-automatic pistol. Close by lay a Bowie knife.

One of the rare witnesses said that a man approached, claiming to be a cop, which no one believed. The shooting started right after that. Another said the man claiming to be a cop had some kind of machine gun. He was hit and staggered back to a parked Ford. His partner got shot helping him, but he managed to drive away.

Shannon put down the newspaper and looked at Clancy asleep in his hospital bed, a blood-stained bandage surrounding his middle. She had heard about his plight when she arrived for work, rushed out to Mount Sinai, and had been at his side ever since. He was registered as a John Doe who had shot himself in a home accident. Reporters were not allowed to approach; anyone asking was told he was in a coma. The police were taking great care not to be connected to the slaughter.

Clancy woke with a groan and flickered his eyes into focus. "Sorry," he said in a dry voice. "Looks like you were right, lass."

"Sean, what happened? How in God's name were you able to drive to headquarters with that wound?"

"Weren't a long drive. Doc says I'll recover." He gave a feeble wink and drifted back into a drugged sleep.

She was only able to piece together the story when Clancy

regained consciousness later that afternoon. When Wood and Muldoon reached for their weapons, Clancy unleashed a sustained burst that dropped them immediately and wounded several others. All the men around them froze except one, who ducked away from the tommy gun and drew a revolver. "That man had military training," Clancy said, his voice growing excited. "He jumped onto his stomach behind a dead body for protection. His first shot got me in the gut. Great shot — it woulda gone fine if he weren't there." Clancy's eyes started to close.

After a break, Clancy continued. "I backed away, firing the tommy gun with one hand, and holding the wound with the other. My bullets ripped into the dead body protecting the shooter. He stayed calm and fired back. When I reached the car, Abbott got out to help me, and the shooter nailed him."

Clancy looked up at Shannon sadly. "Do you know Abbott is dead?"

Chapter 25
The Same Man

Mount Sinai Hospital, New York City: July 1918

10 p.m.: Shannon left Clancy asleep in his bed to confer with his doctor. Her old friend and partner had been lucky: The gunshot had passed through his body, nicking the kidney. He had lost blood but would be on his feet in a few days.

Armed with her indomitable resolve and seething anger at the death of Red and Abbott, Shannon felt renewed determination to crack the case. Clancy had managed to describe the shooter in an interlude of consciousness, but other details about the incident remained murky. The conflicting statements from the few witnesses at the scene ranged from a few terse words to useless rants. None of the stories matched, except everyone blamed the man with the automatic rifle for the confrontation and bloodbath.

Shannon returned to headquarters and fell asleep at her desk, her forehead resting on her folded arms. She woke up at sunrise, washed up, and went directly to Mass. She remained a half-hour after the service to pray, seeking forgiveness for not stopping Clancy from his obvious recklessness. Abbott's death had jolted her. She felt responsible, and added special words for his soul. In her three years working with the New York Police, she had never before lost a colleague. *How does Paul handle the death of his men,* she wondered? *There must be an avalanche of them. Does one ever get used to death, or does one just stop feeling?*

Shannon returned from church feeling guilty and alone. Her husband was in France, and, except for Sergeant Fernandez, whom she had started to like, she had no one else to talk to. Confession had provided little solace, and she vowed to stop going.

Two cups of black coffee later, Shannon settled down to work, the best medicine she could prescribe. Her first task took her to the police morgue to see the men Clancy had shot. Her head jerked back at the caustic post-autopsy smell of death as the coroner rolled out their bodies. Clancy's tommy gun had delivered shocking damage. Their bullet-ridden chests looked like sausage and Swiss cheese. If one hand-held weapon could inflict such damage, she was witnessing the advent of a new era in killing power.

Acclimatizing herself to the sights and smells, Shannon studied Muldoon's face. And then it dawned on her: This was the man who had confronted her on the stairs of the Hanover. Her understanding of the circle surrounding Kittridge grew. She spit on Wood's corpse and left.

~

Later, back at headquarters, Shannon kept coming back to Clancy's description of the man who had shot him. Not his physical details so much as how he acted. *Was there a connection to the dandy?* She had heard Fishbait talk about the dandy, but Fishbait was neither reliable nor observant, and she had largely ignored his words. And yet, added to Clancy's observations, Fishbait's account took on new meaning. She made two columns and wrote down everything she had heard about each man.

Both the dandy and the shooter wore fancy clothes, but their physical descriptions were not much to go on. Fishbait had said he was tall, a bit over six feet; older, maybe forty; had slicked-back black hair, and was built like a football lineman. He'd also suggested the man might have "unnatural leanings," something that Shannon admitted had biased her. Fishbait's fear of the man might have also influenced his perceptions. Clancy put the shooter's age at thirty, but described his hair as brown and short. He had a build like a baseball infielder.

Putting aside physical characteristics, Shannon concentrated on the observers' impressions. Fishbait described the man as relaxed, confident, and bullying. He possessed a good knowledge of firearms and explosives, and his eyes scared him. Fishbait's survival skills sensed the dandy's potential for violence, and he stayed away. Clancy's recollection was similar. The shooter was fearless, with quick reflexes. This he had proven during the gunfight, causing Clancy to keep insisting that the man was a former soldier. He was an excellent shot with a Colt 32-20 revolver, a weapon a street thug would neither possess nor know how to handle.

Used to making calculated guesses, Shannon bet that the dandy and Clancy's shooter were one and the same. But who was he?

~

The dandy, Ronny Ellison, got off the train in Washington, D.C. and headed to the designated meeting place, a park bench a block away from the station. Smartly dressed and wearing his bowler hat, he backtracked twice to make sure no one was following him. Certain he was free of shadows, he would neither need the revolver tucked inside the shoulder harness pressed against his ribs nor his hand-to-hand fighting skills. Ellison was a killer. He could incapacitate a man with any number of moves, learned through years of training that allowed him to thrive in gun-running and services-for-hire professions. His expertise in explosives and skill in martial arts, combined with a keen intelligence, the ability to manipulate people, and a lust for danger, made him much in demand in the underworld of crime and fast money.

He approached his boss, Leon Lewis, the only man he considered an equal. Lewis paid well, something important to Ellison, who spent lavishly on clothes, cards, and women. Their arrangement was mutually beneficial: Ellison worked exclusively for Lewis in exchange for good pay and protection from the law. He never knew how Lewis did it, but once he had started to work for him, Ellison's past criminal problems disappeared. Danger was part of Ellison's life; he might as well be paid for his talents. Besides, working for Lewis was fun, and nothing more so than his current assignment.

Ellison neared the park bench where Lewis was sitting, scattering crumbs to the birds. He reached into a bag again, then looked up at Ellison with squinting eyes. "Did you have to kill that cop?"

"If you had done what you'd said and stopped those cops from interfering, I wouldn't have had to."

"It complicates things," Lewis said. "We'll have to do something else to chase them off."

Ellison sat next to Lewis and shielded his mouth with his hand to make it hard for anyone passing by to hear him. "What do your contacts say about what's happening at Police Headquarters?"

Lewis continued to toss crumbs to the pigeons, whose cooing attracted more of their friends. "Hard to say. The mayor's office has been quiet since the shooting. Everyone's upset, but they got no leads. We still have time to finish the deal." He kicked at some pigeons pecking near his shoe. "Was it really necessary to chop off that cop's head?"

"That was that crazy Wood. He and that useless Fishbait botched the job. I nearly got killed cleaning up their mess. How in God's name did Clancy get hold of a tommy gun?"

"How's Kittridge doing?"

"Nervous, but still committed. No telling when Tammany Hall's going to figure out he's stealing from them and send someone better than Wood to kill him. We still need him to make the final payments." An overhead pigeon dropped a load on Ellison. "Shit, that's a new coat. Goddamn birds." He contemptuously wiped the muck off with a handkerchief and tossed it away. "I had to promise Kittridge we'd get him out of the country when the deal is done," he continued. "And he believed me." Ellison let out a belly laugh.

"I don't give a damn about him. He's just the banker, a means to an end," Lewis said. "Where do we stand with the goods? The final buyer is lined up in Estonia. General Tarvas is still loyal to the remaining imperialists and is organizing to fight the Bolsheviks."

"Everything's on schedule. The cache is being assembled outside Hoboken."

"What about Gibson?"

"He's doing his part. Still thinks this is a legitimate deal. When it all goes down and he's caught in the middle, do you care what happens to him?"

"No."

"What's your next play?"

"Michael Donnelly has invited me to a meeting with his Irish sympathizers and the American money men."

"Good. Learn what you can. We want to catch as many of those renegade Micks as possible. Stop their revolutionary nonsense. Does Donnelly suspect anything?"

"No, they trust me completely."

"Good work." Lewis reached in his coat and handed Ellison a thick envelope.

Without looking inside, Ellison tucked the envelope deftly inside his coat. "One last thing. That red-haired bitch working for the cops worries me. She's smart and don't scare."

Lewis stood up and kicked the pigeons away. Ellison waited a minute and hailed a taxi, smiling at Lewis's last words: "I'll take care of her."

~

The wind rushed into the Grace Reformed Church as Lewis entered through the stone archway. It was conveniently empty except for the man in a front pew, Allen Dulles — Lewis's direct superior in the Kittridge affair, the man who had conceived the counter-plot to trap Kittridge and the Irish revolutionaries, and who had recruited the mercenary Ellison for the project.

Despite his relative youth, the twenty-five-year-old Dulles, a Princeton graduate, was forming an American spy agency. He had the right pedigree: His grandfather, John W. Foster, had been secretary of state under Benjamin Harrison, and his uncle, Robert Lansing, was currently secretary of state. Dulles himself had worked several years in the diplomatic service, and had just returned from an assignment in Switzerland when he was asked to start a spy service. He had direct contact with U.S. Army Military Intelligence and the Bureau of Investigation. Leon Lewis was one of his first domestic associates.

Lewis sat down in the pew just behind Dulles, leaned forward, and listened. "Have we picked the right man for this job, Leon?" Dulles asked.

"Ellison is difficult, but good. He'll see this through."

"We're paying him enough. I'm angry about this interference with the New York Police. I did not like to muscle the mayor and parade into Police Headquarters to order them to stop. We need to use stealth, not outward displays of power."

"It had to be done. Thank you, sir."

"And these dead cops? That's caused all sorts of problems."

"Shannon Keller could ruin this for us, Mr. Dulles. Do I have permission to deal with her?"

"Yes, proceed as we've discussed, Leon. I've made the arrangements. Remember, she's a heroine. I didn't want us to reach this point, but we have to consider the greater good. If she's a casualty, well … ."

Chapter 26
A New Mark

Chaumont, France: July 1918

"Have you found a new source for me?" Emily asked Uncle André, speaking under her breath as they sat on their favorite bench three days after they last met. The trees provided shade, the location privacy.

"How are you making out with that Captain Martin?"

Emily sighed. "That's tough. He's always guarded around me. He misses nothing. Like he's still a detective. Martin is obsessed with his work and seems to regard fun as something for other people." She had worked hard to pull him into her web but was certain he would not succumb to her feminine wiles. Although she was sure he was attracted to her, she was taking a different approach. The way into his confidence was to find his friend, Keller. She thought she had a promising lead, but even with that, luring him in would take time.

"Time we don't have, Emily."

"Any other ideas, Uncle?"

"I'd like someone higher than Major Jameson. I've been thinking about Brigadier General Prescott. Our side considers him one of their weaker generals and easily controlled. He seems the type who'd be susceptible to your charms. But take care, Emily. Don't go too far. We'd rather have him in command. A replacement may well be a better general."

Emily's quick mind jumped at the possibility. Prescott was the kind of egotistical upper-class ass she had manipulated since she first donned silk stockings. She was sure he had noticed her, and if she was sure of anything, it was how men looked at her. According to rumors, he liked to think of himself as a lady's man. "He'd be a good mark, but Captain Martin could be a problem."

"We can get rid of Martin if you like."

"Too soon, but Martin's always watching Prescott. I gather they detest each other. I can't get too close to the general without Martin noticing. I think he's also aware of my friendship with Jameson, so I need to be careful where I rendezvous with the general."

"We can handle that."

"I'm sure Martin still has contacts with the New York Police. That's just too close to my father's work in Manhattan. Someday, he might make the connection."

"Get close to Martin so we can monitor him. Do what you can with General Prescott. In the meantime, let me find out what he does outside of work, where he goes. I'll get back to you."

~

Martin awoke at 04:50 in a daze. He had been traveling so much he was not sure where he was and what he had to do today. His life had become a tedious round of inspections, intelligence briefings, training sessions, strategy discussions, and relationship-smoothing with the French.

He rubbed the drowsiness out of his eyes. Today he had a meeting with Major Fauchaux at the French XXI Corps, which needed another U.S. division to supplement their losses. Pershing didn't want to give one up, and Martin had to broker a compromise. Pershing was proposing to offer the French one of his Negro regiments.

Martin rolled over. He had a few more minutes to rest. Two thoughts dominated: Where was Keller, or his grave; and what should he do about Emily Lange?

~

Two days later, Emily bicycled out of town after Sunday Mass to meet Uncle André in a clearing in the woods away from the main road. As usual, her picnic basket was full of food and other tidbits. André had learned that Prescott supported the local parish priest, Father Sebastian, in his work with orphans. The Yankee papers had gobbled up the news about "the American warrior general who did bereavement work." Whenever he was in Chaumont on Friday evenings, he met Father Sebastian privately at his parish.

"That's strange, Uncle. I don't think Prescott is Catholic."

"He's not, but he thrives on the publicity. I gather he has political ambitions. He's building his post-war credentials."

"Maybe, but why private meetings with the priest? You'd think he'd bring reporters to witness his benevolence. Something doesn't make sense."

"It's worth investigating, Emily. Scout out that parish first."

~

The opportunity to ensnare Prescott arose when Martin was away on a visit to a front-line sector. A call Emily had handled gave her the news that Prescott was planning to visit the parish this Friday, two days from now. She talked her matron into giving her the night off so she could reconnoiter.

Emily bicycled to André's barn outside of town, where she changed into a widow's black dress and headed to confession with Father Sebastian. She entered the church at early evening and pretended to pray, bending low in the pews to conceal herself. Twenty minutes later Prescott arrived alone, wearing an oversized civilian trench coat and a fedora pulled low. He looked around as if he were assessing the few parishioners present, but hardly gave her a look.

Father Sebastian appeared from a corner door, and he and Prescott kissed each other on the cheek, French-style. Their embrace lasted seconds beyond what was proper. Turning, they walked to the door of the priest's private quarters with overly familiar closeness. *Got you.*

Emily drew a small camera from her bag, waited for the two men to become absorbed in each other, then crept through the hallway guided by the male sounds coming from the end of the corridor. No one was about. Just as she suspected, the good father had orchestrated privacy. The door was slightly ajar — she spotted them naked. Prescott was on his knees. Sebastian stood over him, his mouth agape, his eyes fixed on the ceiling, his moans in rhythm with Prescott's labors.

Hoping the light was good enough, she snapped three pictures and left.

Chapter 27

Ellison

Flatiron District, Manhattan: July 1918

Ellison headed out early to his rendezvous with Michael Donnelly in a back alley behind O'Malley's bar in the Flatiron district on 22nd Street. He liked to scout out unfamiliar territory. Most people had gone to bed, and the quiet night was marred by scavenging dogs fighting over something and a couple who insisted on sharing their marital incompatibilities with the neighborhood. He chuckled at their foolishness. Human foibles amused him, and his understanding of them had taught him how to spot and exploit the weaknesses of other men. The fickle fair sex was an even easier mark.

The garbage-filled, vermin-infested alleyway, whose eerie blackness was interrupted by streaks of light from a half moon, would have unnerved a normal man. But Ellison was not a normal man. He relished walking in the shadows and invited danger as an antidote to the boredom that came so easily to him. Death, his or others', was part of the game of life he played so well.

Ellison trusted Donnelly, as far as Ellison trusted any man, which was not very far. Donnelly needed him and, more importantly, needed his weapons. This put Ellison at an advantage. Tonight, he was pushing that advantage further than prudence would suggest, but that was part of his mission and his fun. Just in case — and Ellison had survived this long thinking about "just in cases" — he had slipped a knife into his boot that now pressed reassuringly against his leg, and tucked a .45 into the back of his trousers and undershorts. Its cold metal barrel felt good against his skin.

At first, Donnelly was reluctant to comply when Ellison suggested that he meet his Irish-American contacts, but he finally accepted the request. Ellison was so gifted a liar he could talk a nun into his bed and make her think it was her own idea, something he had done more than once. Ellison, who knew Irish history better than Donnelly, had changed Donnelly's mind by appealing to his Irish patriotism with tales of British atrocities. Ellison riled at the 1801 Act of the Union that abolished the Irish Parliament, cried about the potato famine that killed a generation of Irish, and praised Charles Parnell's efforts to bring Home Rule back to Ireland. He passionately supported Sinn Féin's current political efforts. Lewis had provided Ellison with the material to study, but in mastering it like the accomplished schemer he was, Ellison had transformed himself into a passionate Irish nationalist, or so he made it seem.

Ellison considered Donnelly's blind patriotism his weakness. *Imagine being willing to die for a cause.* Ellison never could, but as long as Donnelly believed Ellison embraced the Irish cause as his own, he could be manipulated. Tonight was a test of how much. Ellison hoped Donnelly would introduce him to his full cadre of Irish-American nationalists and financial backers. If he got their names, Lewis had promised him a big bonus, enough for Ellison to purchase the social status he had never known since his days as an unwanted orphan.

Ellison sat waiting, hidden on a narrow stoop, ready to fend off any drunk or robber foolish enough to approach. No dandy tonight, he was dressed in dark wool clothing purchased that morning from a store that sold used goods. They itched and smelled of cigar smoke and liquor. Better to fit in with these Irish hooligans. Minutes later, Donnelly turned into the alley and walked right past him. Before Ellison could stand, Donnelly whipped around and pressed a revolver to his head. "Think you could trick me, my friend? I saw you from the street. I've survived more street battles than you." Donnelly holstered his gun and smiled. "Let's go."

This man is better than I thought. Give him more respect next time. Ellison followed Donnelly for several blocks. They exchanged no words. Donnelly's face muscles tensed, his hand never straying from the Colt. He walked with a deliberate gait, backtracking twice. He stopped to listen every fifty yards, looking around with owl eyes, making certain no one followed. Such caution signaled to Ellison that this was indeed the important meeting he had hoped for.

~

The two men stopped at an old dilapidated warehouse. Its front window had more tape than glass and whatever paint remained was blistered and cracked. The roof sagged and lacked shingles. Donnelly turned to Ellison and said, "We're here. I've told them you would be coming and that you are invaluable to our struggle. But no specifics. Remember, these people distrust everybody and rile quickly."

"Sure. Thank you, Michael." *I'll be too busy remembering names and faces*, Ellison thought, and imagined himself counting Lewis's money.

They walked deep into the warehouse. Voices emanated from a dank area blocked off by stacks of crates nine feet high. Inside, eight men sat on chairs arranged like a courtroom. Ellison immediately recognized three men: the man in front — the judge, Ellison presumed — was Dylan Moran, a Boston newspaper editor and the son of a wealthy Boston socialite. The man standing and pointing an accusing finger was New York Congressman Ethan Doyle. To his side, the older gentleman recording the proceedings was Patrick Gallagher, a J.P. Morgan vice president and a prominent New York City philanthropist. Getting his name alone was worth the risk.

Ellison did not recognize the three men sitting in the jury box, or the unfortunate red-faced man roped to a chair, pleading innocence between violent fits of sobbing. The last man stood up from his chair next to the accused and shook Donnelly's hand. Ellison overheard him whisper, "It'll all be over soon, Michael. Glad you arrived in time. Everything's happened just as you said."

"Thank you, Liam."

Liam nodded to Ellison, pointed to a spot in the back of the area, and returned to his seat.

"I didn't betray you! He's the man to fear." The accused pointed to Donnelly. "He'll get us all killed."

"Liar. He'd say anything to save himself," Donnelly retorted.

"Prisoner Mason Maguire, please stand," the judge said. "Judgment has been determined."

Liam pulled the prisoner up by the armpit.

"We find you guilty of treason and sentence you to die. Hanging is in order, but we don't have the time. Liam?"

Maguire sank to his knees.

"With pleasure, your honor, but I believe that privilege should go to the man he betrayed, Michael Donnelly."

Donnelly stepped forward. "I have brought the friend I mentioned to you. He says he's an Irish patriot. I think he should carry out the sentence to prove his loyalty to our cause." He handed Ellison a dockworker baling hook.

A test. Obviously a demonstration about betrayal. Were they saying, "We know what you're up to, and this will be your fate," or was it merely a ploy to intimidate? No matter. Whoever the unfortunate Maguire might be, Ellison didn't care.

Without hesitation, he clutched the round wooden handle of the baling hook and glided his finger along the eight-inch metal hook that projected at a right angle from the center of the handle. He placed the weapon to his lips and said, "It will be an honor to administer justice." He raised the hook over his head and, in a pitcher's motion, drove the curved bottom of the hook into Maguire's head with a satisfying crack. Before Maguire keeled over, Ellison lowered the hook to the level of the guilty man's chest and jerked it into his neck. It dug deep. Ellison twisted the hook, forcing Maguire's head to an odd angle. Ellison yanked it out, taking with it half the neck. Blood gushed. Ellison raised the red-stained hook in triumph.

Donnelly patted him on the back. "I was uncertain about you. Not now."

Chapter 28

Obstacles

Police Headquarters: July 1918

Certain the dandy and Clancy's shooter were one and the same, Shannon escorted a police sketch artist to Mount Sinai, to hear Clancy describe the dandy's features. The artist sketched them out to Clancy's displeasure. Ornery and itching to get back to work, Clancy complained the artist worked too fast and wasn't listening.

"You know how to do this, Sean," Shannon chastised. "What details stood out? We'll get this."

Clancy calmed down, provided additional specifics, and proclaimed the second drawing an excellent likeness. They added the dandy's height, build, and coloring to the bottom of the drawing and noted he was an extravagant dresser. Shannon had copies printed up to pass around the various precincts and nearby police departments, and cautioned everyone that the suspect was a potential key witness in a police homicide.

Over the next two days, Shannon's efforts met no success. Reactions ranged from "don't want to get involved" to "never seen him before." Some people hardly looked at the drawing and excused themselves as fast as possible. She knew something was up when a precinct captain advised, "Drop it, Mrs. Keller. For your own good."

That night she confided to Fernandez that there was a systematic attempt to thwart her. Someone powerful was conspiring against her.

~

Shannon wanted friendly company after another frustrating day at work. She went across Centre Street to The Headquarters, where she was always welcomed, and ordered a beer. Standing at the bar, she sensed something was amiss when two nearby cops avoided eye contact, then walked away when she started to ask questions. Those who stayed remained polite and friendly, but did not want to engage in discussion.

She was trying to catch a cop killer — *what was going on?*

After a few minutes, Charlie Rooney, an old Irish roundsman like Clancy, approached Shannon. "Go see Bill Dewey at the far table," he whispered. "White hair, whiskers, brown coat. He'll help you. Pretend like I insulted you and walk away."

"You rude man. How dare you! My husband may be German-American, but he's every bit as patriotic as you," Shannon said. Feeling all eyes on her, she moved to the end of the bar and ordered another beer. She would wait to approach Dewey. A few of the men nodded their heads and flashed quick smiles. She still had friends.

Shannon waited twenty minutes or so as patrons flowed out of the bar and new ones appeared, then walked over to Dewey's small table and sat down. "I understand you worked with roundsman Sean Clancy a while back."

Dewey grunted and looked down at his empty glass. "Sure could use another."

"After we talk."

"Don't got much to say."

"You mean you're like the rest of these cowards?" Shannon asked. "Not willing to help your friend and find a cop killer?"

"The word is out not to help you. Whatever you're involved in, it's got people all riled up."

"So, what about you? You riled?"

"Do you know who I am?"

"Sean Clancy's old friend."

"That don't matter. I'm retired. They got no leverage on me."

"Who's *they?*"

"I understand you got a drawing you want me to look at."

Shannon put the folded police sketch on the table and furtively slid it over. "Gun runner. Hired killer. Shot Clancy and killed Abbott. He's involved in something important."

Dewey studied the picture for a long time. He looked up and

whistled quietly. "That's a bad man. We had a problem with him a few years back. Thought he was selling guns to German sailors coming off their boats. Maybe start an uprising in New York. Rumors say he killed some Eye-talian who was trying to steal some of his customers. We wanted him bad back then, but never could prove nothin'. Haven't heard from him since. You sure that's who you're after?"

"Yes. Who is he?"

"Ronny Ellison."

~

Armed with Ellison's name, but stymied by her active-duty colleagues, Shannon followed Fernandez's suggestion and went to Washington, D.C. to consult with the new national police Bureau of Investigation. A risky move, but Shannon refused to be stopped.

Shannon sat on the train, wishing Clancy had been able to join her. Her mission could not wait for him to recover, so she set out alone, accompanied only by her determination. The surprise was that she felt so vulnerable.

Desperate men do desperate things, and Shannon had no doubt she was facing desperate men. *Surely, no one would attack her on a train — or would they?* She took a deep breath and recalled her Uncle Thomas's advice on how to handle such a situation: remain calm, don't bring attention to yourself or signal you're nervous, keep to crowded areas, and be prepared to act fast. She checked the Webley in her purse and breathed deeply several more times to lower her blood pressure. She checked everyone in the coach and, satisfied they presented no immediate threats, she settled down to plan her next step.

Shannon stayed with the bulk of the people exiting the train at Washington and followed them to the main concourse. She then broke free and darted to the taxi stand. Unwilling to signal her intentions, she had made no appointment, but trusted a persuasive feminine approach and the unwillingness to take no for an answer would secure her an interview with the ranking heads.

The man at the front desk refused to help until she pulled out her New York Police identification. "I can create a scene if you wish," she said. "I'm here on important business and demand to see your superior."

He lifted the phone, mouthed the word "bitch," and said something into the receiver that Shannon could not hear. A young man in civilian clothes soon came out to greet her. She talked her way through a series of progressively higher-ranked senior officials until out of sheer will and persuasion, she managed to reach the desk of the assistant director, Abner Hicks.

She entered just as a man in an army colonel's uniform was exiting the office. Rather than ceding to the fairer sex, he gave her a sharp look and rudely brushed against her as he passed.

Hicks pushed some papers under his desk blotter as she approached. Looking up with an obsequious smile, he stared at her silently before gradually rising to his feet.

Shannon brushed the insult aside and held out her hand. "Thank you for seeing me, Mr. Hicks."

Hicks shook her hand lightly and pulled away. He sat back down, then gestured limply to a chair in front of the desk, inviting her to sit as well. "I only agreed to see you because of what you have done to help us stop the German sabotage ring in New York."

Help us? What nerve. The Bomb Squad did the work. You had nothing to do with it.

"So — what is it you want from us, Mrs. Keller?"

She detailed the circumstances surrounding the Kittridge investigation and the shooting of her friends. He seemed bored and yawned twice. Shannon finished, saying, "I believe this man, Ronny Ellison, is responsible. Here." She handed him the police sketch. "He's a cop killer from Los Angeles. I'm hoping you can help me locate him."

Hicks gave the sketch a cursory look. "I do not recognize him, Mrs. Keller, and I have never heard of Ronny Ellison. The drawing could be any number of men. The description is too vague."

No, it's not. He's lying.

Hicks handed back the drawing. "Let me do this. To help put your concerns to rest, I'll have my people go through our records of gun merchants and hired killers to see if we can find your Mr. Ellison."

"Thank you. Let me help."

"That will not be necessary."

"I'll wait. I won't go back to New York without some answers."

"It might take several hours."

"I'm not in a hurry."

"You can wait in the small conference room. I'll have my assistant see that you have what you need. Tea?"

~

Hicks was right. Shannon's tea was good and cold by the time the assistant came in at 4:48 p.m. and apologized. They had not found anything on Ronnie Ellison or anyone else who matched Shannon's sketch. "It's best if you return to New York. We'll inform you of any further developments." He thanked her for her commitment to the case and wished her the best.

~

Shannon was waiting to board the train when two rough-looking men in suits approached her on the platform. "Please come with us, Mrs. Keller," the taller man said. "Don't reach for that Webley in your purse. You're under arrest."

Chapter 29
Pershing's Train

AEF Headquarters, Chaumont, France: July 1918
No sooner had General Pershing declared victory in Belleau Wood than he began to plan the next phase of the war. The AEF had helped stymie the German Aisne offensive in June, but everyone expected one last German thrust. The British, French, and Americans needed to coordinate their efforts.

To accomplish this, Generalissimo Foch organized a strategy meeting in Paris. Ordered to join General Pershing as a translator, Martin reluctantly turned over the search for Keller to Emily Lange. He did not like the idea of owing her a favor. Something about her bothered him. Maybe her relationship with Major Jameson, or maybe his fear of getting too close to someone so ... , well ..., attractive. Desperate for help, he had accepted her assistance despite his misgivings.

When he left his barracks, Martin was startled by gunfire and shouts coming from the central square. He readied his .45 and ran to the commotion, only to find three privates laughing and firing their pistols in the air. "It's the 4th of July! Happy birthday, America!"

Was it? Martin had lost track of what day it was. He gave the privates a severe dressing down and took their names, though he had no intention of reporting them.

Before he boarded Pershing's train, Martin stopped by Emily's station and learned she was on break, walking with her uncle in the nearby woods. He found them deep in conversation on Emily's favorite bench. Not wanting to disturb them, he watched for a moment, then backed away, just as they, too, were parting. Emily kissed André on both cheeks, and the old man hobbled to his bicycle, weighed down by a large picnic basket.

Officially designated "the Commander-in-Chief's Field Headquarters Train," General Pershing's ten-car train had no distinguishing markings. One car provided power and light and ran the telephone and telegraph equipment. Others included a dining carriage, a meeting and war room complete with up-to-the-minute situational maps, sleeping quarters for General Pershing and key staff, a carriage for the enlisted personnel who provided security, and a transportation car for the general's auto. As Martin boarded, General Prescott appeared and immediately followed him on. A sergeant closed the door behind them.

Martin was directed to the dining car. To his chagrin, the only unoccupied seats were side-by-side facing the back of the train. Prescott pushed Martin aside and sat down on the more comfortable window seat with a loud *plumf,* as the air from the thick leather cushion groaned under his weight. Martin squeezed in next to him. Prescott removed his cap and scratched his bristly white hair. Turning to Martin, he asked, "What is a junior officer doing on this train, Captain?"

"Orders from General Pershing, sir."

"Oh." Prescott pulled some papers from his valise, lit a fat Cuban cigar, and set about reading, blowing eye-watering smoke in Martin's direction. The carriage quickly filled with the pungent fumes, causing Martin to cough. Prescott shot him a sharp look. "Couldn't you keep that down, Captain? I'm concentrating."

~

Half an hour into the journey, the tracks led the train into a vulnerable area not far from the front lines. As they slowed down at a bend, artillery shells rained down on the path of the train. Martin instinctively took charge. He instructed everyone to pull down the shades and close the curtains to black out the train. Within seconds, lights were extinguished and the train came to a halt. Martin then directed everyone to move from the windows and cover their heads.

"What's happening?" Prescott asked. The glowing red and orange tip of his cigar quivered in the darkness.

"Long-range German artillery," Martin replied. "I assure you, they can hit us."

The boom of successive shells drew closer. Martin strained to listen to the incoming sounds and realized they were not yet a threat. "It's hard to tell if this is a nuisance attack or if they are targeting us," he said to Prescott. "If they are, I don't know how."

"Shouldn't we go outside and take cover?" Prescott asked.

"It's safer here. It shouldn't last long."

Colonel Earl Thornton, who managed Pershing's train, entered the carriage and announced the tracks ahead had been damaged. All they could do was hunker down and wait.

Ten minutes later, the bombardment ceased as quickly as it had started. Martin drew his .45 and disembarked. A sergeant leading the security team confirmed the danger had passed. The train had suffered a few broken windows and damage to the sleeping cars, but no one had been injured.

"What happened here, Sergeant?" Martin asked.

"We were the target, that's for sure, Captain. The Huns tossed over a hundred shells in our direction. They don't waste shells like that for nothing. They knew we was here."

"Has this happened before?"

"Yes, sir. Ten days ago."

~

The color had not yet returned to Prescott's face when Martin got back to his seat. "You get used to the shelling, General," Martin said, as the train picked up speed.

The bombardment had apparently dimmed Prescott's arrogance. He smiled and seemed inclined to talk. "I hear you disagree with our tactics to fight this war. Is that so, Captain Martin?"

"Permission to speak freely, General?" Martin reached for a cigarette.

Prescott leaned back and crossed his arms. "Proceed."

"We do not have to condemn so many soldiers to die. Bunched units attacking *en masse* is murder."

"You think the French and British have a better way?"

"Yes. They've learned how to attack a position and keep it."

"I haven't seen any great successes from them in the last four years. The Huns have beaten them back at every turn. Only we, the Americans, have gained ground, using the tactics you criticize. Take Belleau Wood. A marvelous success. Look at the great news coverage."

Martin did not want to argue. "With better use of artillery, more firepower in the front lines — particularly grenades — and coordination of adjacent units, Belleau Wood did not have to be a bloodbath."

"You are forgetting one important factor, Captain. Time. America needs to make an impact on the Western Front immediately. Show that we have the best men, the best generals, the best army. That's the only way we can dictate the terms of the peace and control the post-war world."

So that's it. Political priorities by the higher-ups. "Time is more important than lives?"

"Yes. Once I get my division, I'll push the men hard and fast. I plan to set the example in my sector. A straightforward battering ram, that's what I'll be. The rest of the army can follow my backside."

While you rake in the glory and undeserved commendations, regardless of the men.

"The French and British are too timid. Hard-charging American boys with fixed bayonets will drive Fritz off the field. We have the stomach for battle, they don't."

"You sound like our Allies in 1914. But they have learned."

"We have the numbers, and more are coming every month. I intend to be at the front of victory. The losses are merely the price."

Martin bit his tongue hard before replying. "Time will tell."

"So it shall. And it will favor me. I'm glad you agree. People back home expect victories, and that's what I intend to give them. Generals make good senators, Captain. Now, let me return to my papers."

Mules are less stubborn, thought Martin, and vowed to do what he could to thwart the cost of Prescott's ego and arrogance.

A sergeant walked through the carriage, informing the passengers they would reach their destination in ninety minutes. Martin sat in silence for the rest of the trip.

~

The meeting went smoothly, considering the different aspirations and problems of the participants. Martin liked Foch's confidence and aggressive, calculating manner. For once, the various intelligence sources — air reconnaissance, front-line patrols, captured German soldiers, local French civilians, and Allied soldiers who had escaped capture — had supported Foch's strategic assessment.

"They will strike here." Foch thrust his pointer at the map, indicating the Champagne region, east of Belleau Wood. "The only question is the strength of remaining German reserves. They've suffered huge casualties over the last two months, just as we have. I believe they are weaker than our intelligence estimates."

A British general spoke up. "If you're wrong, General —"

"I'm not." Foch was confident the French and Americans could absorb the blow. He had set a trap. He would let the German army attack and weaken itself against the Allied defenses. When their momentum stalled, he would launch a massive counter-attack with reserves and stockpiled munitions and regain the territory the Huns had taken since March.

Foch promised Pershing at the end of the meeting that he would soon be able to mount his own offensive, in his own sector, with his own U.S. Army. Pershing was delighted.

For the first time since he had arrived in France, Martin began to sense the beginnings of final victory.

~

Just as Martin was about to board the train for Chaumont, a corporal ran up waving a note. "Captain Martin," he cried between heaving breaths. "Urgent message for you, sir."

Martin turned, his foot still on the stairs. "From whom, Corporal?"

"An Emily Lange. Signal Corps."

Martin ripped open the message. *Found him. Keller's alive.*

Chapter 30
Escape

Somewhere Behind the American Lines, France: June 1918
Keller lay in the hospital, confused and alone, his memory blurred. His head ached and his ears rang. The shades were drawn, leaving the room so dark he could not tell if it was day or night. He heard no voices from the hallway or noises outside. The blankets were plush and warm, his scratchy pajamas standard army issue. The room was private and secluded. Such accommodations were usually reserved for generals, not lieutenants.

He struggled to stand but could not maintain his balance and fell back into bed. Nauseated, he vomited into the basin by his bedside. Later, feeling somewhat better, he leaned over and looked at the chart at his feet. Some numbers — blood pressure and temperature, Keller gathered — and a doctor's scribbles. And something curious. The chart listed the patient as Marine Lieutenant Peter Keltner. *What's going on? Why am I listed as someone else?* He flopped back onto the soft mattress and struggled to remember how he got here. Wherever "here" was.

The nurses spoke American English. The doctors' white gowns showed American markings. He was safe and in friendly hands, but how long had he been here? Dreamlike memories of an AEF colonel named Mortimer and a short visit by a pretty young woman in a Signal Corps uniform flashed repeatedly in his head.

His last full memory was a German soldier hitting him with a trench club. After that, bits and pieces. Angry voices — German and American. Man-to-man fighting. Gunfire. Gas. A rifle pointed at him. Marching. Digging. Drawing his knife. Creeping in the woods. Falling. Explosions. Blackness. He drifted back to sleep, fatigued and scared.

He woke again, sat up, and looked around. On the hook over the door was a mud-stained German army tunic. And then it all came back to him.

~

June 6, 1918: A German had just attempted to cave in his head. Blood dripped from his head wound onto his uniform, stained with the flesh of others. He struggled to stay awake. Sleep meant death, and he was not ready to die.

He dared not move, such was the danger surrounding him. The fighting around the machine-gun nest seesawed for what seemed like hours. Streams of bullets, thick as swarms of locusts, passed over him in both directions. Many pounded into the earth embankment protecting him, *thud, thud, thud,* as the dirt absorbed the impact.

Desperate for water, he reached for his canteen, but a bullet hole had drained it. He searched the body of the dead Marine next to him and found a partially filled one. He poured half of it over his sweating face and emptied the rest down his throat. The cool water revived him. He pulled the Marine's limp body over himself for cover.

Neither side would concede ground. Dead or wounded bodies, American and German, were stacked up three-high. This was not war; it was bestiality. Keller wavered in and out of awareness during the struggle. Time seemed to march at its own erratic pace.

He blinked away his unconsciousness and suppressed the urge to cry out. His head throbbed, but he could manage the pain. The sky was light, so not much time had passed since the beginning of the attack. Field-gray and khaki-green uniformed bodies co-mingled around him, motionless or writhing in pre-death agony. Steam poured from the machine gun. It, too, was near death. A nearby tree had been cut in two by the intensity of the crossfire. One of its limbs had caught fire and fallen onto the bodies of the dead. The smoke from the conflagration stung his eyes and choked his lungs. Triumphant German voices reached his ears, and Keller crawled into a ditch behind a clump of trees ten yards from the dugout.

The fighting along the flanks signaled that the battle was continuing. The Americans were attacking again in strength. Germans appeared and frantically began to pull bodies away from the machine gun; they refilled its water jacket and replaced the barrel. Yards away, Keller watched silently.

The Maxim spit out empty shell casings by the hundreds. They piled on top of each other like coins cascading out of a robber's sack. Americans kept coming; the Germans fought back but were losing ground. "Retreat!" a loud voice ordered in German, and it dawned on Keller that the Huns were about to stop the advance with an artillery barrage, including gas. Reaching for his gas mask, he discovered gunfire had turned it into Swiss cheese.

The shriek of artillery shells forced him to hunker down in his ditch. The rough surface scratched his face. The attackers' cries filled his ears as the high-explosive shells knocked them down. The next rounds sounded different, not whizz-bangs, but ... . The smell of moldy hay. Phosgene, *Green Cross*. Gas to drive the enemy above ground, explosives to finish him off.

Keller's eyes watered; his throat burned; he began to cough. Holding his breath, he pulled out a cloth, urinated into it, then placed it over his mouth and sucked in air, gaining a few seconds of relief. Despite the shelling, he had no choice but to leave the ditch and pull a mask from a dead German soldier. Ducking and weaving low, he made it back to his rock and tree-protected safety. His breathing eased.

An incoming shell landed five feet from his position. Its vibrations pulsated across the area, but the shrapnel passed overhead. When the bombardment ceased and the phosgene dissipated, the Germans were bound to reoccupy this strongpoint, but running across no-man's-land would be certain death. He decided to wait for the cover of night to crawl back to American lines.

His chance never came. German reinforcements moved to solidify the position. In minutes, they would be on top of him. *Surrender or die?*

Keller instinctively wanted to fight it out, but thoughts of

Shannon made him release his .45. His life was no longer only his own. He had no right to die a thoughtless death. Clasping his locket for a moment, he stood up, removed his gas mask, and called out. "*Kamerad!*" Wary of a uniformed American speaking perfect German, the soldiers moved toward him, guns at the ready.

"Don't shoot. I surrender," he called in German, raising his hands.

An *Unteroffizier* pointed his Mauser at Keller's chest. "*Amerikaner?*" Keller nodded. The German waved his rifle in the direction of the rear. Someone gave him a bucket of water and soap to wash away the phosgene that had collected on him. On the march toward the rear of the enemy lines, Keller mentally noted the locations of command posts, strong points, artillery positions, and a cache of weapons.

When he arrived at the collection area, two other Yanks, clearly demoralized, were sitting in the clearing. One, a private with heavy black stubble, head hanging down, mumbled something in Italian. The only word Keller understood was "mama."

The other, a kid who looked about eighteen, was shaking uncontrollably.

"Wh—, what we going to do, Lieutenant?"

"Do whatever they say. Don't try to be heroes. Your job is to stay alive," Keller said, his mind already busy figuring out how to escape. He had garnered precious information that could help the AEF and would not include these men in his plans.

They were forced to carry stretchers and dig shallow pits. When they had finished, the *Unteroffizier* tied their feet and hands, saying they would not be harmed as long as they caused no trouble. Tomorrow they would be moved with other prisoners to a holding area miles behind the front lines. A corporal approached; his nostrils flared like a challenged bull. He pointed his pistol at Keller. "I just lost half my platoon. You Yanks just shot us without mercy. You deserve the same."

Saliva dripped from his mouth.

"Halt!" a *Leutnant* ordered. "We need to interrogate these men. We are not murderers. Report to your company commander, soldier. Get ready for the next attack. We need every man." The *Leutnant* turned to Keller and nodded. "We cannot move you tonight. All roads are occupied, but you'll be safe. I'll post a guard."

"*Danke,*" Keller mouthed.

For the next several hours, Keller observed activities in the camp as his dizziness and nausea gradually subsided. His breathing was steady. German reinforcements were moving into the area; if he was going to escape, it had to be tonight.

As the hours crept into late night, his fellow prisoners and the German guard dozed off. He bent forward, reached down with bound hands, and felt his lower leg. His knife still rested between his puttees and his inner leg. The Germans had failed to detect it during their cursory search, so well had he wrapped his cloth leggings. He shifted around so his back faced outward, and with his hands tied, he reached for his knife. After freeing his feet first, Keller placed his knife firmly between them and cut away the bonds on his wrists.

Keller eyed the sleeping guard. If he could steal his tunic and helmet, he could sneak through enemy lines in the dark by impersonating a German officer. He had interrogated enough of them to know how to imitate them. He could do nothing to hide his trousers and American leggings, but hoped no one would notice if he moved fast and kept his distance.

Wait for an opportunity. He would either be killed or escape.

~

At 02:46, the area was still, the sky cloudy and starless. Keller clenched his knife in his teeth and crept on all fours to the sleeping guard. He placed his left hand over the German's mouth and jabbed his knife lightly into his neck. Just enough to draw blood. The guard awakened with a start.

"Take off your tunic," Keller said softly in German. "Keep quiet and I will not kill you." The frightened guard handed over his jacket, equipment belt, and helmet without a word. Keller immobilized him with a knock on the head and disappeared into the night.

He crept toward the woods, retracing the route he had taken to the holding area. Stopping twice to hide when sentries came too close, he reached the weapons cache near the wood line he had noted coming in. Finding the area unguarded, he stole wire cutters, dynamite, and a good number of fuses, and planted bombs with long delays around the area and along his way.

Once in the dark woods, Keller relied on the natural camouflage of the thick forest and the chaotic nature of men scrambling to prepare for battle. Focused on their tasks, the Germans paid him no heed. He was just one more soldier doing a different job.

Keller continued undeterred until he reached a gap in the German front defenses. He looked across no-man's-land, three-hundred yards deep, then checked his watch. Eight minutes to go before his bombs would detonate. Alert snipers on either side surveyed the ground, ready to shoot anything larger than a rat. He studied the area to determine the best way through the barbed wire and cratered field.

Voices. Footsteps. Whispers. The Germans were looking for him. An *Unteroffizier* pointed in the direction he had traveled. With four minutes before detonation, Keller crawled to the nearest crater outside the woods.

Chaos erupted in the German rear as his explosions did their job. As an extra bonus, an inexperienced American artillery officer misconstrued the explosions as an enemy attack and ordered a counter-barrage. The shells from the ensuing artillery duel flew over Keller's head as he raced for the Allied side. Barbed wire blocked him twice but he frantically cut through it, suffering several cuts in his struggle.

One hundred yards from his line, Keller called out. "I'm a Yank. Don't shoot!" he pleaded, casting aside his helmet and ripping open the enemy blouse as he raced across the treacherous terrain. The Germans, now alerted, sent up flares and began to shoot and shell him with *Minenwerfer* trench mortars, their accuracy improving as he ran. His bad leg gave out, and he tripped into a shell hole. He looked up just in time to see the flaming tail of a shell heading right at him. He folded himself into a ball and —

~

Later: Keller's dreams morphed into reality when he woke to discover the actual Colonel Mortimer at his bedside. The colonel looked down on him familiarly, as if this was not his first visit. Keller could not remember previous discussions, although he clearly recalled the man himself: the jet-black hair and pencil-thin mustache; the long, thin nose that highlighted his foxlike features; the inquisitive bloodshot eyes that never seemed to blink; and the smooth, pale skin that made it difficult to guess his age. Confidence oozed from his compact body. He looked like a man who could win at poker with a pair of twos.

"How are you feeling today, Lieutenant?" Mortimer asked with the scratchy voice of a man who smoked too much. "Your recollection better?"

"Yes, Colonel. Thank you. I remember some woman in a Signal Corps uniform. Who was she?"

"Emily Lange, a friend of your Captain Martin. Came asking about you. Persistent. Armed with a note signed by Martin authorizing her to investigate your whereabouts. She was pushy, but since you said the captain was the one person you wanted to see, we let her visit for five minutes. I kept her on a short leash and told her to say nothing about you except to Martin."

"Can't remember our discussion. She was pretty. I remember that." Keller fought off a dizzy spell. "Can you tell me where I am, and why I'm listed as Lieutenant Keltner?"

A knowing amusement crept over Mortimer's face. "The Huns have informers everywhere. We want them to think you died in their mortar attack."

"Colonel?"

"You've been behind enemy lines. Crossing back, you got caught in a mortar attack. About a hundred yards from our front, you fell into a shell hole as a mortar shell exploded. It knocked you out and aggravated your previous head injury, I'm afraid. Lucky for you, one of our men recognized you. He risked his life to pull you back and ..., well, here you are."

"Where, Colonel? I don't remember much after that mortar shell came at me."

"Outside the town of Meaux. We've put you into this château and given you the best care to accelerate your recovery. The doctors report you're feeling better, and your memory is improving. Your exposure to phosgene gas has left no lingering effects, but you'll be here for a while."

Mortimer hesitated and looked at Keller the way a salesman assesses a mark before he makes his pitch. "In truth, we need your help. We are having a bloody time of it in Belleau Wood. Can you give us some insight into the German defenses and dispositions?"

Keller propped himself up. "The details are coming back to me, but my information is days old. The situation was fluid and probably has changed by now."

"Yes, but their strongpoints are still strongpoints. Command bunkers don't move unless there's a retreat, and the Germans are not retreating."

By the end of Keller's report, Mortimer's face showed a predator's glee at a likely kill. "Thank you, Lieutenant," he said, "That will help us enormously."

Chapter 31
The Letter

Chaumont, France: July 1918

More than a week had gone by since Emily had visited Lieutenant Keller in Meaux. She was pleased to have ingratiated herself with Captain Martin, the one person in the AEF who could unmask her. Now he was indebted to her, and better yet, he seemed attracted to her in a new way. She had to be careful, though: He was perceptive and somehow seemed conflicted toward her. But why? Her looks? That happened frequently enough. Her confidence? Lesser men were easily intimidated by her, but the captain? No, it was something else. She would continue to see him around headquarters and guile the answers out of him. The closer she became with him, the less likely he'd become a threat.

The compromising pictures of Prescott and Father Sebastian had worked perfectly. She had carefully hidden her identity as the blackmailer, insisting all communications were written and exchanged in a secret place in the parish. Prescott began immediately passing on information about troop movements, logistics, and scuttlebutt. He continued to visit Father Sebastian, and Emily continued to permit it. Unfortunately, the information had proved too general and untimely to make a real difference in the war. Emily suspected he was holding something back, passing on just enough to keep her from revealing his secret. It was time to resort to other, more drastic means. She just needed the authorization.

Switchboard activity had picked up again. Something big was about to happen. Prescott had mentioned a big push, but anyone around headquarters could figure that out. She wanted to know more. As Prescott was conveniently away, she tried to find out from Captain Martin, but all he said was that he was leaving again and could not discuss his mission.

When Emily left her switchboard at the end of her shift, her matron handed her a letter from her father in New York. She checked the postmark. It had taken weeks to arrive. Had military censors intercepted it? Suspicion came easily to Emily. Even if someone had read it, she reassured herself, he would not discern her father's hidden meanings.

She thanked her supervisor and headed outside to be alone, excited and nervous to discover her next instructions. Along the way, she heard someone walking up fast behind her. "Miss Lange. Wait. Do you have a moment?"

Captain Martin. Remaining calm, she shoved the letter into her coat and looked up. "Yes, Captain. How can I help you?"

"A letter?" He pointed to her pocket.

Damn. She smiled blankly. "My father. I haven't heard from him in a long time."

"I hope things are well back home." Polite words, but Martin looked agitated.

"Thank you, Captain. I'm sure they are," Emily stiffly replied, and turned to walk away, hoping he would not follow.

Martin kept pace. "What does your father do?"

Innocent question from a friend? Or something else? Be nice, but firm. Emily stopped, crossed her arms across her chest, and said. "I'm sorry, Captain Martin. I'm in a hurry. Could we talk later?"

"Wait, Miss Lange." Martin stepped in front of her. "I'm sorry, but I have some bad news."

Emily froze. *Play along. Act distressed.*

"It's Lieutenant Colonel Jameson. He's dead — an artillery shell caught him in the open. I gather you were friends."

He's after something. Does he know about my rendezvous with Jameson in Paris? "Thank you, Captain. I'm so sorry to hear that. Please convey my condolences to his family. I did not know him long. I haven't seen him since his transfer." She feigned appropriate distress and dabbed her eye with a tissue, glad that Martin could not see it remained dry.

"Thank you for your time, Miss Lange." Martin tipped his cap and walked away.

Emily guessed this was not some chance meeting. She apparently did not have as much control over him as she had thought. *What did he know? Was he asking about Jameson or her? Had he found out about their tryst in Paris? Was it mere coincidence that he appeared the same day as the letter?*

Emily walked to her favorite spot in the woods, her mind ill at ease. She tore open her father's letter and examined the sheet of tissue-thin paper. She fingered it and lifted it to the sky No hidden message, just words plainly on the page. Her father did not favor magicians' tricks.

She read it three times to make sure she understood the meaning behind the innocuous family chatter, encouraging words, and the reference to "putting down" the dog. *Proceed with the mission.* Her authorization to kill General Pershing. *At last.* She burned the letter and scattered the ashes.

~

Sunday, three days later, was Emily's day off. She met Uncle André at the town square for Mass at the Eglise Saint-Etienne, which she regularly attended. After the service, they walked along the canal to the *Parc de l'Hôtel* and spread a blanket in a shady, quiet spot under an apple tree. Emily carried a picnic lunch in her large wicker basket, which also proved handy for transporting more than food. Today, tucked into the napkins under the bread and cheese lay the coded report she had written based on the intelligence she had gathered since their last meeting. As she shook out the cloth to lay the picnic, a few laughing children ran by chasing a ball. Their voices transported her to a gentler place half a lifetime ago.

André seemed worried.

"Is something wrong, Uncle?" she asked.

"U.S. Army personnel and vehicles are everywhere. Movement is restricted." He closed his eyes and rubbed the bridge of his nose.

"Communication across the lines are harder than ever."

"We must execute our plan before it's too late," Emily said between bites of her apple.

"We must first make sure you come out of this alive. This will help." He pulled an envelope from his coat and slipped it into the basket. "Dollars, Swiss Francs, French Francs. To help you escape when the time comes. Do you have a place to hide it?"

"Yes."

"I'll arrange to have a bicycle and some local clothes placed in the church. The priest is a friend. I helped him restore his church when it was shelled two years ago. He's not too smart."

"What about you, Uncle?"

"I've got Swiss citizenship papers. I can make it across the border. I've scouted the route. We'll meet in Lausanne when this is all over. Remember the place?"

"The Beau Rivage, where we summered in 1912." Emily glanced around, then whispered, "The plan is approved. I heard from Father."

"Good."

"No one will expect a woman assassin."

"That's the main reason you were selected for this assignment." André looked at her with affection and sadness. "So far, air and artillery efforts targeting Pershing have failed. The information you provide is outdated before we receive it. Is there any way you can use the communications system at the Signal Corps?"

"Impossible. The switchboards are manned twenty-four hours a day. My matron notices everything. I have no spare time during my shift."

Emily hesitated, not sure she wanted to cross her own Rubicon. *Mission first*, she decided. "We may need a direct approach."

"I wish the task had not fallen on you," André said, a touch of sadness in his voice.

"I'll need a bomb."

SECTION IV

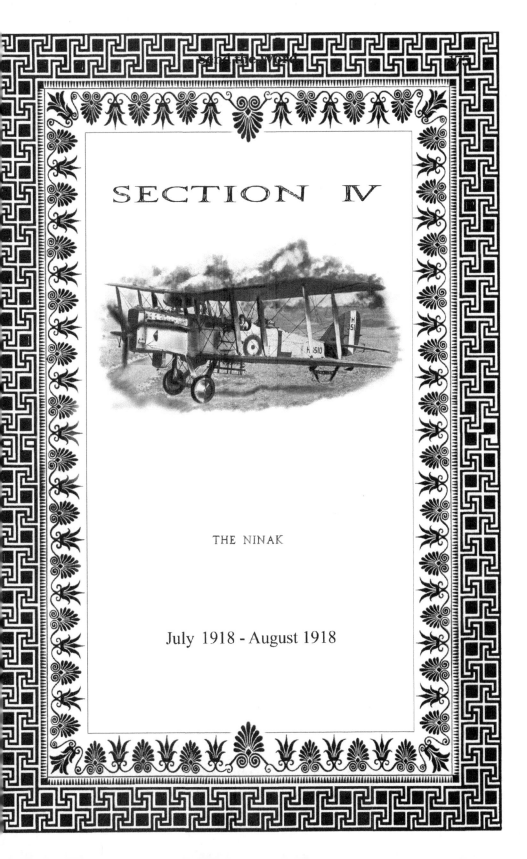

THE NINAK

July 1918 - August 1918

Chapter 32
The Ninak

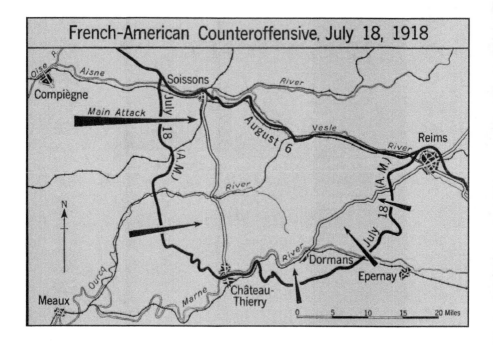

French-American Counteroffensive, July 18, 1918

Champagne Sector, France: July 17, 1918

Dizzy from the height, Martin crossed over no-man's-land at 9,000 feet in the rear observer's seat of the DeHavilland DH 9A two-seat reconnaissance plane. Taller than most airmen, Martin fought back cramps in the confined space. The shoulders of his bulky flight suit brushed against the scarf ring where a Lewis machine gun was mounted. The noise from the engine bored into his head like a drill, obliterating all other sound. His hungry lungs begged for oxygen in the thin air. Fighting lightheadedness, he concentrated on the landscape speeding below him, anxious to understand the direction and strength of enemy troops in a scene that had shrunk to the size of an anthill.

He leaned over and activated the aerial reconnaissance camera mounted on the side of the plane to photograph the battle area. The work forced him to forget the numbing cold, his fear of heights, and the danger. What was he, an intelligence officer who had never flown in an airplane before, doing in a flying machine over no-man's-land? Newly promoted to command the 25th Division, Major General Prescott had specifically requested Martin to assess the front-line situation first-hand as an experienced combat officer. The expected German offensive had been raging for two days — *Friedenssturm*, a captured Hamburg lieutenant had called it. *Peace offensive*. What German reserves remained to prosecute the fight? How depleted were their ordnance stockpiles? When could the Allies counter-attack? Where?

Martin believed Prescott wanted him dead. That was the real reason he was assigned to the mission. Mortality rates among airmen were even higher than those of front-line officers; their expected life span was only a few weeks. And the DH 9A, known as the "Ninak," claimed a higher percentage than most. The men called it a flying coffin. The sixty-seven-gallon fuel tank located between the pilot and the observer was prone to catch fire, especially under attack. The castor oil used to lubricate the engine sometimes leaked and sprayed into their faces, blinding the pilot. Martin didn't like his chances of survival. Crashing to the ground from thousands of feet or burning alive in the air were terrifying ways to die.

The German communication trenches and secondary lines looked like jagged gouges ripped into the earth, lined with barbed-wire nooses. Escorted by two SPAD XIII pursuit planes, the Ninak passed over them unopposed as shells exploded along the front, their horror impossible to judge at that altitude.

Martin thanked God that his pilot, Colonel Billy Mitchell, commander of the U.S. Air Service Group, AEF, was the very best. He flew over the access roads feeding the slaughter, then turned north to observe German movement all along the sector. Excitement raced up Martin's spine — the flow of enemy reinforcements was thinning. The Germans had already committed the bulk of their forces. Contrary to the opinion of most senior Allied officers, Foch had been right: The Huns were vulnerable to the massive counter-attack the generalissimo had planned.

As Mitchell steered the Ninak back toward American lines, three Fokker D-VII biplanes pounced out of the blue. The SPADs peeled off and engaged. The whine of their engines and percussion of their machine guns reverberated in Martin's ears. A green Fokker with a skull-and-crossbones and fifteen Allied rondel markings on its side broke through and raced toward them.

Mitchell pointed his hand to two o'clock in the sky, but Martin's tight-fitting goggles constricted his view. Unable to see the Fokker, but certain that Mitchell had seen something, Martin struggled to ready the Lewis machine gun. Mitchell strained to escape his faster enemy. The Ninak's frame creaked in protest, sending a surge of vibrations up Martin's body.

Mitchell banked hard left and down. Martin braced against the cowling to keep from falling out as a line of machine-gun bullets danced over his head. He swiveled the Lewis gun and aimed at the Fokker diving toward him, its twin Maxim machine guns chattering away. Bullets pierced through the fragile fuselage, but the plane flew on, its engine undamaged.

The Fokker sped under them before he could fire off a burst. Mitchell countered and rolled in the opposite direction, trying to give Martin a clear shot. Martin twisted and rotated the Lewis gun to target the enemy, but the Fokker was too agile and countered every move. He took his best guess at the German's next position and fired enough rounds to keep the Fokker off his tail.

The German maneuvered again. Bullets zipped past Martin's head. He squeezed off a wild burst. No effect. The Fokker accelerated under his sights.

Mitchell circled around. Martin could not see the Fokker, but the bark of its engine betrayed its location below. Mitchell slowed and leaned the plane sideways, giving Martin a visual. He fired a sustained burst, but the Fokker zigged away, looped above them again, then dived down through the clouds from ten o'clock high.

Mitchell steadied the plane and tried to move away. Straining to keep eye contact, Martin rotated the gun, hoping for a clean shot but was too slow. The German turned, circled back, his machine guns firing relentlessly. Bullets passed in front of them, each burst closer.

Mitchell banked down and right, barely avoiding the danger, as the Fokker drove the outclassed Ninak closer to the earth. Ground fire began to pierce through the Ninak's flimsy canvas-covered wings and up through the fuselage. Death above and below. Martin was acutely aware of his vulnerable groin as bullets pierced the body of the plane. Mitchell weaved, anticipating his adversary's moves, his skills preventing a direct shot. Martin glimpsed the frustrated German smack his fist against his fuselage, but it was only a question of time.

Mitchell weaved again, pushing the shuddering DeHavilland to its limit. Martin sensed it could break apart at any second. They continued to spar for a minute, as Mitchell dodged and Martin fired wildly, trying to drive the German back.

Just as they crossed over no-man's-land, a bullet struck the Ninak's engine. The unmistakable rasp of metal against metal. The engine sputtered and slowed. Oil spilled out, blinding Mitchell, painting Martin's helmet and goggles black. Mitchell wiped away the sticky goo with his sleeve and regained control of the plane. Martin tossed off his goggles. The Fokker closed directly behind them, giving the German a clear shot. Martin could sense the victory grin on his rival's face.

Martin slumped down and spread his arms over the fuselage, pretending to be shot, hoping to draw the German closer. He took the bait, certain of the kill, and positioned himself for the final shot. Martin rose up and emptied the Lewis gun into the Fokker. The pilot's arms flew up wildly, trailed by a red mist.

Over American lines now, the Ninak bucked wildly as Mitchell lost the struggle to stay aloft. The engine groaned a death knell and stopped. Martin accepted death and mumbled a few words to God.

Somehow Mitchell kept the plane in a level glide as a narrow, tree-lined access road opened up to the front. Was it wide enough? Smooth enough? Straight enough? Men scrambled to move horses and trucks from their path as gravity pulled down the Ninak faster than Mitchell could control it. One hundred feet, seventy-five — they were descending too fast. The plane clipped the tops of the trees, slicing off its landing wheels. Mitchell yelled something. It went into a spin when the wing brushed against a tree, tearing through the fuselage. Martin blacked out.

He awoke on the ground and smelled fire.

Chapter 33
The Human Cost of the War

Field Hospital Behind American Lines, France: July 1918
Martin awoke to the sound of coughing. The smell of gangrene, iodine
and hydrogen peroxide antiseptics, soiled bedsheets, muddy floors, and
body waste invaded his nose. *Still alive. No pain. Blessed morphine.
Can't remember anything.* Moans and pleas for help filled his ears. He
slowly opened a gluey eyelid, squinting against the sharp light. Dirty,
sweaty men pressed bandages to unattended wounds. The human cost
of war.

Roughly starched sheets chafed against his naked legs. *Still
whole?* He felt around. *Not paralyzed. Couldn't live like that.* His eyes
blinked away the fog. Both of them. He lifted his head, raised the sheet,
and looked down at his body. *Testicles in place. Thank God. Limbs
all there.*

A band was pounding a John Philip Sousa march into his brain.
He reached up and felt a thick bandage wrapped around half his face.
*Disfigured? Burned beyond recognition? A freak. Forced to wear a
mask. What happened? How long have I been here? I need to ..., oh,
hell, what does it matter?* Despondent and disoriented, he fell back
into a drug-induced rest, more oblivion than sleep.

~

The sensation of someone removing the bandage from his head woke
him up. *How long have I been asleep?* The white-robed nurse with a
tarnished silver crucifix hanging from her neck silently rolled away the
cotton cloth. She wore the detached, expressionless face of a woman
who had been caring too long for the wounded. Deep lines around her
eyes told of lack of sleep, and her pallid complexion masked her age.
When she finished removing the bandage, he touched his face. Stitch
marks. No burns. He mumbled a silent prayer. "How long have I been
here?" he croaked.

"Just rest, I'll get you water."

He lifted himself up on his elbows. "I have vital information. I must get to ... ." Fatigued by the exertion, he fell back.

Heavy soled shoes scratched across the floor. "Doctor!"

~

A gentle touch to his shoulder. Martin struggled to unscramble his brain. His nurse backed away as a doctor and a colonel he did not recognize approached. "How is Colonel Mitchell?" Martin asked before they could speak. "Did he survive the crash? Did you get the photographs we shot? I need to —"

"Please lie back, Captain. Let me examine you." The doctor checked Martin's vital signs, then smiled. "Improving."

The colonel gestured for the doctor and nurse to leave. He leaned close to Martin and said in a low tone, "You were shot down a day and a half ago. We were worried you might have suffered brain damage, but apparently not. Just lacerations to your head. Don't ask me how, but Colonel Mitchell walked away from the crash with some bad bruises. Somehow, he landed the plane but couldn't control it. The side of the plane rammed into a stack of crates by the road and broke apart. The front spun 180 degrees but stayed upright. Your end flipped on its side and threw you into the air. The plane ignited, but soldiers pulled you away before the flames reached you. The doctor tells me you'll be fine in a few days."

"But the German offensive. We need to counter-attack. I must ... ." Martin struggled to swing his legs from the bed, but the colonel guided him back.

"We know. Colonel Mitchell relayed the information. American forces are leading an attack as we speak. They're making excellent progress. Headquarters is optimistic. There is nothing more for you to do but rest."

"And you are?"

"Colonel Aloysius Mortimer, your new commander. I've replaced

Colonel Ewell at GHQ in Intelligence. He's been sent back stateside. Had the shakes, I gather. Now rest."

~

Martin awoke feeling better. The headaches had become intermittent and less severe. His limbs felt stronger. His stomach was full after a meal of puréed something and boiled horsemeat. Still thirsty, he gulped down the glass of water on his bedstand as a visitor was announced. To his surprise, it was Emily Lange, as fetching as ever. Emily had enhanced her drab Signal Corps uniform with a dashing black, silver, and red silk scarf. "How are you today, Captain Martin?" she asked, flashing a smile as she walked to his bedside. "I was worried about you. Everyone was talking about the crash. This is the first chance I've had to visit. She noticed his empty glass and refilled it. Martin gestured for her to sit down.

"Where is Lieutenant Keller? I haven't seen him yet. Thank you for helping to locate him."

"Can't say. Could be anywhere, but I gather he's back on duty. GHQ has been busy with the latest push. We've captured thousands of prisoners. He's an interpreter, isn't he? Is there anything I can do for you?"

"A cigarette?"

"Thought so." She surreptitiously slid him a pack of Camels.

Emily chatted briefly about nothing, then mentioned that cafeteria scuttlebutt claimed Martin's mission was critical to the Allies.

How would she know that?

"Is it true? You and Colonel Mitchell are heroes. What did you see?"

Martin declined to say anything more, saying he needed to rest. He fell asleep quickly, still wondering what she was trying to find out.

~

Emily remained at Martin's bedside until she had assured herself he was deep in sleep. She looked around. No one. She picked up a pillow next to his bed and lifted it above his face, just as a nurse scurried in with a heavy chart and a big needle. "What are you doing, Miss?"

"He looked uncomfortable. I thought I'd ... ."

"That's my job. Thank you, anyway." She smiled.

"Just trying to help." Emily handed the pillow to the nurse and left. *Scheisse.*

~

Later that afternoon, amidst the moans and cries for "mother," Martin considered the plight of the sick and wounded around him. "Do you know why you are here?" he asked those who could speak. Draftees and volunteers alike replied they were not fighting for the cause that had brought them there; the reason was the man next to them. Fight hard to keep your buddy safe, and he'll do the same for you.

French-bred Martin had his own reasons for fighting, but time in the hospital was changing his beliefs. President Wilson's declaration that this was "a war to end all wars" held little meaning for front-line troops. Their war was not about honor or glory or patriotism. A private with blood-stained bandages wrapped around his chest looked at Martin wearily. "I just want to get home safe in one piece. 'Heaven, Hell, or Hoboken,' right?" Minutes later, he closed his eyes, never to return to Hoboken.

Vic, the Aussie captain, had been right: It was a general's war, but an enlisted man's fight.

~

The next morning, Martin was determined to view *this*, the other side of the war — not the grand strategy and massive assaults, but the grisly human cost. The head matron insisted he wear a surgical mask as he followed her on her rounds. "Who knows what germs you could pick up, Captain? In your weakened condition, you are vulnerable. The Spanish flu is spreading fast. It's striking down our men at an alarming rate. Civilians too, and the Germans we capture."

"I've seen the reports."

"Yes, but numbers alone don't tell the *true* reality." Her head slumped as if weighted by her convictions. "It could be our biggest medical problem yet. It's highly contagious and deadly. It's disabling more soldiers than the Huns are, and the numbers are growing every day. Weakness, chest pain, headache, high fever — some men don't last a day, others just recover on their own."

"Out of the way!" A stretcher bearer barreled past Martin and into the influenza ward. The matron eyed the soldier on the litter and shook her head. "See his face? He's turning blue. He'll be gone in a few hours."

"What can we do?"

"Pray. We've got no miracle cure for this disease."

Martin followed the matron into the main ward. Rubber umbilical cords connected men to bottles of clear liquid; mechanical pulleys raised splinted legs. A man leaned over to throw up and choked on his vomit. A nurse rushed to help. In the next bed, a soldier in gray flannel pajamas with a bandage over his eyes dictated to a Red Cross volunteer. She scratched out the words with one hand and wiped her eyes with the other.

A few beds down the corridor, a man looked toward the ceiling, staring like a marble statue, his mouth half-open. The matron ordered the head stretcher-bearer to take the body to the moribund tent. She turned to Martin. "We need the space. A new batch of wounded is coming in."

Martin returned to his cot with the understanding that the true cost of war is measured by the number of occupied beds in the wards and stacks of metal identification tags waiting for an officer to compose condolence letters. He tried to rest but his thoughts shifted to the men. Their shattered minds. Their shattered bodies. Their shattered hopes. He vowed to do everything in his power to minimize casualties, prayed for a quick end to the war, and drifted into a fitful rest.

~

Early the next morning, a major in a dusty uniform with MP patches on his shoulders stood at Martin's bedside. "I understand you are almost recovered, Captain Martin. How do you feel?"

"Fit for duty, Major."

"Good. You were a bomb expert with the New York Police before the war, correct?"

"Yes, but — "

"We have an emergency. Come with me immediately."

Chapter 34
The Interrogation

Somewhere in Washington, D.C.: July 1918

Shannon sat in a place she had never wished to be: the wrong side of the table during an interrogation. The tiny room was stifling; she had no escape. The noise of people and traffic from the street above her suggested she was in a basement. *But where? How had she ended up here?* Swallowing her fear, she relived the last hours and tried to piece together what had happened.

~

"Don't reach for that Webley in your purse. You are under arrest," the tall man had said.

Shannon's indignation masked her shock. "Under whose authority?"

The second man grabbed her purse and said, "We'll ask the questions." The tall man gripped her arm.

Shannon tried to pull away. "I work for the New York Police. You have no right to —"

"I have every right." The second man flashed his identification. "Bureau of Investigation. You are in violation of the Espionage Act. You have conspired against our country."

My God. How is this possible? She fought off dizziness. "What have I done wrong?"

"Please don't make a scene." He squeezed her arm tighter.

"There must be some mistake." Shannon's legs buckled, but the tall man held her up. The other man clamped on cuffs that cut into her wrists as she struggled against them. *Paul, help me.*

They guided her to a sedan, where they gagged her and pulled a stinking poison gas mask over her head, its eye slots blacked over. She labored to breathe and realized with a start that she would drown if she vomited. Intimidation. Break the suspect. She knew the game but never expected to be the target. They drove for several minutes, stopping and turning frequently.

This is not happening, she told herself.

~

It was. The driver stopped and turned off the engine. Sounds echoing off nearby walls told Shannon she was in an alleyway. The tall man next to her in the back seat removed the vision-blocking gas mask, handcuffs, and gag. "Come quietly, Mrs. Keller, or I'll break your arm. Understood?"

She nodded. They moved her into the tiny room where she sat across from a thick-necked man with fat lips and muscular arms. Dirt filled his cracked fingernails; his unshaven whiskers were rough and uneven. Shannon smelled peppermint and tobacco on his breath, and the stale, musky odor of an unwashed man. She knew the type; Red had been one of them. She did not know if they would beat a woman, but she did not expect mercy.

Assistant Director Abner Hicks entered with a steely look, his arms crossed. The tall man watched from behind him.

"What have I done wrong?" Shannon spit out with the last of her saliva. "You know I'm with the New York Police, Mr. Hicks."

"No, you are not," Hicks said. "You just work for them. They provide you no legal protection."

"I'm looking for a cop killer. You hiding him?" As soon as she said it, she realized her mistake.

The tall man raised his arm, but Hicks gestured for him to stop. "No, Mrs. Keller, *you* are the criminal."

"A *criminal*?" It was simply unbelievable. "For what? Investigating a murder?"

"You were warned," Hicks said.

"Someone tried to kill me when I was going home. No one warned me about that." *Had all this started with the incident in Bronxville when she first confronted Silas Wood?*

"Your superior, Sergeant Fernandez, was specifically instructed to drop his investigation of Kittridge."

"We did. Until Red got killed. You ever see a decapitated body with vermin crawling through its carcass? A weakling like you would get sick." Shannon had moved from fear to bewilderment to anger. "Is that what this is about? A Tammany Hall thief?" She stood up, her face turning Irish-red.

"Sit." The tall man forced her down by the shoulders so hard that she almost broke the flimsy chair.

Hicks put his hands on the table and leaned in close. "It's more than that."

"So, who was that man who strutted into headquarters acting like the King of Siam, telling everyone what to do? A spy? Your boss? Both?"

Hicks seemed startled by the comment. *Close to the truth?* He backed away as if planning a new approach. "You want to win this war, Mrs. Keller?"

"Which one?"

"The one that matters. The one against Germany."

"What are you talking about?"

"Shut up!" The tall man readied a mighty slap. She ducked and his hand passed over her head in a swoosh, ruffling her hair.

"Are you going to beat me up? Arrest me? I'll willingly face twelve good men. I'll tell my story. What story are you going to tell?"

The tall man drew his hand back again and looked to Hicks for direction. Hicks shook his head. "We need to get Lewis," he said flatly, and turned to leave. The thick-necked man tied Shannon's arms to the chair back with a forceful tug and a gleeful sneer. She grimaced but refused to cry out. He shut off the lights and clanged the metal door shut. A lock turned with a sturdy click.

In the dark room no bigger than a cell, Shannon had never felt more alone in her life. The walls seemed to move in closer with each tick of the overhead clock. She had been arrested, legally apparently, and detained in some godforsaken cellar. No one was coming to save her: Her husband was in France; Clancy was in the hospital; and Fernandez was under orders to stay away. The tightened rope numbed her hands, the hard chair hurt her backside, and her head ached from breathing through that wretched gas mask. Her cheek itched from the burlap gag. She rubbed it against her shoulder but got little relief.

She fought off desperation and gathered her thoughts. She would need her wits to confront Lewis, whoever he was. *Confess no wrongdoing,* she lectured herself. *You have broken no law, despite what these people say, unless they know something you don't.*

~

Twenty minutes later, a well-dressed man led Hicks into Shannon's holding room. He took one look and said, "My, my, my, this will never do. Turn on the lights and untie this good woman." They hesitated, and he raised his voice. "Immediately."

Surprised but grateful for the relief, Shannon merely said, "Thank you," and scratched away the itch tormenting her cheek.

"May we get you something, Mrs. Keller? Water? Would you like to use a toilet?"

Was this a deception to trick her into something? "Water, please," she croaked. The tall man left to fetch it. Hicks looked on from the back, his head bowed like a scolded schoolboy.

The well-dressed man was young, about thirty. Despite his law-school appearance and patrician manners, she guessed he was born on the Lower East Side. Jewish? Something in his voice. She had met several such men in New York. He would be hard to defeat. *He's dangerous and smart. Be honest and respectful. Deal with the facts. No emotions.* She forced a smile and tried to look relaxed.

"I am most sorry that things have developed in this way, Mrs. Keller, but you have complicated things for us."

"How?" Shannon asked. "Aren't we on the same side? I assume

you are from the Bureau too."

"Me? No, no, no. I am not law enforcement."

"Then what are you, if I may ask?"

"I cannot divulge that, and even if I could, it would take too long to explain."

"Then you do not have the authority to arrest me, but he does?" Shannon nodded toward Hicks, who narrowed his eyes.

"Yes." The Jewish man said nothing more.

Shannon broke the silence. "Then who the hell are you?" She regretted her choice of words, but they did not seem to faze him.

He leaned back and crossed his legs in a relaxed fashion. "My name is Leonard Lewis. I do special work for the U.S. government. That is all you need to know. It is in my current project that you and I have, uh, ... our problems."

Taken aback, Shannon composed herself. "You mean the Kittridge investigation?"

"Precisely."

"But what have I done wrong?"

"Mrs. Keller, after discussing the situation with my superiors and reaching up to the highest levels of government, I want us to come to an agreement."

He must have spoken with Treasury Secretary McAdoo.

"My contacts vouch for your patriotism and discretion. You have proven these qualities over and over these last few years. We have decided to trust you. Can we?"

"Of course." The conversation was leading in unexpected directions.

"It was either arrest you under the Espionage Act, which you have indeed violated, as Mr. Hicks has stated, or let you into our little secret. I chose the latter, on one condition."

Here it comes.

"You will work for me until this Kittridge business concludes."

"How can I agree to that until I know the details? I will not betray my friends."

"We do not expect you to. Let me elaborate. Mr. Hicks, would you and your assistant kindly leave us alone? Mrs. Keller will be more comfortable that way."

The two men left, disgruntled, and Lewis continued. "Working from two different directions, you and my team have uncovered some, shall we say, illegalities, concerning Mr. Kittridge's affairs. Or, to put it differently, your excellent detective work has stumbled into my operation to ensnare Mr. Kittridge in his plot."

"What plot? This is what I am trying to discover."

"And we were trying to stop you from doing so. Unfortunately, things have become a bit — how should I say it? — complicated. I regret the loss of your men and the wounding of your friend. Where, may I ask, did he get a tommy gun?"

"He has many contacts."

"Anyway, your interference has compromised my work."

"Which is?"

"Mr. Kittridge is merely a middle man in a larger problem. I assume you want Britain to stay in the war?"

"Why would it not?"

"Remember the 1916 Easter Rebellion? What most people do not know is that Germany shipped a large quantity of weapons to the Irish revolutionaries just before the uprising. Luckily, the shipment was intercepted or the rebellion might well have had a different outcome."

"So that's what Kittridge is doing? Supplying weapons to Ireland."

"Most perceptive, Mrs. Keller. But there is one difference."

"That being?"

"We — specifically, my colleague Mr. Ellison — are the ones supplying him."

What? "Why?"

"We want to identify his financial backers here, roll up his network, and shut down these Irish revolutionaries for good. We can't allow them to force Britain to pull troops from the war to suppress an Irish revolt. Not when the situation on the Western Front is so delicate. This is more than Kittridge. It is the fate of the war itself. For the sake of a tiny island of Micks? Preposterous. Do you see?"

"What do you want me to do?"

He told her, whispering softly. Shannon thought a while before speaking. "I'll cooperate," she agreed, "but on one condition. I want that dandy Ellison."

~

Hicks met Lewis in the hallway after Shannon had gone. "You tell her everything?" he asked.

"Enough, not all."

"What do we do with her?"

"If she becomes a problem," Lewis said, "I don't care what you do. Just make sure nothing gets back to us."

Chapter 35
The Belligerents

Plaza Hotel, New York City: July 1918

Shannon returned from the Capital in a quandary. Unable to sleep, she forced herself to believe the last three days had not been a dream. She was sickened by the revelation that Lewis and the Bureau of Investigation had hired that murderer Ellison to thwart an Irish revolt, which planned to use weapons financed by Kittridge with stolen Tammany money. Worse, she felt violated by her arrest and the common criminal interrogation by the Bureau.

She wrestled with the bed covers not knowing what to do. Abner Hicks had given her instructions, but would she, or her colleagues, comply? She guessed he had only told her part of the story. That was dangerous enough, but the part she did not know could get her killed. *Walk away.* Hicks had given her the option: "Leave. Go back to New York," he had said. "Tell Fernandez to close the case. This is too big for you. Let the Bureau take care of it. If you don't, we'll blame any mistakes on you."

Shannon knew he was not bluffing. If something went sour, the Bureau would, no doubt, accuse her and the New York Police of wrongdoing. But she would not walk away. That was the only thing she was certain of. She had scores to settle and criminals to arrest. Stubborn? *No.* Reckless? *Maybe.* Righteous? *Definitely.*

Hicks had forced her to swear not to discuss the matter with anyone, including her husband and uncle. Fernandez and Clancy were the exception, and she needed their agreement to move forward. She was certain how they would decide, although their careers, and maybe their lives, were at stake. Hicks had promised they would handle New York City's mayor and police commissioner.

She got up from her bed too anxious to sleep.

~

The following day, Shannon detailed her arrest and encounter in private with Fernandez and Clancy. The three shared silent looks. For several moments, Fernandez squeezed his fingers together; Clancy rubbed his nose; and Shannon toyed with her hair. She spoke first, trying to keep her voice steady. "We are all in this together. If we decide to go forward, it must be unanimous. A no from one is a no for all. Agreed?"

"Nobody pushes us around." Clancy stood and leaned forward, his hands placed resolutely on the table. "I'm in. I want to send Ellison to Sing Sing for life. I don't care who he's working for. We owe it to Red and Abbott. Justice must be served, and I don't trust those Federals to do it." He hesitated for a moment. "If there's going to be a fight, I'm ready."

"This was our case from the start," Fernandez said, his fingers tightened white.

Shannon felt the determination of her friends. "So we agree to stay with this?"

"Aye."

"Of course, but there'll be trouble," Fernandez said. "Do you know when and where Ellison will deliver the goods?"

"Some warehouse in Jersey. "Two weeks, no more. Hicks plans to make the arrest there when Kittridge and Donnelly are together."

"What about Brown?" Clancy asked. "We need to talk to him about that Wall Street attack two years ago."

"I don't think he's aware of the double-cross," Shannon said. "He's being set up."

"How many men will Hicks bring?" Fernandez asked. "This is —"

Clancy cut in. "Shannon, this is too dangerous. Let us handle this."

"No."

"Hicks will have his men; Kittridge his; Brown too. There's sure to be shooting," Clancy said. "We could get caught in the crossfire."

"We'll need a plan," said Shannon. "Sean, can you still get that tommy gun?"

~

While Shannon and her friends were forming a plan, Jelly Brown stood at the open door of a partially burnt-out warehouse in Kingsland, surveying a blighted landscape littered with unexploded artillery shells. Located in the Jersey meadowlands, the warehouse, or what was left of it, was about five hundred yards along the main road from the site of a massive explosion.

Now, a year and a half later, Jelly could still smell traces of cordite. The remains of a brick chimney stood defiant, the lone remnant of the Canadian Car and Foundry Company that had produced materiel for the Russian army until 500,000 artillery shells blasted into an inferno that lasted four hours. Witnesses in Manhattan across the Hudson River claimed the spectacle surpassed that of the Black Tom Island explosion in July 1916.

Accident or arson? Investigators disagreed, and Jelly didn't give a damn. The swarms of mosquitoes didn't discourage him none, neither. The fewer people around the better. He didn't want no one prying into his business.

Jelly had discovered the site when he was searching for a place to store Kittridge's goods. That it survived the blast at all was amazing. Jelly figured the wind had something to do with it. The fire had ravaged the area, leaving Jelly's gutted warehouse a carcass without commercial use until he'd showed up and paid two months' rent in advance, pre-explosion rate, no questions asked. The owner took his money gleefully and said to use it as long as he liked. Wouldn't be much use come winter, but Brown did not intend to use it that long: two weeks, maybe three — just the time it would take to collect the weapons and get them to his ship in Hoboken.

Jelly put his hands on his hips and cussed. Murdock Kittridge and Michael Donnelly were late again. He went back to the area that served as his office and sat behind his desk, a door resting on wooden boxes. He swatted away a few mosquitoes and smoked a Cuban cigar, a pleasure he had acquired living in Havana. He reviewed his itinerary and how he would store the weapons in his cargo ship. Jelly planned to transport Kittridge's weapons to a secluded cove in the west coast of Ireland and sail on to Norway a rich and free man.

Jelly reviewed the risks. *The British fleet.* Donnelly would only tell him which cove was his destination at the last minute. The chance of being intercepted at sea loomed large. If the ship were boarded, his sole hope was that Ellison's measures to disguise the cargo would be successful. *Transporting the weapons to Hoboken.* Jelly hired reliable men and paid them well; they knew enough not to cross him. The trucks were rented and ready. *Mistakes.* Errors were part of any job like this, but Jelly trusted his men and his arrangements. Donnelly had excellent commando experience, and Ellison was an experienced gun runner. Kittridge, who seemed nervous, was just the money man, not part of operations. *Betrayal.* His biggest fear. It could come from any number of people: Ellison's name was at the top of his list. Only thing to do was be ready for anything.

While Jelly waited, he planted a shotgun near the main warehouse entrance and placed pistols and grenades by his desk and on the truck he would drive. He inspected the hidden defenses his men had built. *What else?* He had an idea.

A few minutes later, Kittridge and Donnelly drove up in a Cadillac roadster. *Stupid. Why draw attention to yourself in a fancy car?* Kittridge made no excuses for the delay. "You ready, Gibson?" were his only words.

Jelly felt the pang of his distrust and dislike of Kittridge. "You got my money?" An uncertain feeling he had had about this job from the start washed over him again, but the money and the lavish life it would bring trumped his concern.

"When I see your final plans."

"I'm ready. You?" Jelly motioned them inside the warehouse, pausing behind them before he closed the door to survey the area in case Kittridge had brought friends.

"Don't trust us, Gibson?" Kittridge asked.

"Just being careful-like." Jelly flashed a crooked smile full of teeth. "We all in this together. Someone messes up, we all suffer. Over there." He pointed to his office.

"You still planning to officially sail to Norway?" Kittridge asked.

"Yeah. Got the route planned all the way out to Bergen. Explains why we sailing by the Irish coast. Goin' have some engine problems right where Mr. Donnelly tells me. Come night, duck into that cove of yours. Make sure it's deep enough for my ship. You and your men, Mr. Donnelly, do the offloading."

"We'll handle it. I've got small boats arranged to take the weapons to shore."

"Got to be done lickety-split."

"Do not worry yourself."

"Ain't as easy as it looks. Any problems, my men will chuck everything overboard and skedaddle."

They reviewed all the details, and Kittridge handed over the cargo list, several pages long. "Full inventory. No changes from last time. Four columns, just like you wanted."

Jelly inspected the list without comment. The first column detailed the actual goods: rifles, machine guns, bullets, grenades, mortars. The second itemized their false descriptions — how they would be listed on the manifest: machinery, spare parts, hospital equipment, and farm tools. The last two catalogued the size and weight of the boxes and crates. "This all?" Jelly looked up.

"You expecting something else?" Donnelly asked.

"Just making sure."

Donnelly moved closer to Jelly. "If your people chicken out on us, I'll chase you to Kingdom Come if I have to."

"My men don't scare." Jelly stood his ground and flexed his chest muscles.

Kittridge stood between them. "No time for this. Any other questions, Michael?"

"How many men are you bringing?"

"Once we load up, I'm sailing with eleven men plus you, Mr. Donnelly, and your two men."

"What about U-boats?"

"That covered."

"How?"

"My business. I ain't lost a cargo to U-boats yet. If no more questions, I want my money, Mr. Kittridge."

"In the Cadillac. One-quarter. That makes half you already have. You get another quarter before you sail, and Mr. Donnelly will give you the rest upon delivery in Ireland. One last thing," Kittridge said. "Do either of you expect trouble when Ellison delivers the goods?"

"Why would there be?" Donnelly asked.

"Never know," Kittridge said.

Jelly added, "Those weapons will attract trouble. Me and my men will be fully armed. Anyone interfering better be ready to meet his maker."

~

That same afternoon, Ronny Ellison sat in Schrafft's on Manhattan's West 23rd Street with Abner Hicks, waiting for Leon Lewis. The lunch crowd was coming in, but Ellison had tipped the hostess two bucks to procure a quiet booth in the far corner by a window overlooking the street that gave them sufficient privacy. Ellison had gulped down a cup of coffee and was feasting on a large slice of apple pie, feeling pretty good. The trap was about to be sprung. Hicks sipped tea between drags on a cigarette, carelessly flipping ashes in the direction of a half-filled tray. Lewis rarely respected rendezvous times. He liked to say unpredictability kept one's adversaries at a disadvantage.

Eight minutes later, Lewis entered wearing an oversized coat with the collar turned up, fake glasses, and a hat pulled low to his ears. He slid in next to Hicks and hip-bumped him for extra room. "Afternoon, gentlemen." He then thumbed through a small notebook, saying nothing more until the waiter came over. Still absorbed in his notebook, Lewis ordered a hamburger and coffee and did not look up until the waiter left. "There's news?" he asked.

"Kittridge contacted me," Ellison reported. "I'm to deliver the goods to a warehouse in Kingsland, New Jersey."

"It's perfect for our plans, Mr. Lewis," Hicks assured him. "Isolated. Nobody working nearby. My men have already scouted it."

"We're ready for final delivery," Ellison said.

"Excellent. What about the warrants, Abner?" Lewis asked.

"We have enough to arrest Kittridge right now," Hicks said. "When we catch him with the weapons, we can add smuggling. Gibson too."

"I don't care about him. What about Donnelly?" Ellison asked.

"I wouldn't call it kidnapping exactly, but ... ." Hicks waved his arm casually. "My boys will grab him and deliver him to you in whatever condition you say."

"Once we have him safe, we can move on his rich Irish-American friends," Lewis said. "Good work, Ronny. Now let me enjoy my meal."

Lewis ate heartily, down to the last crumbs, then ordered a hot fudge sundae. "One last thing, Abner. You got enough men?" he asked, wiping his mouth with a napkin.

"We expect a fight, but I've deputized twenty men. Bureau men don't work like that — these men do."

"I figure on having six delivery trucks there. Twelve men," Ellison said.

"Thirty-two in all," Lewis reckoned. "Should be enough. What about the New York Police?" He eyed the waiter approaching with dessert, and the men fell silent for a moment.

"We expect they'll be there despite our warnings," Hicks continued in hushed tones. "I told Mrs. Keller in no uncertain terms to keep out of our way. Doubt they will."

"I've already made separate plans to ship the weapons to General Tarvas. A White Russian émigré will pay us. We get to stop a revolution from occurring in Ireland and help a counter-revolution against the Bolsheviks at the same time. And get paid twice. Excellent work," Lewis said, levering a big spoonful of ice cream into his mouth.

"I hope there'll be a fight," Ellison ventured.

"If the police get in the way, push them aside. I can cover up anything we have to." Lewis picked the cherry up between his thumb and forefinger and popped it into his mouth. "But just to be sure, bring an armored car."

Chapter 36
Pershing's Cadillac

Chaumont, France: July 1918

Martin sat silently on the drive back to AEF headquarters with Colonel Mortimer. He tried to forget the hospital and his aching body and focus on the new danger. German agents had infiltrated the inner workings of the AEF. The bomb was too sophisticated for the AEF explosive specialists on hand, and they hoped Martin's experience would allow him to disarm the bomb and tell them who had made it.

Mortimer stopped the car near the main entrance to the headquarters. Pershing's Cadillac was parked by the woods next to his train a few hundred yards away from the main compound. The faces of the nervous MPs who had cordoned off the area flooded with relief when Martin appeared and crossed over the rope into the danger zone.

Colonel Thornton, Pershing's train commander, extended his hand as Martin approached. "Glad you're here, Captain. The bomb is in the engine block. No one has touched it."

"Who discovered it?"

"General Pershing's driver, Sergeant Santini. He says the car was fine yesterday when he changed the oil. This morning after the bombing raid, he —"

"Wait. What bombing raid?"

"About 06:30. They happen. Earlier than usual. Everyone scrambled. Santini was having breakfast." Thornton scratched his head. "You think that has something to do with this?"

"How long did it last?"

"Maybe ten minutes."

Martin paused to consider the implications. "What happened next?"

"After the raid, Santini drove the Cadillac off the train at 07:10. Everything seemed normal, no strange sounds, but he wanted to check the engine just in case. He opened up the hood and noticed some external wires connected to the cooling fan. He didn't touch anything and ran for help. We cordoned off the area and called one of our bomb guys, but he was completely baffled. Wouldn't go near it. Said whoever designed it was smarter than he was. We asked the French too, but they couldn't spare anyone. That's when we called you."

Martin lit a cigarette and studied the Cadillac, seventy yards away. Someone very good had planted this bomb. His mind drifted, searching for answers.

"Captain? Captain Martin?" Thornton inquired. "What are you going to do?"

"Yes, sorry, Colonel." Martin dropped the burning stub of his Camel next to the first butt still glowing on the ground. "Let me take a look."

As Martin approached the Cadillac, images of the first time he had had to single-handedly defuse an unexploded bomb flooded his mind. Old fears returned. Not fear of an explosion — he didn't care if he got blown into pieces — but fear of failure. Familiar sensations reappeared: his mouth became dry, his palms sweated, the hair on the back of his neck bristled, he needed to urinate. He pushed them aside and breathed deeply, concentrating on the bomb eighty paces away. It could explode any second.

A dog barking in the distance momentarily distracted him. Fifty paces. The surface under his feet felt uneven. He nearly tripped on a rock. Thirty. Head down, he placed his hands in his pockets and continued to walk like a man on a march to the gallows. Twenty. He slowed his pace to gather his thoughts. Ten. He crossed himself and remembered he had not made a confession in a long time. Five. No turning back. His fate the fate of a frontline soldier about to go over the top.

He stopped two feet from the Cadillac and rolled his head and neck to relieve the built-up stress. He curled his arms behind his back, looked up, and stretched his arms out behind him, draining away more tension.

Martin took his time and carefully considered the engine block from every angle. The bomb consisted of four sticks of dynamite, enough to assassinate anyone in the car two times over, attached by wires to a casing, presumably the timing device and trigger. Wires led from the casing to the cooling fan. He looked for booby traps but did not spot any hidden devices.

He listened for sounds. No ticking. He lightly touched the casing. Not hot, good sign. No scent of unstable nitroglycerine or leaking gas. He tasted his finger. A bit of grease, but no residue or bomb-making odors. He sketched a detailed diagram of the bomb and returned to the perimeter and an anxious Colonel Thornton.

~

Emily exited the mess hall with her picnic basket in hand and twenty minutes left on her lunch break. Seeing Martin walk away from the Cadillac, she realized her plan had failed. She disguised her disappointment with a composed disregard and sauntered by the scene. *What had gone wrong?* The operation had been meticulously planned and carefully executed: routines studied to the second and rechecked; the positions of the train sentries known at all times; practice runs performed that no one had noticed. Emily had analyzed the timing and how to sneak from the barracks at dawn, slip undetected into the train carriage housing the Cadillac, and plant the bomb in the engine, while André had orchestrated a well-timed bombing run to cover her return as she mingled into the confusion from the raid.

Despite his missing hand, André, the former card shark, had shown her how to pick a lock and watched her practice setting and activating the bomb in an abandoned barn outside of town. She had done it so many times, she could do it in the dark railroad carriage. Why had that meddling driver, a mere enlisted man, rechecked the engine? Had she made a mistake?

She urgently had to retrieve her picnic basket, which she'd hidden near the bench in the woods. She had stashed it there at five that morning, switching it out for an identical basket containing the bomb and some stones that André had left the previous evening. Emily had slipped into the train as scheduled and planted and activated the bomb in Pershing's Cadillac before Santini drove it off the transport carriage. After the bombing run, the Americans had flocked around the area faster than anticipated, leaving her no time to dispose of the bomb-carrying basket with its tell-tale traces of explosive material. Her plot foiled, she hurried to the river, the incriminating basket over her arm, and dumped it in, watching it sink, pre-weighted with stones. She retrieved her customary basket near the bench and returned, no one the wiser.

I should have smothered Captain Martin when I had the chance.

~

"You can disarm it, can't you, Captain? You must," Thornton said. "General Pershing has a full schedule today and can't be delayed."

"You're the bomb expert. Get cracking," Mortimer said.

Martin withheld his temper, but Thornton kept pressing. Finally, Martin had heard enough. "Colonel Thornton, let me explain the situation. You may think I'm just another disposable captain, but whoever made that bomb is highly skilled. If I go in without a plan, I'll likely be blown up, scrapping your precious Cadillac and the General's schedule along with it. I have an idea, but I need to discuss it with my old colleague, Lieutenant Keller. Can you bring him here?"

~

Two hours later, Keller arrived from interrogating prisoners. Colonel Thornton had not stopped pacing until Mortimer suggested he sit down and do something useful.

After an emotional greeting, Keller studied Martin's drawing, and they debated the details. "The secret is inside that casing," Martin said, "but if I pry it open, I might trigger an explosion."

Keller agreed. "This looks like the same concept as the rudder bomb we encountered a couple of years ago," he noted, "but it's much smaller than the one that German agent, Frisch, used."

"Agreed, but I wanted to hear it from you," Martin said. "Somehow Frisch's design has gotten back to Germany. Frisch connected the timing device to the rudder of a ship; after so many revolutions, the bomb would ignite. Here, the principle's the same: The cooling fan rotates a certain number of times, then after a predetermined number count that corresponds to a number of minutes, it detonates the bomb — guaranteeing the bomb will ignite when the vehicle is in motion. That's why the car didn't explode when Santini drove it off the railroad car."

"There must be a clock-like mechanism inside that casing," Keller said. "Each rotation of the cooling fan winds up the mechanism until the alarm 'rings' and explodes the bomb. You said there were no signs of a booby trap outside the casing, right, Gil?"

"No signs."

"So, we should be able to neutralize it pretty safely."

"Always the optimist. Okay, but only one of us, Paul. Me. You have Shannon. I have only memories."

"Flip a coin?"

"No, me. I'll defuse it. You're not ready to die." Martin swallowed hard. "I'll cut the blue wire first. Remember that if something goes wrong."

~

Martin held his breath and cut the blue wire between the casing and the cooling fan. Nothing happened. He wiped his hand over his hair as much out of relief as surprise to still be alive. As he walked away from the cordoned area, Colonel Mortimer patted him on the shoulder. "You are now assigned to this case exclusively. Find the bastard who did this and stop him before he tries again."

~

That night, plagued by failure, Emily could not sleep. *I must find another way, and soon.*

Chapter 37
The Interview

Chaumont, France: July 1918

In an old shed commandeered for use in the investigation, Martin looked up from the disassembled bomb and said to Keller, "We know from Shannon's investigation that a spy is lurking in our midst. I assume he planted the bomb, but who is he?"

"Someone familiar with our routines," Keller said.

"One person acting alone? Don't think so. Our bomber had help."

"But who? Hundreds of people come in and out of our headquarters."

Martin fingered the bomb fragments as if they might reveal a clue. "How many could have planted that bomb?"

"We've never handled a more important case," Keller said. "Losing General Pershing would have been a catastrophe." He stood up and hobbled to the window. His bad leg continued to hurt from his run across no-man's-land. He wiped at the grime on the glass, leaving greasy streaks. A sparrow chirped from a nearby tree. "Shut up," he said.

Martin joined him at the window. "This was a well-planned operation, timed to the minute," he said, eyeing the sparrow as it flew away. He paused to collect his thoughts. Gazing into the distance, he said, "We'll solve this."

~

Over the next few days and on into August, Martin and Keller interviewed everyone who was in the vicinity of Pershing's Cadillac. Many witnesses were unreliable, others contradictory, some had been so confused by the bombing raid that they recalled nothing. The most useful was Sergeant Santini, who had given them a timeline to work with. *The bomb must have been placed when the car was in the carriage overnight*, thought Martin. *I'm sure the bombing run had something to do with it. But how?* The puzzle remained.

They interviewed Santini for a third time. "Let's go over this one more time, Sergeant," Martin said. "Just to confirm, anyone else have a key to the lock on the train carriage?"

Santini confirmed that he and Colonel Thompson had the only keys. He saw no signs of tampering when he unlocked the carriage that morning.

Our bomber knows how to pick a lock. How many can do that? "Did you do anything differently that morning?"

"No." Santini confirmed he had followed the usual routine. "The general is a precise man. I saw no one suspicious. Can't imagine who coulda done it."

"Was the train guarded?"

"Two men patrol the tracks at night. Four-hour shifts: 22:00, 02:00, 06:00."

"Could someone have snuck past them?"

"Guess so, but the guards didn't hear no sound. Not from the carriage or around it."

After so many days, their interview room had become as uncomfortable as a Number 1 Manhattan subway train stalled at Times Square in an August heat wave. Fatigued and frustrated, Martin pinched the bridge of his nose. The clock on his desk ticked away like a metronome. He looked at the MP sentry by the door. "Who's next, Sergeant?"

"Miss Emily Lange, Signal Corps."

~

Emily breathed deeply and forced herself to relax as she sat in the lobby waiting to be called. Legs crossed, hands folded over her lap, she was outwardly composed, the picture of unconcerned calm. Despite the heat, she stayed dry. Her father had prepared her for such interrogations. "Act like a lady, and they will treat you like one. Demand nothing less. Don't show emotion. Stick to your story. Listen carefully. Keep your answers short and to the point. Do not speculate or argue. Confess nothing, even if trapped. In case of trouble, forget selectively (*in all this excitement ...*), but keep the story credible. Don't get caught in a false timeline."

An MP sergeant appeared at the doorway and called her name. Emily stood up and smoothed her hair with a single gesture, confident. *Remain demure, highlight your patriotism, underline your excellent pedigree and outstanding performance. Never let them forget you are the cream of American womanhood.*

~

Torn between suspicion and attraction, Martin shifted in his chair at the sound of Emily's name. She had proven helpful and stalwart when Keller was missing in action. Lonely since the death of his wife and fearful for the safety of his best friend, Martin had found comfort in her company. On several occasions over the past few weeks, alone together in the cafeteria, Martin had found her conversation a welcome distraction from the war. They shared a love of New York City. He admired her gumption, persistence, and sharp intellect. Yet something about her bothered him. He did not quite trust her. *Was she too attractive? Maybe jealousy play a part?* Anyone seen often with General Prescott was suspect in his mind.

~

The previous evening, Martin had told Keller to take the lead on Emily's interview.

"You're smitten with her, aren't you, Gil?" his old friend replied. It was more an observation than a question.

"Nonsense. How can you say that? I'm too busy to worry about a woman." Martin deflected the question, unwilling to admit the extent to which Keller was right. Worse, he feared he would fumble the interview.

"How can you deny it?"

"Leave it be. We need to discuss which questions to ask her."

~

"She's coming," Martin said, standing up.

"The gallant French knight, Gilbert," Keller remarked. "Always a gentleman."

An affront from anyone else but Keller. Well, he was right, wasn't he? "And you're not?"

"Not when —"

"Am I interrupting something, officers?" Emily's silky voice flowed into the room. She showed no signs of the oppressive humidity. Her heels tapped across the wooden floor with a lively beat. She walked toward them with the grace of a ballerina, her well-proportioned curves obvious despite her drab gray uniform, her gaze disarming.

Martin flashed a brief smile. "Thank you for coming, Miss Lange. Allow me to introduce my colleague, Lieutenant Paul Keller."

"It's good to meet you, finally," Keller said, with a slight incline of the head. "Thank you for helping to find me,"

~

"It is good to meet you too, Lieutenant. You were a bit groggy when I last saw you," she said innocently. "Captain Martin has told me many stories about you." Emily made a half-curtsy. "It was a pleasure to help. I hope you're fully recovered."

"Pretty much. Please take a seat, Miss Lange. We have some routine questions."

Emily smiled, hiding her surprise as she realized Keller, an unknown adversary, would be her main inquisitor. *Were they arguing when I came in?*

~

"Just as a matter of record, Miss Lange," Keller asked, "we would like to establish your whereabouts between 22:00 the night before the incident and 07:30 after the bombing run ended."

Emily explained that she had left her room at daybreak for a stroll. The morning air refreshed her. That was her routine. The air raid had happened so suddenly she did not have the chance to find proper shelter, so she hid in the woods. She neither encountered anyone nor saw anything suspicious there.

Martin observed her reactions while Keller probed deeper,

rattling off a series of more specific questions: "What time did you go to bed?" "Were you in your room the entire night?" "When did you wake up?" "Take breakfast?" "Anyone see you leave the barracks?" "Where were you when the bombing raid happened?"

~

Emily responded quickly and precisely. She had followed her regular pattern of activity that night. Went to bed early, about 21:30, and stayed there all night, except once to use the toilet.

"Could anyone confirm this?"

"I don't think so. I was alone the whole night." She paused to dab her face with a handkerchief, wondering if they knew about her liaisons.

Played my role well, she thought. *Father would be pleased.*

~

Although her statements confirmed what they had previously heard, Keller probed deeper. "Do you have any knowledge of automobiles, Miss Lange?"

"Oh my, no. My father owned one, but I was never interested. Not something a lady would worry about."

"You studied mathematics in college, didn't you?" Keller pressed.

"And languages."

"And locks. Ever interested in those?"

~

The question caught Emily off guard. Her pulse jumped, but she managed to prevent the rest of her body from betraying her. "I'm sorry, Lieutenant. I don't understand your point."

"No matter." Keller waved away the comment as if he were not making progress. He hesitated long enough to get her attention, then leaned forward. "On another point, would it trouble you to show us your hands?"

"What?" Emily shrugged and held out well-scrubbed hands and neatly shaped nails. No cuts or unexplained marks. *Watch it, he's sly.*

~

She's careful. Keller changed his line of questioning again. "What do you do on that park bench?" he asked. "We often see you there."

~

Emily folded her hands tightly to prevent her fingers from trembling. "Collect my thoughts. Find the energy to carry me through the day. Uncle André likes it there. The shade. Sometimes I do a little sewing to relieve the tension. You might have seen me there with the picnic basket I use to carry things that need repair?" *Better to volunteer the information, appear completely honest. Don't let them ask first.*

~

"Were you near General Pershing's car that morning?" Keller pressed.

"Near there, it would be fair to say. I was in the woods."

"One last question. Can you think of anyone who might be involved in this affair?"

"Goodness, no."

"That's all, Miss Lange. Thank you," Keller said.

"Yes, thank you. You've been most cooperative," Martin said in a neutral tone.

~

After she left, Martin turned to Keller and said, "Either she's telling the truth or she's as good a liar as we've ever seen."

"She seemed forthcoming, but I wouldn't want to play poker against her," Keller said. "Can't rule her out, but I don't see a reason to pursue her for now. Her background was thoroughly checked before she joined the Signal Corps. We might need to talk to her again after we learn more."

~

That night Emily finished dinner and went for a walk under a clear, star-filled night. She looked up and wondered how the Teutonic gods would decide her fate.

~

As Emily walked under the stars, Martin sat at his desk trying to write to Shannon. He composed two sentences, looked at them a moment, then ripped the letter in two. *What to say? How to say it?* The war was beyond words. He ran his hand though his hair. It seemed thinner. He went to the bathroom and looked in the mirror. Yes, thinner and a bit of gray, he admitted. Furrows cut deeper into his cheeks. In less than five months, the war had carved its imprint into his face as surely as a shrapnel cut.

He returned to his desk but could not find the right combination of words. Was it fatigue? Did he sense his own mortality? Was this investigation one too many? Though he had defused the cooling-fan bomb, luck had played a part. Cutting the blue wire was just a guess. He spilled into his bed, his thoughts in conflict.

~

On the other side of the Atlantic, Shannon wondered if the AEF was close to catching her spy. Somehow, she sensed Paul had dodged something terrible, but feared he would face something worse. She was emotionally drained.

~

Several days after the interview, Emily bicycled out of Chaumont to talk to Uncle André in secret. "I feel the bloodhounds on my back. Those detectives are closing in. I'm sure of it," she said, breathing hard. "Our efforts to eliminate Pershing at a distance have failed. We need to do something drastic."

"Like what?"

"Shoot him."

"*No.* Too dangerous, Emily. You'll be killed. I can't allow it."

"We don't have a choice — it's our last option, and there's not much time before I'm arrested. Besides, we are losing the war. We must take risks."

"You think by killing the general, we can achieve victory?"

"No, but removing him gives Germany time. It will take weeks for a new commander to reorganize the AEF. In the meantime, we can improve our military situation. Tighten our lines. Maybe we can seek an equitable peace."

"Nothing I can do to change your mind?" André waited for a response; he received nothing but a determined look. "I promised your father —"

"*I* choose to do this. It is what he would want. Help me and you'll be fulfilling your promise to him and our cause."

André rubbed his temple. "What do you want?"

"A pistol."

Chapter 38
They're Coming

The Ferry to Weehawken: August 1918
Shannon leaned against the cold metal rails of the Manhattan ferry bound for Weehawken, New Jersey. The boat crashed against the rough waters of the Hudson as a strong wind whistled above, chafing her face. She winced when the boat jerked suddenly, sending a stabbing jolt down her back. She ignored the pain and looked at the cliffs of the Palisades rising up before the ferry. A deep sense of foreboding overtook her.

~

Her day had started poorly. The chilly night had turned warm; the thick air portended a muggy afternoon. During the night, her nervous tossing and turning had strained her back, and she now moved cautiously to avoid a wrong turn. Despite the stiffening spasms, she managed to dress but despaired when she reached the hallway and found the elevator broken. She descended the stairs to the hotel lobby, gripping the handrails and stopping frequently as she navigated down five full flights. Running late, she skipped breakfast and gulped down a cup of bitter coffee. Her sole stroke of luck was to find a taxicab within minutes.

To her alarm, Shannon did not see Clancy at the ferry. Without him, they could not possibly succeed. The ferry's shrill whistle pierced her ears, announcing two minutes to departure. Shannon reluctantly boarded the boat, grimly resolved to meet Fernandez and a New Jersey-based marshal alone on the other side. They needed the marshal, who had jurisdiction there, since the New York cops did not have authority to arrest suspects across state lines.

At the last minute, Clancy sauntered up the gangplank, carrying a long flower box under his arm. Shannon felt relieved and confused. "You ready, lass?" he said as he approached.

"Long-stemmed roses?" Why in God's name —"

"The *Annihilator*," Clancy said. "You wanted me to bring her.

Well, here she is." He glanced down at the box, then up into Shannon's eyes. "Couldn't think of no other way to carry her without nobody seeing. Pretty clever, don't you think?"

"Thank God you made it, Sean. Promise me you won't be reckless with that gun again. You're still recovering from your wound."

"No, lass, I won't. But this is a fight I intend to finish."

Shannon moved to the back of the ferry where there were fewer people. She needed to concentrate on the fight to come. People would likely die unless Kittridge and Ellison gave up easily, which was unlikely. She herself might not survive. That did not worry her as much as the possibility she would fail to protect her friends. Although she was an excellent shot, she had never killed another person. Clancy had told her not to fret. "When the time comes, your training will take over, and you'll do good." Her instincts and religion told her the opposite. *Killing someone is a sin. Isn't that what the Bible says? Yet good people kill all the time. Make a mistake, and my friends die. Shoot straight, and I'm a murderer.*

~

The wind rocked the ferry, forcing Shannon to look away from the Palisades and cover her eyes. The ferry lurched forward against the cresting waves and passengers heaved their guts into whatever buckets were available. Shannon's stomach churned, but her coffee stayed down. She remained topside, preferring to battle the elements than to breathe the engine's noxious fumes and stale air inside. She tightened her grip on the guardrails as a gust sprayed up murky river water. She wiped the droplets from her face with her silk handkerchief, then returned it to her purse, weighed down by the fully loaded Webley and a supply of the Webley's unusual .455 bullets she had taken from the police inventory.

Clancy approached and insisted she fasten the gun inside her boot. "Won't do much good if you lose your purse. Easy to do in a fight." Not wanting an argument, Shannon felt a searing jolt of pain as she bent to follow his instructions. She suppressed a wince and forced herself upright, hoping Clancy didn't notice.

Clancy clutched Shannon's arm and guided her off the ferry. She needed a few minutes to regain her strength before proceeding to Weehawken. By the time they reached the meeting place where Fernandez and Marshal Purvis Duvall awaited, she was physically exhausted from mounting the long, steep hill.

The graying around the marshal's temples and the bulge around his middle suggested a man past his prime. A bend in his nose, most likely from a fight, and his leathery skin told of a hard, outdoor life. Fernandez had said that Duvall, a weapons expert, claimed he had fought with Teddy Roosevelt's Rough Riders.

Shannon weakly extended her arm and shook his hand. "Good to meet you."

Duvall smiled and said, "We're going to arrest some bad men today, ain't we?"

She did not appreciate his levity.

Clancy countered. "Not as easy as that, lad."

Fernandez directed them to the auto. "Weapons are in the car. Get in and I'll tell you the plan."

~

The wind had dissipated, and the late summer heat and humidity turned the air heavy. Jelly stood in front of the main door to the warehouse and mopped his brow. He had grown up in hot, swampy fields and liked the weather. The underarms of his shirt were wet. He wiped his forehead again with his right hand and tasted his salty sweat. A mosquito raced toward his neck but landed in his bear-sized hand. Jelly crushed it and rubbed his palm down the side of his trousers.

Jelly scouted the area for intruders. He did not expect them but knew a smuggled weapons cache, especially one this size, attracted unwanted guests. *Prepare for anything. Always did. Always will.* Who would arrive first: Kittridge or Ellison?

~

Fernandez parked on a 125-foot-high ridge in the Hillside Cemetery overlooking the devastated Kingsland manufacturing and warehouse complex. Twenty months after the calamity, the odors of charred wood, rot, and gunpowder still lingered faintly over the network of muddy roads, broken glass, scattered debris, and twisted wreckage. Bent telephone poles stood like disoriented stick figures, frozen and useless. Busted railroad ties and bent iron rails would never again support a locomotive. Cut telephone lines swayed in the breeze.

Though the location provided excellent concealment and an unobstructed view, the unexploded shells that littered the area made it dangerous. It was impossible to guess where they lay, but Fernandez confirmed they were indeed there.

Walking from the auto, Clancy said to Shannon, "If you have to shoot, imagine you're aiming at targets, not men." He patted her gently on the shoulder. "You'll do fine, but stay here and let us approach Kittridge and Ellison."

He turned and said something to Duvall. With a .45 on each hip and a full bandolier of ammunition across his chest, the marshal looked ready to take on the whole German army. One hand carried a satchel of hand grenades and the other held a shotgun, just for good measure.

Shannon's stomach had settled, but her windburned face felt as if it had been rubbed raw with sandpaper. Her jumpy nerves and painful back caused her to walk deliberately, lest she fall. She could not let the men see her weakness, but Clancy knew her too well. He leaned close and whispered in her ear. "It's natural to have the jitters, lass. We all got them in some way. We just know how to hide them."

His words helped Shannon calm down as they moved to the lookout spot. She inspected her Springfield and expertly fed a clip into the rifle, as she had done so often in practice. She felt her confidence rise, diverting her fear, as she fixed the scope to the rifle barrel and scanned the wide area. The towers of Manhattan came into view in the distance. To her surprise, she spotted the top of the Statue of Liberty farther south. Closer in, a chimney stuck out from the ruins of the Canadian Car factory. To its left, she noticed activity in front of a partially destroyed warehouse. Fernandez came over and pointed. "I checked the area yesterday. That's where they're delivering the arms." She turned slightly and focused on a large black man giving orders. Jelly Brown, for sure.

~

Jelly noticed something move in the cemetery above the warehouse and ordered one of his men to investigate. A minute later, a blast occurred along the road the man had walked; he had likely tripped an unexploded bomb. Jelly called to his men. "Stay near the warehouse and you'll be safe."

~

Fernandez and Clancy ducked at the sound of the explosion. Shannon froze, but Clancy pulled her down. "What was that?" She asked, her face turning white.

Duvall stood calmly. "A .76mm shell most likely. Area's full of them. I was part of the investigation right after the incident. Someone set it off."

The explosion had unnerved Shannon. "My God. That's what our boys are facing in France?"

"That times a thousand. Poison gas too. Hours at a time. Right on top of you. Can drive a man crazy," Duvall said.

Shannon's concern for her husband grew a hundredfold.

~

Losing a man this early was regrettable, but the goods would arrive anytime, and Jelly did not want to risk another man to investigate. *If somethin's goin' to happen, it'll happen soon,* he thought. He increased his watchfulness. This would be Ellison's final delivery. After that, Jelly was responsible for moving the weapons to his ship in Hoboken. After today, he was through with Ellison. The man talked too fast and dressed too fancy. What would his life be like when he arrived in Norway a rich man? Would he return to Cuba? *Never*. Maybe Paris after the war. *They treat us pretty good there.*

Jelly looked over his twelve men, who had settled down after his warning and were waiting to receive the delivery. Hand carts and small wagons were spread out neatly in front of the warehouse. Each man carried a crowbar, a chain, or anything else useful in a fight. They seemed to have forgotten their lost man. Part of the job. These were proud, good family men, used to physical labor, fisticuffs, and prejudice. Trust did not come easily to them, but they trusted Jelly, to a degree. No one else. They had accepted the job because of the money. If it succeeded, they would have more cash than they had ever seen in their lives, but everyone understood that paydays like this were risky.

Jelly's ears, sharpened by years on the water, picked up the sound of approaching trucks, coming up from the main road leading to the warehouse. He went inside, hustled the weapon he called his *Equalizer* to the entrance, and hid it behind some burlap inside the doorway. One man who saw it looked dumfounded. Another shook his head and whistled. "Things going to get mighty hot around here."

Jelly winked. "Git to your post."

~

Fernandez took out his binoculars and adjusted its wheel to focus on the warehouse down the road from the cemetery. "Get ready. They're coming."

~

Facing down to the warehouse, Ellison set the brake on the lead truck on the ridge. He turned to Hicks, sitting next to him. "Let's talk outside." Behind Ellison's truck were five more trucks carrying weapons supplied by Lewis, and two similar trucks, one a disguised paddy wagon, carrying Hicks's convoy of Bureau of Investigation troops. The armored car idled loudly at the back of the line.

Ellison described the layout in front of them. "We're on the east side of this ridge," he pointed. "Warehouse is about 500 yards from that chimney. A cemetery is less than half a mile west of us on this ridge, but no one's there but boxes of bones."

They walked back to the line of halted trucks. "I'll go in first with the weapons," Ellison said to Hicks. "Get your men ready. I want Donnelly and Kittridge together. Don't screw this up."

"We'll move in fast on your signal," Hicks said.

Ellison nodded and returned to the lead truck as Hicks walked past the paddy wagon and grabbed a megaphone. He peered into each truck. His deputies, badges flashing, signaled they were ready. He said something to the driver of the armored car, its heavy machine gun pointed forward.

Chapter 39
That's the Signal

Kingsland, New Jersey: August 1918

Shannon stood with Clancy, Sergeant Fernandez, and Marshal Duval behind the remnants of a three-foot stone wall running along the cemetery boundaries. They were under orders from Bureau Director Hicks not to interfere. *Not likely.* They fully intended to arrest the cop-killer and gun-runner Ellison and the 1916 Manhattan terrorist Brown. Ellison was due to arrive momentarily with a posse of Hicks's men. From her talk with Lewis, Shannon knew Ellison and Hicks planned to double-cross and arrest the warehouse man Brown, the Irish revolutionary Donnelly, and his Tammany Hall benefactor Kittridge.

Shannon looked down at the warehouse. Brown stood vigilant in front, seemingly unaware of the forces aligning against him: Shannon and her police colleagues, Ellison and his men, and Hicks and his Bureau deputies.

The sun burned hot. Shannon could feel the damp patches blooming on the back of her dress. The wind picked up, aggravating her skin, already raw from the river crossing. Her hair was pulled back tightly out of the way in preparation for shooting. She glanced down at the Springfield reassuringly resting against the wall.

Before the explosion in 1917, the warehouse had served a major function for the entire area, but it now contained the only activity in a mile radius. Central yet isolated, it was dangerous enough to discourage the curious, but functional enough to serve the intrepid, with good access roads.

Shannon peered through her scope. "They're coming," she said to Duvall. "Black Super-Six up from the southwest road. Looks like Kittridge and Donnelly."

Clancy shaded his eyes with his hand and squinted. "Yep, that's his car, but what about Ellison? He should be here by now."

"What road will Ellison use?" Fernandez asked.

"Far side of this ridge, I think," Duvall said. "Can't see where exactly. Let me check."

Nine minutes later, Duvall returned. He looked worried. "They're there all right. Perched on the same ridge as us. Half a mile away. Lots of trucks. Men in uniform, heavily armed. They got an armored car."

"What in the name of the Blessed Virgin ... ?" Clancy, startled, stopped short.

~

The Super-Six bumped across the road and approached the warehouse from the main entrance. Jelly waited with his hands on his hips, his eyes scanning every direction. Two of his men flanked him, rifles in hand. Donnelly jumped out of the driver's side and approached Jelly, a heavy-looking rucksack over his shoulder. "They here yet?" Anxiety in his voice.

"Soon," Jelly said.

Kittridge exited the Hudson. Two scarred, tight-faced men with red hair followed. Donnelly pointed to them. "Patrick and Connor. They're coming with us."

Jelly shrugged, trying to act nonchalant, all the time assessing the new Irish soldiers, suspicious of this unexpected addition to Kittridge's crew. One had long unkempt hair; the other the sparse whiskers of youth. They were dressed in the uniform tunic and trousers of a British soldier. Undoubtedly stolen. No insignias or uniform markings; side-arm holsters; equipment belts with extra magazine cartridges and grenades.

Kittridge sidled up to Jelly. "Everything ready, Gibson?"

"Jus' waiting for Ellison."

~

What was left of the warehouse roof had blistered. Sweat rolled down from Jelly's forehead, stinging his eye. He patted his brow with a red kerchief. His other men moved into the shade. Jelly watched as Ellison drove the lead truck into the main entrance. Five more followed, low on their wheels, and parked in a crescent, starting twenty yards from the entrance. Ellison stepped out and looked at Jelly, Kittridge, and Donnelly. "We're all here. Let's conclude our business." Ellison glanced over his shoulder to the northeast and scratched his cheek.

Jelly pretended to ignore the curious gesture. He leaned over to his man Satch and whispered. Satch nodded and headed away.

Jelly led the men into the warehouse.

~

"They're heading inside," Shannon said quietly. "When do we arrest Ellison?"

"Stay out of sight, Shannon," Fernandez warned. "Let Hicks make the first move. We'll react accordingly."

"Hicks's men must be getting ready," Duvall said. "I counted about twenty of them."

"What are they waiting for?" Shannon checked her rifle for the third time in six minutes.

"A signal."

~

Twenty-two minutes later, Jelly emerged from the warehouse followed by Ellison, Donnelly, and Kittridge. He gestured to his men to start unloading and studied the scene with the look of a man expecting trouble. If it was coming, it would be now. Ellison moved close to the front door of his truck and seemed to count Jelly's men. Appearing calm, he glanced up toward the western road and lit a cigarette.

~

"That's the signal," Duvall said.

~

Instinctively, Jelly understood the cigarette's meaning. "Ambush! Run!" he yelled to his men. He whipped around and hit Ellison in the face with a haymaker. The dandy keeled over as Jelly scrambled to the warehouse.

Kittridge and Donnelly looked at each other, momentarily stunned by the turn of events. Recovering quickly, the Irish commando pulled out his revolver as Patrick and Connor ran to join them.

Ellison's men raced to their trucks to grab their guns and began firing at Jelly's men. Two charged recklessly armed only with knives and were cut down. The rest of Jelly's men retreated to well-prepared defensive positions concealed by dirt embankments and shallow pits. Having driven Jelly's men back to their defenses, Ellison's mercenaries concentrated on the Irishmen. Patrick and Connor protected Kittridge and Donnelly's front, firing back and cursing like demons. Connor rolled a grenade under the nearest truck, eliminating two of Ellison's drivers as Patrick wounded another. A concentrated burst of retaliatory fire riddled them both, but not before their standoff had bought the time for Kittridge and Donnelly to scramble to safety behind the farthest truck along the crescent line.

Donnelly dug into his rucksack for more ammunition and resumed firing, stopping the drivers' advance. He tossed another grenade, forcing them to retreat. Kittridge joined him but fumbled his gun.

Two more trucks drove into the main entrance and stopped behind the last of Ellison's trucks. Twenty well-armed men jumped out, badges flashing in the hot sun. To Jelly's surprise, an armored car rolled up and stopped forty yards east of the main entrance. Its machine gun pointed at Kittridge and Donnelly. They dived under the truck.

A man emerged from the armored car and yelled into a megaphone. "This is Assistant Bureau Director Hicks. You are all under arrest. Put down your guns and surrender peacefully." Still groggy from the punch, Ellison ran over to join Hicks. The deputies spread out and pointed their weapons at Jelly's men. As did Ellison's mercenaries.

Jelly's men responded with gunfire.

~

From her position behind the cemetery wall, Shannon watched the cops and Ellison's men shoot it out with Jelly's crew. Outnumbered three to one, Jelly's men began to fall. Soon only five remained fighting.

At the top of the line of trucks, Kittridge and Donnelly were caught between Ellison's men, who had regrouped and were advancing. Ellison, Hicks, and two other cops maneuvered toward them. The armored car followed. Not sure which threat was greater, Kittridge panicked, crawled away from the truck, and attempted to flee. Bullets hit him in the shoulder and gut, spinning him around.

Donnelly ignored the armored car, which was too far away to use a grenade, and dropped to one knee. He fired a well-placed shot that passed through Hicks's neck, leaving him gasping for his last breaths. Ellison dived behind Hicks's dying body and returned fire but missed.

Stepping over the wounded Kittridge, Donnelly moved up along the line of trucks and tossed a grenade in front of the charging mercenaries. He turned and threw himself over Kittridge's body, protecting it with his own. The blast killed three men instantly.

Donnelly pumped out his last rounds, wounding one of Hicks's deputies and driving Ellison and the others back to the armored car. He snatched Kittridge by the belt and managed to drag him back as he crawled under the truck. The armored car inched forward. Its machine gun blasted away, sending the top half of the truck flying into a thousand fragments, but Donnelly and Kittridge remained, for the moment, safe.

~

Shannon, shocked by the carnage of the battle, tried to tally the dead. Hicks's body was frozen in agony, his hands clutching his neck as the two Irish revolutionaries convulsed with fatal wounds nearby. Several of Ellison's mercenaries lay ripped to pieces by grenades. Six of Jelly's men sprawled motionless along their defensive line; and the remains of at least seven deputies and mercenaries lay strewn around the line of trucks. Fifteen men or more dead or dying.

She had witnessed Donnelly drag the wounded Kittridge under the now-shattered truck while Ellison sat protected inside the armored car. It advanced toward them, intent on delivering imminent death. Jelly and his four remaining men continued to exchange gunfire with a good dozen cops and mercenaries, protected behind the trucks.

"We can't let Ellison win!" Shannon cried. "We can't!"

"We were ordered to observe." Fernandez said. "If we go in, we'll never survive that fury."

"We must!" Clancy shouted.

Chapter 40
The Equalizer

Kingsland: August 1918
Cradled under the truck, Michael Donnelly checked Kittridge's wounds. *No hope*, he judged. Donnelly stopped shooting and waited to die. *It's all over*, he thought. Not his life — that didn't matter — but his dream for a free Ireland.

~

Jelly fed another box magazine into his Lee-Enfield and fired off three rounds in quick succession from his sandbagged position in the warehouse. He called out to his men. Only two responded. He cursed his greed for taking on such a wild, high-risk job, but somehow, deep down, he had suspected it would end this way. Better to die fighting like a man than to die a drunk on a beach in Cuba.

Deadly splinters flew in all directions as bullets pounded into the warehouse. Ellison's mercenaries were closing in. In minutes, they would be in range to reach him with grenades. Concentrated fire bored through Jelly's makeshift loophole, forcing him to huddle behind his barricade. The old wood could not last much longer. With no chance to reach his *Equalizer*, he needed a distraction, something. He'd fight on until ... .

A tap on his shoulder. He recoiled and swung his rifle around. Only his keen reflexes prevented him from pulling the trigger.

"Stop! It's me!" Satch raised his hands protectively.

"What? You still alive? You take that trip round the back?"

"Took some bullets, but can still walk."

Jelly poked his head up, emptied his rifle, and ducked to reload.

"Down!" He pushed Satch to the floor as bullets ripped through the walls. One clipped his cheek as he was giving Satch new instructions, causing them both to recoil.

"Git!" Jelly shouted and returned fire.

~

Ellison sat laughing in the passenger seat of the armored car. He liked to win, and he was having a good time. He did not care about the others. Hicks was a useless bureaucrat; Kittridge was a fool; and dead men came with the job. Gibson was trapped, and that tiresome red-haired bitch and her police friends had stayed out of it. *Kill the Irishmen and secure the weapons — both close to done. And me without a scratch.*

~

Jelly tried to stay alive as Satch circled around the warehouse to flank Ellison's men. Jelly's barricade could collapse at any minute. Two daring cops inched forward, confident that suppressing fire would pin the black bastard down. Jelly raised his rifle over his head and fired blindly from a crouch. He peered from around the remnants of his barricade. The cops kept coming. One raised his arm to throw a grenade and Jelly closed his eyes. *Lord, I'm ready. It's been a good life, considering.*

His eyes flew open at the sound of Satch's shotgun blasting. One cop was down, the live grenade right next to him. Satch charged the other, unloading the second barrel of his shotgun as he ran with no concern for himself. The cop fell, his chest a mess of purple-red meat and buckshot. Gunfire from the trucks plowed into Satch, striking him repeatedly. He died before he hit the ground. The grenade exploded among the fallen men.

Jelly had his chance. He dashed to the entranceway, grabbed his *Equalizer*, strapped it on in a flash with practiced hands, and released a torrent of flame as he stepped across the threshold. Fire spit across the row of trucks, igniting them immediately. Huddled beneath the farthest vehicle, the dying Kittridge and Donnelly had no escape. The remaining mercenaries and cops scattered in panic. Flames quickly extinguished their horrific screams.

The armored car jolted to a halt, but reversed away as Jelly ran toward it and aimed his flamethrower. The stream of fire fell short.

~

Shannon could taste the cordite and smoke. Cinders landed on her clothes, but she patted them out.

Next to her, Fernandez and Duvall argued.

"No! I'm ordering you to stay," Fernandez said.

"Hicks is dead," Duvall said. "All our promises to him are void. I say we move in."

"Aye." Clancy stood up and raised his tommy gun. "I came to arrest Ellison, and that's what I intend to do." He gestured with his weapon toward the inferno. "Who's coming with me?"

~

Jelly dodged the erratic machine-gun fire from the armored car and raced back into the relative safety of the warehouse. One bullet to the fuel tank on his back would cremate him. He reached the entrance just as the machine gun cut down the last of his men.

~

To Shannon, it seemed like she was watching a movie from the back row, but this was real. The heat from the fires cooked her brow. The acrid smoke dried her tongue and made her gag. The smell of roasting flesh and burning trucks irritated her nose. The sounds were the worst of all: the wounded men's pleas, the crackling fire from the burning trucks, the straining engine of the armored car, the bark of rifle exchange.

"Sean, stop!" Shannon cried as Clancy charged down the crest into the battle. She picked up her rifle and put her foot on the wall, but before she could jump over, Fernandez pulled her back.

"You stay here. It's his choice." He grabbed her shoulder. Shannon tried to elbow him away, but he slapped her in return. "He made me promise to protect you. He does not want you to die."

The sting brought Shannon to her senses. She wiped her face and watched, blood boiling and speechless, as Clancy ran toward the fray, whooping like an Indian. "He'll be killed!" she cried.

"No, he won't." Duvall followed him down.

Shannon turned to plead with Fernandez. "Stop them."

"Cover them with that rifle."

"But ... ." Shannon watched her friends. They had made half the distance to the warehouse, but in the melee below, no one appeared to notice.

Fernandez looked amazed. "He might just succeed."

~

Out of the corner of his eye, Jelly saw two men running down the crest from the graveyard, one brandishing an oddly shaped rifle, the other pulling his arm back — that a grenade? *What the shit?*

~

Ninety yards from the burning trucks, Clancy stopped, raised his tommy gun, and sprayed a full burst. Duvall threw two grenades to get their attention. "Stop your firing!" he yelled. "This is U.S. Marshal Purvis Duvall. Drop your weapons — all of you. That's an order."

A few men stopped shooting and looked at the spectacle unfolding from the crest; others continued sporadic gunfire. Clancy unleashed another burst and all the curse words in his vocabulary, bringing the shooting to a halt. "Ronny Ellison!" he called out. "Come here! You other men, all of you: Get out!" he shouted to the drivers and deputies.

Duvall stood beside him. "Don't get in our way." He fired his shotgun again and again.

~

Furious at the sudden reversal, Ellison jumped out of the armored car. "Go to Hell!" he screamed at Clancy. Gibson in the warehouse was no immediate threat, but these Goddamn New York coppers had butted in once too often. "Keep him at bay," he ordered his last three deputies, nodding toward Gibson sheltered in the warehouse. "You. All of you." He waved a hand at the half-dozen mercenaries who still could walk and pointed to the hill. "Take those two fuckers out! *Do it!*"

Ellison climbed back into the armored car. "Turn around," he commanded the driver, then turned to his machine gunner, eyes narrowed. "Give 'em all you've got," he snarled.

~

Shannon watched the armored car turn toward Clancy and Duvall and the adversaries running to confront them. Caught in the open, Clancy returned fire with his tommy gun, stopping one man short and driving the others to ground.

"Watch out, Clancy!" Duvall shouted, diving into a shallow crater as a phalanx of machine-gun bullets cracked around him. One clipped Clancy in the shoulder, another buried in his gut. He dropped the tommy gun and fell awkwardly.

"Sean!" Shannon shouted.

~

Half-stunned, Clancy watched the blood pool in his shirt. *Strange,* he thought, *no pain. Just light-headed ... .* Suddenly overwhelmed by nausea, he weakly struggled halfway to his knees and keeled over. Duvall rushed to protect his fallen partner.

~

Shooting furiously from the stone wall, Fernandez downed another attacker. "Shannon, fire!"

Thou shalt not kill.

"Pull the trigger."

Fernandez's words connected. Shannon took careful aim. The bullet nicked her target's arm, just as she had intended. *I won't kill them, but I can damn well stop them.*

Shannon and Fernandez pinned down Ellison's men, giving Duvall time to reach the *Annihilator.* Seizing the tommy gun, he sprayed his attackers with a continuous burst. The field in front of him fell silent.

Not for long. The armored car churned up the muddy road, engine growling, machine gun chattering. A swath of bullets ripped through Duvall.

Sickened by the grisly sight, Shannon vomited. She lifted her head, wiped her mouth with the back of her hand, reloaded the

Springfield, and fired her entire clip at Ellison inside that steel monster. Her bullets pinged off its metal skin like harmless stones. The beast turned and moved up the road to the cemetery.

"Run, Shannon. We can't stop it!" Fernandez said. "Come. I'm gonna try something."

Shannon fired another clip. The beast turned, unharmed, and headed right toward them, its machine gun growing more accurate. Bullets skipped around her. The stone wall could save them only so long, and it now began to crumble under the unrelenting slew of bullets. Shannon crouched low and followed Fernandez out of the cemetery along the ridge of the crest.

Ninety seconds of the hardest running Shannon had ever done forced her to stop. A blinding pain cut up her side as she gasped and fought for breath. "Come, Shannon," Fernandez pleaded. "You *must*."

"I can't. My back."

Fernandez glanced around the deserted roadside. "Hide there," he said, pointing to a large shell crater.

"What are you going to do?"

"I investigated this area, remember?"

Shannon could not have run another yard. Safe in the crater, she withdrew the Webley she had secured in her boot. *Thank you, Sean.* She peeked over the lip of the crater as the armored car muscled by.

Two sights startled her: Jelly Brown with a shotgun in hand was hustling up the crest, chasing the armored car. The flamethrower was too heavy to run with, she guessed. Thirty yards ahead, Fernandez briefly moved into the main road and waved his arms to draw the car's attention, then dashed onto a side road before the gunner could react. The metal monster accelerated and followed him.

Sweet Jesus, Shannon whispered aloud as she suddenly realized Fernandez's intention. *No, Sergeant. Noooo —*

A massive explosion rocked the area as the armored car hit a live shell along the road. The force of the blast lifted the car so high that Shannon heard it crash back down on its side. The passenger door swung open, pointing to the sky. A bloody arm reached out. The rest of Ellison followed.

Brown ran by Shannon panting, brokenly repeating between jagged breaths, "Goin' kill that son-of-a-bitch."

Clutching the Webley, Shannon followed him to the explosion, adrenaline overriding all sense of pain. The pop of bullets and crackle of flames were the only sounds from inside the beast. The fumes were overpowering. Fernandez's body was nowhere to be seen.

A raspy voice, seemingly from some other world, shocked her. "So it has come to this." Ellison limped toward her, his face covered with oily grime and blistered from the explosion, his arm bleeding. "I underestimated you, Mrs. Keller." He pointed his .45 at Shannon, then at Brown.

~

Jelly recognized Shannon from newspaper accounts and pictures of her suffragette work. From the details, he had connected her to the Bomb Squad men who had foiled his attack on New York, but he held no grudges. His vendetta was with Ellison, not past failures. "I shoulda killed you when I first saw you, Ellison. You treacherous snake," Jelly said, a wide grin revealing his gold tooth. His finger rested on the trigger of the shotgun.

Shannon did not know where to point the Webley. She looked at Brown. "You fiend. You almost blew up Wall Street."

"Yes, we did." Jelly continued to point his shotgun at Ellison. "But, I'm no threat to you, ma'am."

Raising her Webley, Shannon ordered, "Give yourself up, Mr. Brown."

A three-way standoff. Jelly aimed at Ellison. Ellison at Shannon. Shannon at Brown.

Ellison moved first. He feinted left, but Brown was faster and calmly pulled the trigger. His first round staggered Ellison before he could shoot. His second round lifted him off his feet. He fell to the ground and spit out blood. He raised himself half up on an elbow and reached for his .45 as Jelly reloaded and moved in close. After he kicked the pistol away, he pointed the shotgun six inches from Ellison's head and pulled the trigger. "That's for my men."

Jelly turned to Shannon and lowered his shotgun. His face and clothing dripped with gray and red splat. "I mean you no harm, Mrs. Keller," he said softly, and started to walk away.

"Stop. I should arrest you for the Wall Street attack." Shannon's voice was firm, but her hand trembled.

Jelly turned and looked her in the eye. "That was a lifetime ago. I ain't goin' to no prison. Never kilt a man, have you? Pull that trigger, an' you'll regret it for the rest of your life." He looked tired and seemed to age before Shannon's eyes. "Ain't there been enough dying today, Mrs. Keller?"

Shannon lowered her Webley. "Go."

Chapter 41

We Did Pretty Well

Washington, D.C.: August 1918

Three days after the battle in Kingsland, Leon Lewis walked into Allen Dulles's office, uncertain how his employer had reacted to the events. He found Dulles with his feet on his desk, munching on a fat chicken drumstick. "Sit down, my friend," Dulles said.

How should he interpret Dulles's seemingly good mood? His agent Ellison and all of his men were dead or hospitalized. The Bureau had suffered worse, losing Hicks and twenty deputies.

Dulles finished the drumstick, tossed the bone into his rubbish bin, and licked his fingers. "I guess no operation can be one hundred-percent successful, but I'd say we did pretty well, eh? On U.S. soil, no less." A wry smile crept onto his face.

"Sir? But the men?"

"What of them? We need to assess the results of the overall mission. We stopped the flow of arms to the Irish revolutionaries and made a profit on the side. Discovered useful information about some less-than-American citizens too."

"Where are the arms now?"

"We recovered about half after the police cleared away the bodies. They objected when we showed up, but we presented some legal papers and they had no recourse. They left us alone to cart away the goods. The arms are now on their way to Estonia. General Vargas will make good use of them. I hate those Bolshevik bastards," Dulles said.

"What about the money we paid Ellison?" Lewis asked. "That was a lot of —"

"My, uh, ... specialists, let's call them, have relieved Ellison's family of its burden."

Lewis laughed. "You mean you stole it back?"

"Stole? Heavens, no. We merely reclaimed what was rightfully ours. The banks were surprisingly cooperative. Ellison failed to fulfill his contract, so we had every right to claim the payment. And Mr. Ellison is no longer present to contest it, is he?"

"And the dead men?"

"Hicks was worse than useless. He created this mess. His losses are the Bureau's concern. They were upset, but what could they do? Admit their men were incompetent or involved in gun-smuggling? I'd argue my people had nothing to do with it — there are no provable connections between Ellison and us. The Bureau would surely take the blame."

"But Ellison's men?"

"Trickier, but solved. Lawyers from an obscure firm in D.C. paid the families a little visit. Said their men died in a trucking accident and gave them a thousand bucks to help them over their loss. Paid the funeral expenses too. We were *so* sorry to have to cremate the bodies, but it was the only practical solution given the nature of their unfortunate loved ones' injuries. A few folks protested, but when details were explained, they pocketed the cash and signed the papers. No one will ever hear from them again."

"And the New York Police? What are they saying?" Lewis asked, impressed by Dulles's efficiency.

"What *can* they say? They got the justice they wanted when Ellison died. Unfortunately, their man sacrificed his life when he triggered an unexploded bomb. They're making him into a hero. Secretary McAdoo has spoken to Mrs. Keller and secured her cooperation."

"That still leaves Donnelly's Irish-American contacts. Most are highly placed, important people."

"Nobody wants a scandal in the midst of a war. So let's say we visited some and are watching others. All know it's against their best interests to support an Irish revolt. It would be such a pity if an unforeseen catastrophe or bankruptcy befell them."

"One last question. The press?"

Dulles snickered. "How gullible. Well-trained puppets. They swallowed our explanation hook, line, and sinker." He read out the headlines from a newspaper on his desk. "*New Explosions in Kingsland.* An investigation by the New York Police into the affairs of Tammany Hall banker Murdock Kittridge led officers to the old Canadian Car Company plant. Unexploded ordnance ignited during the investigation. A detective sergeant and a New Jersey marshal died heroically in the line of duty." He tossed the paper on his desk and smiled. "No mention of Bureau involvement."

"I've enjoyed working with you." Lewis smiled. "I trust we will have a long relationship."

Both men stood to shake hands. "Yes, an excellent partnership, Mr. Lewis," Dulles agreed. "Welcome to the 20th century. Undercover operations outside government interference. This is just the beginning." He rubbed his hands together. "Now I can go back to my work in Bern."

~

The threat to her life was over, but Shannon, back in Bronxville, woke up feeling depressed. It was good to be home, but she sorely missed the camaraderie of her now-depleted unit. Three important tasks, none joyous, would occupy her day: the memorial service for Joe Fernandez; a hospital visit to Sean, who was still in critical condition; and a search of Murdock Kittridge's apartment.

~

The Fernandez family had requested a small service, limited to family and close friends. The police commissioner agreed, eager to attract as little attention as possible to events that had transpired at Kingston. No casket. The only remains were a few bone fragments and the sergeant's wedding ring. Shannon approached his widow after the service. "Your husband saved my life," she said warmly. "I don't know how to thank you, but I'll be in your debt forever. He was a fine man and an excellent detective."

Mrs. Fernandez lifted her veil, her face white, her cheeks red.

"We were trying to have a baby, but never made it. I guess it was God's will that I join the other childless war widows." She paused and took a deep breath. "Joe considered you his little sister. He loved working with you. He would consider saving you the noblest thing he ever did. Given the same circumstances, I'm sure he would do it again. Bless you, Mrs. Keller." She extended her hand.

Shannon gripped it tight, but could find no words.

"May your husband get home safely from the war. Goodbye."

Shannon sat quietly in the back pew while everyone else filed out of church. An hour later, she still remained, sitting alone and gazing at the crucifix.

~

Shannon brought Clancy a package of Oreo cookies, his favorite, even though she knew he shouldn't eat them. He was groggy from the medicine and still in obvious pain, but trying to keep up his usual good spirits.

"Can't be a cop no more, I guess," Clancy said when he opened his eyes and discovered Shannon at his bedside. "Always wanted to fish. Think I'll buy a cabin upstate by some lake. Maybe marry some rich widow. You'll visit me, won't you, lass?"

"Every Sunday."

He smiled. "Memory's not too good. Remind me, Shannon. We got them, didn't we?"

"Yes, Sean, we got them." She said nothing about her encounter with Brown. She had told the investigators she thought he had died in the warehouse.

"Good," Clancy said, and immediately fell back to sleep. Shannon waited, watching over her old friend a good long time before leaving.

~

Shannon approached the door to Kittridge's apartment with two detectives newly assigned to the investigation. A uniformed cop was standing in front, part of the twenty-four-hour guard the New York

Police had posted immediately after the Kingsland battle. The officer let them into the sealed-off apartment, and Shannon cast a careful look around. To her relief, it looked as if no one from the Bureau of Investigation had entered.

Though Kittridge was dead, many questions remained. Now the unofficial head of her detective unit, Shannon was anxious to discover his secrets.

The apartment was smaller than she would have imagined, but the view overlooking Central Park was magnificent. The place was richly furnished with red Persian carpets, antique mahogany furniture, and a hutch full of gold-rimmed crystal glasses. Lingering odors of pipe smoke and burning logs filled the rooms, which were not as tidy as one would expect from someone of his means. No maid, Shannon guessed. Kittridge seemed to have protected his inside world as well as he protected his outside world from intruders. A half-empty bottle of Irish whiskey rested on top of the liquor cabinet. She was tempted to take it for Clancy, but did not touch it.

The pictures on the piano intrigued her. Who was the man on skis next to Kittridge? The pretty young girl was probably his daughter, but where was she now? The bride was presumably his wife, but why was the picture cracked? Had something happened to her?

Shannon next examined the papers on his desk. To her disappointment, she found no financial ledgers or notebooks, but several papers in German caught her eye. Fluent in German, she quickly saw the contents revealed nothing to help her. But she had not known that Kittridge read German. *There's much to this story I still don't know.*

She looked around the apartment again with new focus. Signs of Germany were everywhere: an etching of Heidelberg; books by Goethe and the military strategist von Clausewitz; a painting of Frederick the Great; local *Fatherland* newspapers. *So, you were more German than Irish, weren't you?* She silently addressed Kittridge's ghost. *No wonder you wanted to send weapons to revolutionaries plotting to overthrow British rule. What else were you up to, Murdock?*

When a thorough search of the apartment turned up nothing of interest to the investigation, Shannon sent her assistants back to search the bedroom and returned to Kittridge's study herself. As she carefully reconsidered each object, her gaze came to rest on Kittridge's armchair. The heavy bottom fringe touched the floor. Cautious of her weakened back, she knelt, lifted the fringe, and bent to peer underneath as best she could. Nothing. Gingerly stretching her arm as far as possible under the chair, she patted her hand around the gritty floor. Her fingers touched a piece of paper. Pinching it between her fingertips, she dragged out a sheet of crumpled onionskin stationery.

A page from a letter, obviously a draft, addressed to someone named Andy. *His son?* "I trust your final days at Camp Merrick were not too stressful, and your journey across the ocean was uneventful … . I'm sorry to say that your dog McKinley is sick." *Dog? What dog? He doesn't have a dog.* "This should all be over by the year-end, and God willing we will see a righteous end to all this slaughter."

Shannon reread the letter several times and concluded it conveyed a coded message. *She let her mind roam over the possibilities. Yes, that's it. Kittridge was a German agent. I doubt Hicks knew that. He must have a son in the U.S. Army — the Camp Merrick reference. This is an order to carry out a mission.*

Shannon was positive she had discovered a new threat to the AEF from a German agent named Andy.

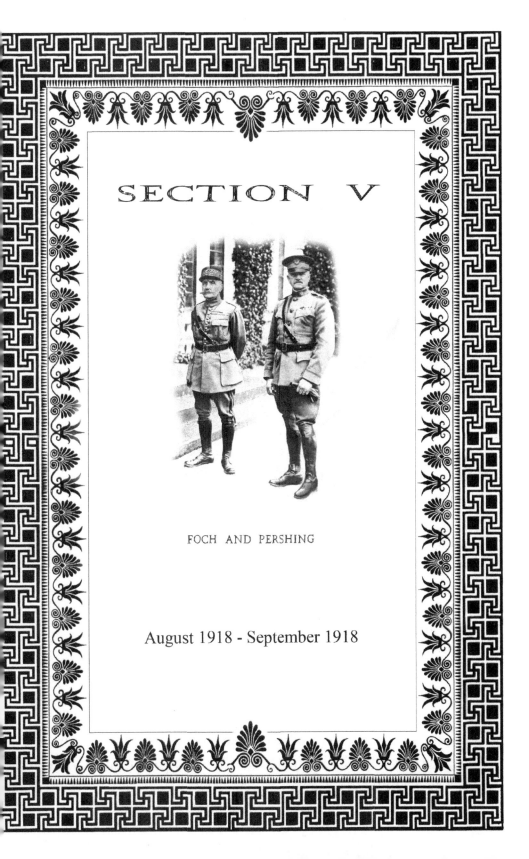

SECTION V

FOCH AND PERSHING

August 1918 - September 1918

Chapter 42
A New Question

Chaumont, France: August 1918

Colonel Mortimer put his hands on his hips and glared down at Martin and Keller. "Nothing? Eleven days since the assassination attempt, and that's all you've got to say? Nothing. Not one suspect? What have you been doing?" In the confined office, his voice magnified to twice its normal boom. "You're missing something. Something so obvious it's invisible."

Martin folded his hands on his desk and absorbed the rebuke. Keller tapped his hand against his chair and looked ready to jump into the fray. Martin spoke to intercept any chance Keller might say something reckless. "Let me explain the situation, if I may, Colonel."

Mortimer grunted something and sat down. He rearranged his chair, its legs scraping against the wooden floor. "Okay, explain."

"Our first thought was that Major Jameson was the spy. We know from Kittridge's letter that we were looking for someone called 'Andy.' The major was the only Andrew of rank at headquarters. But Jameson was killed in action."

"So, where to next?" Martin answered his own question by succinctly summarizing the status of the case and finished with suggestions for further investigation.

"Methodical. That's what everyone says about you, Captain Martin. Thorough. But all you've told me is what we already know. Dead ends. What don't you know, and why don't you know it?"

"Investigations take time, Colonel."

"Time we don't have. General Pershing is scheduled to meet Generalissimo Foch in eleven days. Our general's importance grows every day. His loss would deadlock the war."

"If you want someone else to conduct this investigation, just say so," Martin said with bitter coldness. "There are other ways for me to help our cause."

"Can you guarantee that no further attempts will be made on his life?"

"You know I can't guarantee that."

"The general has requested you act as his translator again on this trip. You go, and we compromise the investigation. Don't go, and we anger the general."

"How can I refuse?"

"How can you accept if you haven't found the assassin? We'll decide later." Mortimer rose and forced his cap low on his brow. "AEF headquarters is packing up and moving to a new sector. I want this wrapped up before then."

~

In a barn along a dirt road behind a stand of trees, André handed Emily a U.S. Colt .45 semi-automatic. "Here, girl. It's what you asked for. It has the kick of an angry mule but great stopping power. A bullet from one of these can knock a man down. Take it. It's empty."

Used to handling all types of firearms, Emily was surprised by the weight of the gun and nearly dropped it, but she recovered and examined it, sensing its lethality. The double diamond grip felt comfortable in her hand. Good balance. She extended her arm and looked down the sight. "This will do fine."

"I thought a Yank pistol would be best. Fewer explanations needed if discovered. Easier to obtain too. Here, bullets." He handed her a seven-round magazine. "They leave a nice round hole. About the size of the end of a cork."

Emily eased the magazine into the gun and worked the slide. "What is the effective range?"

"Fifty yards for an expert marksman. Best to be within twenty."

"I won't need more."

"Take a shot." André pointed to a row of bottles set up on haystacks fifteen yards away.

Emily pulled off a round. The .45 recoiled powerfully, but she managed to hold the gun steady. Her aim was poor, and she missed.

André chuckled. "It's not a lady's gun."

"Who said I was a lady?" She held the .45 up to her face and looked at it as if it was a naughty child. "What am I doing wrong?"

"Hold it in both hands. You can control it better that way. Take a boxer's stance, like this." André demonstrated. "See? You're about to throw a punch — one foot in front, the other to the side and back. Spread your feet. Get comfortable. Crouch a bit. Derriere back. Stay balanced."

Her next shot buried into the hay five inches below the bottle. Fragments of hay sprayed in all directions. "Humph."

"Better," André said. "The sights on this gun are first-rate. Concentrate on the front one. Squeeze slowly. Press the trigger steady all the way back."

Emily lowered the .45 and processed everything her uncle had said. At the end of an hour's practice, she moved into shooting stance, aimed, and fired three rounds in quick succession. Three bottles disintegrated. She was ready.

André clapped. "Excellent. You were always a fast learner. I've loaded your picnic basket with grenades. Thought you'd need them. Do you know when you'll go hunting?"

"Next week, when Pershing is scheduled to return from Paris. I'll be there as he leaves his train."

"Go up to him and just fire away?"

"Yes."

"If I hadn't lost my arm at the Marne, I would be doing this."

"Don't worry, Uncle, I'm ready."

"You were destined for greater things." André looked away.

~

Martin stared at his ashtray overflowing with butts while Keller finished off another cup of cold black coffee. A dank smell of tobacco, sweat, and weariness permeated the room. Outside, trucks rumbled and officers shouted orders. "Mortimer is right about one thing," Keller said. "We need to rethink our approach."

"We've been concentrating on who was there," Martin said. "It's time we thought about who was *not* there."

"What do you mean?"

"What bothers me is that bomb. Where did it come from?" Martin placed his left elbow on his desk and rested his head in thought. "I don't think our bomber built it himself, so how did he get his hands on it?"

"Same person who organized the bombing run?"

Martin's eyes lit up. "Of course. The man who delivered the bomb must be the same man who orchestrated the bombing run." He bounded up from his chair. "Let's step back a second. How would he communicate with our assassin? He can't cross no-man's-land. A secret code?"

"Probably, but how is it exchanged?"

"Radio? Telephone? Letters? In person?"

"A U.S. military person maybe. You asked if our man was a traitor or a spy. How about both?"

"Or one of each. Our bomber on the inside, and someone else on the outside," Martin said.

"The outside man must be a civilian. Someone in the AEF would have no time, but someone on the outside who has access to our activities and —"

"Or can observe them. Someone who knows weapons, locks, codes."

"Who would know all that?"

"We know our bomber has a direct link to Germany, presumably through an intermediary, but who?"

They tossed out various names but rejected them all. Martin closed his eyes for a moment. They flashed open as an idea struck him. "What do we really know about Uncle André?"

Chapter 43
The Barn

Chaumont, France: August 1918

"Maybe Uncle André isn't so kindly." Martin's detective instincts were aroused. "He walks around and observes our movements and nobody says *boo*. He leaves and goes where? We don't know. He must be at the center of all this."

"That makes Emily Lange an accomplice, doesn't it?" Keller asked.

"Not necessarily. Her background was thoroughly investigated. Maybe she's just unknowing."

"But don't forget Shannon's spy, Gil. We have a traitor inside the AEF. Could be Miss Lange."

Martin reeled. "No, damn it. She's an *Emily*, not an *Andy*." *Had Emily duped him?* That horrible possibility added to his growing disillusion with humanity. And yet, her connection to André was undeniable. "I refuse to believe she would betray us. Not until we have proof."

"You've had doubts about Miss Lange since I returned from Belleau Wood. Look at this like a detective. She has the brains — that gives her the ability to commit the crime — and as a Hello Girl she listens into all AEF communications — that gives her the opportunity. That's two strikes against her."

"But so far, no motive."

"Who knows her true loyalties."

Martin masked his doubts with a stony expression. "André first. See where he leads us."

"But watch her?" Keller asked, more demand than question.

"I'll put Sergeant Wilcox on it."

"She must not suspect she's under suspicion."

"If she's our traitor, she'll already know."

"I've already talked with her matron," Keller confessed. "She said Miss Lange works extra shifts before her uncle's visits, so she can have more time with him."

Martin wrinkled his brow and gave Keller a serious look.

"Sorry, Gil. Part of our investigation. Just routine. Somebody had to ask. The matron will tell me when she expects André's next visit. She fully understands she must keep the inquiry quiet. She has given me her word she will speak to no one."

The next morning, Martin and Keller snuck into Emily's room and sifted through her possessions while she was at work. They looked into every corner and checked every possible hiding place, but found nothing incriminating. Her picnic basket was full of sewing material as she had claimed. The only marginally curious items were a guide book to Paris, a pad of paper with several missing pages, and a well-worn copy of *Uncle Tom's Cabin*. Martin guessed the guide book had to do with her liaisons with Major Jameson. If Emily was a traitor, Martin would have to prove it elsewhere.

Another setback.

Colonel Mortimer's deadline loomed closer and with it the possible end of Martin's intelligence career and a transfer to all but certain death at the front. He did not want his name to become one among thousands in a newspaper obituary.

~

That night Keller was called to 2nd Division headquarters to help sort out an issue between rival Army and Marine brigades. Martin traipsed back to his quarters, glad to be alone. He slumped over his desk and began to write.

> *Dear Shannon:*
>
> *These letters help me as much as I'm sure you're glad to receive them. I can speak to you more freely than to anyone else except Paul.*
>
> *I'm acting as a detective again on a sensitive matter. I can't say much, but we're threatened from within. You are aware of the*

details, as the lead has come from you. We're building a case against one of our own; almost too incredible to believe. I don't like where it is heading. It's a great weight pressing on me.

I wish you were here to help, but we both know that's impossible. This is a military matter, and, even if you were allowed to come, the incident would be resolved before you got here.

We are about to shadow a key suspect in this conspiracy. If I am right, the case could break fast.

I am happy to be working again with Paul since the battle at Belleau Wood — a victory, but a costly one. He's in fine spirits. The locket you gave him never leaves his neck.

I'm tired and wish this war would end, whether I get back to America or not.

— Yours, Gil

~

Three days after a tip from the matron, Martin stood on the roof of the Hôtel de Ville waiting for André. Located at the end of a two-hundred-and-fifty-yard row of one- and two-story stone houses, the Hôtel de Ville was set high enough to provide an unobstructed view of the whole area: a public square below, a large grassy knoll across the street, and, beyond the row of houses, the train tracks and the woods behind them. The AEF GHQ and its compound of barracks, Signal Corps station, latrines, and a few hastily erected buildings and tents, were located to the right of the grassy area. Someone could walk from the compound to the train stop in five minutes.

André appeared as he always did: bicycling down the road parallel to the train tracks on his right. He crossed over the tracks and went into the woods, undoubtedly heading for the bench that overlooked the grassy area across the street. The old man showed no sign of concern. All smiles despite the difficulty of navigating with one good hand and a prosthesis. He likely carried his usual gift of fresh farm eggs and vegetables in baskets hung on either side of his rear wheel. Martin had often seen them before, but today he wondered what else they might contain.

Picnic basket in hand, Emily ran to meet him. They hugged and acted as if the war were a million miles away. They showed no fear of any threats. Martin cringed, wondering if she was André's unwitting pawn or disciple.

So many questions needed to be answered. If André was a spy, who was he? What was his real connection to Emily? How did he run his operation? How could he be stopped? And at what price?

Martin pushed the last question out of his mind. His mission was to solve the case; he would face the repercussions later. But he suspected the emotional price of this case would cost him dearly. When André looked ready to leave, Martin signaled Keller and a corporal, both dressed as farmers standing at the near edge of the grassy area. They stood up, careful to conceal their faces, ready to pursue on foot or bicycle.

~

The movement of the two farmers he had never seen before caught André's attention. "I fear they are watching us, niece."

"I told you they were getting close. But they still don't know for sure, or they would have arrested us. In a few more hours, the mission will be completed. We can manage until then."

"Where is the .45?"

"Safe. Nearby. With the money and grenades you gave me and a knife I stole from the kitchen. They won't find them."

"Are you ready?"

"Of course."

"You don't have to do this, Emily."

"Who else will?"

André's body slumped in resignation. "Continue as planned. I'll distract them."

"Thank you for everything, Uncle."

"Your father would be proud. I hate goodbyes. Kiss me and go."

~

Martin watched Emily and André emerge from the woods and fondly part company. She headed back to her station and the old man pedaled out of town. They had spoken but a few minutes.

Martin motioned Keller and the corporal to follow André. He returned to GHQ and told Sergeant Wilcox to keep Emily in view and record her every movement. "Assume she is dangerous."

~

The road from town was rutted and crumbling from the weight of heavy AEF traffic. Dust wafted so thickly in the air that Keller needed goggles. Fine with Keller, as it hindered André's ability to spot him. Not that it mattered. André maintained a slow pace, which to Keller meant that André was either innocent — unlikely — or he wanted to be followed. Keller was sure the old man was executing a plan.

Three miles out of town, André stopped to drink some water and look around. The kind of look only a trained spy would make. Keller steered his bike off the road before André saw him. He ordered the corporal to ride past André and wave as he pedaled by. "Go up ahead of him five hundred yards, then wait for me to catch up. Let's see how he reacts."

André played this stop-and-go game two more times. Keller, now certain the old man was leading them on, watched from a distance as André bicycled off the road and disappeared into a thick clump of trees. Keller and his corporal dropped their bikes, drew their pistols, and moved forward silently. They stopped and observed André enter a small barn.

"You're mine, you rat," Keller muttered under his breath as he

reached for his binoculars. He sent the corporal back to tell Martin to join him with a squad of soldiers, then settled into a well-concealed spot that allowed him good visibility.

Six minutes later a homing pigeon flew out of the barn. *So that's how you get your messages out.*

~

Martin parked an army truck six-hundred yards from the barn and joined Keller with six heavily armed MPs. Keller crouched behind a tree, adjusted his binoculars, and studied the barn.

"André's still in there, Gil. Alone. Haven't heard any sounds. He's waiting for us to make the first move."

"Why would he do that?"

"Anyone's guess. Maybe he's stalling. Out of options. Knows he's trapped."

"Whatever he's doing, he's doing it deliberately." Martin shaded his eyes against the sun.

"Only choice is to rush him," Keller said. "A one-handed man can't operate a machine gun."

Martin ordered the squad leader to deploy his men around the barn. "No one comes in or out. Hold your fire until we move in."

"We need to end this quickly, Gil. Get back to Chaumont. Right now, *he's* controlling the situation."

"Let's shake him up. He doesn't know what happened after he left town." Martin cuffed his hands around his mouth. "André!" he shouted. "This is Captain Martin. Come out peacefully. No one has to die. We've arrested your niece. She's confessed."

Silence.

"Look, smoke." Keller pointed to the back of the barn.

"He's burning the evidence." A shot rang from the barn. "He's making a final stand." Martin signaled his soldiers to shoot. The MPs released volley after volley as André unsteadily fired from the barn.

"Let's go." Martin and Keller charged amidst intensifying

smoke. André's shots missed them widely. Martin signaled his men to stop shooting when he reached the barn. Keller muscled open the door and Martin charged through, firing his .45.

A dozen yards away, André stood in bloodstained clothes, fumbling with his Mauser in an attempt to reload with his one good hand. Dazed, he dropped to one knee and raised his weapon, but shots from Martin and Keller knocked him to the floor, blood pouring from his stomach and shoulder. He tried to stand. "You will never defeat us," he said, and collapsed.

Martin kicked the gun away and stood over him. André smiled victoriously.

"Who are you?" Martin yelled.

André raised himself up with his good arm, rested against the wall, and spat out a red gob. "Whoever you think, you will be wrong."

"Talk and you might not die."

"Go to Hell."

"I'm already there," Martin said. "Maybe we can convince you to cooperate." He gestured to Keller, who pressed his finger into André's shoulder wound.

"Where's Miss Lange?" Keller demanded.

André grimaced, then cursed, then snickered. Keller pressed again. André gritted his teeth but couldn't suppress a howl. A flood of pain spilled from his eyes. He emitted a demonic cackle.

Puzzled, Keller looked at Martin. What more could he do?

Martin's rage exploded. "What are you planning?" Martin shoved his .45 into André's good elbow. Talk or I'll leave you armless."

"You've lost." André struggled to speak again, but his head slackened and flopped to the side. His mouth agape; his eyes frozen.

Realization seeped into Martin's face. *Pershing.* Martin raised his sleeve and checked his trench watch. "He's scheduled to arrive in thirty-five minutes. Lange's waiting to ambush him."

"We'll be too late."

Chapter 44
Proof

Chaumont, France: August 1918

"Wait!" Martin cried. Keller was already halfway out the door. "We've got to look for evidence."

"No time," Keller said. "Pershing's more important."

Martin searched frantically through André's pockets — nothing but a few coins; a picture of Emily, André, and another man; and some matches. The picture appeared to be taken in New York City.

"Gil, the fire is spreading. We've got to go." Keller grabbed Martin's coat and tried to pull him away.

Martin placed his hand on Keller's shoulder. "You go. I'll be a minute. I have to prove Emily is the traitor."

"She is. You know it as well as me. She's not worth dying for."

"I'm not doing this for her." Martin needed to understand how he had erred so badly. For that, he wanted to know how André and Lange had managed their duplicity. He looked around and focused on the smoldering pile of papers near the back of the barn. He grabbed a stick and began to rake through them.

The fire intensified. Embers swirled through the air, igniting anything that would burn. Martin brushed them off his coat, continuing to stir through the pile. Remnants of a book cover came into view, just as the title disappeared into ash. *Uncle's Tom Cabin*. Lange had the same book. No coincidence. They must have used it as the key to their code: page numbers, number of lines down, number of characters across — all referenced a letter or word. No one could decipher the numerical code without this exact copy of the book. He had his proof.

The barn's support structure groaned. Martin looked up, startled by the noise.

"Get out!" Keller yelled from the entrance. "The barn's giving way."

A burning beam cracked and dropped, glancing off Martin's

shoulder in a rain of debris. He tripped and fell, surrounded by flames. "Help!"

~

Keller looked at his men, "You stay here. We all don't have to die," and ran inside. Heavy smoke had reduced visibility to feet, effectively blinding him. "Gil, where are you?" As he headed toward Martin's voice, the hay burning on the floor seared his boot soles like a hot summer street. Keller found Martin sitting on his knees struggling for air. Keller kneeled, gave Martin a handkerchief, and put his arm around his friend's waist. "We've got to move."

Martin wobbled, but he managed to stand with Keller's help.

"Hurry." Keller tried to quicken the pace, but Martin stumbled, nearly forcing them both to the floor. Keller managed to keep him upright but realized Martin was too fatigued to move. He stopped, lifted Martin up in a fireman's carry, and ran as the fire began to nip at his legs. The crackle of flames behind him sounded like gunfire.

By the time Keller reached the entrance, the fire had burned patches through his trousers. It felt like dozens of leeches were feasting on his flesh. Two of the soldiers ran to help. Together they struggled forward thirty more yards until they were safe. Martin asked for a canteen. He drank half and poured the rest of the water over his blistered hands. One of the soldiers patted down glowing embers burning through his clothes.

Keller ripped off his smoking uniform blouse, grabbed another canteen, and poured water on his pants where raw skin was cooking. Relief was immediate. He laughed wildly at their improbable escape, prompting confused looks from the soldiers clustered around Martin. Suddenly, a huge blast erupted behind them. The men dove to the ground and covered their heads with their hands as a storm of wreckage and splinters washed over them. Keller remained flattened, face in the dirt, until a diminishing series of smaller explosions finally played itself out. Keller shakily lifted his head and peered back at the barn. Nothing was left but burning tinder.

~

"Are we going to be too late?" Martin kept asking as Keller sped into Chaumont.

"I'm going as fast as I can, Gil. Let's hope Sergeant Wilcox can stop her."

"She'll be as willing to die as André."

"Where to first? Intercept Lange or protect Pershing?"

"Split up. You alert Colonel Thornton at the train. Tell him to remain inside. I'll go after Lange."

Keller eyed his bandaged but determined friend. "Wouldn't it be better if I go after Lange? You're —"

"No. She's my problem. I need to fix my own mistake. Stop here."

Keller braked hard, let Martin off in front of the Hôtel de Ville, and accelerated down the street toward the tracks.

~

Emily operated her switchboard with her usual efficiency, casting covert glances at her timepiece. She mourned Uncle André, most likely dead. Pershing's train was due to arrive in ten minutes. Calls to headquarters confirmed he was on time. Her only fears were Martin and Keller. Sergeant Wilcox was merely an annoyance. *So predictable. So easy to trick.* But the detectives would be a challenge if André hadn't managed to divert them long enough. All the same, she felt she was more than their match. Three minutes more, and she'd go to the toilet and get André's money, her knife, the .45, and the picnic basket full of grenades.

~

Martin knew Emily would either be at work, in her barracks, or outside waiting for Pershing. Moving slowly due to injuries and smoke inhalation, Martin headed to Lange's quarters thanking God that Pershing had not yet arrived. Fighting for breath, he asked for the strength to complete his mission and prayed for Keller's safety as he helped guard Pershing's train. He looked down at his damaged hands. The left was well-wrapped, but despite painful blisters, his right remained unbandaged, as he'd insisted. He needed the freedom to handle his .45. His other injuries were dressed and numbed. "Just a nuisance. Won't slow me down," he had told the medic who'd treated him at the barn.

He did not want help apprehending Lange. This was personal. So far, she had manipulated and outsmarted him. Not today. He kicked open the door to her room. Empty. Neat. Ready for her return, though he knew she never would. He found neither a weapon nor her picnic basket.

Martin headed to the Signal Corps exchange. As he passed the women's latrine, intuition told him to investigate. He studied the entrance; something did not seem right. No activity. He drew his arm and called out. "Anyone in there?" No sound but a leaking pipe. He called twice more, then cautiously opened the door, wary of a trap. A reddish-brown puddle spilling from the toilets caught his attention. It led to Sergeant Wilcox's lifeless body, whose face gaped back, shock and anguish carved into it. His neck had been sliced half-way through. Lange was still ahead of him. The whistle of Pershing's train announced its imminent arrival, loudly interrupting Martin's curse.

Martin ran to meet the train. *What was Lange's plan? Explosives? A rifle? Pistol up close? Could Keller stop her?* Maybe, but he knew that a determined assassin held many advantages.

~

Emily left the AEF compound and strolled along the grassy area, looking for all the world like her usual aloof, but friendly self. Her .45 weighed down the pocket of her coat next to the blood-stained kitchen knife and André's money. Wilcox's side arm sat in her basket atop six grenades: one smoke, five explosive. Knowing Martin and Keller could be hunting her, she relied on her hat and uniform to afford her some anonymity. Despite her hurried attempts to wipe Wilcox's blood off her sleeves, they were partially visible. She'd ignore any busybody questions and hurry along. If need be, she'd silence them with the knife.

Emily crossed over the tracks and headed into the woods, turning left when she neared her bench. She walked parallel to the tracks for another ninety seconds until she reached her ambush point, a dense thicket of brush and undergrowth. It was ten yards behind the normal resting stop of the last train carriage, across the street from a stone wall and row of buildings that partially blocked the view from the Hôtel de Ville, where a sniper could present a threat when she moved into the open. This was the closest she could get to her point of attack without being seen.

Keller and a dozen men patrolled the spot where Pershing would exit the train. Their presence eliminated her first assassination option — jumping out from her hiding spot and shooting the general and his bodyguard. Unfazed, she looked down at her picnic basket. *Thank you, Uncle.*

The train whistle neared. Any minute now.

~

Still breathing hard, Keller instructed his men to maintain a tight perimeter. He surveyed the area, searching for the best position from which to launch an ambush. He turned and shifted focus when Martin yelled his name.

~

Martin ran over to Keller to inform him of Wilcox's murder. "She's around here, Paul," he warned between coughs.

"I'll send out men."

"They'll never find her in time. She's already where she wants to be."

"We're ready. But the next move is hers."

Chapter 45

In Another World

Chaumont, France: August 1918

"We can't give her the initiative," Martin said. "I'm going after her."

"Stay here, Gil. We need all the men we have to protect the general. I've got a sniper on top of the Hôtel de Ville with orders to shoot her on sight."

"Bombs?"

"She didn't have time to plant them. I've got three men looking just in case."

"Get on that train and tell the general to stay there until we secure the area."

"He won't listen. He'll —"

"Die if he doesn't. Lange is close. Have the men circle the general as he gets off. No one gets near here."

"And you?"

"She's got to be in those woods."

"Be careful, Gil."

Martin turned and, hindered by his injuries, moved slowly into the woods, thinking Lange might be near the bench.

~

Emily remained hidden in the dense thicket of underbrush and saw Martin disappear across the tracks. *Wrong direction — I'm near the back of the train, not the front. Fool. I still have time.*

Her mouth was so dry she had no spit. She was surprised by her body's nervous betrayal, so strong was her usual control over it. She took several deep breaths to calm herself, then removed the grenades and Wilcox's gun from the picnic basket and placed them in her coat pockets. She fingered André's fully loaded .45 and calculated her next move.

~

Martin moved cautiously, his .45 drawn. When he approached the bench, he shouted, "Emily Lange. Surrender. You don't have to die like André." No response. He continued on through the woods, the train tracks to his left. "Emily Lange!"

~

Stop shouting my name. The train steamed to a stop and men began jumping off. Emily faced one opportunity and one threat. Martin neared. She looked to the train, then back toward Martin's voice, estimating distances, guessing timing, determining whether to go after Pershing or eliminate Martin first. His voice told her he was out of range. The general, then. She sprinted out of the woods, past the last carriage of the train, and angled closer to the stone wall, away from the threat of a possible rooftop sniper. A grenade in one hand, her .45 in the other.

~

Keller confronted Colonel Thornton as he prepared to leave the train. "General Pershing is in danger."

"The general's always in danger," Thornton scowled. "We've got a full schedule. No delays. General's orders."

"Where's his chief of security? He must not descend the train."

"What the hell is going on, Lieutenant?" Thornton's voice dropped an octave lower and harsher.

Keller spied Pershing approaching the exit. "General, stop!"

Too late.

~

As Emily ran toward Pershing's carriage, she counted many heavily armed men standing guard. More were running to join them. Behind her, Martin was yelling out to the soldiers. A bullet from the Hôtel de Ville streaked over her head. She saw Pershing exiting the train. Keller right behind. The soldiers looked around, confused.

Now.

Emily lobbed a grenade in front of Pershing's carriage and jumped over the stone wall across the street to safety. Keller pushed the general down and covered him with his body. The grenade landed short but exploded with enough force to fell the five men moving toward her. Emily rose and starting shooting.

Ignoring the bullets, Keller pulled the general off the ground and shielded him amidst the chaos, preventing Emily from taking a clean shot. Two soldiers leapt off the train and yanked Pershing back into the carriage with Keller. Several more came running down the grassy area and peppered the street with bullets. Emily crouched low behind the wall and kept shooting, eliminating one more soldier.

The remaining men rushed in her direction. She was dead if she stayed where she was, and Pershing was still alive. Exposing herself, Emily stood, tossed her second grenade, and ducked, stopping the attack. She threw her third grenade with more force and wiped out the rest of the soldiers around the train. *Now.* She charged into the clear, powered by some inner strength greater than even she had ever felt. Vulnerable in open ground, she dropped her smoke grenade to reduce visibility.

Bullets from the Hôtel de Ville continued to miss high and gunfire from soldiers coming from the AEF compound whizzed by as she zigged and zagged toward Pershing's carriage. A soldier moved to cut her off. He aimed. She was faster and shot him twice.

A bullet nicked her arm, but she hardly noticed the pain. Emily glanced over her shoulder and saw Martin coming up the street through the smoke. She turned and drove him back, emptying her Colt.

~

Martin dived just as Lange pulled the trigger. The first bullet missed, the second drilled into his upper thigh. He spilled over, firing back awkwardly, his bullets off the mark.

~

Martin's down. Emily rapidly reloaded, dashed to the carriage and fired into the window, shattering the remaining glass. She pulled the pin on her fourth grenade, tossed it in and ran. Three seconds. Two seconds.

Martin hobbled toward her, shooting. One second. She rolled to the ground as the grenade ripped the carriage apart. She eliminated all immediate threats with her last grenade and ran.

~

"No!" Martin screamed. His heart raced. His leg throbbed. His anger intensified. His failure complete. He looked up through the smoke and saw Lange sprint away. Before she rounded the train, he fired wildly. A lucky shot knocked the .45 out of her hand. The ground was red, gray, and dusty, strewn with body parts and dying men. The wreckage of the carriage was aflame, smoke pouring from its naked windows.

Martin forced himself up and followed Lange into the woods, joined in pursuit by several U.S. soldiers. Lange wove, staying low and moving fast. Martin stopped to staunch his wound with a handkerchief. *Not serious.* A couple of soldiers caught up with him. Their faces cried for revenge.

"Don't shoot," Martin ordered. "We need to arrest her."

Silent curses.

"General Pershing?"

Blank looks. "I saw his doctors working on him," one man said.

Martin split the men into groups: three to organize a roadblock out of town; four to circle around and cut off her escape; and two to come with him in pursuit. "She dropped her gun. She may be unarmed, but consider her extremely dangerous."

~

No one could have escaped that blast. Pershing is dead. Emily began to think she'd survive. She had never expected to get this far. Her lungs protested, but she willed herself on. In three minutes, she would reach the little church on the other side of the woods where André had placed a bicycle and a new set of clothes. If she could just get out of Chaumont, she'd disappear into the crowded market at the next town.

Emily was tiring, and the soldiers were gaining on her. They had had some clear shots but hadn't taken them. *Why not? Hah. They want to arrest me. What weakness. The great American justice system. The German military is better: guilty — firing squad — move on.*

Weakening, Emily slowed down, allowing her pursuers to catch up. Had the ploy to drop her .45 make them think she was unarmed? She tucked her other gun in her pocket, stopped, and raised her hands. "I surrender. I surrender," she pleaded, her eyes full of crocodile tears. She began to sob in fake desperation, and the solders took the bait. They lowered their weapons.

Emily heard Martin running to catch up. "No! Don't. She's —"

Too late. She pulled out Wilcox's .45 and fired twice before the soldiers could react. Their lifeless bodies tumbled to the ground.

~

Martin watched the scene in disbelief. Two more men down. Lange, too far for him to take a shot, was getting away. Rage and adrenaline propelled Martin forward, his leg a forgotten hindrance. He emerged from the woods behind her, just as she jumped on a bike. She pointed her .45 and fired two rounds. He felt the bullets zip by but refused to be stopped.

She started to pedal away, but three soldiers at a roadblock forced her back. Another group arrived with guns blazing.

~

Emily stopped and searched for an escape route. Nothing. The street offered certain death; bullets were finding their range. A shot clipped her side, knocking her off the bike. She hobbled through the side door of the church.

The church was empty except for an old woman waiting to make a confession. "Get down!" Emily hollered as she eyed the interior, frantically looking for a spot to make her last stand. She retreated to the altar, the only place safe from crossfire.

A priest emerged from the confessional. "*Que faîtes-vous ici?*" he demanded. "What are you doing here? This is the house of God. Get out."

Whatever else her crimes, Emily did not want to be held responsible for a priest's death. "Please, Father," she pleaded. "I don't want you to die. Take your parishioners and move to safety."

Martin was barking orders outside. She envisioned his men preparing to storm the sanctuary. *They will not want to wreck the church. My one advantage.* She tipped the alter table over, ducked behind it and checked her ammunition. *Two full clips and a few bullets in the .45. Maybe twenty. Enough if I make them all count.*

Knowing Martin, she expected he'd try some trick. Minutes ticked by. Every minute meant additional reinforcements and heightened anxiety. Six minutes crawled by. Emily stifled her breath as the church door opened. Martin entered. Alone. Arms raised. His gun still in his hand. She lowered her pistol in disbelief, then raised it, fearing a ruse.

~

Martin approached the altar at a snail's pace, outwardly calm, but ready to react in an instant. Ignoring the advice of his men, he hoped to defuse the situation alone and end the standoff with minimal loss of life. If he became a casualty, well ..., he deserved it. He should have caught her weeks ago. Besides, this was a sacred place, not a battlefield. Lange had chosen her Alamo well.

"This is no place to die, Emily," he said in a reassuring voice. "Please, give up. We can work something out."

"I don't want to hang. I'm not a traitor."

"I didn't say you were. I assume you're a patriot ... for your country. Germany, I believe." Martin continued to advance slowly.

"I'll shoot."

"What good would that do? My men are right behind me. The only question left is how many more need to die today. Me? You? The priest?"

~

"Stop right there, Captain."

Martin's calm approach had unnerved and confused Emily, weakened with the loss of blood. He was getting too close. She wanted a fight, not a chat. Her index finger tapped the trigger guard.

"You're a Catholic aren't you, Emily? Remember your teachings."

Stop lecturing.

"Thou shalt not kill."

Shut up.

"Yea, though I walk through the valley of the shadow of death ... ."

The face of the priest who spoke at her mother's funeral flashed through Emily's mind. For the briefest of moments, she longed to be an innocent girl again, before her father began to indoctrinate her.

"Surrender, Emily. I'll make sure you're treated fairly."

Emily took a deep breath. Ever so slowly, she started to rise when half a dozen soldiers burst into the church.

"No!" Martin shouted.

With a surge of adrenaline, Emily stood upright, aimed at Martin, and fired. He dodged and pulled his trigger. Two slugs hit her midsection. She collapsed.

Emily felt cold but no pain. She didn't need to look down to know her insides were leaking out. She gazed at the crucifix above her. *Good place to die.* Martin stood over her, victorious, confused, pained. He looked at his gun with disbelief and horror.

Emily spit up blood. "I liked you, Captain," she smiled faintly. "You're a decent man." She fought for breath. "In another world − ," she coughed, "we could have been ... ." Her lips stopped moving.

~

That night Martin sat down to write Shannon. Deeply distraught over the day's events, he had drunk three glasses of cognac and was on his sixth cigarette. *How much could he tell her about Pershing's escape?* Emotionally, he felt at his lowest point since his arrival in France.

Dear Shannon,

I can only say so much, as the censors will undoubtedly inspect this letter, but I trust you can fill in the gaps. First, your husband is a hero, though you will never read about it in the papers. His quick actions prevented a military disaster and saved an important person.
He has also managed to escape a seemingly fatal situation. The incident relates to the problem you warned us about. That threat is eliminated.

During the action, I was forced to confront a woman (we were all looking for a man). She died at my hand. Her death was completely justified, but she is the first woman I have ever killed. It happened in a church. A woman. In a church. I cannot describe how awful I feel. I wonder if, had I acted sooner, been smarter, or been a better detective, I might have prevented her death. I made sure she received last rites, if that means anything.

So, for me, the war has come to this: killing a woman in a church. I talked to the division chaplain at length afterward, but his words provided little comfort. I do not regret what I did, only that the war put me in the position to have to do it.

When will it end? I'm committed to seeing the war through, but after, I'll need a long rest in a remote cabin. It will be a long time before I like the man I've become.

— Yours, Gil

Chapter 46
Unified Command

Bombon, France: August 24, 1918
Martin sat next to General Pershing in his staff car on the way to a meeting with Generalissimo Foch at the Château de Bombon, twenty-five miles southeast of Paris. Still shaken by the violent conclusion of the Lange affair, just two days past, Martin was glad to escape from Chaumont and was once again acting as Pershing's translator for this crucial meeting.

Martin marveled at the flourishing garden and well-trimmed rose bushes as he followed the general to the main entrance of the centuries-old brick château Foch had chosen as his headquarters. A quiet respite from the harsh daily demands incumbent on the Supreme General Allied Commander, the regal château with its slate roof and large, rectangular windows seemed far removed from the war. The very embodiment of French elegance past, it reminded Martin of a better world to be regained once this cursed war was over.

Martin and Pershing proceeded past heavily armed French Alpine troops at the entrance and were led to a large dining room. Other top-ranking French and British commanders were already there. It was here that Foch would determine the strategic direction for the fall battle campaign and coordinate Allied efforts now that General Pershing was scheduled to command his own autonomous sector. Martin imagined meetings in times past when other dignitaries gathered in this very room to discuss matters that shaped the world. No more so than today.

The high-ceilinged room was covered in tapestries and hunting trophies: the heads of boar, deer, and bears, all magnificent specimens. A gleaming medieval suit of armor stood rigidly in the corner, a guardian of past glory. It reminded Martin how military advances become obsolete, replaced by ever more frightening weapons — flamethrowers, tanks, poison gas. *What's next?* He shivered at the thought.

The room smelled of cigarettes, fine wine, and highly polished furniture. Allied generals waited for the generalissimo to arrive. Aides mingled among them, whispering important (to them) rubbish and clutching inconsequential papers with fancy seals. Martin started up a conversation with an AEF officer he had not met before, Colonel George Marshall, whom rumors suggested would have a role of importance in the coming campaign. Martin took the measure of the man and was duly impressed.

The mood was upbeat. High casualties aside, the summer's fighting had gone well. Despite its lack of experience, the U.S. Army had made a difference and was learning fast. Logistical problems and tactical deficiencies remained to be rectified, but the consensus was that the Doughboy was brave, steadfast, and aggressive. American soldiers had the makings of a fine army.

"*Attention!*" The command issued loudly from the hallway. Everyone snapped into parade-ground posture and military academy salutes as Generalissimo Foch, a punctilious man, strode into the room at precisely 14:00 and saluted back. The commander-in-chief had the dignified bearing of a head of state. His grizzled mustache filled his face beneath gray-blue eyes that reminded Martin of the steel in the finest Japanese swords. Surprisingly, his boots lacked polish. Maybe the generalissimo was more of a common man than his rank and title would suggest.

After an hour of talk, Foch led the group to a large room, where they stood around a massive oak table covered in maps. Martin translated as Foch summarized the actions the Allies would have to take to reconfigure their armies.

The British would naturally be responsible for the northern sector of the Western Front, as it was closest to their base of supplies coming from England. But the BEF would have to return five U.S. divisions that had proved useful during the summer counter-offensive. A glance at Pershing told Martin he was pleased.

In turn, the French would continue to hold the center of the line, the direct route to Paris. Because America prioritized sending troops over equipment, the AEF lacked heavy weapons. The French army would transfer 3,000 guns, 150 tanks, and 1,400 aircraft to General Pershing's newly formed U.S. First Army.

First Army was to take over portions of the southern and eastern line, centered on Saint Mihiel, south of Verdun. It overlooked the Woëvre Plain, an area of marshlands and streams surrounded by woods. The Germans had occupied this area since September 1914, despite several costly attempts by the French to take it back. The German position formed a salient that knifed into the Allied position. For the last year, the French had considered this a "quiet" sector as the fighting moved north following Ludendorff's Spring Offensive, but the salient now had to be eliminated if Pershing's planned offensives in his sector were to succeed.

Meetings at AEF high command made Martin aware that Pershing had lobbied for the responsibility of this sector. It presented many challenges due to stout defenses and forbidding terrain, but it also presented Pershing with an outstanding strategic opportunity. Behind Saint Mihiel stood Metz, a vital rail link that fed the German army. The loss of Metz would be disastrous for Germany; taking it would provide Pershing with the chance for the decisive victory he sought.

~

On the way back to AEF headquarters, General Pershing invited a few key generals, Colonel George Marshall, and Martin for dinner in the dining car of his train. The rumors were true. Marshall outlined the logistical challenges facing First Army, but Pershing called them "manageable" and expressed complete confidence in the colonel.

Pershing complained about his relationship with Foch. Difficult man. Stubborn. Seemed to have a low opinion of the American army: units too large and cumbersome, attacks foolish and uncoordinated. The AEF officer corps was inexperienced and overeager. Martin silently agreed.

"Foch never seems interested when I discuss First Army's problems," Pershing said. "He is essentially a student and teacher of history and strategy."

The other men nodded. It was a bad idea to confront the general in such an open forum. From what Martin had heard, those who did went back stateside, disgraced.

Pershing continued: "I am eager to prosecute this attack. We'll show the French and British what brave American boys can do with a bayonet once we force the Huns out in the open. We'll drive them out of the salient and speed toward Metz. Once we take it, and the Germans are trapped with no supply, they are *done*. What our Allies couldn't do in four years, we'll do in weeks: *Win the war*." He pulled out a cigar.

Martin winced. *If it were only that easy. Haven't we learned anything since Belleau Wood?* He mentally began to count the fresh graves.

Chapter 47
Fismette

Fismes, France: August 26, 1918
Martin's staff car pulled up to the 28th Division's advance regimental command post in Fismes, along the Vesle River. With the staff at AEF General Headquarters preoccupied with organizing the fully combined American First Army and planning the upcoming offensive, Pershing needed an officer from his own staff to assess a worrisome problem developing in Champagne. Lower-ranking Captain Martin drew the lot.

Having spent the last few weeks tracking down Lange, Martin was unfamiliar with the situation. He read the tactical report summary in the car:

> *The French 6th Army, commanded by French General Jean Degoutte, defends the Aisne-Marne salient. The 6th Army includes the AEF III Corps and its 28th Division as part of the unified Allied command introduced in May. III Corps commander Robert Bullard reports directly to General Degoutte, not General Pershing.*
>
> *Units of the 28th Division, mostly men from Pennsylvania, hold positions in Fismes on the south side of the Vesle River along the main Allied line and a bridgehead on the north side in the small town of Fismette. The situation is a direct result of Generalissimo Foch's July counter-offensive that pushed the Germans back to the positions they held before their Spring Offensive.*
>
> *During this time, fighting in the Aisne-Marne sector has been vicious, seesawing*

*back and forth in August. Fismes has changed
hands five times. Finally, the Germans have
established their defensive position along
the Vesle, with the exception of the American
bridgehead at Fismette, an intolerable tactical
situation which 6th Army must rectify.*

*General Degoutte maintains that the
bridgehead at Fismette is vital as a base for
further offensives. The U.S. III Corps high
command disagrees and believes their troops
in Fismette are unnecessarily exposed. General
Bullard has requested GHQ to intercede.*

Martin lowered the report, wondering why he always drew these thankless assignments. Through General Pershing, Colonel Mortimer had ordered him to assess the situation, report back with recommendations, liaise with the French, and, if possible, arrange a mutually acceptable solution. "It's nothing too difficult, wouldn't you agree, Captain?"

~

When Martin arrived in Fismes late that afternoon, he learned that 232 American soldiers were holding Fismette across the river. The bridge linking Fismette with the 28th Division's main line at Fismes was partially destroyed, making it difficult to reinforce the bridgehead. The commanding AEF colonel at Fismes saw no point in throwing more soldiers into a tactically deadly and strategically valueless position and requested permission from division headquarters to withdraw his men from Fismette. Unfortunately, with orders from Degoutte's 6th Army headquarters to hold the bridgehead, the 28th Division had to stay where it was.

After talking with the junior officers and inspecting the front line, Martin agreed that withdrawal was the sensible course. Several men confided to him that the French would never leave their soldiers so exposed. *Who cared about American boys?* Not the French.

Martin decided to drive to 6th Army headquarters the following day to discuss the situation with the French.

~

An artillery bombardment across the river woke Martin at dawn. Heavy guns: 150s and 210s. He watched the flashes stream into Fismette. Their ferocity signaled that the Germans were determined to sweep every American off the north bank of the river. The first casualty was the bridge over the Vesle. It collapsed, cutting off the men defending Fismette. The pattern of the explosions told Martin the Germans were using a "box barrage," designed first to isolate an area by shelling the perimeter, then, once the defenders hunkered down inside the target box, pound them into oblivion, like an elephant stomping ants.

The barrage went on for an interminable twenty minutes. Martin witnessed the disaster unfold, observing through field glasses from his fortified position on the riverbank like a mere spectator at a well-choreographed play. Helpless to affect the outcome, he raged at his impotence.

Continuing his surveillance after the barrage had ceased, Martin observed a company of more than one hundred Germans approaching along the river in an attempt to flank the American position. The professionalism of their movements indicated they were first-echelon soldiers. Overhead, a squadron of low-flying German planes bombed and strafed the defenders, sparing nothing in their attack.

In the midst of all of it, his ears distinguished the surprising crackle of small-arms fire. *How could anyone possibly have survived such savagery?* he wondered, but somehow, the Americans were fighting back. The gunfire continued for a long time.

The next surprise was even more stunning. An American soldier raced through the death trap and dived into the river, as the men in Fismes cheered him on. Swimming through shelling, rifle fire, and a tough current, the soldier reached the south bank exhausted but unharmed. Two Doughboys rushed to drag him to safety at the risk of their own lives and carried him to the protection of the fortified position that served as a command post.

After medics revived the soldier, Martin listened as he described the attack, at first incoherently, his eyes blank as he spoke. He looked and sounded as if he had seen ghosts. Hesitantly, and stopping frequently to inhale deeply on his cigarette, bit by bit, he spewed out the terrible facts.

"After the air attack, they assaulted from the north in three directions. Battalion strength at least. Came at us hard, rifle fire, lots of grenades. Our right flank held and inflicted heavy costs on them. Buildings provided good cover. We got more of them than they did us, but they kept coming. Our center and left flank began to retreat. Light machine guns hammered away. Men dropped all around me. They unleashed the flamethrowers next. We had nothing to stop them. Some men tried. Others ran. You couldn't escape the stench of burning flesh. The screams of a man cooking are different than anything else you'll ever hear. Makes your skin crawl and you shit your pants.

"Then our captain shouted, 'Every man for himself!' He asked those of us standing who was the best swimmer. I won some competitions in high school. I said, 'Guess that's me.' 'Get across, son,' he told me. 'Tell them what happened here. Tell them we did not give up.'"

By the time he finished, twenty-nine more men had swum across. By 10:00, the tumult of battle had ceased. The regimental colonel approached and announced the butcher's bill: 75 killed, 127 missing, presumed captured. He spit on the ground. "Those Goddamned French killed my men just as surely as the Germans. We could never hold that position. This isn't the first time those fucking Frogs have sacrificed American boys. It won't be the last. I'll tell you this, Captain Martin: Every American unit in Europe will know about this atrocity by tomorrow."

~

Goddamned French, thought Martin on the way back to AEF headquarters. He had heard many whispers about how the French risked the Yanks to save the lives of their own boys, now confirmed. The regimental colonel was also correct. The news of the incident reverberated across the AEF.

Martin had great respect for the French *poilu*, but the tragedy at Fismette made him lose his confidence in French high command. *Last week, an American woman turns out to be a German agent. This week our Allies get us killed at Fismette.* How many more depressing things were yet to be revealed in this increasingly hideous war?

Chapter 48
Saint Mihiel

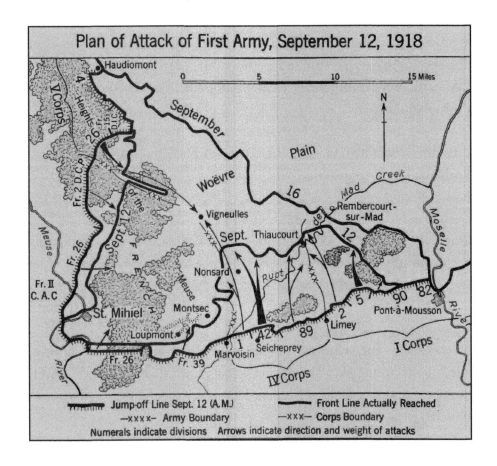

Plan of Attack of First Army, September 12, 1918

Fort de Gironville, Saint Mihiel Salient, France: September 12, 1918 04:00: Having returned from Fismette, Martin stood next to General Pershing, Colonel Mortimer, and several other AEF staff officers at Fort Gironville. The fort was situated on heights overlooking First Army's jumping off position and provided an excellent observation point from which to assess its progress. As an intelligence officer, Martin was responsible for assessing the German defenses, understanding their potential order of battle, and determining what was needed to win and at what cost. His job was done. He hoped he had performed it well. The attack was about to begin.

Pre-attack conditions were not favorable. Heavy rain had soaked the area, filled the trenches, and threatened to compromise the artillery's effectiveness. Several hours earlier, the AEF's chief engineer and several division commanders, including Martin's nemesis, the 25th Division's new commander General Donald Prescott, recommended postponement.

At the meeting, Martin had remained silent but knew the tight timetable Pershing had established to meet both his and Generalissimo Foch's fall campaign objectives. Delay was impossible. Billy Mitchell, now a Brigadier General, and Colonel Mortimer had argued that the Germans faced the same conditions. Besides, reports compiled by Martin and the rest of the intelligence staff indicated that First Army vastly outnumbered the defenders. Now was the time to strike.

General Pershing agreed and forcefully rejected any delay. "We attack as planned. Go to your units and don't let me see you again until we are victorious."

From Fort Gironville, Martin watched streams of American shells light up the sky. The ground shook from their explosive power. Somewhere down there, Keller waited to go over the top. *God be with you, my friend.*

~

Keller waited in his forward position ankle-deep in water. He checked his watch: 04:48. Twelve minutes to go. *It never gets easier.* Ordered at the last minute to replace Company A's commander, who had contracted influenza and was hospitalized, Keller watched the artillery shells pound into the German lines. He hoped the bombardment would eliminate initial resistance but knew its effect was likely limited. He spied the maze of barbed wire in front of him, certain that enemy machine guns covered whatever gaps existed.

He wiped his hand on his trousers and crunched the Pep O Mint

Life Saver in his mouth. The burst of flavor was a welcome distraction. He looked at the men in his command. All eyes were on him, some questioning, some scared, all looking for reassurance. None of them had ever seen combat. A few had only three days of practice with their Springfield rifles. Others wore partial uniforms supplemented with civilian clothes. They were eager. And nervous.

When Colonel Mortimer assigned him to this posting, he said, "We need an experienced man to lead this company, Lieutenant. You're it. I know you're officially an intelligence officer and we'll bring you back into the fold as soon as possible, but First Army must succeed. Under your command, we expect Company A to function as a veteran unit. Don't let me down." Mortimer hesitated for a moment, then added, "Oh, by the way. You've been recommended for the Distinguished Service Cross for your action at Belleau Wood."

Keller faked a smile. He didn't care about medals.

Mortimer scratched his nose. "Unofficially, the recommendation came from me for protecting General Pershing during that spy business. Can't let the press know about that." A humorless chuckle. "Quick thinking flipping that stout table over. Made an effective shield against that grenade. The general didn't appreciate you lying on top of him, though. Kicked your way out before the fire engulfed the carriage. Well done."

Mortimer's final words caught Keller off guard: "Don't die."

~

04:59: Don't die? What did that Aussie captain say? "Live today, die tomorrow. Can't think about the future. Luck and the man upstairs decide." Good advice. Keller stopped worrying and checked his watch. He popped another Life Saver in his mouth and sucked on it furiously. *Last thing I'll ever taste?* Ten seconds, ... three, two, one. He kissed his locket, blew his whistle, and shouted, "Follow me, boys!"

Across American lines, Doughboys soaked in rain and tension climbed out of their trenches. Company A crossed into no-man's-land

and maneuvered into fields packed with barbed wire. The five men Keller had assigned to cut through the wire worked quickly, helping to spearhead the attack. He had not divulged his concerns but was surprised they managed to survive the first ten minutes. No German machine gun fire. The German counter-barrage was weak. Company A advanced with little resistance. *A trap?*

Confused, the men looked at Keller. "Keep moving, men," he ordered them, all the time wondering when Fritz would release his fury. He didn't. To Keller's amazement — maybe the man upstairs was saving him for another day — Company A reached the German lines and found them empty. They had pulled back.

Keller ordered his men to press on. Company A moved forward steadily during the day, encountering light resistance. The company incurred only four casualties: two men who suffered shrapnel wounds, a man who broke his leg after falling into a crater, and another who was badly cut when he got caught in barbed wire. They pushed into a small fortified town but concentrated rifle fire and accurate artillery drove the Huns from their positions. Keller noticed a few German soldiers fleeing in disarray, some without weapons, a sight he never expected to see. This was not the enemy he had come to respect but was thankful they were his opposition today.

By the end of the day, German resistance stiffened and a counter-barrage forced Keller to halt his company's advance. In the distance, he spotted German troops feverishly building earthwork defenses, *Stellungen*, the Germans called them. They would become formidable obstacles quickly.

~

At GHQ, cheers erupted each time Martin, who was manning the telephone lines, relayed progress reports. First Army was advancing and meeting its objectives. In many areas, German units were routed and in full retreat. General Pershing acted like an excited football coach watching his team drive toward the goal line with a succession of straight-ahead fullback rushes against a tired and undermanned defense. Some German units fought back tenaciously, but the attack in the southern sector reached its objectives in only seven hours. The day had gone splendidly.

The rest of the battle continued just as favorably. In four days, First Army had retaken the 200 square miles of the salient. Mood at GHQ was jubilant. "We figure we engaged at least seven front-line divisions. Took 1,500 prisoners. Only suffered 7,000 casualties," Colonel Mortimer reported.

"The newspapers will be delighted," he told Martin. "This will be a propaganda gold mine. The public back home will be ecstatic. The Brits and the Frogs will eat crow. The AEF can fight and win on its own. What do you say, Captain Martin?"

Knowing better than to devalue an obvious victory, regardless of why, Martin merely said, "We did well."

"We have the German army on the ropes. One more push and we can end this war."

"Yes, Colonel." *1914 Allied optimism all over again.*

~

Two nights later, Martin embraced Keller with a bear hug when he returned to GHQ. Keller mentioned he had spent the last half-day interrogating prisoners. Martin was anxious to understand what really happened in the trenches, not the manufactured propaganda filtered to the press.

"Don't believe what you're hearing," Keller said.

"Everyone at GHQ is happy. What do you think?" Martin asked.

Keller frowned. "I'll tell you who's happy. The French. They were starving. German occupation was terrible. This was not some great military victory."

"What do you mean? I know we massively outnumbered them, but the higher-ups claim we achieved all our objectives within the planned time frame."

"True, but a bunch of Girl Scouts could have done what we did. The troops we faced were third class. No fight in them. They were battle-weary. Many were raw recruits. The Germans were pulling back when we hit them."

"But they wouldn't sacrifice Metz," Martin said. "They can't. It's too strategic."

"My guess is as good as yours. By withdrawing from the salient, the Germans were consolidating their line. Making it easier to defend with the same number of troops. Their retreat from the salient was scorched earth. They destroyed everything we need: bridges, railroad lines, communication networks. That will slow us down. Apparently, they believed that, if Metz was threatened, they could move enough soldiers fast enough to defend it. They've done this time and time again."

"But you have to agree it was a success."

"A partial one. Tactical, maybe." Keller rubbed his face.

"But from what you've said, we had them reeling. If we had pushed farther —"

"Yes, *if*. We should have. They might have been in the middle of pulling back, but we surprised them. They were disorganized. We should not have let them regroup. They're masters at that. A concerted push with all of First Army might have taken Metz. Not many opportunities like that present themselves in this war. We missed a big one."

"Maybe."

"You were at GHQ. What was going on?"

"First Army was ordered to take the salient and regroup."

"To do what? Bury more dead?"

"We're moving into the Meuse-Argonne sector," Martin said.

"When?"

"Attack in two weeks."

Keller shook his head. "We're going to move our entire army fifty miles and start a major engagement after just finishing one? In two weeks? That's crazy."

"It's part of Foch's overall strategy for the fall campaign: Attack the Germans across all fronts. Don't give them a chance to recover from any one blow."

"We're not ready," Keller said. "Logistics are a problem. At Saint Mihiel resupply was slow to reach us. Air support was spotty. Infantry and tanks need to work together. We don't have enough junior officers. Communications are poor. All we have are brave men and arrogant generals."

"I agree with you, Paul, but we have no choice. Our job is to help us win, at the lowest cost possible."

"It will be a fearsome cost, Gil. Meuse-Argonne will be a much harder nut to crack than Saint Mihiel. First Army will confront the real German army there. Backs against the wall, they'll fight. Battle-hardened troops. Tenacious. Professional. Well dug-in. We haven't confronted anything like that yet. The French couldn't crack it in four years. They're happy to let us try. We're going into a meat grinder."

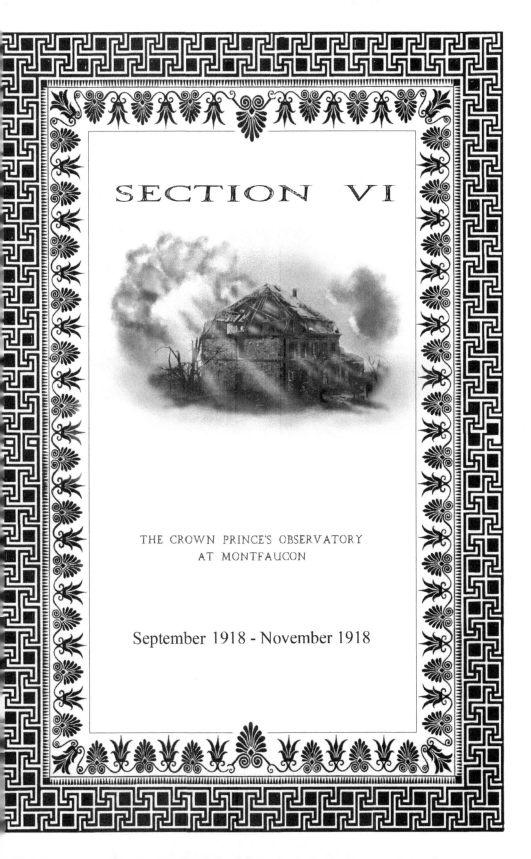

SECTION VI

THE CROWN PRINCE'S OBSERVATORY
AT MONTFAUCON

September 1918 - November 1918

Chapter 49
Pershing's Plan

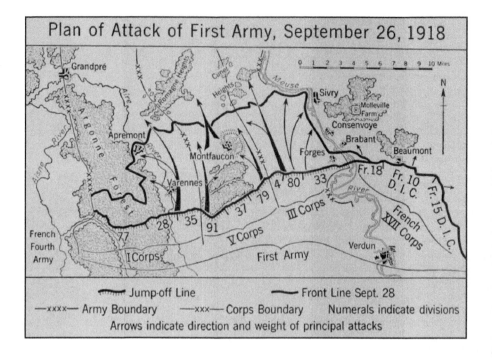

Plan of Attack of First Army, September 26, 1918

Jump-off Line — Front Line Sept. 28
—xxxx— Army Boundary —xxx— Corps Boundary Numerals indicate divisions
Arrows indicate direction and weight of principal attacks

Souilly, France: September 1918

General Pershing's staff assembled in the large room that covered the length of First Army's new GHQ at Souilly, located behind the Meuse-Argonne sector. Staircases flush against either side of the outside wall led to the main entrance on the middle floor. French and American flags waved over the patio in front of the main door. Windows about the height of two men dominated the facade of the top two floors. Gray smoke rising lazily from each of the two chimneys provided a calming element to the bustle below. Automobiles and military vehicles came and went faster than taxis at a Manhattan stand. Uniformed men with grim and determined faces hustled around like anxious brokers in the New York City Stock Exchange.

The modest town hall building had served as General Pétain's headquarters during the height of the Verdun battle two years before. As with so many things in France, the war had left its mark. The structure needed paint, its floorboards creaked, and its furniture needed repair. Standing in the back of the room, Martin shivered as he thought about First Army moving into that same merciless killing ground that had cost the French and German armies one million casualties in total. He prayed the First Army would not incur the same fate.

He was the lowest-ranking officer present. The other officers basked in their perceived glorious victory at Saint Mihiel and marveled at the brilliant planning and logistical achievements Colonel Marshall had orchestrated in moving First Army to its present location.

General Pershing glided to the large map detailing the target area: the eighteen-mile-wide front sandwiched between the Meuse River on the east and the Argonne Forest on the west. In his perfectly pressed uniform studded with decorations and gold braid, he looked like a president at his inaugural podium. He beamed with confidence and basked in his audience's admiring looks.

He outlined his plan.

Phase 1, 36 hours: Drive up the Aire River, threatening the German position in the Argonne Forest. Flank and cut off Montfaucon, the highest position in this sector and the key to this phase of the battle. During the battle of Verdun, the French were certain the head of the German 5th Army, Crown Prince Wilhelm, the Kaiser's son, maintained an observation post in the town that looked down on the entire area, giving them an unprecedented artillery advantage. As long as the Huns maintained that post, they could shell First Army with accurate and merciless fire. Taking it would be a prize in itself. Aerial reconnaissance had failed to identify the observation post's exact location, so it would be up to the infantry to find and eliminate it. With Montfaucon in its hands, First Army could advance across the entire front to the next line of defense: the *Kriemhilde Stellung*.

Phase 2: Advance 10 miles along the western bank of the

Meuse, forcing the Germans out of the Argonne. Tie down the enemy along the Aire, allowing the Fourth French Army to his west to seize the vital rail connections farther north at Mézières and Sedan.

Phase 3: Cross the Meuse River, capture the heights behind it and advance, threatening to trap the German army, which would be forced to retreat to its next defendable position, the Rhine River.

"With that, gentlemen, the war is as good as won," Pershing concluded. "In weeks. Thanks to the AEF."

Martin was incredulous. Pershing's plan was dramatically different from the one he had supported. He knew what First Army faced. Last night, he and Colonel Mortimer argued as they reviewed aerial reconnaissance photographs, intelligence reports, and information Martin had gathered from French officers who had fought in this sector: "With all due respect, Colonel, I think the general staff is wildly optimistic in its planning."

"Your input has been considered. General Pershing disagrees. And, I believe, he outranks you."

"Of course, Colonel. I am not trying to be disrespectful. I am thinking of the men's lives and the best way to achieve our objectives."

Mortimer seemed to calm down. "Speed will be critical to the campaign."

"On that we agree," Martin said. "The question is whether we can achieve it. General Pershing's timetable requires rapid movement and resupply. Our units are large and unwieldy. The terrain is perfect for defense. The roads are narrow and in poor condition. The Germans will surely wreck them before they retreat. The terrain we'll cross is woodlands, hills, and ravines dotted with heavy underbrush. Eighteen hours isn't enough time to take half of what he plans."

"But you are forgetting the general is relying on 'open warfare' tactics, Captain."

Did Mortimer believe this or was he just repeating words? Martin tried with limited success to hide his contempt for the general's preferred method of fighting and his fixation on insufficiently supported rifle and bayonet attacks. "The Meuse-Argonne does not lend itself to this type of warfare."

"You're not telling me anything I don't know, Captain." Mortimer sighed. He seemed more hunched over and weary.

"You *know*, but you don't understand."

Mortimer's look signaled to Martin he should shut up, but fearing the inevitable senseless cost in lives, Martin continued: "Open warfare is a nice concept, but don't forget the German counter-tactics." Martin hesitated. *I've crossed a line.*

Mortimer folded his arms and scowled, but let Martin carry on.

"The Boches employ an elastic defense. They defend the front lines weakly, let the attackers use up their strength. When it weakens, they counter-attack in force, pushing the enemy back. We'll never get our men into the open without a real fight. It hasn't happened yet on the Allied side of the line, and it won't happen here."

"Captain Martin, may I remind you that you are a junior officer."

"I understand, Colonel, and I apologize if I am out of line, but —"

"You are."

"Too many lives are at stake. I have to finish what I have to say or I won't be able to live with myself."

"Because of everything you have done and the experience you have gained, I'll give you one more minute."

"We will have to fight through multiple lines fortified with trenches, endless fields of barbed wire, redoubts, and thousands of well-placed machine guns. The Germans have excellent artillery positions on the high ground above the Meuse. It will take weeks to clear those out. In the meantime, they will shell our men mercilessly. Our troops are raw. First Army has never encountered the logistical problems we'll confront. Our men will advance under constant threat."

"Noted, Captain. Thank you for your input. First Army will jump off in two days as planned."

~

While Martin was listening to General Pershing summarize his plans for the upcoming offensive, Keller drove to his new command: Company C, 313 Infantry Regiment, 79th Division. Two days before, Colonel Mortimer had reassigned him temporarily to this green unit. Keller protested vigorously, but to no avail.

"For whatever reason, the 79th Division is to form the center of First Army's advance," Mortimer said. "We need experienced junior officers to lead the attack. The 79th doesn't have many, and Company C had one of the few. Fool contracted syphilis and is out of the fight."

"Mission?"

"Montfaucon, first day. After that? Continue advancing."

What? Keller couldn't believe his ears. The 79th Division, which had never seen combat, was to take "Little Gibraltar" in one day. "Impossible."

"Nothing's impossible. We are asking a lot, but with tank and artillery support, the mission is feasible. We know the 79th Division needs experienced line officers. Your troops did splendidly at Saint Mihiel."

"You're forgetting something, Colonel."

"*I am, am I?*"

"The Germans were already withdrawing when we hit them. Their troops were poor. Montfaucon will be something entirely different. The Boches will not give it up without a fight."

"Here are your orders, Lieutenant. Report there tomorrow. If all goes well, you'll be back at GHQ in a few days."

"And you expect all will go well?"

"See that it does."

"And who can I go to when I don't get enough ammo and water? When there's no air support? When German artillery goes unchallenged? When communications break down?"

"We are all learning," Mortimer said sternly.

"What the Germans already know."

After Mortimer left, Keller knew the odds of survival were stacking up against him. He didn't have nine lives like a cat, and if he did, he'd already used three. Miraculously, he was hardly scratched when he fought with the Australians. He should have died at Belleau Wood either on day one or during his escape. Saint Mihiel had gone better than anyone could have expected. No doubt Montfaucon would go worse.

~

When Keller reviewed Company C the next day, he felt sick. Attached to the 79th Division, it had been in France only two months. Most of the men had come from Pennsylvania, Maryland, and the District of Columbia. They were draftees and had been called into service four months ago. The men had completed only half of the required twelve weeks of combat infantry training. Many had drilled with wooden rifles. Others were given Spanish-American War vintage Krag Jorgensen rifles. Bayonet training — *ye Gods, haven't we learned anything?* — was emphasized, not the necessary instruction they needed with heavy weapons, tanks, and unit coordination. General Joseph Kuhn, the division commander, had never led troops into combat.

Company C's lieutenant and Keller's executive officer-to-be, Roscoe Farnsworth, came from prominent Baltimore society. Keller had seen plenty of his like in New York. Farnsworth's aristocratic upbringing disguised a mediocre mind and a timid spirit. The enlisted men did not respect him, and he looked down on them. Promotion and personal safety were his main concerns. He would be of little use once the shooting started.

After talking with every soldier, Keller understood they were keen to "do good." Many were recent immigrants who spoke poor English. A few were of German descent and questioned the need to "kill their cousins." Keller changed their minds quickly. Physically, the men were strong. Many had worked in the western farmlands and factories in Pittsburgh and Philadelphia. Unfortunately, dysentery was common in the ranks.

Four men stood out from the rest: Sven the alleged murderer, Tony the moonshiner, Francis the actor, and Frank the professional baseball player. Keller figured Sven, who knew how to kill, could lead an attack, but men like him were unpredictable. He gave Tony the responsibility for supplies, knowing they would be scarce, and an accomplished thief was the best man to obtain them. Keller didn't care about legalities. He cared about winning and keeping his men safe. He didn't know what to think of Francis but liked his nonchalant attitude. When Keller learned he and Frank shared talents on the ball field, he challenged him to a pitching contest. Frank won, and he and Keller became friends. Frank would be his main grenade man.

Not much to work with and only a day or two to get them ready. *What kind of slaughter awaits us?*

That night, Keller got drunk.

Chapter 50
Montfaucon: Day 1, *La Redoubte du Golfe*

Jump-off Point, 79ᵗʰ Division, France: September 26, 1918
01:30: Squeezed into a front-line attack trench, Keller knew he would not sleep. Too much to do to get Company C ready to go over the top at H-hour, 05:00. Besides, who could rest once the American artillery bombardment started? 2,775 guns along the front, Martin had told him.

Company commanders were instructed to "move fast and don't give the Huns a chance to reinforce." The optimistic words of a staff officer who could stay behind the lines. *His glory, our blood.* The Aussie had got that right, Keller told himself, careful not to let the untried men of Company C know his true feelings.

He removed Shannon's locket from his neck and squeezed it so tight it left an impression on his hand. He welcomed the feeling. Shannon was still with him. After a minute, he returned the locket to its place under his uniform blouse where it rubbed up against his heart and identity tags. Metal on metal. One warm. One cold.

Francis the actor looked up and said, "Got someone special, I guess." He shuffled his feet to some silent rhythm.

Keller grinned.

"Lucky man." Francis returned to his dance.

Rain pelted down, adding to the misery. A few men in Company C pretended to sleep. One man read a Bible. Sven the murderer slid a sharpening stone across his bayonet. Tony the moonshiner flipped a coin. Again and again. Sven threatened him if he didn't stop. Francis did a jig. Frank the ballplayer swung his arm as if he were pitching an imaginary ball. Lieutenant Farnsworth was nowhere to be seen. Another trip to the latrine, Keller supposed. A private began to light a cigarette, but Keller grabbed it out of his mouth and threw it to the ground. "You want to get us killed? Give away our position before we start?"

In the moonlight, Keller saw the silhouette of their objective: Montfaucon. It sat on a 1,122-foot butte, a little more than three miles away. The highest point in the area, it dominated the horizon. An artillery spotter's dream, Montfaucon offered an unparalleled view of the area. Keller imagined a German officer spying down on them from an observation tower somewhere up there. *How many men will it cost to take you?* Keller tried but could not stop thinking about it.

~

02:00: With a deafening roar, fiery hell spat from the barrels of First Army's artillery pieces. Keller had never before witnessed anything that matched its ferocity. Streaks of light flashed across the sky in unending blazes. Explosions followed, some reaching several stories high. The butte in the far distance disappeared amidst the smoke. Keller's head ached; his ears rang; and his eyes stung as the contaminated air on the other side of no-man's-land wafted toward him.

~

04:30: A half-hour to go. Anxiety began to build. The men in Company C became quiet. They adjusted their helmet straps, fidgeted with their equipment belts, and tightened their grip on their rifles. A few men hopped up and down. Three men folded their hands and bowed down with closed eyes. Sven picked his teeth. Tony kept flipping his coin. Francis continued his dance. Frank adjusted his crotch.

Keller talked to every one of his men. Their equipment ready? Their assignments clear? Their nerves steady? He kept telling himself: *Behind that butte is the finish line. Win this battle, and we're close to winning the war.*

~

05:00: The familiar sound of whistles shrieked across the 79th Division's jump-off point. The men shouted and cheered. The creeping barrage started. Flairs lit up the ground. The men were expected to follow but stay behind the advancing explosions at a pace of one hundred yards every four minutes. By sticking with the bombardment so closely, the attacking forces would be upon the enemy before it could rise up into their defensive lines.

Company C waited in the third attack line. Keller tried to calm the men with fake confidence and relaxed gestures. When their turn came to go over the top, Keller led the way. "Give 'em Hell! Keep moving! Don't bunch up! Stay behind the barrage!" He pointed the way and shouted directions. The two men assigned to cut through the barbed wire stayed with him.

Keller's life stood at the brink, but he felt exhilarated. The stakes were incalculable: victory or defeat; glory or dishonor; mutilation or preservation; life or death.

They moved steadily forward. The German counter-barrage was light. The ground, cratered from fighting during the battle of Verdun and littered with broken trees, made progress slow. The rolling barrage began to advance too far ahead of them. Keller told Tony to run back to battalion headquarters and relay the situation, but he had little hope either that the moonshiner would get through or that headquarters would do anything with the information. Out here, a soldier balances on his own precipice.

Except for Sven, the men seemed uncertain. They looked to Keller for guidance. After four hundred yards, Company C waded knee-deep into a bog. Progress was exhausting.

Despite the slow pace, Keller was pleased with Company C's advance after one hour, but worries began to plague him. First Army had blanketed the area with black smoke that covered their advance, blinding friend and foe alike. Visibility was reduced to a few yards, forcing Keller to proceed by dead reckoning. He lost contact with the units on either side of him. If Germans were there, he would not know it, nor would they detect him. Barbed wire and other obstacles further hindered their progress.

When the smoke started to clear, snipers claimed their first victims. The cigarette-smoking private took a bullet in the lung. He suffocated on his own blood. The next bullet killed the medic helping him. Keller was glad he had removed his lieutenant's bars and carried a rifle instead of an officer's pistol. He longed to fix the scope on his Springfield and take out the sniper, but his mission was to lead the men.

Company C slowed down considerably. At the slightest sound, the men ducked behind tree stumps, cowered in craters, and froze with indecision. No one wanted to be the next casualty, and who could blame them? Ignoring the danger, Keller ordered the men up. They pressed ahead, moving in erratic patterns to confuse the snipers. He was playing bad odds against the house, and he was losing.

Despite the problems, Keller kept Company C pressing on. They soon confronted a forward defensive position manned by German "suicide troops," as the Brits called them: fanatical men pledged to fight to the death. Keller spotted the ambush and ordered Frank to circle around while his men fired everything they had at them. Fog provided additional cover. Scampering across the kill zone and jumping from crater to crater, Frank got within grenade-throwing range and eliminated the threat with one toss. Keller lost three men in the process.

Not five minutes later, they faced a machine-gun position hidden behind a rock. Instead of firing, one of the Huns stood up and lifted his hands. "*Kamerad.*" Before Keller could warn them, two Doughboys walked out in the open to accept his surrender. The German lowered his hands and ducked. His machine gunner fired. The two Yanks had no chance. Company C countered with curses, heavy fire, and grenades. The survivors bayonetted the bodies of the treacherous Germans as they passed.

The next threat came from mortars. The Germans lobbed shells into the 79th Division across the front. The men in Company C hunkered into craters and refused to move. "Get going," Keller commanded. "The Germans want you here so they can drop the next rounds on your heads."

Keller sensed a shell heading right toward him and dived into the safety of a shell hole. Lieutenant Farnsworth reacted slowly. The explosion caught him in open ground. It ignited the grenades attached to his equipment belt, creating secondary explosions. One minute ago, he was there. The next, all physical trace of him was obliterated. The men gawked in stunned silence. *Where did he go?*

Somehow, Keller led Company C onward. Two machine guns stopped them until First Army artillery eliminated the threat. As Company C drew closer to Montfaucon, First Army's medium-range artillery failed to move up in concert. Keller had lost his artillery protection just as German artillery intensified.

Two things became clear. Company C was behind schedule, and they had yet to confront the main German position in front of Montfaucon. The men ran out of water. Resupply was a fool's hope. More dying was certain.

~

14:38: Martin sat at GHQ processing the information from the field. Despite admirable progress from General Robert Bullard's III Corps on the eastern flank, and General Liggett's I Corps on the west, the news was dismal. A principal problem was the 79th Division, stalled by formidable resistance in front of Montfaucon. Frenzied desperation whirled all around Martin as the planned timetable slipped away.

General Pershing raged. From across the room, Martin overheard him call General Kuhn, the 79th Division commander: "You're holding up the entire front. Get your men moving. I don't care what you're up against. No excuses. Take Montfaucon. Now!" The general slammed down the phone and glared across the room with the face of a wounded grizzly.

Martin turned quiet and left his station to seek out Colonel Mortimer. He was leaning over a table full of maps, drumming his large ring against the wood. The pressure had obviously gotten to him, changing him from a stalwart intelligence officer into another one of First Army's many "ring-knockers," officers who tapped their large

West Point rings nervously.

"Where is the 25ᵗʰ Division?" Martin asked. "They're in position to flank Montfaucon. Wasn't that the plan? What is General Prescott doing?"

"My office," Mortimer said. "*Now*, Captain." Mortimer escorted Martin into his office and slammed the door so hard Martin thought it would break off its hinges. "We're in a crisis, and you're questioning the general staff?" Mortimer shook with rage.

"The 79ᵗʰ Division is getting slaughtered. They need help."

"It's common knowledge that you and General Prescott don't get along. Your criticism isn't influenced by that, is it?"

Normally mindful of rank, Martin was not shy when men's lives were at stake. "Absolutely not."

"The 25ᵗʰ Division is making excellent progress. One of the few divisions to meet its objectives. General Prescott has said he will not sacrifice his excellent work to help another general who's failing to measure up."

"I understand, Colonel, but the plan called for them to aid the 79ᵗʰ if necessary. And it *is* necessary. The 25ᵗʰ Division needs to —"

"They're showing why they're one of our best, whatever you think."

"Classic military doctrine, you know it as well as me. Attack with a weaker force while the stronger force flanks and crushes the enemy from the side."

"The situation is more complicated than you understand, Captain. Communication between units is spotty. There's confusion up and down the line. The 25ᵗʰ and 79ᵗʰ Divisions are fighting in different operational zones."

"I am right, and you know it."

"I'll look into it. Return to the war room. Dismissed."

Martin returned to the war room to the sound of Pershing's shout, "What's holding up that damned 79ᵗʰ Division?"

~

Fatigued, thirsty, and with 30% of its men out of action or dead, Company C reached the main German defense line in front of Montfaucon, the *Redoubte du Golfe*, the French had called it. Keller's stomach tightened with terror when he saw it. Despite seeing aerial photographs, it was more formidable than he had imagined.

A deep valley and open field lay between the redoubt and his position. He and his men faced a combination of interlocking machine-gun nests that commanded the valley, concrete pillboxes impervious to shelling, trench lines bristling with infantrymen, more rushing in by the minute, and a spider's web of barbed-wire obstacles.

How in God's name are we supposed to take that? Just as Keller began to assess his impossible options, a runner from battalion headquarters delivered his orders. "Here, Lieutenant. I'm the third man sent to you today."

"First to arrive."

"It's been a nightmare of a day."

Keller opened the orders without comment or expression. *Attack butte without delay. Lack of progress unacceptable.* He folded the orders and said to himself, "Madness." He ordered Sven to take a head count and to instruct the platoon leaders to report to him immediately.

No sooner had Sven left than German artillery began to concentrate on his position. The explosions screeched toward him. Keller hunkered down as best he could. Hands over ears. Head tucked low. Helmet tightly fastened. Whizz-bangs exploded nearby. *Where's the 25th Division?* Suicide to advance, but advance they must. Keller accepted his inevitable death.

The shells dropped on Company C with the power of an avalanche. The concussive force of the explosions sucked away the air. Keller's skin tightened and his eyes pulsated. Shock waves followed, creating a vacuum. He struggled to breathe. A powerful burst of energy jolted his innermost organs. Men closer to the blast died instantly from massive internal damage. Others suffered ruptured eardrums and hemorrhaged internally. Two men were hurled into the air like helpless dolls. Shrapnel spread across the area, slicing into everything in its path.

Volley after volley continued for several minutes, a torture more diabolical than any medieval instrument of pain.

Wait it out. Wait it out. Keller lost track of time, every second an hour. The bombardment moved to another sector, remarkably leaving him alive. He looked around, dazed, but all he saw among the living were shaking men with "thousand-yard stares."

A rough roll call indicated that only half of Company C was fit to fight. With Sven's help, Keller organized an attack with the survivors. Hearing the mechanical rumbling of tanks, he hesitated a moment, listening. *Thank God.* His hopes were obliterated one by one as the tanks were eliminated by German artillery fire. Their burning carcasses added their own distinctive metallic stench to the battlefield.

~

16:00: Reinforced with the remnants of three other companies, Keller outlined an attack plan: half the men would lay down suppressing fire while the other half would move ahead a short distance. They were then to change roles. The suppressing group would leapfrog forward while the attackers provided support. Repeat. Leapfrog. Attack. Repeat. Each advance cost Keller men, but his plan was working.

Frank led the way, throwing grenades so fast he emptied two sacks full in minutes. Interlocking machine-gun fire cut him down, but his bravery opened a gap in the defenses. A squad of Keller's men rushed to exploit their advantage, but they were stopped when a German soldier with a flamethrower emerged from a bunker and doused the Doughboys with liquid fire. Those who could, ran. Those on fire uttered interminable, unearthly, high-pitched wails. The smell and sounds reminded Keller of bacon frying. He shot one of his men to put him out of his misery and retreated.

More Huns arrived to drive the Yanks back.

Badly burned and trapped between the Germans and his friends, Sven kept fighting. More Germans appeared. Before he collapsed, Sven fired one last shot. It hit the gas tank on the back of the flamethrower, igniting a fireball. Everyone within twenty yards was incinerated.

Keller and two other men reached the safety of a large crater. Company C was spent. He ordered the forty-seven men left to dig fox holes and stay alert. Keller found Francis in a shell hole. He was bent in a fetal position; his body shook. His legs were gone, victims of the last mortar attack. He looked up at Keller with a childlike expression. "Don't think I can walk, Lieutenant. Won't make it to Broadway now."

"I'll see that you do. *Medic!*"

Francis's mouth curled into a smile. "I can still sing good. Maybe ... ." His head drooped. Keller took his identification tag and gently covered his body with a coat.

Now trapped, Keller did not know if or when help would arrive.

~

19:30: No German counter-attacks. Exhausted, wet, and furious, Keller received word that the 79th Division attacks were halted for the night. Preparations should be made to continue them the next morning. With the respite, he had time to realize he had suffered numerous wounds. None serious if tended. All he could do was bandage himself and wait. Maybe he was already in Hell and didn't know it.

~

Midnight: Martin tallied the day's butcher bill and helped communicate tomorrow's orders. Preliminary estimates calculated First Army's losses at more than four thousand. Three of the nine attack divisions had been shattered. German reinforcements were rushing in. The Yanks had lost the initiative. Speed, the critical element in Pershing's plan, had been lost. This was going to be a long and bloody campaign.

Martin lay down knowing this was the second-worst day of his life.

Chapter 51
Montfaucon: Day 2, Daybreak

In Front of Montfaucon, France: September 27, 1918
03:30: Keller realized he was alive when fat droplets of rain splashed on his face. He rubbed his eyes and reached for the locket around his neck. Something real. Something beautiful. Something to help him forget the horror of the last twenty-four hours. Sheltering in the safety of a shell crater, he was soaked on the outside and parched on the inside. He had not tasted water in over twelve hours. He cupped his hand and dipped it into the puddle at the bottom of the crater and sucked up the water: grime, bugs, and all. He repeated the process four more times.

Keller was surprised but grateful he had lived through last night's artillery barrage. Every second that passed was another second on Earth. He figured he didn't have many more. By his count, he should have used up the time allotted him, but the Devil's arithmetic added up in mysterious ways. Whatever seconds he had left, he meant for them to count. He checked his ammunition pouches and counted the remaining grenades.

Attacks were to resume in thirty minutes. Impossible to survive another day. He poked his head over the lip of the crater and tried to assess the situation. Fog and darkness limited his vision. "Sve—" He stopped himself. Sven was dead. So were Frank and Francis. His best men. He had failed them. He pushed aside his gloom; he had other men to save.

"That you, Lieutenant Keller?" Tony.

"What are you doing here?"

Tony crawled into Keller's hole and collapsed, almost certainly from exhaustion. "I've been looking for you for hours. Not many left in Company C. I'm coming back from battalion headquarters. New orders."

"Another suicide attack?"

"No, you're being relieved. Company F is taking over here. You and the remains of Company C are to report back to the battalion command post."

A reprieve or a new death sentence?

~

Eighteen minutes after he left his position, Keller heard heavy gunfire behind him. Tony led them back to the command post, hidden in the woods. The officer in charge, a major Keller had never seen before, wore a clean uniform with shiny buttons. A replacement officer, hopefully someone with some brains. Keller was so tired he hardly had the strength to salute. The major informed Keller that Company C was being merged with Company H on the eastern flank. They were fighting through a well-defended cemetery and needed help. The major drew a map and pointed out directions. Keller started to move away, but the major called him back. "Lieutenant Keller. One more thing."

"Yes, Major?"

"I understand you're a sharpshooter."

Keller squinted, not sure what the major wanted.

"When you find whoever's in charge over there, hand your command over to him. I want you to act as a counter-sniper. The Krauts are picking us off fast. I figure you can kill more that way than leading a charge into Hades. Acceptable to you?"

"Yes, Major." Energy returned to Keller's voice. No longer destined for the slaughterhouse, he controlled his own fate. Man against man; sniper against sniper. If he lost to a better man, well, ...

~

09:00: At GHQ, General Pershing prowled around like a frustrated lion after an unsuccessful hunt. "What's wrong? Why aren't we moving? Who's to blame?" He dictated a message that Martin sent out.

> *The Commander-in-Chief commands that*
> *Division commanders take forward positions*
> *and push troops energetically, and the Corps*

and Division commanders be relieved of
whatever rank who fail to show energy.

No doubt General Pershing was referring to General Kuhn, commanding the 79th Division, still held up in front of Montfaucon, but Martin knew the commander-in-chief would fire anyone who failed to measure up. The problem was not the bravery of the Doughboys but their lack of adequate training and experienced leadership. The Germans' skilled and stubborn defense exacerbated the situation. Chaos behind First Army's lines contributed to the delays. It was a question of the head not matching the heart, but after yesterday's confrontation with Colonel Mortimer, Martin decided to keep quiet.

"Captain Martin?"

Colonel Mortimer. Not good.

"Follow me."

Martin tried to read Mortimer's expression in the hallway but couldn't. He had nothing to apologize for but prepared for the rebuke to come.

"Hell of a situation, wouldn't you agree, Captain?" Mortimer's tone sounded deceptively friendly.

"Colonel?"

"Worried about Lieutenant Keller?"

"Yes, Colonel. And the thousands more men who will die today."

"We have no word if Keller is alive or dead. We know the company he led saw front-line action. However, the 79th Division is continuing to press forward against Montfaucon as we speak. The 37th Division is sweeping in from the west. You have your flanking movement. We've also called up a platoon of French tanks. We expect to take Montfaucon today."

A bit late. "Good news."

"The delay has cost us, but the French thought we couldn't take it until December. I'm proud of what we're achieving."

Martin faked a smile.

"Your work in the last two days has been exemplary. I have an assignment for you. It's important."

"However I can help, Colonel."

"We have reports of problems all along our supply lines. Traffic jams. Artillery can't move up. See what you can do."

~

09:45: Keller stood atop a captured German bunker and scanned the southeast corner of the Montfaucon butte. Fighting in the cemetery was raging, vicious hand-to-hand combat. The Germans refused to yield ground without inflicting pain. The in-close fighting worked to the Americans' advantage. The Germans were reluctant to fire artillery and mortars so near to their own men, and this lack of enemy artillery support gave the Doughboys a chance.

The regimental commander approached. "Lieutenant Keller, I've appointed a new company commander. You're ordered to act as our counter-sniper. The Germans are well concealed. Their snipers are murdering us. We've already lost three of our sharpshooters. You may operate as you see fit, but I want you to kill as many of those bastards as you can."

Keller went to work immediately. He needed to get close to the fighting. The inexperienced Doughboys' observations were incomplete and often contradictory. *Better to go on a one-man hunt.* He crawled as close as he could to the front line, which shifted between one gravestone and another depending on who was attacking or retreating that minute. Bullets passed over his head in both directions. The fighting resembled a no-holds-barred wrestling match, each side determined to kill the other. Men fought with knives, clubs, and pistols. They kicked, bit, and punched. No quarter asked. No quarter given.

When the Yanks got a look at the scope on Keller's rifle, they saw him as a savior. Before he could set up, a squad of valiant Doughboys charged. A machine gun opened up from nowhere and cut them down in seconds. It took Keller a few minutes to realize the nest was located deep inside a mausoleum. It singlehandedly stopped any further American advance. A few Yanks threw grenades, but they exploded outside the mausoleum, creating nothing but dust and ineffective shrapnel. The machine-gun crew kept firing.

Knowing where they were and doing something about it were two different matters until Keller realized the mausoleum was nothing but a marble box. Well-placed bullets might ricochet inside it with lethal effect. Aiming high to avoid the sandbags protecting the front of the machine gun nest, Keller squeezed off his entire clip. He reloaded and shot another five rounds into the mausoleum. Screams issued from the mouth of the mausoleum, then silence. A corporal ran and tossed a grenade inside to make sure the threat was eliminated. The Yanks advanced.

Seven seconds later, a shot. The lead man fell instantly. A second dropped moments later. Keller followed the trajectory of the shots to a tree four hundred yards away. He caught some movement halfway up, adjusted his sights, and waited. A brief look at a field-gray uniform was all Keller needed. He fired. A limp body plunged to the ground. Cheers from the American line. They moved forward again. No shortage of bravery today.

Keller heard something to his right. Germans. In force. Moving fast. Keller was the only one between them and the advancing Americans. They'd be cut off and slaughtered. He called out loudly in German, causing confusion among the Huns and signaling danger to the Americans. He hustled away just before concentrated gunfire hit his former position. He found a safe spot twenty yards away, eliminated another Hun, and moved again.

For the next hour, Keller continued to pick off Germans, switching from position to position. He was making a difference in the battle. Finally, the weight of the American numbers began to prevail; Keller saw the Germans pull back. Just before 11:00, the enemy made a final counter-attack and started to hurl rifle grenades at the Doughboys.

Keller shot two of them out of the air, saving at least eight men. *No harder than hunting birds in flight.* Keller's grandfather had taught him well in the Pennsylvania woods.

A final push by the Americans drove the Germans out of the cemetery and off the crest of the butte. They were in full retreat.

~

The traffic snarl-up on the road feeding First Army's front lines was infinitely worse than anything Martin had ever seen in New York City: miles of paralyzed vehicles, angry officers, and total confusion. Even on a motorcycle, Martin could not get through. Out of desperation, he steered the bike onto the field paralleling the congestion, only to confront muddy holes, ruts bigger than tractor tires, and hidden rocks. The bike's suspension groaned, the rough ride bruising his backside. He felt like he was riding a bucking bronco. Press on he must. Press on he did.

Four times he had to ask soldiers on the road to pull him out of a quagmire. Later, when his bike stalled and refused to start, he needed the aid of a mechanic. Luckily, an ambulance driver heading to the front had the tools and skill to fix it. After another breakdown, someone offered a horse, but as a city kid he had never ridden one, so he declined the offer. A private walking by somehow got the bike working.

By the time Martin reached his destination near the town of Malancourt, halfway to Montfaucon, his arms ached, his backside protested, and his balls felt numb. His strength had dwindled to zero.

The problem was obvious. The roads were too narrow to handle the volume of traffic. The huge size of American divisions provided extra firepower in the attack but demanded more materiel than their logistics could reasonably supply. Worse, the roads were in terrible shape, cratered from two years of bombing and rutted from overuse. Mud had turned sections into impassable bogs. In their retreat, the Germans had planted mines and erected obstacles. The closer to the fighting, the worse the damage.

No one was in charge. Trucks from different regiments competed for the same space. Everyone had his own priorities. No one yielded. Tempers raged. Accusations were made; threats followed. Vehicles overheated. Pack animals protested. Danger from artillery was ever-present.

The human suffering caused by the snarl-up disturbed Martin the most. Ambulances returning from the front filled with wounded soldiers couldn't move, stuck as dying men pleaded for help. None came. Many died needlessly. Stragglers sat on the road in a daze and asked where their units were. Some men walked along aimlessly, undoubtedly the victims of shell shock. Infantry replacements, ordered to get to the front pronto, slogged along the side of the road. They'd be too exhausted to fight once they reached there, doomed to die for no good reason.

Martin heard the battle raging ahead. Desperate to solve the problem, he knew one man could do little more than direct traffic. Yet, up there, American boys were dying.

Chapter 52
Montfaucon: Day 2, The Prize

Montfaucon, France: September 27, 1918

11:35: Keller stood at the crest of the butte at the top of the cemetery and looked at the town of Montfaucon. The Germans had pulled back, but the ruins of the stone buildings provided excellent defense. Keller, the third-highest-ranking officer present, formed the Doughboys around him into an attack formation. Germans who surrendered slowed them down. Old men and soldiers too tired to continue the fight. Keller briefly interrogated them and sent them back to battalion HQ with a sentry even though he could not afford to lose a single soldier.

Nearby, Keller heard someone shout, *"Kamerad."* Then a Springfield rifle shot. Vengeance. The Yanks had learned.

To his relief, he heard gunfire from the other side of the butte. The division was closing in from both directions, squeezing the defenders in a vice. Keller was sure the Germans would withdraw unless the Yanks could encircle them first, but they had to move fast. *I want to find that German observation post that's killing us.* "Come on, men. We're after a prize. Follow me."

Keller led about fifty men over the top of the butte into Montfaucon. Resistance was light. The retreating Germans were escaping the trap. On the way into town, they found a garden the Germans had cultivated. The famished men broke ranks and rushed toward it. *The observation post will have to wait.* One man ripped open a cabbage and offered a section to Keller. He bit into it. It tasted better than his mother's sauerkraut. The slightly bitter flavor made his taste buds come alive. He let the men finish enjoying their unexpected delicacies before ordering them forward.

As they moved through the rubble, Keller's main concern was snipers. His unit had already incurred enough casualties, so he moved cautiously, trying to anticipate and eliminate possible ambush positions with hand grenades. Not the first Americans there, his unit encountered few threats. He lost two wounded, a tribute to his leadership and the growing presence of Doughboys edging into town.

Keller led his men through the main street. When he reached the eastern end of town, a major stood in front of a three-story château and shouted, "We found it. The Crown Prince's observatory. Took us a day and cost a lot of men." He allowed Keller inside where, on the ground floor, he saw a huge telescopic periscope that protruded through the roof. A cement casing protected it. Unimpressed with the technical feat of building such a contraption, Keller instead contemplated the number of French and American soldiers it had killed.

Keller exited and led a patrol down the remnants of Montfaucon's *Grand Rue.* He heard a lone voice singing from inside the remains of a shelled-out café. A trap? Keller tapped the door ajar lightly with his rifle and peered inside. As he snuck closer, Keller recognized Tony's voice. The moonshiner who had brought back the message from HQ was singing, "One hundred bottles of beer on the wall." He was down to eighty-two.

Tony leaned against the wall with a bottle of wine in one hand and his rifle in the other. A dead German lay at his feet. He looked up with tired eyes. "That you, Lieutenant? I got separated from our unit. Still a bad soldier, I guess." He took a healthy swig and offered Keller the bottle.

A red patch was spreading on the side of Tony's uniform blouse, near his liver. "Tony, you're hurt."

"We did good today, didn't we?"

"I'll get you a medic."

"Too late for that. Me and Fritzy here had a bit of a disagreement. Don't know who was more scared when I walked in, him or me. Came looking for a drink. Always knew booze would get me in the end."

Keller tried to inspect the wound, but Tony pushed him away and laughed.

"He shot first. Merely clipped me, I thought. Got him good with my bayonet. One thrust. 'Yahhhhha,' just like in training. The drill instructor said I couldn't handle a rifle good. Guess I showed him." Tony finished the bottle and tossed it away. "Get me another, will ya, Lieutenant?"

Keller found a corked bottle, pried it open with his knife, and handed it to Tony. "You're a good soldier, Private. What can I do for you?"

"Nothin'. Got no relatives or anyone I'd call a friend back home." He stopped to cough. "I wasn't no good a person before I joined the army. No regrets. Had some good times. I ... ." Tony spit out a wad of coppery blood and raised the bottle. "Eighty-one bottles of b..." He got no further.

Keller removed his identification tag, covered him up, said a quick prayer, and resumed his patrol. He turned a corner and looked up at the church steeple. An American flag waved over it, the most visible location in the area. German troops had evacuated the town, giving their artillery freedom to pound Montfaucon. And the flag gave them a perfect target. *Idiots!*

He called out, "Find cover. Get down now!" and ran back to the shelter of the café. The incoming barrage sounded like a rushing New York subway train roaring above him on the elevated line, only a hundred times louder.

All Keller could do was hunker down and hope he did not get buried in rubble. The barrage lasted ten minutes, covering Keller with dust and debris. Tony's body was no longer visible. Keller struggled out, knowing his quick reaction had saved his own life and his men.

Though they had no more fight in them today, Keller had orders to continue. He gathered those able and some stragglers looking for an officer, about ninety men, and walked down a road heading north to Nantillois, less than half a mile outside of Montfaucon. A German observation plane marked his progress and flew away. *Only a matter of time. We're exposed.* He ordered his men to dig in and prepare to use their gas masks at a moment's notice.

The barrage began almost immediately. "Gas! Get on your masks." This was the most dangerous threat Keller had faced all day. Cunning with their use of different gas combinations, the Germans hurled irritants that would cause men to sneeze or shed tears followed by mustard or phosgene gas. The first induced the men to remove their gas masks; the second exposed them to the killer. Often, they added a third element, explosives in what Keller called a "hurricane barrage." Heavier than air, the poison drove soldiers above ground only to be obliterated by anti-personnel projectiles.

Keller flipped off his helmet and fixed the wretched gas mask over his face. He hated the three-pound contraption and felt claustrophobic as soon as he had put it on. If given the option, he would have preferred sticking his head into a jack-o-lantern. He clipped his nose so he was forced to breathe through his mouth, something he, an athlete, adjusted to better than the other men. The odor of the rubbery mask mixed with the charcoal in the filter and his own sweat created a repugnant smell. The stale filtered air made him want to gag and remove the mask. It took all his training and self-discipline not to tear it off.

Unfortunately, three men succumbed to the distress and removed their masks. They choked immediately and screamed in blind panic. Keller helped them put on their masks, calmed them down, and called for a medic. Even as they were led away, Keller knew they were walking dead, but he said encouraging words to settle them down and reassure the rest of his troops.

He tried to direct his men, but neither he nor his men could hear well. He relied on hand signals, but those proved inadequate when their eyes watered and the goggles in the mask fogged up. The men continued but tired quickly, hampered by their masks. Keller figured they operated at less than 50% effectiveness. Keller kept the pace, and the men relied on him. Failure on his part could doom them all.

Machine-gun fire stopped his progress just south of Nantillois. He had orders to advance, but he looked at his men, assessed the situation, and decided to dig in. They were too few, too exhausted, and too emotionally drained to attack another stronghold. Besides, they were short of food, water, ammo, and grenades. He'd only move forward with tanks, reinforcements, and decent artillery support. No one would question his or his men's courage, grit, and sacrifice over the last two days. If someone did, so be it. At least he was still breathing.

~

23:19: Despite the late hour, activity at GHQ continued at the same frantic pace it had maintained all day: Evaluate situation; issue orders; realign units; fix problems; fire commanders not measuring up. Above all, push, push, push. General Pershing had ordered continued attacks along the entire front without letup.

In two days of fighting, First Army had accomplished a lot despite losses of more than 8,000 men. III Corps had advanced nicely along the west bank of the Meuse River, thus protecting First Army's right flank. I Corps had moved into the Argonne Forest on the left with mixed results. V Corps had finally taken Montfaucon and moved up another mile or so to the towns of Nantillois and Cierges, where they confronted formidable German defenses.

One thought kept stabbing at Martin throughout the day. First Army had squandered a great opportunity yesterday when the 25th Division elected to press forward instead of flanking left to help the 79th Division take Montfaucon. Updated situation maps showed Martin that the 79th had died today for the same ground that Prescott's 25th Division had passed through unopposed the day before. *Damn him.* Aside from the unnecessary loss of 79th Division lives, the one-day delay had allowed the Huns to absorb the initial Yankee attack. Yesterday, their forces were weak. Now, with reinforcements, the Germans presented a much stronger opposition. First Army had lost its tactical advantage.

The Germans had also suffered, but their strategy of "defense-in-depth" worked and had blunted the Yanks' momentum: Inflict as many casualties as possible in the front lines. Counter-attack in strength as opportunities arise. Use artillery to inflict maximum casualties. Retreat, leaving the abandoned area as unfit for the attackers as possible. Repeat process. Push the enemy to exhaustion until he was unwilling or unable to fight. It had worked well before; it would work well in Meuse-Argonne.

With the vital rail connections between Metz and Sedan at their backs, the Huns would fight ferociously to defend it. The rest of the campaign would repeat the French and British experiences on the Western Front: attack, die, counter-attack, attack again until one side or the other could no longer take the punishment. From here on out, it would be a foot-by-foot brawl, not the open battle General Pershing had envisioned.

In Martin's estimation, First Army had had a chance to show what it could do as a separate all-American force at the start of the campaign. It had failed to measure up. At Fismette, he had lost confidence in French command. Now, he was losing confidence in American command.

At 02:45 Martin went to his room for a brief rest. He was too spent to sleep. He wanted to write Shannon but had no words to express his feelings. What could he say anyway? Keller was likely dead. He couldn't manage the thought and wondered if he himself would soon be dead. Tonight, he didn't care. If he did survive, what condition would he be in? Alive? Maybe on the outside, but on the inside, he was hollowing out every day.

Chapter 53

Clemenceau

GHQ, Souilly, France: September 29, 1918

09:14: It was turning into another bleak day for Martin. Nothing was going according to plan — the situation maps confirmed it. For four days, First Army had pounded the German defenses and had gained only eight miles. In the western sector, I Corps was hung up in the Argonne Forest. In the center, V Corps was facing the formidable *Kriemhilde Stellung*, which showed no sign of cracking. In the east, III Corps could advance no further without exposing its flanks. Ground was gained in yards and blood, if at all. Logistical problems continued, and the German artillery perched on the commanding heights above the eastern bank of the Meuse River dominated the battlefield and shredded American infantry.

No solution presented itself except continued frontal assaults, a formula for death. Martin had had enough of the carnage but was helpless to stop it. Anytime now, he'd receive confirmation of Keller's death. What would he say to Shannon, except that he had failed them? He was in deep thought when Colonel Mortimer called him over. "Something urgent has come up, Captain. My office."

"Yes, Colonel. Whatever I can do to help."

Mortimer hesitated as if he didn't want to broach the subject. "It's a highly sensitive matter. The most important request General Pershing has received today."

Martin's curiosity exploded with possibilities, but he stayed mum.

"Prime Minister Clemenceau has asked to visit Montfaucon. Our French liaison has requested you accompany his entourage. They know and trust you. Frankly, I'd rather a more senior man, but we know you've dealt with high-ranking dignitaries before so you won't fumble the ball."

"That's crazy. The most important man in all of France?

German artillery is still shelling Montfaucon. Our roads are still jammed. Can't we —"

"If the French Prime Minister wants to visit a place, which we took in two days and their army couldn't take in four years, we can't say no. This could be a publicity gold mine. You're to act as translator to a First Army delegation. I can't stress how politically sensitive this is. I want to hear a glowing report from the French by the end of today. Understood?"

Martin gulped. Today just got a whole lot worse.

~

13:46: Keller surveyed what was left of his men. Too exhausted to advance, they had dug in on the front line above Nantillois. Keller guessed their effective combat strength was 25% what it was when they moved into Montfaucon two days ago. Many suffered from dysentery, the result of bad water, uncooked rations, and captured "Kanned Wilhelm."

Keller felt personally responsible for the losses. Sven was a good soldier if not a good man. Frank had a great baseball career ahead of him. He liked Tony. Francis? Well, he deserved his chance on stage. No time for remorse. He had to keep the rest of the men alive. Despite heavy German artillery and determined machine gunners, his company had advanced with the rest of the battalion above Nantillois, but could go no farther. He'd resist any order to attack without more help, even if threatened with court-martial.

A runner arrived and gave Keller written orders to report to battalion headquarters. Keller ripped up the note and ground the remnants with his toe like they were cigarette butts. *Might as well ask me to run naked through barbed wire.*

~

Three hours later, Keller stood in a captured German officer's quarters with all the amenities. He ordered the room cleared and scrutinized a music box, sure it was booby-trapped. The Germans had planted many cleverly disguised bombs during their withdrawal: hand grenades attached to food satchels or canteens, mines buried in horse shit, and explosives wired to Lugers or ceremonial knives. The bombs were costing lives and sapping already flagging morale. Keller, the former Bomb Squad detective, was badly needed here.

The music box rested on a table next to a piano where he had just defused a bomb. Drained from four days of constant fighting and little sleep, Keller knew he was too tired to think clearly. One wrong move and ... . The music box was cool to the touch. There were no visible wires. Keller dared not disturb it. He considered his next move for several minutes.

Uncertain how to proceed without further risk, Keller ordered a long rope and tied it to the table. When he walked outside with the rope in hand, the major in charge demanded what he was doing.

"Find some cover," Keller said as he ducked behind a brick wall.

"You can't blow it up. We need that room to —"

Keller tugged on the rope. The force of the explosion blew the outside door off its hinges. He looked at the major and said, "It's safe now. What's next?"

~

17:25: Martin returned to GHQ after his day with Clemenceau. It had been a debacle. Martin had driven his staff car to meet the prime minister on the outskirts of Souilly, where he followed Clemenceau's retinue on the narrow road to Montfaucon. Almost immediately, they encountered delays. The road was clogged with trucks, horses, wagons, and artillery. Soldiers lingered on the side of the road waiting for orders. Horns honked. Men shouted. MPs tried unsuccessfully to restore order. Martin enlisted the aid of two of them to make a path for the prime minister, but little helped.

Five miles south of Montfaucon, traffic stopped altogether. Clemenceau got out of his car and pointed at the idle Doughboys. "*Regardez-les,*" he said, outraged. He gestured disdainfully at a group of Doughboys smoking by the side of the road, and said in French, "The

French and the British have been fighting nonstop for the last three months, and you Americans look like you're having a picnic. Why isn't General Pershing deploying these men?"

Martin was aware of French concerns about his commander-in-chief, but hearing it so openly from the French Prime Minister was a shock.

Clemenceau walked across a field to fume with his staff. Martin thought it best to leave them alone. He overheard enough of their angry discussion to know Clemenceau intended to complain to Generalissimo Foch and ask that Pershing be relieved.

As they walked to their cars, a lieutenant colonel on Clemenceau's staff pulled Martin aside. Martin had worked with him at Belleau Wood and knew him to be a good man. "Black Jack has tried to do too much," he said. "We believe he is unfit for high command." Martin shook his head silently. This was hardly the publicity Pershing had been expecting.

Back at GHQ, Martin reluctantly sat down to write his report. *Where to start? And how to say the French Prime Minister intended to have Pershing dismissed?* He wished he could omit the remarks he had overheard, but their very sensitivity required him to include them. On the other hand, he decided to leave out the nugget the lieutenant colonel had offered and instead would mention it to Mortimer verbally.

Martin left the report on Mortimer's desk and headed to the map room, anxious to see what had transpired since the morning. "Developments," he was told.

Aside from the problems in front of Montfaucon, First Army had suffered other significant setbacks during the day. The 35th Division in the eastern sector had been mauled in a well-orchestrated counter-attack. Casualties were increasing. First Army's losses had now approached 20,000 men. Four of the nine original attack divisions were being replaced. No political razzle dazzle or fake bravado to the press could mask the disheartening reality.

After Pershing returned to his office, word quickly spread that all attacks would be halted tomorrow. First Army needed to regroup and bring up fresh troops.

No stronger admission of a beating than that.

~

03:00: Martin returned to his quarters for a two-hour rest. He was mentally and physically as spent as the men in the 79th Division. Working tirelessly toward a winning goal was one thing; working to exhaustion in the face of a looming disaster was another. *All those wasted lives. For what? Six miles?* He didn't know if it was worse tabulating the number of wounded and distributing the names of the dead to the newspapers or being a casualty himself. He decided he'd prefer the latter.

He fell onto his unforgiving mattress and closed his eyes. A familiar voice came from nowhere. Had to be a ghost. No other possibility, but it seemed real. Someone nudged his shoulder. "Gil, you awake?"

"Paul?"

~

At New York Police Headquarters, Shannon gaped at the empty desks: Fernandez, Clancy, Red, and Muldoon. With her friends dead or retired, she felt alone and conflicted about the whole Kittridge affair. Why had she survived? Sure, she had helped thwart a dangerous plot, but the cost was high. She questioned letting Jelly Brown go but decided if she were faced with the same situation, she would do it again. After all, he had saved her life. *Maybe issues of life and death are not as black and white as they seem.* Did her husband feel the same way about his fight?

Wondering what her next assignment would be — Fernandez had not yet been replaced — she was surprised to be summoned to the police commissioner's office.

"Sit down," the commissioner said.

Shannon couldn't gauge his tone. Worried that he would dismiss her because of the costly incident in Kingsland, she told herself to keep calm.

The commissioner cleared his throat and offered water. *Positive sign.*

"I've been cleared by the highest authorities to discuss the matter of Murdock Kittridge and the episode at Kingsland with you. Provided, that is, if you agree to keep everything we say confidential." He changed to a more forceful tone. "That includes your uncle, your husband, and Gil Martin."

"Yes, Commissioner."

"Good. I'm pleased to say that the matter concerning Kittridge's accomplice in France has been resolved. However, there are a few loose ends we need your help with." He pushed a photograph across the desk. A postmortem shot of a pretty young woman. "That's your Andy."

"A woman?"

"Miss Emily Lange. Real name, to the extent we can determine it, is Andrea Kittridge von Stolberg, his daughter. She worked in the AEF Signal Corps. Her cause of death was reported as 'influenza.' Her treachery will never be revealed. Here is a second picture, taken off the body of her accomplice. Looks like it was taken in Battery Park. Obviously, that's her in the middle. The man on her right is her accomplice. Her real uncle, we believe. Swiss. Do you recognize the man on her left?"

"Kittridge. No question. The dead woman looks like the picture of the young girl I saw in his apartment."

"Excellent. We had to make sure. His body was pretty charred after Kingsland. You're the only one we can ask who saw him before the, uh, ... We needed confirmation. Kittridge, von Stolberg, really, was a longtime undercover German agent. Taught his daughter to be a spy. A good one. Couldn't have stopped her without you. Once again, the country owes you a great debt." He stood to dismiss her.

Shannon stood as well. "Thank you, Commissioner. But I have a few questions."

"Yes?" The commissioner looked peeved.

"I still don't know who was behind Ellison's gun-running operation. Why were we told to stop the investigation? What was the Bureau of Investigation's role in all of this?"

"Mrs. Keller. You are smart enough to know that you should not be asking those things. These are sensitive matters that don't concern you."

Shannon tensed. *My friends died in this investigation. I almost did.* "I believe I have a right to know."

"You do not." The commissioner softened his tone. "I expect the war will be over soon. Take a week off. Best to forget the Bureau and these other matters. Good day, Mrs. Keller."

~

On the train back home, Shannon pushed the conversation she had had with the commissioner out of her mind. Worried she had received no letters from Martin in weeks, she scoured the papers, hungry for news but dreading seeing the latest casualty reports.

Chapter 54
Phase 2

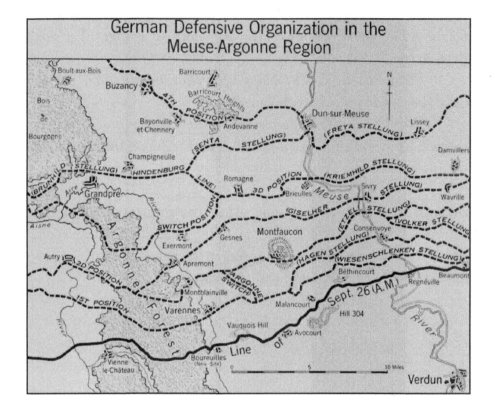

GHQ, Souilly, France: October 3, 1918

With the introduction of fresh veteran troops numbering more than 150,000, First Army's combat strength exceeded one million soldiers. Martin sensed the mood at GHQ had turned optimistic. "Attack on all fronts" was the order from General Pershing.

Martin remained skeptical. The twelve-mile-wide front presented formidable obstacles. The Boches were heavily entrenched in depth. Their line, protected with barbed wire, bristled with machine guns and had been stiffened with reinforcements. Its real strength was its long-range artillery bolstered by excellent observation points on the heights above the eastern bank of the Meuse River. It dominated the battlefield.

Yet, the commander-in-chief continued to favor the rifle and bayonet over a 210mm German howitzer, thinking that aggressiveness and numbers would prevail over 20th-century technology. Martin understood the consequences.

~

After another four days of bloody fighting, First Army had gained little ground. The weather had turned chilly. Combined with constant rain, it made life miserable for the troops. Even their blankets were soaked. Fighting in the Argonne Forest was relentless, confusing, and terrible. The terrain proved more treacherous than anticipated. A battalion from New York was cut off. East of the Argonne, the *Kriemhilde* defenses appeared impregnable. German artillery continued to exact a fearful toll: An estimated 80% of U.S. casualties fell from artillery and mortars, a figure Martin had verified.

With strong recommendations from French observers and some of his advisors, Pershing finally ordered an attack against the eastern Meuse heights, whose defenses were as formidable as those on the western bank. Martin recognized the success of the entire campaign depended on taking those heights. Costs be damned, sadly.

~

A mile away from Souilly, Keller finished interrogating another captured prisoner. He was glad to be back at GHQ, away from the front-line meat grinder and his ticket-to-oblivion bomb disposal duties. He had gotten used to talking to men who had tried to kill him a few days ago. Some could have been his cousins.

The stories they related were much the same. Keller felt compassion for fellow warriors. Universally, they were demoralized, hungry, and fed up with the war. Many had been in constant combat for three months and were exhausted. They called themselves *Frontschwein*. Influenza had hit them as hard as it had the Doughboys.

They were overwhelmed by the number of Americans coming at them day in and day out with unparalleled courage. "It's like we're fighting all of Europe," a *Leutnant* told him. "We've captured Swedes, Italians, Poles, and Greeks. Even German-Americans like you."

Keller offered him a cigarette. He closed his eyes and savored it. "We would have stopped the French a week ago, but you Yanks keep coming. We can kill you, but we can't *stop* you. Relentless. It's breaking our spirit."

A *Hauptmann* admitted that he knew Germany was fighting alone. "Bulgaria is out and Austria-Hungary is finished. I've never seen a Turk. You have millions of men to send here. We're calling up kids and old men."

"Why do you keep fighting?" Keller asked.

The *Hauptmann* looked at Keller with a bewildered look. "You know why. Why are you fighting, Lieutenant?"

"My country."

"Yes. The *Fatherland*, right or wrong. What choice do we have?"

Keller knew he was right.

A sergeant interrupted Keller with a written message: "Urgent. Colonel Mortimer needs a translator immediately."

Keller sprinted to the communications building and was pulled into a private room. "I was just given this," Colonel Mortimer said. "A field order from the German commander, General von der Marwitz, to his divisions. An alert corporal found it in a captured command post. Keller's hand quivered when he held the paper. Keller translated it as he read.

> *According to recent intelligence, the enemy*
> *is going to attack the 5th Army and try*
> *to push to Longuyon-Sedan, the most*
> *important artery of the army of the west.*

Keller stopped and looked at Mortimer with disbelief. "This is real, isn't it?"

"We believe so. Continue."

*It is on the invincible resistance of the
Verdun Front, that the fate of a great part
of the Western Front depends, and perhaps
the fate of our people.*

"If the Germans think the Meuse Heights are that important," Mortimer said, "we must make every effort to take them. I'll inform General Pershing's chief of staff of our little discovery. The contest along the eastern bank may be a slog, but even if we get bogged down, our attacks will draw their forces into the cauldron. Weaken them on the Meuse, destroy them elsewhere. Foch is right: They can't fight the British, French, and us at the same time. We'll get a breakthrough somewhere."

"I don't care. I just want to win. And win fast," Keller said, memories of Montfaucon still vivid.

"But high command wants *us* to make the breakthrough. Now." Mortimer knocked his ring on his desk.

"I suppose we'll count the bodies afterward."

~

The next day, October 8, First Army planned to attack hard along both banks of the Meuse River. Martin understood the war would be decided there. The Americans wanted a breakthrough that would sever the railroad artery feeding the German army on the Western Front; the Boches needed a stalemate to secure favorable terms in the inevitable peace negotiations.

Martin dragged his stiff body out of bed after three hours of something close to sleep. Since the start of Phase 2 one week ago, First Army had pounded the German positions, brought up fresh troops, replaced commanders, and saw soldiers die in disturbing numbers. The 126th Regiment alone had gone into action with 1,000 men. Only 66 remained. Losses mounted with no tangible success.

Rubbing his red eyes, Martin headed to the situation room on the second floor when he heard a disturbance at the main entrance downstairs.

"I demand to speak to General Pershing."

Prescott again. Violating protocol. Breaking the chain of command. Insisting on seeing the commander-in-chief. Martin rolled his eyes. *How does he think he'll get away with this stunt? Political backing? Or is he just a fool? Probably both.*

Colonel Mortimer ran to intercept Prescott. He caught him halfway up the landing to the main floor and General Pershing's office. Martin stayed close enough to hear.

"What is the meaning of this interruption, General?" Mortimer asked. "Why are you not with your division?"

"My division is frozen. I need men and ammunition. I face excellent opportunities. Give me the tools I need and I'll crack open the *Kriemhilde* line like a hollowed-out nut."

"I see you're concerned about your men. You didn't ask for food or water."

"They can eat later. I have victories to seize. *Now*."

"Direct your concerns to your corps commander. Not us. We have challenges all along the front. Orders are the same for all of us: 'Advance.' You must make do like everyone else."

"How can I move forward if I don't have the means?"

General Hugh Drum, Pershing's latest chief of staff, exited the general's office and confronted Prescott. "General, leave now and I might forget you were here. Otherwise, you will be relieved of your command."

Outranked and chastised, Prescott left.

Martin overheard Drum say to Mortimer, "He's one of the most disagreeable men in the AEF. Unfortunately, he has powerful friends in Washington."

Martin could not have agreed more.

~

For three more days, First Army continued to bash away at the German defenses. Martin placed pins on the situation maps to mark the current positions as best as he could determine based on aerial reconnaissance and obsolete field reports. He was handed some papers and moved the pins a quarter-inch forward. The Huns were staggering back, foot by foot. The Argonne was fully in I Corps hands, forcing a German retreat and rescuing a New York battalion that was cut off. The papers were calling them "the Lost Battalion," creating much-needed positive publicity.

Martin noted with sadness that First Army had finally reached its planned objectives for day two almost two weeks behind schedule. But the Germans controlled the high ground, and its *Stellung* remained strong. Mortimer insisted that the Huns were in trouble too. He instructed Martin to prepare a situation report detailing the current status.

Martin passed General Pershing in the hallway. The commander-in-chief's tanned complexion, gained from his Pancho Villa expedition into Mexico, had faded to a pallid gray. His belt was notched two holes tighter, and his muscular physique looked flabby. Martin caught the general say to General Drum, "This is putting a heavy burden on me and the army."

Martin could only guess at the pressure Pershing was under. Clemenceau wanted him relieved. President Wilson and the American public expected victories he had failed to achieve. The French high command doubted his ability. And, worst of all, the army was reported to be "used up."

The mood at GHQ had turned bleak.

~

That night, Martin looked downcast when he handed his intelligence report to Colonel Mortimer and said, "We lost the race." Everyone in GHQ knew the situation was bad, but the actual facts were shocking. Since the spring, priority on Allied shipping coming from America was troop transport, not equipment and supplies. Now, First Army needed both. Based on Martin's calculations, 90,000 replacements were needed to compensate for the losses suffered in the last two weeks. Only half that was available. Functioning motor transport, the most important component of the logistical chain feeding troops and supplies to the front, was functioning at less than half its September 25th capacity. Cruelest of all was medical. 150,000 cases of flu and the vast number of wounded had overwhelmed the system. Hospitals lacked much of their needed supplies. The thought of wounded or gassed soldiers suffering without morphine, bandages, and salves, angered Martin.

Mortimer adjusted his new glasses and glanced through the report without comment. He was the head intelligence officer who had to present the dire news to the generals. From Martin's perspective, he would have preferred to attack the *Kriemhilde* line with a slingshot than to give the report to Pershing.

Mortimer said, "If I didn't know any better, I'd say that we have been fighting for four years, just like the Tommies and the Frogs, instead of four months. It seems as if a division loses its effectiveness after two days of fighting. At that rate, we'll run out of divisions. Something has to change."

Chapter 55
Liggett

En Route to Bombon, France: October 13, 1918
The climax of the great battle of the Great War had arrived. The adversaries were like two groggy boxers staggering back into the ring for the 14th round. The U.S. First Army was exhausted; the German Fifth Army was reeling but still deadly.

The mood in General Pershing's train was tense. Once again they were headed to Generalissimo Foch's supreme headquarters in Bombon to discuss the AEF's reorganization. Martin would act as liaison and translator.

He had just learned that General Pershing would cede direct command of First Army. He would continue to lead the AEF, having overall authority of all U.S. forces in Europe, but First Army would be split in two. General Hunter Liggett would command the First Army, fighting on the western bank of the Meuse, and General Robert Lee Bullard would lead the newly formed Second Army, with troops on the eastern bank.

Finally, hope. Martin had long thought Pershing was stretched too thin running the army and commanding field operations. He was better suited as the overall army head. His tactics were outdated and simplistic, and First Army needed a jolt of new energy and thinking. Liggett was an excellent choice. He had led I Corps superbly in the campaign. The only criticism against him was he weighed three hundred pounds. His response was always a wry smile. "But the fat is below the neck."

How would Foch react?

~

Martin stood by Foch, waiting to translate. Foch looked coldly at the Americans. "Results. I only judge by results," he declared. His following reproach of Pershing was so harsh it sounded like a West Point instructor lecturing a plebe on military organization and tactics.

Martin felt embarrassed delivering Foch's hard words into acceptable English, especially given the total lack of enthusiasm for the revised AEF command structure that those words implied.

Despite the caustic rebuke, Pershing held his ground and refused to concede either incompetence or failure. Across the Western Front, the AEF contributed mightily to the Allied effort. It held more than 20% of the line, about the same as the British. The Meuse-Argonne campaign had engaged parts of 44 German divisions. By drawing them in from other fronts, the Americans had created German weaknesses elsewhere. At the same time, the AEF was starting to crack through Germany's depleted defenses. The French and British were also exploiting Germany's overstretched front. They were poised to break through the Hindenburg line, Germany's strongest defenses west of the Rhine River.

The meeting ended on a positive note. Everyone agreed that German forces were close to the breaking point. A combined push might deliver final victory *if* the Allies could find the fortitude. An American victory in Meuse-Argonne could win the war.

"If." So near, yet so far away.

~

One more blow, one more blow, Martin repeated to himself on the train heading back to GHQ. With Liggett conducting the offensive, it might just succeed. He desperately wanted to end the war and go home. He was sick of the misery and the dying.

He dozed off. An image of Corinne, his dead wife, appeared in her wedding dress. *Don't give up hope, Gil. Stay strong. I am with you always. I know you killed a woman, but you had to. Feel no regret. The end of this horrible war is near. You have saved many lives and will save more. The men need you.*

He woke up feeling better than he had in months.

~

Three days later, General Liggett took formal command of First Army.

He called for a staff meeting to outline his approach. "First Army has accomplished much since we attacked Saint Mihiel. I want to thank General Pershing for his leadership and devotion. He continues to have total responsibility for all AEF forces in Europe."

He paused, looked across his audience, then continued. "Many demand the army continue the push. I disagree. The army needs rest, resupply, and training. However, this does not mean we will stop pressuring the Huns. No, we will attack selectively in key areas and build positional advantages at critical points. Then, when we attack in force, I expect by the end of the month, we will be able to knock them back across the Meuse."

Liggett elaborated. He proposed bringing in more MPs to round up the stragglers, numbering in the tens of thousands. That alone would compensate for their losses. He aimed to improve coordination between the air service and the army and also teach the soldiers how to attack with tank support and how to take a fortified position with grenades and light automatic weapons. No more Pickett's charges.

"Gentlemen, when we next attack, the Huns will know it. We'll be an army fully equipped, professionally led, and damned scary."

The room erupted in cheers.

~

After the meeting, Colonel Mortimer pulled Martin aside for a private conference with General Liggett. Mortimer closed the door and nodded to the new commander.

Liggett stood up, signaled Martin to sit, and offered a cigarette, which Martin declined.

"Your work at GHQ has been outstanding, Captain," the general said.

Mortimer followed. "General Liggett wants to make a few changes beyond what he said at the meeting."

"Yes," Liggett said with the authority of his new responsibilities. "I understand, Captain, that you have been critical of the AEF's tactics from the start. 'Outdated' might be a word you've used. Would you agree?"

Martin cleared his throat, unsure what Liggett was suggesting. He wished he had taken the cigarette. Unable to read Liggett's expression, he calculated his words. "As I am sure the general knows, my partner and I —"

"Lieutenant Keller," Mortimer added.

"I've heard of him. Continue, Captain."

"I've made my suggestions based on experience. We fought with the Australians this spring. They taught us a lot. Their methods of fighting differ from those used by the AEF. We saw that in Belleau Wood. Too many casualties for too little gain. I try to be constructive when I advocate my views."

"Not always diplomatically, I understand," Liggett said.

"I am not casual with lives, General. I hate to see men die needlessly."

"We all do."

Apparently, Martin had inadvertently raised his eyebrow just enough to catch the general's attention. He said, "I gather you have been particularly critical of General Prescott."

Martin glanced at Mortimer, who shrugged, then back at Liggett. *How to answer?* "I believe First Army missed the best opportunity for a quick victory when we failed to flank Montfaucon on day one. We have paid the price ever since."

"Are you specifically pointing your finger at Prescott?"

"It's not my place to judge, General."

"Colonel Mortimer tells me you do not like Prescott personally. Has that clouded your opinion of him?"

"My personal feelings about the man do not affect my assessment of him as a general."

"And what would those be? Do you think he is fit to command a division? Your honest opinion, Captain."

"I believe we have better division commanders."

"Okay, sure. But how would you rank him? Good? Average? Poor?"

There's no way out. I have to answer. No doubt Keller would give 'em both barrels. "I don't think he cares about his men as much as he should."

Mortimer chuckled. Liggett smiled and said, "Would it surprise you to hear that we share your opinion, Captain?"

"I'm not in a position to say."

"Humm. Diplomatic fellow when you want to be. I can see why the French like you. I'll let Colonel Mortimer explain why you are here."

"General Liggett is as concerned about the men as you are. We want to win, but the costs so far have been unacceptable. We want to change things."

"And that concerns General Prescott?" Martin asked.

"No. You and Lieutenant Keller," Mortimer said. "We want to keep an eye on him."

"I don't understand."

"General Prescott will continue to head the 25th Division. We can't change that. But we want someone we can trust in his headquarters. That's you two."

"To do what? Prescott won't want me around."

"You're smart. The men respect you. I'm sure you will be able to figure out what's going on. Prescott's not popular," Liggett said. "We can win this war if we do things right."

"You will continue to report to me," Mortimer said, "but you will be an 'observer' on Prescott's staff. Inform me if he is about to do anything reckless you think we should know about."

"Isn't there someone better qualified to do this, General Liggett? General Prescott will call me a spy."

"No, Captain," Mortimer said. "Here are your orders. We're counting on you."

Martin's chest tightened. *Until Prescott arranges to get me killed.*

Chapter 56
Prescott

25th Division Headquarters, France: October 1918
Martin insisted that Keller and he dress in their best uniforms, crisply ironed with smartly polished brass buttons, when they reported to General Prescott. Martin himself had taken meticulous care to present well, knowing the egotistical general demanded by-the-book deportment and West Point neatness. Keller protested, but Martin saw no sense in giving Prescott further cause to rebuke them — their assignment to his staff was antagonizing enough. Martin warned Keller one more time to control his temper as they exited the car. "Best to say nothing, Paul. Neither one of us wants this detail, but the commander-in-chief has ordered us here for a reason. Maybe we can do some good."

"Humph. I don't trust Prescott. And he won't trust us. We'll be in trouble the minute we report to him."

Martin didn't disagree but knew he had to calm down his righteous and quick-tempered friend. To succeed and stay alive, Martin had to gain the respect and trust of Prescott's general staff. There'd be enough problems without Keller creating more.

Martin and Keller were instructed to wait on a hard bench in the hallway. They sat for twenty-five minutes before the major escorted them into another room. Forced to stand because there were no chairs, they waited another fifteen. The major's harsh voice broke the boredom. "General Prescott will see you now."

They followed him through a long, dark corridor lined with closed doors that reminded Martin of prison cell row at New York Police Headquarters. He led them into the general's office, which smelled of cigars, stale coffee, and disinfectant.

Martin and Keller stood straight and saluted with army-manual correctness.

Prescott eyed them for a moment, like a buzzard inspecting a lion's leftovers, and saluted back with equal parts disdain and hubris and left them standing at attention. He remained seated at his desk. *Trying to catch us with some infraction,* Martin figured, hoping Keller would not give him cause.

Martin noticed Keller flex his hand, like a pitcher adjusting his grip on a baseball. The gesture indicated Keller was about to explode. He reached over and lightly placed his finger on Keller's hand.

Prescott didn't seem to notice. "So, you're the officers assigned to my staff from General Pershing, are you? I thought I was rid of you, Captain Martin."

"We've handed our orders to your major, General."

"What am I going to do with you?"

"We're here to observe and advise."

"No. You are here to *spy*, Captain." Prescott's expression turned cold. "They're jealous of me at GHQ. I should be running the show. Go back to your masters and tell them I don't want their trained monkeys. Dismissed."

Keller rocked side-to-side but remained silent.

"I am sorry, General, but those are not my orders. You can clearly see that Lieutenant Keller and I continue to report to Colonel Mortimer. And through him to Generals Liggett and Pershing."

Prescott frowned. "So you won't leave?"

"No, sir."

Keller relaxed. A silent duel between Martin and the general ensued for several seconds.

"You want to spy on me, go ahead. But I'm watching you. Please make one mistake. All I need is one to send you to Leavenworth." Prescott looked down and fumbled with some papers, finally saying, "I am the division commander. Remember that. The major will show you to your quarters."

On the way out, the major patted Martin on his back and whispered, "You don't know how much I've wanted to stand up to *Iron Head* like that."

~

That evening, Martin and Keller ate alone in the officer's mess. Obviously, word about Prescott's contempt for "Pershing's spies" had contaminated the division's officer staff. Even the cook had been infected. Their steak, probably a dead army nag, was tough and overcooked; their potatoes were cold; their carrots were mush. Keller insisted on opening his own bottle of wine, concerned the waiters might try to add a personal touch to it. "What are we doing here, Gil?"

"Prescott is dangerous."

"Dangerous to whom? First Army?" Keller asked. "He's more dangerous to us. He already tried to get you killed on that Ninak mission. You said so yourself."

"Listen, Paul. Our job is to get Prescott's staff to trust us, to work with us. Prescott will slaughter his men without a thought. His arrogance and stupidity could ruin the entire operation. That's why we're here. The 25th Division is at the center of First Army's position. It will lead the attack on the Huns. If it fails, we're back to Montfaucon."

Keller winced. "We can't let that happen."

"We won't," Martin said. "Let's help finish this God-awful war."

~

In their bunks that night, Martin pleaded with Keller: "Don't volunteer for the front, Paul. I beg of you. How many times can you tempt fate? Keep at it and you'll surely die."

"If I don't volunteer, Prescott will find a way to get me there. This way, I can pick my unit. I hear Major Ricketts runs a good battalion."

"There's a lot we can teach these people. Help me. Stay here."

"You don't want me here at division. You're good at these political games. I'm not. I'm more likely to cause you problems and get us both arrested. Better I fight on the front line. First Army needs experienced officers to ramrod this attack."

"Haven't you done enough fighting?"

"Forget Prescott. I need to go. I can't imagine the excitement I'll have when we crack the German lines once and for all."

"You've already done your part."

"Don't you see? It's a challenge, and I'm good at it. I'm alive on the battlefield in a way I've never been before."

"So it's glory you seek?"

"Personal glory, maybe. What's wrong with that? I'm not Prescott."

"You're being selfish."

"Why? Because I'm the best man to lead a company? We don't have many who can. Maybe I can save lives too. Some green officer in my place will make a mistake."

"What about Shannon?"

Keller paused and reached for the locket. "She'll understand."

"What if you die?"

"Then I'll die doing the right thing. On my terms."

"Dying for what? I don't see right from wrong any more in this senseless war. French, German, American — we're all the same. Some good, some bad. I see that now. We breathe the same air. Have the same hopes, fears. This war is just a slaughterhouse. We've all become animals scratching for survival."

"It ends with victory. Compel Germany to surrender. No other way."

"And you'll do this all by yourself?"

"Let me go, Gil."

"You know I can't stop you." Martin tried to hide his sadness.

~

Martin awoke the next morning to find a note on his friend's bunk. *Off to find Major Ricketts. See you in Hell or Hoboken. Paul.* Martin didn't find it funny.

At breakfast, Martin tried to talk to some of Prescott's staffers. Three of them sat at his table, looking down at their plates and shoveling in their eggs. The major from yesterday, Wentworth was his name, sat on an opposite bench with his back turned.

Martin figured the only way to befriend them was to appeal to the one thing they cared about: themselves. He looked up and quietly asked, "How many of you staffers have been to the front line?" *Silence.* "Do you know how to attack a fortified position?" *One glance up.* "Coordinate with tanks and artillery?" *Two grunts.* "Ever seen combat?" *Frowns.*

"We've all fought in Meuse-Argonne, Captain," a first lieutenant said. "We're a veteran division. We have done well."

"With General Prescott in command?" Martin asked.

"Mainly."

"What were your casualties?"

"High, like the rest."

"Yes, too high. Did it have to be so bloody? I've had a lot of experience leading men into battle. That's no brag. I'm here to keep you and your men alive." Martin knew he had their attention when Major Wentworth joined their table.

~

After breakfast, Martin received a request to report to General Prescott.

"Captain Martin. Thank you for coming. It appears you might be useful to me after all. Please sit."

Martin declined the offer of a cigarette and lit up one of his own Camels, wondering what plot the general was hatching against him.

Iron Head explained he had been ordered to visit the troops. "Build up their spirit and confidence. General Liggett was adamant." Prescott took a big pull on his cigar and flicked the ashes toward his overfilled tray. "The men respect you. I want you to talk to them. Teach them a few things. Make them believe I'm looking after them."

"Am I to talk propaganda for you?" Martin asked.

Prescott snarled. "I can't make you say anything. Just convince them we'll keep them alive."

"May I pull them aside and teach them infantry tactics?"

"I don't care what you do. Get them into the fight. Just don't undermine my authority. There's a life after this war. A good one for me if my division does well."

"And for your men?"

"Every man has his destiny. Mine's the Senate. What's yours?"

I only wish I knew.

~

Five days later, Martin was gaining support among Prescott's staff. They were listening to his words and learning to appreciate the tactics of modern warfare. While Keller was working with Ricketts's 1st Battalion, Martin had no time to worry about him and what to do after the war. Even if he survived. As if that mattered.

Rumors that the Germans were seeking peace were spreading through the units faster than influenza. They convinced him that the end was near. Wherever he went, Martin was asked if the rumors were true. "You work for GHQ. You must know, Captain."

He didn't, but his answer was always the same: "The Boches are still capable and must be defeated. One last push. The great climactic battle. The day is fast approaching."

~

That night, Martin wrote Shannon a letter. He hoped this would be the last one he would have to write before the war ended. Maybe it would be his last one ever.

> *Dear Shannon,*
>
> *The eve of a great battle is upon us. We have been fighting continuously for 35 days, but I feel this fight could end the war. By the time you get this letter, I hope the war will be over, and that Paul will return to you, safe.*
>
> *As for me, I'm sick of this whole thing and frankly not sure if I care to see the aftermath of this Great War. Maybe President Wilson will*

be right: This war will end them all. Forgive
me if I'm skeptical. I've seen too much horror.
   My beloved France is like those sad,
maimed men who fill our hospitals: frightened,
blinded, missing body and soul. I hope I never
have to return to Europe again.
                    — Yours, Gil

                              ~

That same night, Keller learned that the great push would start in two days. He did something he had not done since his rookie days as a cop: He visited a chaplain.

Chapter 57
November 1

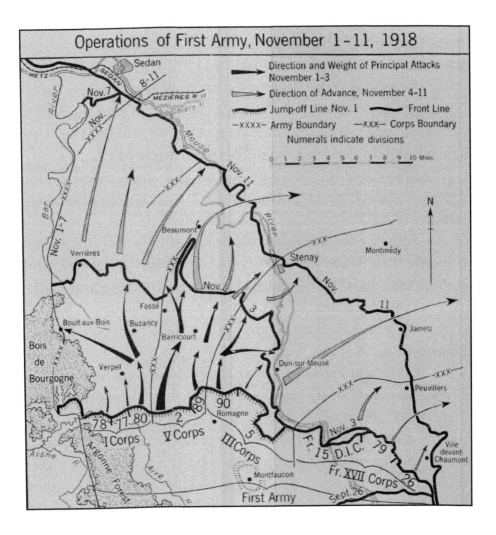

25th Division's Attack Position, France: November 1, 1918

03:25: Keller checked his watch. Five minutes before First Army would start its bombardment. He felt as excited as if he were the starting shortstop for the New York Giants in the World Series. The Polo Grounds are full; the crowd excited; the tension electric. He felt more confident than he had facing Montfaucon. And more alive. His vision seemed sharper; his rifle felt lighter; his reflexes were quicker. Despite the danger, he felt invincible.

He sensed this was the final battle of the war. Everything he had done so far had come to this. He could not imagine being anywhere else.

A volcano erupted behind him. A thousand angry comets streamed across the sky, turning night into day. Wave after wave of American shells crashed into the German position with stunning force. The explosions shook the ground. The noise ear-piercing.

Yellow and Green Cross poison gas shells followed. The American gunners were pounding the Huns. A rat couldn't survive such ferocity.

Keller walked among the two hundred or so men of Company D. Corporal Joe Fisher had a mutt on a leash. "Rags has been with me through thick and thin, Lieutenant. He's the best messenger we got."

Keller petted the dog. "The noise doesn't bother him?"

"He's been in the fight before, Lieutenant. He's saved us more than once."

Keller scratched the dog's ears. "I think you'll be our lucky charm." Rags jumped up and licked Keller's face. "Where did you get him?" Keller asked.

"Along the Marne. We were mopping up an area near Château-Thierry. We found him wandering around. Starving. Poor dog." Fisher reached down and patted Rags's side. "You got a nose for Germans, don't you, boy?" Rags wagged his tail, somehow knowing a treat was coming. Fisher fed him a dollop of something from a can labeled "beef." The dog lapped it up. "He likes it. Gives me the trots." Fisher gave him another serving. "I'll tell you what, Lieutenant, I'd rather have Rags next to me in a fight than anyone else in my platoon."

The other men came up and patted his head. He was the calmest creature on the battlefield.

"What's that?" Fisher pointed to a bulge in Keller's pocket.

"Breechblock from a German machine gun. Trick I learned from the Aussies. Every one of their platoons carried one in case they found a spiked machine gun. Surprised the hell out of the Huns when the Diggers opened up on them with their own gun."

~

05:30: Keller blew his whistle. "Go! Stay with the creeping barrage just like we practiced!" Keller was the first man over the top. Flares lit up the ground in front of him.

~

Martin stood at the most dangerous spot in the 25th Division, its forward artillery position. He could still not believe how easily he had been blindsided.

"If you want to know what's going on, Captain," Prescott had said, "you need to be with our batteries. They will determine the success of this operation."

Yes, and they'll be the main target of German retaliation.

"Of course, you can refuse, Captain, but if you do, I will be forced to make a report highlighting your cowardice."

Yes, that bastard Prescott outplayed me, Martin thought as he rechecked his artillery coordinates. He may be foolish on the battlefield, but he's a shrewd political operator.

The American 75mms opened up to deafening effect, belching fire and spitting destruction. The German counter-barrage would strike at any moment. The gun crews worked with Henry Ford efficiency. The shell casings piled up like so many dead bodies outside a field hospital.

The artillery men began to lay down their creeping barrage.

Twenty minutes later, incoming shells streaked toward them from the heights east of the Meuse. Martin looked with impotent horror as one headed right for the battery's main ammo dump. No time to run or even pray. Three blinks and it would be over. He relaxed and accepted his fate.

A flash. Martin seemed paralyzed, caught between this life and the next. "Yellow Cross!" A voice pulled him back to reality. Through his confused thoughts, Martin realized that the incoming ordnance was a mustard gas shell, not a high explosive. More through instinct than conscious action, he put on his gas mask and covered as much exposed skin as he could.

Some men choked and others yelled for help, but the gun crews continued to man their 75mms despite the constraints of their masks. The battery commander tapped Martin on the shoulder and gestured to abandon the position. Spooked horses protested, but Martin and the others managed to hitch them to the caissons and haul away the guns.

High-explosive rounds saturated the area they had just evacuated. "Duck!" Martin yelled and dived for cover. Anyone standing was eviscerated. One fragment caught Martin in the neck. He covered the wound with his hand, which quickly filled with sticky wetness. He kept pressure on it, fearing the worst and refused to move his hand when a medic rushed over. Feeling lightheaded, he finally relaxed his grip.

"It's deep, Captain, but hasn't severed anything critical. You're lucky. I'll patch you up. Go to the field hospital and you'll be okay after some stitches."

~

For the next few hours, Keller's Company D advanced steadily. The American artillery had torn gaps through the barbed wire and pulverized the German front line. Crossing no-man's-land, the company encountered no machine-gun opposition and shoved aside what little resistance they met without suffering casualties. The units on either flank advanced unhindered as well. When they reached the second defense line, many Germans popped up with hands raised. Mostly old men and boys who didn't want to die.

By late morning, Keller's men were spearheading the 25th Division's main thrust. Company D had pierced the *Kriemhilde Stellung*.

The enemy was in full retreat but extracted a price for every yard they sacrificed. Soldiers destined to die fought to the end. Booby traps, fallen trees, and wrecked vehicles forced precious delays but proved more nuisance than full barrier. Nothing could stop the Americans.

Keller knew these were desperation tactics designed to buy time, not victory. He sensed a lack of willpower in the German soldiers he had not seen before. Three miles into his advance, his unit approached a stone house that Keller suspected was a stronghold. Rags's barking confirmed his intuition.

The lead squad crept forward, ready for anything. When no one fired back, Keller scanned every inch of the house and saw no enemy. He approached and called out in German. No response.

He learned why they were not opposed when he opened the door to the basement and found four German soldiers passed out drunk. He kicked them awake and was surprised when they smiled at him and greeted him as if he were a long-lost cousin. A *Leutnant* said, "My friend. We're glad to see you. We surrender. We're sick of this war."

"Where's the rest of your unit?" Keller asked.

"Ordered back to the *Freya Stellung*. Like that would hold you. It's only half built. We volunteered to stay and die, but drank wine instead. You have any food? We're starving."

Keller sent them back with an armed guard, though one was hardly needed. With a wink, he grabbed a spare German coat, put it in his pack, and ordered his company to advance.

One hundred yards down the road, Rags started barking and struggling against his leash. "He sees something," Fisher said. "Watch out." The crack of a Mauser broke from the woods. The sergeant in front of Keller dropped. The rest of the men scattered. Keller looked at Fisher, who pointed his hand toward two o'clock, the direction Rags wanted to go. Keller ordered his BAR man to spray the area. The sniper got him first.

Keller ordered a retreat back to the house. He instructed

one squad to flank the sniper while the rest pinned him down with suppressing fire. The mortar team set up and blasted the area. Six rounds were all it took. The flanking team reported that all they found were a German helmet, parts of a rifle, and something that looked like discarded scraps from a meat packing plant.

Keller took the helmet and attached it to his equipment belt. He told Fisher that Rags deserved a medal. At dusk, Company D dug in for the night after advancing five miles. The day had gone well. Losses were relatively light. The Germans were in retreat. It had been easy. Tomorrow would be harder. The weak have surrendered. The strong remained.

~

Martin returned to division headquarters after he was treated at the hospital. He was surprised to find the mood upbeat. First Army was progressing in all sectors. Despite the setback in Martin's rear area, the American artillery had performed well. Billy Mitchell's airplanes dominated the skies. Infantry was moving toward the Meuse on the west bank and fighting through German strongholds on the heights above the eastern bank. It was the best day for the Americans since the start of the campaign.

Even Prescott's demeanor had moderated. When they happened to meet in the corridor, the general looked askance at Martin and said, "A wound I see." He shrugged." But, you're alive." He hesitated as if he wasn't sure what to say next, then added, "Good day anyway. You might as well go help monitor the communications from the front. Maybe your report to GHQ will praise my triumph."

The last thought Martin had before falling into bed was *where is Keller?*

Chapter 58
Crossing the Meuse

1ˢᵗ Battalion Advance Position, France: November 2, 1918

The next day started as the day before had ended: Germans in retreat. An early morning artillery duel that had gone in America's favor threw the Huns in disarray. At close to its full strength, Company D moved forward with little resistance. Joe Fisher and Rags stayed by Keller's side, the dog always alert for danger.

"He did good at the farmhouse," Keller said. "Maybe we should call him Sergeant Rags."

Rags's ears perked up.

"Let's go, men," Keller ordered. Rags scampered out front.

Danger struck twice in the next hour. The first came in a four-minute mortar attack. Luckily, the first salvo veered off-target, giving Company D a chance to find cover. *The Huns are running low on ammunition,* Keller figured. *Or not. They were clever.*

The second incident was more diabolical. One of the men began to vomit uncontrollably after he had drunk from a well. The Germans had poisoned it. The poor soldier writhed in agony, finally retching up his vitals.

Fifteen minutes later, Company D proceeded up a road where a large German column had been shelled in the open. The first hint of horror was streams of blood flowing toward them. Up the hill, the remains of trucks, equipment, and artillery were scattered like driftwood on the shore. Patches of body parts, a combination of pack animals and humans — Keller could not tell which was which — stained the ground. The victims' remains were pasted everywhere. The lingering smell of explosives mixed with the carnage caused some of his men to heave and vomit.

Keller moved his men on quickly. By the end of the day, they had advanced another four miles, a distance unimaginable weeks ago, with minimal losses.

~

In a 25th Division forward command post, Martin struggled to verify the locations of the lead units. Telephone communications were garbled and information sent by carrier pigeon was outdated before it arrived. But one thing was certain: The Yanks were winning.

Martin relayed orders to the units at sunset: Consolidate your positions, regroup, and hit the Boches hard tomorrow. A belief the end was near gave him hope for the first time in a long while.

~

The next morning Keller studied his map and calculated he was less than a mile from the river. German resistance had stiffened, and Keller proceeded cautiously. Whenever the company encountered a strong point, usually signaled by Rags, they stopped and let the heavy weapons teams pound the Huns until they retreated, surrendered, or died.

After another push, a farmhouse on a crest was all that separated Keller from the western bank of the Meuse. Company D swept aside thirty or so Germans defending it, and Keller walked the top of the crest and looked down at the river.

There it was! The Holy Grail: the Meuse River about two hundred yards away. Keller had reached his objective: a mile down river from the town of Dun-sur-Meuse near Brieulles. A breakthrough on the other side would annihilate the German army.

Both sides knew it, but the terrain favored the Huns. Twenty yards beyond the eastern side of the Meuse and parallel to it was a canal. Behind that a small hill and some woods. *Get through those and we'll win.* Keller was elated. He could return to Hoboken. And Shannon. He reached for his locket and lightly kissed it.

~

At the forward command post, Martin told the engineers, waiting for orders, to be ready to move out at a moment's notice. The next phase was about to start: the crossing of the Meuse.

~

Keller was eager for the engineers to arrive. He ordered his heavy weapons teams to dig in and set up on the crest. He tried to call in artillery support, but the communication lines were down. No matter — Company D was up to the task. Through his field glasses, he assessed the German position and looked for the best place to cross the river and, after that, the canal. The German-occupied eastern bank looked quiet, too quiet.

When an engineering team reached his position in late afternoon, the captain in charge suggested they wait until evening. Keller agreed, choosing the benefit of darkness over the chance the enemy could reinforce.

Rain began to fall during the night, further masking the engineers as they prepared their bridging equipment. Company D saturated the German position with mortar, machine gun, and rifle fire. Smoke grenades cloaked the engineers. At 03:00, the engineers signaled they had finished a walkway three wooden planks wide at a cost of six casualties.

Keller called for his runner. "Send the word to the battalion," he said as he jotted down a message. "Company D is crossing the Meuse. Bring up the reserves."

~

No one at Martin's forward division command post slept that night. He was trying to coordinate ground efforts with the air forces, but he was worried. Information was sketchy. Runners were not getting through, and the situation was uncertain. No one had heard from Company D. General Prescott kept sending orders: More men to the front. More men to the front.

~

At daybreak, Keller led all his men except the mortar and machine-gun teams Indian file across the narrow and rickety walkway. As soon as they reached the opposite side of the river, a mortar round destroyed the walkway, preventing reinforcements from moving across the river to help. At the same time, a Maxim came alive, stopping any advance across the canal and pinning them down with lethal fire. Four Doughboys went down in seconds. Company D responded, to no avail. The machine gun was well positioned and impervious to American mortars.

Caught between the Meuse and the canal in front of them, some men backed into the freezing river up to their chests. Die now of bullets or hypothermia later. Keller had to silence that machine gun. Do nothing and they would die.

Desperate, Keller outlined his plan to his trapped men. He crouched and added three grenades to his waterproof knapsack that already contained the German coat he had taken from the stone house. He checked the German helmet hitched to his equipment belt, readied his .45, and crawled away. "You're crazy, Lieutenant, you can't ... ," Fisher cried.

Keller ignored him and stayed close enough to the ground to kiss it. A short embankment by the canal's edge absorbed the bullets fired directly at him, and he kept low enough to avoid the swarms flying over him. Mortar shells landed in the water, dousing him with icy sprays.

Crawling was slow, exhausting work. His face rubbed against the gravel, scratching his cheeks. His butt shifted from side to side as he lurched forward. He brushed against a protruding rock that jammed into his groin. The pain nearly knocked him out.

Each minute cost another American casualty. Keller forced himself onward until he reached a slight bend that offered concealment. He waited two minutes, then signaled his mortar team on the western bank to drop smoke along the canal. He held his breath and slipped into the water. It was almost six feet deep. The cold stabbed through him like icicles. The brackish water tasted like muck. He swam as far away from the machine gun as he could and reached the bank on the other side. He put on the German coat and helmet. The easy part was done.

He heaved himself to his feet and ran one hundred and fifty yards to the machine gun, crying *"Hilfe! Kamerad, hilfe!"* Shots from some of his men plowed up the earth around him, close enough to make the Germans think they were aiming at him, but missing. The rest of Company D continued to pour fire into the machine gun position, hoping to confuse them long enough ...

... for Keller to reach grenade-throwing distance. He pulled the pin, tossed it into the nest, and ducked. Explosion. Dying voices. Silence. The American side stopped shooting. Filled with adrenaline, Keller rushed over and finished off whoever was still alive. He signaled the Yankee engineers to start their work. An hour later, they had repaired the spans across the river and canal. Fisher ran to Keller, but Rags beat him to it.

~

Passed out from exhaustion, Keller dreamed a nurse was washing his face. He awoke with a start to Rags's hairy mug and scratchy tongue licking his cheek. Relieved, Keller collected his thoughts and ordered his men to fortify their new bridgehead on the eastern bank. He was horrified to learn Company D was down to half strength.

~

At his command post, Martin saw medics carry the body of a soldier they had found along the road to the front. "A runner," one of the medics said. "He's from this unit."

"Check his pockets," Martin ordered.

The medic pulled a note from the man's uniform blouse and gave it to Martin, who ripped it open. "From Keller. He's crossing the Meuse."

That was hours ago, thought Martin. *Where is he now?* He inquired, only to learn no one at division headquarters had any more information. Fighting was raging all across the front; all reinforcements were committed.

~

For the next hour, Company D fought off weak counter-attacks and snipers, but the unit was too depleted to launch an attack. Keller needed men and ammunition. Company D was running low on both.

As if the Germans were reading Keller's thoughts, they hit his position hard. It was a classic trap, and Keller had fallen for it. Let the forward machine gun take out as many lives as it can, offer little resistance after it's eliminated. Lure them in, then *charge*.

A mortar shell once again destroyed the repaired walkway over the river, making retreat impossible. A few men jumped in the water and tried to swim for safety. They didn't make it. Company D was a sitting duck, its strength dwindling by the minute. Keller scrambled to improve his defenses; they could hold, but only for so long.

Joe Fisher tapped him on the shoulder and said, "No man can get across, but Rags can. He can bring help."

"You sure?"

Fisher nodded. "He'll make it."

Keller penned a note and attached it to Rags's collar. "Good luck, boy," he whispered, looking the dog in the eye. "You're our last chance."

~

At the 25th Division's forward command post, Martin's head jerked up from the little roll of paper he had just removed from the leg of a carrier pigeon. *Barking? Was that a dog?*

"Rags!" a signalman shouted. "Come here, boy."

Martin handed his message to another officer and ran to investigate. He found Rags licking the specialist's face. "I know this dog," the specialist said. The dog was bleeding from cuts to his paws and a gash to his side, but otherwise he looked fine despite his grimy fur.

"No idea how the dog got through. We've lost eight messengers already. Let's see what he's got for us." Martin agonized at every passing second. The specialist undid the note attached to the dog's collar and read it. "Company D has crossed the river and the adjacent canal. Fighting a determined counter-attack. Low on ammunition. The Germans are pinching our flanks. Need help immediately," he read. The specialist checked his watch. "Less than two hours ago. Anything could have happened by now."

Another Fismette. "Who signed it?"

"A Lieutenant Keller. Know him?"

"Do we know where he is?"

"Between Dun-sur-Meuse and Brieulles, Captain."

Martin jumped in his staff car, Rags at his heels, and sped to division HQ. He pleaded with Prescott's chief of staff and was admitted to Prescott's office, where he summarized Company D's plight and urged the general to send reinforcements.

Prescott barely looked up. "I appreciate your concern for your friend, but I am in a critical situation. We are trying to cross the Meuse in several places. My priority goes to the one that promises the most success."

"But Keller is already across. We have a bridgehead."

"You are not in a position to know that. Thank you for your report, Captain. Dismissed."

"You're going to let those men die?"

"*Dismissed.* If I have to say it again, I'll have you arrested."

"Then may I —"

"You do not report to me. I don't care what you do."

~

Keller's defensive perimeter shrank by the hour. About eighty men, including the lightly wounded, were still able to fight. Only the mortar team was holding back the Huns, but they were using up shells fast. A gunnery sergeant ran up to Keller and reported the light machine guns and BAR men had little ammo left. Help was not coming. Unless he did something, the Germans would close the vice and crush them.

An enemy machine-gun team had set up by a stone wall along

the canal and was raking them from the right. "You got any more explosives?" Keller asked the only engineering officer left.

"That we got plenty."

"Good." Keller explained his plan and asked for volunteers. Every man capable of walking raised his hand. "We need to capture that machine gun intact. Any of you mind getting wet?"

He picked the five unmarried men.

~

Martin angrily returned to his car and was greeted with a wagging tail. Rags, his only ally. *Damn, the dog is smarter than Prescott. And braver too.* Time was running out on Keller. But what could one man do alone? Martin stepped on the gas and accelerated to the advance air field. He had friends there.

General Mitchell was hurrying from the operations hut just as Martin arrived. *Maybe the head of the air combat forces can help.* He caught up to Mitchell.

"Good to see we're both alive, Captain," Mitchell said. "Sorry, I have to run. Got to lead a mission."

"Are you aware, General, that elements of the 25th Division have established a bridgehead across the Meuse?"

The colonel stopped short. "*What?*"

"Hear me out, please."

~

Keller's engineers exploded their last smoke grenades. Company D's defensive perimeter became shrouded in gray, giving Keller and the five volunteers the chance to slip into the canal unnoticed. Fisher remained behind with orders to move the rest of the men when the time came. "Don't worry, Corporal. The plan will work," Keller said, sounding more confident than he felt.

The water was so cold it was nearly paralyzing, but no one complained. The teeth of the soldier behind him chattered so loudly Keller worried the Germans would hear it.

Several minutes later, Keller was close enough to hear the machine-gun crew talking. The Huns were about twenty yards from the canal's edge, protected by the stone wall. Keller signaled his men to ready their clubs, knives, and pistols. Everything depended on taking the machine gun intact.

Just as the Yanks crawled out of the canal, a German flare lit up the area. Exposed, Keller stood and yelled, "Charge!"

One of the crew reacted quickly, but Keller silenced him with his .45. Another German fumbled with the machine gun and ran. Keller tried to shoot him, but the man dodged away. The others fought hand to hand. Keller lost two men, one bayonetted in the gut.

An engineer inspected the Maxim. "We can't use this, Lieutenant. That soldier ran off with the breechblock."

Keller reached into his coat. "Yes, we can. I have a spare." He signaled Fisher to initiate the next part of his plan: abandon your position and bring the rest of Company D to the stone wall and machine-gun position he had just taken.

The Germans charged when Fisher's men appeared in the open. Keller's engineer readied the Maxim and opened up. Surprised, the Germans pulled back and moved into the area Fisher had just vacated. One of the engineers triggered his detonator. The booby trap exploded with the impact of a heavy artillery shell. Nothing within fifty yards survived.

Keller and his men had bought themselves some time.

~

Fifteen minutes passed with no further action. Keller guessed the Germans were regrouping for another attack. "Pass the word," he told Fisher. "Gas masks ready. Conserve ammo."

Out of the corner of his eye, Keller spotted a platoon of stormtroopers moving along the canal. The machine gunner saw movement in front. They were attacking on all sides, outnumbering the remnants of Company D by 4 to 1 at least.

Fisher took a bullet in the shoulder. Keller vowed to kill as many as he could before ... .

~

Martin looked down from the observation seat of the Ninak. In the pilot's seat, Mitchell signaled his SPAD XIII pursuit planes to pounce. They dove over the canal toward the charging stormtroopers and opened up with their machine guns. The planes looped around, dropped bombs on the Huns' heavy weapons positions and circled around for another pass. The surviving stormtroopers scattered, to cheers from the remnants of Company D.

~

Keller looked up at the Ninak in disbelief and was overwhelmed to recognize Martin waving down at him. Amazed, he instinctively reached for his locket. It was gone.

Chapter 59
Sergeant Rags

AEF Advance Air Field, France: November 5, 1918

Martin climbed out of the Ninak and extended a hand to General Mitchell. "Thank you, General. That was a brave decision to change your mission based on my information."

Mitchell chuckled. "I make the calls. My boys did what they need to do. *Iron Head* called my aide and asked for my planes to help units north of Stenay. If he wants me to do something, I figure there's a good reason not to do it. Your information was it." Mitchell removed his headgear and wiped the grease off his brow. "Anyway, it worked out. We landed safely this time. I figured I owed you after I nearly got you killed last time."

"I guess we're even then. You saved my friend."

"No. I helped First Army cross the Meuse." Mitchell walked over to a chalked-up message board. "Sorry, Captain. I see I need to refuel and re-arm."

Martin saluted and headed off to report to Colonel Mortimer, who was there to coordinate with Air Services. He was just about to enter the command post when a communications officer called him over. In his arms was Rags, his paws bandaged, his tail wagging, and his coat shiny clean. Rags greeted Martin with a friendly lick on his face, and happily submitted to a scratch behind the ears as Martin chatted with the officer.

Colonel Mortimer exited the post and approached Martin. "Well done, Captain. Your bombing raid succeeded. We secured the bridgehead." Mortimer cleared his voice. "I've just got off the phone with General Prescott. He complained about you, of course, but when I explained how you and General Mitchell saved his 1st Battalion, he shut up. Old *Iron Head* doesn't do that often."

"Does that mean I can return to GHQ?"

Mortimer laughed. "Of course not. We still need you with the 25th. Who knows what other mistakes Prescott might make?"

Martin frowned, but restrained a groan.

"Don't worry, Captain. The Germans are reeling. The war will be over soon. Between you and me, negotiations for an armistice have started."

"Permission to go to the bridgehead at Dun-sur-Meuse, Colonel?"

"Of course."

~

Barely able to hold up his head, Keller stood with the eastern bank of the Meuse at his back and a cold breeze in his face and assessed the damage. He shivered in his wet uniform, ignoring the pain from numerous wounds and his inner numbness. Being alive was all that mattered.

That and Shannon. He had to find the locket, but right now the men took precedence.

Dozens of dead American and German boys littered the area, and the vermin had already started their banquet. Thirty-eight Doughboys left standing manned Company D's perimeter, but they moved at a cripple's pace. Any attack could push them aside, though Keller expected none. An engineering team had arrived to complete repairs and widen the spans across the Meuse and the canal. Swarms of reinforcements waited to cross.

The lone remaining medic had set up a triage tent by the Meuse. The cries of the wounded echoed widely across the area.

Two men carried Fisher from the stone wall where Company D had made its last stand. When they were near Keller, he asked them to stop.

Keller glanced at the stretcher bearer with a concerned look. The corpsman returned a smile and said, "He's out of the war, but he'll recover."

"Do you know what happened to Rags, Lieutenant?" Fisher

asked. "If I don't make it, take care of him, will ya?"

Keller looked up at the sky and down at Joe. "Don't worry about Rags. Some angel tells me he made it through. That's why we're all alive. I'll let everyone know what Sergeant Rags did. Make sure you go back to Hoboken together."

Joe's young face relaxed into a smile. "Thank you, Lieutenant. Rags did good, but none of us would have survived without you. God bless you. I got a wife and son at home." Joe quietly closed his eyes and breathed comfortably.

Keller gave Joe's hand a squeeze as the stretcher bearers carried him off and walked to a secluded area by some trees. He wiped his eye with his finger, bowed his head, and thanked God.

~

Shannon rode the train into New York City, totally engrossed in the newspaper. The front headline read: *American Victory at the Meuse! Germans predicted to capitulate!* Tears of relief came to her eyes, but she wondered if she was a wife or a widow. Like so many, she would have to wait to find out.

A side article caught her attention: *Messenger dog "Rags" saves American unit at Dun-sur-Meuse.* The story contained few details except that the dog swam across the freezing Meuse River to deliver a message that rescued a company of Doughboys. She blessed the dog and the unknown Americans he had saved. At least their wives still had husbands.

~

Keller continued to search for the locket, obsessively retracing his steps from the canal to the stone wall and machine-gun nest he had captured the day before. *"It's got to be here; it's got to be here,* Keller thought. *It's protected me all this time. Without it ... .* He meticulously sifted through the dirt, debris, and the empty shell casings to no avail. He started to probe with his bayonet when he heard a familiar voice. Martin. Keller froze, speechless.

~

Martin ran to his friend and hugged him. Neither could let go. They were joined by a limping but excited Rags. Keller patted the dog and said, "You're the best soldier in the AEF. Maybe you can help me find my locket?"

Rags seemed to understand and began to sniff around. Martin and Keller followed his wagging tail to the canal's edge. He soon reached the place where Keller had crawled from the water to start his rush at the machine gun. Rags began to bark excitedly as if to urge his human companions forward. Keller was the first to arrive at the spot. The locket sat gleaming in a clump of grass.

Keller fell to his knees and brought it to his heart.

Martin came over and rested his hand on Keller's shoulder. Shannon and Paul were back together. Martin had fulfilled his promise to keep his friend alive. The darkness in his soul lifted.

APPENDIX I
Cast of Main Characters

I. Main Characters
   - Captain Gil Martin, bilingual French-American army officer. Former member of the NYPD Bomb Squad, now working as an American intelligence officer in the American Expeditionary Force's (AEF) General Headquarters (GHQ). Often acts as a translator at key Allied meetings. At the start of the book, he is a liaison officer to the British Second Army.
   - Lieutenant Paul Keller, bilingual German-American army officer. Martin's best friend, former Bomb Squad partner, and right-hand man in AEF intelligence. Interrogates German troops and later leads AEF companies into battle.
   - Shannon Tunney Keller (Keller's wife), a suffragette, had worked with Martin and Keller in the Bomb Squad before the war. Her uncle is former Bomb Squad Head Captain Thomas Tunney (historical figure). At the start of the book, she is working in the NYPD detective bureau investigating Tammany Hall financial irregularities.

II. 1st Australian Division
   - Captain Vic Maddison.
   - Sergeant Bill.
   - Malcolm, the Aboriginal scout.

III. New York City
   a. New York Police Department
      i. Detective Sergeant Joe Fernandez, Shannon's supervisor.
      ii. Officer Sean Clancy, old friend of Martin and the Kellers. Assigned to protect Shannon.
      iii. "Red," former Texas Ranger and NYPD interrogator with a sordid past.

iv. Detective Gordon Abbott, helps Shannon in her investigation.

v. Federal Marshal Purvis Duvall, involved in Kingsland shootout.

b. Tammany Hall Conspirators

i. Murdock Kittridge, Tammany Hall treasurer, involved in secretive plots.

ii. Silas Wood, Tammany hall enforcer. Also known as "Gray Hair."

iii. "Fishbait" Jackson, Tammany Hall tough. Also known as "Acne Face."

iv. Ronny Ellison, "the dandy." Duplicitous gunrunner; goes where the money is. Has powerful connections.

v. Jerome Gibson, intimidating black man with mysterious background.

vi. Edgar "Dusty" Muldoon, notorious ruffian, works with Mr. Wood.

vii. Michael Donnelly, Irish Republican Brotherhood soldier, looking to smuggle weapons into Ireland to start an uprising.

c. Others

i. Allen Dulles (historical figure), well-connected government spy. Hires Lewis to infiltrate Kittridge's operation.

ii. Leon Lewis (historical figure), Jewish adventurer who works with Dulles. Leads sting operation against Kittridge.

iii. Abner Hicks, Assistant Director of the Bureau of Investigation.

IV. Western Front

a. AEF/General Headquarters (GHQ)

      i. General John "Black Jack" Pershing (historical figure), overall AEF commander.

     ii. Emily Lange, U.S. Signal Corps "Hello Girl," bright and ambitious, anxious to work at GHQ. Patriotic but cares nothing for existing social conventions.

    iii. Colonel Aloysius Mortimer, AEF Intelligence Head, becomes the commander of Martin and Keller later in the story.

    iv. General Donald *Iron Head* Prescott, ambitious and politically connected general who has a running feud with Martin.

     v. Colonel (later Brigadier General) Billy Mitchell (historical figure), head of the AEF Air Services.

  b. French army

      i. Generalissimo Ferdinand Foch (historical figure), Overall Allied Commander.

  c. Others

      i. Uncle André, Emily's one-armed elderly uncle. Visits her often at AEF headquarters.

V. Meuse-Argonne, U.S. First Army

  a. GHQ

      i. General Hunter Liggett (historical figure). Former AEF I Corps head, takes over command of First Army in mid-October.

  b. 79th Division (historical unit)

      i. Tony the moonshiner.

     ii. Francis the actor.

    iii. Sven the alleged murderer.

    iv. Frank the ballplayer.

  c. 25th Division (fictitious unit)

      i. Corporal Joe Fisher.

     ii. Rags (historical figure) the messenger dog.

APPENDIX II
U.S. Military Organization

ORGANIZATION	PERSONNEL STRENGTH (a)	RANK OF COMMANDER (b)
Field Army	200,000 – 1,000,000 men	Full General (4 stars)
Corps	50,000 – 250,000	Lieutenant General (3 stars)
Division	10,000 – 20,000	Major General (2 stars)
Brigade	3,000 – 6,000	Brigadier General (1 star) or Colonel
Regiment	1,500 – 4,000	Colonel
Battalion	300 – 1,200	Lt. Colonel or Major
Company	100 – 300	Captain or Lieutenant
Platoon	60 – 80	Lieutenant or Sergeant
Squad	6 – 10	Sergeant or Corporal

a. By the end of the war, German, French, and British units had dwindled considerably in strength. For example, by the fall of 1918, a German division might consist of only 6,000 – 8,000 men. On the other hand, the AEF packed their divisions to include 25,000 men.

b. In reality, a lower rank often took command.

APPENDIX III
Key Terms and Abbreviations

- **.45:** (the ".45") model 1911 Colt semi-automatic pistol is the standard U.S. Army issue sidearm. It is magazine fed (7 rounds of .45 caliber cartridges) and served as the army's main pistol through the 1980s.

- **AEF:** American Expeditionary Force, the American army in Europe.

- **Ami:** French term for an American.

- **ANZAC:** Australian and New Zealand Army Corps fighting with the British army.

- **BAR:** Browning Automatic Rifle, a portable infantry assault rifle with a 20-round magazine that serves as a light machine gun. In service through the Korean War.

- **BEF:** British Expeditionary Force, the British army in Europe.

- **Boches:** expression for Germans, mostly used by French-speaking people.

- **Central Powers:** the four countries/empires that opposed the Allies during WWI: Germany, Austria-Hungary, the Ottoman Empire, and Bulgaria.

- **Digger:** Australian infantryman.

- **Doughboy:** American infantryman.

- **Fritz:** derogatory word for a German soldier.

- **Frog:** derogatory word for a Frenchman.

- **GHQ** (General Headquarters): central headquarters of commanding general; e.g., General Pershing's headquarters would be designated the GHQ for the AEF.

- **Green Cross:** phosgene gas.

- **Hun:** derogatory word for a German.

- **Lewis machine gun:** light portable machine gun used extensively in the British army.

- **Lighter:** small boats used to transport goods to cargo ships for ocean voyages.

- **MP:** Military Police.

- **Mick:** derogatory term for an Irishman.

- **Plonk:** cheap wine.

- ***Poilu*** ("hairy one"): French infantryman.

- **Pommy**: derogatory word for an Englishman.
- **Roundsman:** a New York City term used during this period for a beat cop.
- **Salient:** bulge in a defensive line.
- **Shrapnel:** small flying projectiles released from a bomb.
- **Stellung:** a German term for a well-entrenched defensive position that might consist of pillboxes, trench lines, fortified machine-gun nests, barbed wire, etc.
- **Shadower:** someone who surreptitiously follows someone.
- **Tommy:** British infantryman.
- **Yellow Cross:** mustard gas.

APPENDIX IV
Acknowledgements

Writing a book is a journey. Without the help, encouragement, and guidance of so many, *Send the Word* would still be words on a computer screen.

Once again, my brilliant editor, Gayle Wurst, of the Princeton International Agency for the Arts, has risen to the challenge of taking my manuscript and making it better. Because of her, my narrative is tighter, the dialogue crisper, and the characters more compelling. Her advice was outstanding and artfully presented, always for the better. She is the special sauce behind this book.

Colleen Nugent, my longtime friend and stalwart partner in HN Books LLC, has guided and advised me during every stage in the process. In many ways, this book is as much hers as it is mine.

I give special thanks to Asha Hossain of Asha Hossain Design, LLC, my cover designer; Howard Brower, my inside-artist; and Hope Yelich and Diana Groden, my superb copy editors and proofreaders.

Randy Gaulke, my World War I historian, and his German friend Markus Klauer, who guided me through the Meuse-Argonne battlefield in a memorable and instructive three days, provided historical accuracy and fascinating detail about the battle and World War I tactics and strategy. Randy saved me more than once and pointed me to the U.S. Battlefield Commission, whose maps you see in this book.

I also want to thank Anne Waldron Neumann and her writing group — David, Cecil, Mort, and Sue. The first critics of the chapters as they spilled out, they gave me invaluable insight into the characters and the plot. Their encouragement helped sustain me, and their comments strengthened the book.

My beta readers worked tirelessly and late into the evening to improve this book. Thanks to Hung Do, Glenn Eichen, Greg Schaub, Charlie Watkins, and Mort Zachter. At times, I was surprised by their comments, but always grateful. Glenn was the one who told me about Leon Lewis.

Finally, I am most grateful to my friends and family, who always supported and encouraged me.

APPENDIX V
Author's Note

Did you know that, except for the American cemetery in Manila, the Philippines, the largest overseas U.S. Military cemetery in the world is in the French town of Romagne-sous-Montfaucon, part of the Meuse-Argonne battlefield sector? It is larger than the one at Omaha Beach. After finishing the first two books in my World War One Intrigue Series (*Over Here*, 1915-1916; and *So Beware*, 1919), I was compelled to return to 1918 and tell the story of how so many American boys died at the end of World War I. I trust I have conveyed, in some small way, their sacrifice, bravery, and unparalleled endurance.

As with my other books, I have blended actual characters and events with fictional ones. What is real and what is fiction? I have borrowed much from history, but I created the story. My intention in writing this book was to explore America's role in the last year of the Great War and to examine the emotional impact of the horrors of trench warfare on the main characters, particularly Martin. I have tried to convey the battle scenes realistically and in a way that brings the reader into the terrible experience. At the same time, I could not ignore the home front. Through Shannon's investigation of the Kittridge conspiracy, leading to the spy in AEF headquarters, I connected events in New York with those in France.

The main characters, Gil Martin and Paul and Shannon Keller, live only in my imagination. Along the way they confront several historical characters: General John "Black Jack" Pershing, General Billy Mitchell, Generalissimo Ferdinand Foch, Allen Dulles, Leon Lewis, and Rags the messenger dog. These men play a vital, but secondary role in the book. Their words are mine, except for a few times when I sprinkle in their actual quotes. I have tried to be true to their physical characteristics and well-documented behaviors.

A few words on General Pershing. In this book, several of my characters mention his failings as a commander-in-chief. He did stress the outdated tactics I describe, but the conclusions I render about his combat leadership are my own, though not universally shared. I believe he navigated the treacherous political waters superbly and stood up for the AEF despite harsh and continued criticism. I applaud him for giving direct field command of the army to Generals Liggett and Bullard, when First Army had stalled in mid-October 1918.

The reader might be intrigued by the participation of Allen Dulles and Leon Lewis in this book. Though 1918 was early in their careers, both Dulles and Lewis were on their way to becoming 20th-century American spies. Allen Dulles came from a prominent family and started his career in the Foreign Service with postings in Vienna and Bern. During this time, he expanded his role to less gentlemanly undercover operations. He ended his career as head of the Central Intelligence Agency. His brother, John Foster, became secretary of state under President Dwight D. Eisenhower.

Leon Lewis is a more obscure figure. During World War I, he performed clandestine intelligence work for the U.S. Army. Later, he established a private espionage operation that infiltrated Hitler's Germany and foiled a Nazi plot against Hollywood in the 1930s. Their role in this book is entirely fictional.

The character Murdock Kittridge is entirely made up. To my knowledge, no deep under-cover German agent such as Kittridge ever existed in this time frame.

The plight of the 79th Division dramatized in this book warrants further discussion. Many of the events during its attack on Montfaucon remain contentious. My key source material is William Walker's book, *Betrayal at Little Gibraltar: A German Fortress, A Treacherous General, and the Battle to End World War I*. If interested in further details about the Meuse-Argonne campaign, I direct my readers' attention to these books: *Forty-Seven Days: How Pershing's Warriors Came of Age to Defeat the German Army in World War I*, by Mitchell

Yochelson; *To Conquer Hell: The Meuse-Argonne, 1918: The Epic Battle that Ended World War I*, by Edward Lengel; and *With Their Bare Hands: General Pershing and the 79ᵗʰ Division, and the Battle of Montfaucon*, by Gene Fox.

I have tried to highlight the AEF's key campaigns on the Western Front during 1918. To help the reader better understand the actual battles, I have included several maps prepared by the U.S. Battlefield Commission. Additional comments are in order:

- The situation of the British army on April 10, 1918 was as precarious as I detail. The 1ˢᵗ Australian Division was called upon to help stop the German advance, which the BEF accomplished. No AEF units/soldiers that I am aware of participated in this battle. General Haig's "Back Against the Wall" message is well known and accurately presented here.

- I have tried to convey the strategic importance and consequences of the battle in Belleau Wood. The terrain in and around the battlefield is described to the best of my knowledge. Keller's participation in the battle is fiction. I have not read any story concerning a U.S. soldier who was captured and escaped during the battle.

- The meetings with Foch that Martin attends as a translator happened: Abbeville (May 1) and Bombon (August 24). I have tried to capture the main strategic points in the meetings. However, Martin's observations and the dialogue are fiction. *Amalgamation* is the controversial actual term used to fold American enlisted troops directly into the British and French armies.

- Foch's counter-offensive in mid-July was successful. The Germans never launched another major offensive action after that in First Army's sector.

- The events at Fismette are part of the historical record. Martin's observations of the battle reflect my understanding of the actual events and their subsequent impact.

- The attack on the <u>Saint Mihiel</u> salient is important as it marked the first time the AEF fought as a complete military command, from General Pershing down to the lowliest private. It gave First Army needed experience and confidence (some of it false). Keller claims it could have been a greater victory than it was. Many disagree. The debate continues. True, the AEF caught the Germans pulling back, and they were surprised by the strength of the attack. A continued push may have reached Metz. "May" is the key word. Subsequent fighting in this sector proved difficult. During WWI many immediate gains were ultimately reversed when an army advanced too far from its logistical base. Also, deployment of additional AEF forces into the Saint Mihiel sector would have compromised Foch's overall strategy. My chapter highlights the battle in broad strokes.

- Largely because of *Betrayal at Little Gibraltar*, I chose the attack on <u>Montfaucon</u> as the centerpiece for my final section. The delay in taking Montfaucon overturned Pershing's ambitious timetable for the campaign and allowed the Germans to rush badly needed reinforcements to the battle as I have suggested. Pershing's frustrations on Day 1, which Martin witnesses, are well documented.

- The <u>*Redoute du Golfe*</u> existed, but the book's action there comes from my imagination.

- On Day 2 of the Meuse-Argonne offensive, there was brutal hand-to-hand combat in the cemetery below Montfaucon. The <u>Crown Prince's observatory</u> is real, and its capture was considered a great prize. The periscope is on display at the U.S. Army Museum, Fort Sill, Oklahoma.

- The <u>success of the First and Second Armies</u> from November 1 to the end of the war was as impressive as I describe in the book, though the German army's ability to carry on in the last weeks of the war was remarkable. By the end of the war, the AEF had become an excellent fighting force.

- The <u>Crossing of the Meuse</u> at Dun-sur-Meuse (and later at Stenay) was a significant, but not a solitary, achievement. At the same time, First and Second Armies were advancing across the entire front. Keller's fight at Dun-sur-Meuse and his rescue by Martin was an excellent place to end this book. When Rags finds the locket, my three main characters are finally safe and back together.

Some additional qualifications are in order:

- Regarding the variety of assignments I give to Martin and Keller, my German guide through the Meuse-Argonne, Markus Klauer, insisted that, as intelligence officers, they would not have led front-line companies. They would have interrogated prisoners. Also, I doubt that an army officer would be allowed to lead a Marine company. For the sake of the story, I break "Markus Rules" often but hope my readers accept that Martin's and Keller's talents were much needed across the AEF. By deploying them as I have, I was able to give my story the broad scope it demanded.
- I invented the 25th Division and General Prescott. I have placed the 25th Division fictionally to the right of the 79th Division during the attack on Montfaucon. See further comments above on the actual battle.

The reader might be interested to learn that:

- I grew up in Bronxville, New York. Its layout hasn't changed that much in one hundred years.
- Details concerning Pershing's train are scarce. My principal source is a *North American Newspaper Alliance* article: CHICAGO, January 10 (1918). My friend and WWI historian Randy Gaulke gave it to me. To my knowledge, there was never an attempt to assassinate the general.

- Clemenceau's visit on September 29, 1918 occurred largely as I have described it. His attitude toward General Pershing is part of the historical record.
- General von der Marwitz's captured field order is real, though someone other than Keller translated it.
- Although "Free Ireland" found support in America, I know of no actual plot to fund and ship guns from America to Irish revolutionaries. My representation of Tammany Hall is purely my own.
- The 1916 German weapons shipment to Irish revolutionaries on the cargo vessel *Libau* happened.
- The Kingsland bombing occurred on January 11, 1918, when 500,000 artillery shells ignited. The cause has not been conclusively proven, but there is strong conjecture it was the work of German agents. In magnitude of German sabotage operations, the explosion was second only to that at Black Tom Island the year before. The subsequent events described in this book are fictional. The description of the area is primarily based on a visit I made to Kingsland and my imagination. The damaged chimney is still visible today.
- I direct those readers interested in more information about the rudder bomb to my first book, *Over Here*.
- "Hello Girls" is the actual term used to describe the women who worked for the U.S. Signal Corps. They performed brilliantly. Sadly, their contribution to the AEF's success is little known.

A final word: I have tried hard to be as accurate as I can with the historical facts. Any errors are mine. Of my fictional characters, any connection or resemblance to actual people is purely coincidental.

THE WORLD WAR ONE INTRIGUE SERIES

CONTINUES INTO 1919 with

Read the first chapter.
The book is available at:
www.jameshockenberry.com &
Amazon (book and e-book)

Chapter 1
The Last Day

The Western Front, Meuse-Argonne Sector, France: November 11, 1918
05:00: "Gil, wake up! Now!" Captain Gilbert Martin of Army Military
Intelligence recognized the voice — Lieutenant Paul Keller, his longtime
friend and assistant. Martin, alert and focused despite his all-night trek
from Allied headquarters, lifted himself from his cot in the basement
of an abandoned church. After eight months near the front, he was
accustomed to crises, but he had not expected problems today.

"Paul, what's wrong?" Martin grabbed his boots from under the
bed. He trusted Keller with his life. "What in God's name is it? The
war's almost over." The armistice between Germany and the Allies was
to take effect on the 11th hour of the 11th day of the 11th month. Six hours
away.

"Not yet. The general's sent the reserves up." In General Donald
Prescott's part of the line, American troops had assembled in their
forward positions. They were about to fight for ground the armistice
would grant them for free a few hours later, a senseless waste of blood.
"All hell's about to break loose. We're preparing to — "

The deafening barrage of American artillery commenced. The
explosions rattled Martin's eardrums. "What did you say?" Martin
hollered.

"Prescott has ordered an attack," Keller yelled back.

"He's not that stupid."

"I was on forward watch. I saw the build-up."

The artillery fire intensified. Martin cupped his hands around his
mouth and yelled. "I have to stop him." They rushed to their motorcycle
outside the church. Keller, the fastest driver in the division, grabbed the
handlebars and started it up. Martin hopped on the back, and Keller
skidded away, kicking dirt behind him. They were at Prescott's division
headquarters in five minutes. General Pershing, the Commanding

General of the American Expeditionary Forces (AEF), had assigned Martin and Keller to Prescott. Pershing said he trusted their judgment. Prescott called them Pershing's spies.

Martin and Keller smoothed their uniforms. Prescott was adamant about neatness. Martin marched into the general's tent with as much authority as he could muster. Keller followed. Prescott's aides stood aside and let the intelligence officers through. Everyone liked and respected Martin, and they had witnessed Keller's fearless aggression when provoked. The general, concentrating on his maps, did not look up.

Martin walked right up to the general and saluted. "Excuse me, General. May I have a word?"

Prescott glared at him. "How dare you barge in like this. Leave."

Martin maintained his best parade-ground posture. "Permission to speak freely, General." The request sounded like a demand.

"Denied." Prescott looked back at his maps. He smelled like cigar smoke and expensive Parisian soap.

Keller stepped back and stood at attention with clenched teeth. Martin advanced one step and pointed to Prescott's maps. "Listen, General."

Prescott's chief of staff backed away as if he expected an eruption.

The general's bristly white hair stood at attention. His barrel chest puffed out. "Get out of my way."

"General Prescott, this is slaughter," Martin said grimly.

"Go to Hell. I don't care who you report to. I'm going to give those Fritzes a final kick in the balls."

Martin understood why Prescott's staff called him *Iron Head*. "For Christ's sake. Hasn't there been enough killing? For what? A field we can walk across like it's Central Park in a few hours." Martin knew all too personally the value of human life. "Show some mercy."

"You're wrong, Captain. We've got these bastards on the ropes.

I want to kill as many as I can. I'd march to Berlin if I could."

"But we've won," Keller said.

"Another word out of you, Lieutenant, and I'll have you court-martialed."

Prescott's icy stare failed to intimidate Martin. "I'm calling AEF headquarters." He turned and walked away.

"Stop," Prescott yelled. "That's an order. Sergeant, remove these officers. Keep them under guard until we finish the attack." The sergeant and a burly corporal pulled their Colt .45 semi-automatic pistols and pointed them at Martin and Keller.

On their way out of the tent, Prescott's chief of staff approached them. "Come with me." As he escorted them away, he whispered to Martin, "Sorry."

"Glory will be mine at last!" Prescott shouted behind them.

Once outside, Keller paced. Martin lit up a Camel and smoked it in seconds. His next one went just as fast. The chief of staff returned to the tent. The sergeant looked on apologetically. Minutes later, the barrage stopped and Martin heard distant whistles and yells from the front lines. The inevitable machine gun and rifle fire began to chatter.

"Shit." Keller kicked the ground.

"I failed." Martin shook with rage.

The wounded began to flow back from the front lines. Sick of the butchery, Martin prayed for these men with deep sorrow. The last American soldiers were dying in the war.

~

11:01: Shouts of joy erupted from both lines. Martin and Keller followed General Prescott and his senior officers and staff into no-man's-land. Half-way across, Prescott stepped into a mud hole. He ordered a staff officer to wipe off his boots while everyone waited.

This walk was unlike any other Martin had made across a battlefield. Except for the cries of the wounded, it was so quiet he could hear his timepiece tick. No machine guns, no shells bursting, no confused orders. But some things had not changed. A nine-inch rat ran across his feet with something in its mouth. Another chewed on the face of a soldier blown apart at the waist. Martin was not sure if the man was American or German. The smell of cordite, decaying flesh, and onions filled his nose. He wondered if this field would ever yield crops again.

Martin reached for another Camel. Smoking was his one solace. Since he had landed in France, he had smoked two packs a day. When the war had started, the army transferred Martin and Keller's entire police unit, New York City's elite Bomb Squad, into military intelligence. That was almost a year ago, an eternity. His lungs were still recovering from exposure to poison gas two summers ago, and his doctors had told him to stop smoking. Die now or die later — what difference would it make? Nothing at home to go back to. He had expected to be buried in France.

Martin surveyed the field. He estimated the attack had cost more than forty American casualties. Stretcher bearers continued to carry the wounded back to the field station. A soldier with a Red Cross band around his arm picked up human remains too small to be identifiable and dumped them into a sack. Martin had seen death up close as a New York policeman, but the killing in this war was beyond his comprehension. Industrial murder. He longed to go away. Someplace quiet. Someplace where he could forget.

They followed General Prescott to the German position. The Germans in their tattered gray uniforms stood weaponless. "Bavarians," Keller said when he saw their uniform markings. Although defeated, they looked tough and proud. A one-armed German major stepped forward and saluted crisply. He offered Prescott his Luger. The general grabbed it and pushed him aside. "Where is your commanding officer?"

Keller translated. The German major replied. Keller turned to Prescott. "They're all dead, General. Major von Ohlmann here was ordered here last week to take command of this sector."

Prescott grumbled and shouted orders. Keller and von Ohlmann talked for a few minutes. Martin understood enough German to know that Keller had softened Prescott's orders. Keller turned to Prescott. "These men are hungry, General. Can we bring some food over to their lines?"

"Don't give these bastards a damned thing," Prescott said.

"General, I apologize for saying this, but Major von Ohlmann is from a long line of Prussian officers," Keller said. "He's an honorable man and deserves respect."

"He's lucky I don't shoot him." Prescott looked around and seemed bored. "I'm done here. You so-called intelligence officers can do what you want. You will anyway, Lieutenant." Prescott instructed his master sergeant to supervise the collection of German weapons. He told a corporal to remain with Martin and Keller and left with his staff.

After he was gone, von Ohlmann approached Keller. "Am I to understand you are intelligence officers?"

"Yes. We are part of General Pershing's staff, not his." Keller nodded his head toward Prescott.

"*Gut*. Then, may I speak to you and your captain in private?" the major asked, looking suspiciously at the American corporal standing nearby.

"Of course. Where?"

Von Ohlmann pointed to his command bunker behind a series of communications trenches. The three men walked there in silence followed by the corporal. Three times von Ohlmann looked behind him. Martin followed his eyes to a German sergeant with a red arm band and a curious stare who never took his eyes off them.

"Corporal Wasek, please stand guard outside," Martin ordered. He, Keller, and the German major descended several steps into a 10 x 12 foot bunker. Three layers of stout timbers formed the roof, which was reinforced with layers of sandbags. Keller had to bend down to enter. It smelled of sweat, human waste, and turnips. Two sagging cots, a small table, and a chair were the only furniture. Rats moved unmolested. A dim light completed the bleakness. Von Ohlmann looked nervous but said in good English. "We can speak freely now." His voice was dry. "You noticed that my men are Bavarian, did you not?" Von Ohlmann swallowed hard and stopped. He looked at the entrance to the bunker.

"Is something wrong?" Keller asked.

"Go on," Martin said. "We're alone."

Obviously distraught, von Ohlmann looked toward the entrance again.

"We're safe," Martin said. "That corporal is a good soldier. I know him."

Von Ohlmann breathed deeply and said in a low voice, "I love Germany, but these Bavarians, they are not German. They are traitors." He squeezed his fist so hard his knuckles whitened. "You must tell General Pershing this. It is critical."

"What?" Martin and Keller both said.

"The junior officers. They are planning a coup. They want to break Bavaria away from Germany and make it Communist. That would be a catastrophe. You must stop them!"

Martin heard a faint gasp outside, the sound of a man falling, and footsteps. A shot went off. Von Ohlmann grabbed his chest and slumped to the ground. Martin and Keller reached for their .45s and dived for cover. In the confined bunker, Martin looked up and saw the German sergeant with the red arm band in the entrance. He fired two more bullets from his Luger, but they missed. Martin's return shot bored into his heart.

Keller examined the assassin, while Martin tended to von Ohlmann. His dying words were, "The German Revolution has begun."